W9-AOX-907

THE LAND OF CAIN

BY PETER LAPPIN

the land of cain

1958 DOUBLEDAY & COMPANY, INC., GARDEN CITY, NEW YORK

ACKNOWLEDGMENT: The author and publisher are grateful to The Talbot Press Limited (Dublin) for permission to use two poems by Padraic Pearse: *I Am Ireland* and *The Mother.*

No person now living on earth is portrayed or described in this book. Any resemblance to living beings, either by name or characterization, is wholly fortuitous.

Library of Congress Catalog Card Number 58-5946

First Edition

contents

PART I The Land 7

PART II The Trouble 87

PART III The Flight 197

I the land

1

Brian O'Connell Burke Sheridan Tracey opened his eyes.

The name had been conferred on Brian too early for him to resist. Michael Tracey, his father, had given it to his first-born for, boy and man, he and Father Pat Quinn, the parish priest of Drumree in County Antrim—a village of five hundred souls, four hundred of them Protestants and lost—a great pity to see such neighbors lost!—had read with passionate interest the speeches these great orators had delivered in freedom's cause, and nobody had a more eloquent tongue than Michael Tracey when the liquor loosened it. There had been plenty of fun and a steady flow of liquor at the christening of the first-born and Michael had felt inspired to confer the names of Ireland's great upon his son. His wife Mary, poor creature, lay in bed weeping until they returned to her aching arms the new heir to the kingdom of God.

As soon as Brian had come to realize what had happened to him, he had resented it fiercely and had publicly denied ownership of the name. But what could he do? Against him was the evidence of the baptismal certificate, and from there it was copied into the school registers for all the world and the prying eyes of Miss Eudora Lavin, the schoolteacher, to see. Now when Miss Lavin was certain that Brian had done something wrong behind her back at school, but she had no evidence to prove it, she took revenge when she called out the roll by reading off, to Brian's sorrow, his full name; she also did this when she felt in high spirits and wanted to be funny.

Brian stared at the gray ceiling and was sorry he had wakened up at all. In his dream he had been riding a horse with a coat so black and shiny it was almost blue, across the plains west of Drumree. Sometimes the horse's feet *clump-ata-clumped* over the soft turf; sometimes they did not even touch it but glided over it. When the ground ahead was too difficult to ride on, Brian simply pulled up his chest and shoulders and that made the horse lift and soar over homes and barns to another level stretch of green. Then he came back to the *clump-ata-clump*—a sound and a feeling that made Brian gurgle inside with delight—and the wind whistled past, tickling the inside of his ears and puffing out the sleeves of his coat and making his heart swell until he was so happy he screeched out: "Eeeee! Stardust! Eeeeeee!"

It must have been this cry that had wakened him, thought Brian. He never could figure out how you were able to wake yourself up, because no matter what noise you made when you were sleeping it was the *sleeping* you that made the noise and that had nothing to do with the *waking* you. He lay there trying to understand what Dinny Coleman, the farm hand and his friend, had told him about a man who had dreamed that he was awake and when he had wakened had found himself still sleeping, but he could not figure it out at all, because for a boy of twelve years he was not very clever, as Miss Lavin, "Spudface," was fond of telling him.

Something fluttered inside him, and although he didn't know what caused it, he knew that it was something pleasant for he always had that feeling inside when he ought to be remembering something pleasant. The unpleasant something was quite different; it was like a piece of cold iron placed across your stomach. The pleasant thing was like somebody tickling your stomach with a feather but not quite, for this was hidden away inside where a feather couldn't reach.

He was still thinking about this pleasant something and the ceiling was becoming whiter as the morning grew brighter when he noticed his brother Paul lying almost right across the bed, taking up his own place and most of Brian's as well.

"If Paul thinks I'm going to give in to him the way Ma does, because he's younger, he's daft!" he said to himself.

He already had to give in too much to Sean because Sean was the baby and sometimes even now slept with Ma and Da. Ma always said that he should know better than to hit Sean because he was a big boy of twelve now and Sean was only eight. He did not mind giving in sometimes to Sean because Sean was a good kid now and then, and Brian was fond of him. But Paul was ten and went too far, so that he had to punch Paul for Paul's own good. Now he pushed Paul roughly back to his place and Paul just grunted and complained but did not waken, and that made Brian wonder all over again if it was Paul's *sleeping* him that was complaining or his *waking* him. His mind swung back to what he had heard about the man who had dreamed that he was awake. . . .

All of a sudden he remembered what it was that had made the feather tickle his insides. Today was Saturday and his father had promised to let him spend the whole day on the farm. Besides, since it was Saturday the other two would have to stay in the house to help with the cleaning and would not be allowed to interfere with his fun.

He sat up, feeling his chest and back tingle with the cold, and crawled over Paul's body, still very warm and red outside the nightshirt, as if he were blushing all over. He put his moist soles on the freezing linoleum. The cold did not worry him for he knew that once he had washed, dressed, got something to eat, and raced down to the farm everything would get warmer. Later the sun would come out and it would be a wonderful day the way it had been all week. He had watched the sun shining through the schoolroom window day after day and had seen the birds outside come around and look for likely spots in the thick, leafy parts of the big bay trees for somewhere to build a nest.

"What are you doing, Brian O'Connell Burke Sheridan Tracey, staring out of the window?" had said Miss Lavin.

"I was thinking!" he had said in a dignified way.

"With what?" she had said.

"About the sums."

"I didn't say *about* what; I said *with* what."

"Beg pardon, Miss Lavin?" She liked them to be polite.

"Nothing!" she said.

"Which is not very polite yourself, Spudface," said Brian, only he had not said this out loud. Boy, if he ever had!

Brian pulled his nightshirt over his head, rubbed the skin of his back and chest, already goose-pimpled, and put on his shirt. Then he put on his stockings and trousers and went downstairs with his hobnail boots in his hand, for his father, Michael, was still asleep and he did not want to wake him. His father was easier to get along with when he was sleeping, for when he was awake his favorite word was No. True, his father had promised to let him spend the day at the farm, but his father's idea of spending the day at the farm was to let him go down with Uncle Jamie who owned the farm, before dinner, do some odd jobs, and then come back by dinnertime. Brian's idea was to go there early in the morning, exercise and brush down Stardust, help with the feeding; go out with Dinny to plow the great open fields; eat with him and listen to him and the men talk. There were also the horses, the pigs, the cows, the calves, the fruit. . . . There was everything at the farm, and if you only spent an hour there you saw nothing and did nothing.

Brian was very careful not to make any noise when he passed his father's room. He was walking on the smooth linoleum in his stockinged feet when, at the top of the stairs, his foot slipped from under him and he fell all the way downstairs, making a noise like a roll of thunder.

"God bless and save us!" cried his mother from the kitchen where she was already up and cooking the breakfast. She saw it was Brian. "What on earth made you do that? Are you hurt, darling?"

Brian wasn't sure whether he was hurt or not. The back of his head had hit the last step with a thump. He thought it wiser to say nothing for the moment. He would get something extra if he were hurt.

"What's going on down there?" That was Brian's father.

"It's Brian," said his mother sympathetically. "He fell down the stairs and nearly killed himself."

"What did he do that for, the idiot?" His father was always a bit sour in the mornings until he had had breakfast.

Brian waited to hear if he would say anything about going down to the farm at this early hour, but the news that Brian had hurt himself must have caused him to forget about the rest.

"Here, son," said his mother, as he sat down at the table, "this'll take the pain away."

Mary Tracey was the daughter of farmers from nearby County Cavan. She had been convent-trained to make a wife that could take care of a home and who after thirteen years of married life still believed that Michael's love and the devotion of her three children were the only things that she needed in this life. She loved the foolish ways of the three boys and often, as Brian had told her, seemed to be "laughing inside" at what they did or said. Brian's father loved to play tricks on her, such as leaving rubber spiders on the bed or rubber blots of ink on her fresh white tablecloth. Sometimes he would insist on kissing her and Mary would blush and resist and say: "Not in front of the children." But Brian and the other two would clap hands and cheer Da on.

She now pushed toward Brian's place at the table a plate with two sausages and four or five thick slices of bread that had been dipped in gravy and fried hard and smooth on both sides. Brian knew then that the fall had not been without some use after all. The only way to get Mother on your side was to be suffering from something or somebody. It was through watching the antics of Paul in front of her that he had learned this. Paul was such a sly codger Brian could never figure out how his mother did not catch on to him. Sean, now, could try the very same tricks on her, but she always saw through Sean's game and laughed at him but gave him what he wanted anyway. Brian often heard his father and the men say they never could figure out women, and he supposed that this was what they meant. He also noticed that, oddly enough, Paul never tried any of his tricks on his father.

He sat down to breakfast. His mother looked at him sharply: "Did you forget something?" she said.

"Oh yes," said Brian. He bowed his head very low and *me-me me'd* with his lips as if he were saying grace and wondered if

Dinny would be in a bad mood and not let him near Stardust.

"Up!" said his mother suddenly.

"I'm praying," said Brian, offended. "I'm saying grace."

"Get up and wash that face!" said his mother.

"What's the use?" he complained. "I'm only going down to the farm, and I'll be dirty again in five minutes!"

"At least for five minutes you'll look like a son o' mine!" said his mother. "Up!"

Half sulking, Brian went in to the scullery sink and sloshed the water round noisily, trying to save himself from its icy bite so early in the morning. As he stared in the glass he was almost ready to admit to himself that his face looked, not funny, but different. His thick, black hair came down his forehead in a V like a duenna cap, and his eyebrows worried him. At school his companions kept reminding him of the proverb: "Beware the man whose eyebrows meet, for in his heart there lies deceit." *His* eyebrows not only met but clashed in a thick black V between his eyes. He used to be worse until he made his mother let him cut his hair short instead of bunching it up on top of his head like a Zulu's. That's what the boys at school had called him at first: *Zulu.* Nat Turley was the last one he had made give up saying that. Nat and he had fought so often over it with nobody ever winning that they had got fed up fighting and had begun to like each other, and now Nat would fight anybody who called him Zulu.

After breakfast he pulled on his thick jersey and buttoned his knickers at the knees. He wanted to be all fixed up for the farm. Before he left, his mother tugged this way and that at his jersey and held him up still more while she pressed him very tightly to her the way he always hated when they were in public. At last, after brushing back his hair with her fingers, she let him go.

Outside the sun was coming up over Tara Hill and the ground looked like the house on Sunday morning when the floor had been washed and the brasses polished the night before. Even the green grass around the house was brighter and the tops of the cobblestones in the yard were shining. A mist almost hid the sun, although it was coming through as a big gray ball, and that was a sign that it would be a warm day. The birds were already chirping around the door, waiting for his mother to throw them the breakfast crumbs she carried out in her apron. The birds came down fast enough when she appeared, for they knew that any crumbs that came later during the day would be picked up by the hens. Hens, thought Brian, should have been all neck and belly, for the only thing he ever saw them do was peck and eat, peck and eat.

He shivered slightly when he got outside. But it was only the sort of shiver he often pretended whenever he came home very hungry and it was too early for a meal. It made his mother worry about a cold and she would give him something to eat to keep him warm. The countryside was still lonely, as if the early cold and dampness had lulled the people into a longer sleep than usual.

The Tracey hundred-acre farm lay about a mile to the south of Drumree along the road to Belfast. Brian's family lived in a brick house of two stories that was so small his father called it a cottage, and it lay to the extreme northeast corner of the farm. Two fields below stood the much bigger home of Uncle Jamie. Facing Brian on the northwest was Tara, a hill crowned by a copse of chestnut and larchwood trees. Tara was a favorite haunt of Brian's, for when in the mood he could hide among the trees or gaze down enraptured at the sweeping panorama of checkered fields which sloped away from his feet and which, to Brian's continued admiration, was always clothed appropriately to the seasons. It was not that it merely changed color with the seasons. Everything did that; flowers and leaves and birds and animals changed color with the seasons. What appealed to Brian more than all this was the fact that the great stretch of land before him looked like a bed, it was so peaceful, a bed which in winter nature covered with a heavy brown blanket that slowly became lighter and brighter through spring and when summer came was so light and airy the slightest winds caused ripples to run through it and raise it off the bed.

Below Tara lay the Long Field and further on the farm buildings; to the right of the farm lay Benburb Glen, through which flowed a brook that the people imaginatively called "the river." Beyond that again the road swept to the right, rounding off the farm, and the brook curved round with it. This Tara was not the "Tara of the Kings." Brian used to think so until one day Miss Lavin told the class that the kings of old used to live on Tara but that nobody lived there any more. Brian had whispered to Nat Turley that the Traceys lived there now and that Spudface Lavin didn't know what she was blethering about. Turley laughed, and the teacher saw him and gave him a smack on the ear for disturbing. She asked him what the laugh was for, and Turley told her that Brian had said that the Traceys lived on Tara now and would always live there, no matter who was king of Ireland or what Miss Lavin said.

"God help Ireland if that omadhaun was king!" said Miss Lavin to the class. She told them then that Tara of the Kings was a hundred miles from there, but for a long time afterward she called Brian "King Tracey of Tara Hill."

"To blazes with her!" said Brian defiantly this morning. "The women are a curse!" He had heard Dinny Coleman use the phrase, and it suited well his mood. Digging his hands deep down into his pockets, he pulled his shoulders almost up to his ears the way he had seen the big fellows do when they came to the fairs in their blue serge suits with their trousers slapping high up over their brown boots. He spat on the road and whistled, and a big cock pheasant swooshed out of the ditch not more than fifty yards ahead and whirred away into the trees. After that Brian stopped whistling. If he kept quiet he would spot a lot of game out foraging before the rest of the world woke up. He left the hard cobblestone center of the road and walked on the soft, spongy turf at the side where his hobnailed boots made no sound.

Away over on the other side of the glen the rabbits nibbled the grass and hopped nervously around the big rabbit burrow Mattusalum Molloy used to shoot at. Mattusalum had told Brian he was over a hundred and twenty years old and had lived to that age because he rinsed his guts clean every day with Guinness's stout. He was fond of rabbit shooting, and when he got too old to walk much he took the gun out mornings and came to the Tracey side of Tara Hill, opposite the burrow. There he lit his pipe, stretched himself out flat on his broad belly, and aimed the gun at the hole. When the rabbits came out Mattusalum let fly, killing one or two. Then he went home and told one of his clutter of grandchildren to go out and bring them in.

Grown too old even to come out and shoot rabbits, Mattusalum now lay in bed most of the time, coming out only on warm days to sun himself. He kept his sheep dog, Roger, with him. Brian liked Roger, but Roger, too, was getting old, and he often wondered who would be the first to go, for the one would soon follow the other.

Brian skited another spit thoughtfully through his front teeth in the direction of the rabbits and plucked a thick straw from the side of the ditch. Pretending it was a cigarette, he pulled on it, taking deeper draws than he would have dared if it had been real.

It felt so good going down to the farm he bubbled inside and, to get there faster, began to run out on the hard center of the road, having since forgotten why he had kept to the soft turf at the side. The nails his father had put in his boots—he said that not even cast-iron boots would hold Brian up for long—slid and slithered all over the road and nearly threw him a couple of times. Brian did not mind. He liked to see the sparks fly from the iron nails as they struck the smooth cobblestones. When the sparks did not flash out by themselves he made them by skimming the heads of the cobblestones with the iron tip of his boot.

He must have been running fast, for he came round a corner and surprised a squirrel sitting like a tiny patch of gray cloud on the road, staring at him, his paws in front of his chest with the claws bent inward. The squirrel realized his danger and, with a frightened scurry, dashed up the tree behind him, his claws scraping the bark like the rustle of dry leaves. He raced on up to the very top of the tree, leaped from there to the top of another tree, weaving designs against the blue sky as the treetop swayed in the wind.

"Come on down, you blackguard!" Brian shook his fist at the squirrel. "What did you do to go scootin' off like that for?"

A robin tugging at a clay-colored worm in the ground away from the road did not even bother to notice Brian, and Brian felt too happy to annoy him. He started off again at a run in the direction of the farm.

2

As Brian neared the farm he heard the pigs squealing like the fools they were. Dinny must be bringing the hot swill out to them. They never waited until he poured out the swill but, just like pigs, stepped into the trough and let Dinny pour the food over them. Dinny had told him that was why they were called pigs, "for only pigs would act the way they do." The squealing started the cocks crowing and the cows lowing, and Dinny began to curse them all at the top of his voice.

"Get t'hell outta that!" he cried. The palm of Dinny's hand came down with a smack on the back of a lazy sow, and she let out a frightened squeal. Dinny was in a bad mood.

Brian then heard the one sound he had been waiting for since he had headed for the farm. It was the whinny of a horse. "The greatest, the beautifullest, and if only they'd give him the chance, the fastest horse in the whole world!" The sound set his heart leaping as much as it leaped when he heard Spudface Lavin say in her nasty, squeaky voice: "There'll be no school tomorrow!" Something gurgled inside him, and he ran faster for the rest of the road, and his hobnail boots again drew fire from the heads of the cobblestones.

When he got down to the farmyard, Turnip, the Irish terrier that guarded the farm, barked and snapped bad-temperedly at his feet, and Brian knew that she was protesting over the way he was coming into the farmyard. He stopped and patted her on the head, and Turnip whined with pleasure for she was seeing Brian for the first time that day. He let Turnip lick his face for a while.

"I have to go and see Stardust," said Brian again. When he said "Stardust," Brian could see by the look in Turnip's eye that Turnip was jealous of the horse, so he didn't mention Stardust any more.

There were two stables in front of him at the bottom of the yard, one on each side of the hayloft. Tufts and strands of hay hung out from between the floor of the hayloft and the badly fitting door of the stable to the left. Brian went up to this stable and stood outside the door.

"Stardust!" he called out. Inside, the horse made little noises in his throat and rustled the straw bedding. Brian opened the door and the morning light shone on the black coat of the horse's smooth, round rump.

"Stardust," said Brian again. "You're the most beautiful animal in the whole wide world!"

Brian could have cried with joy when Stardust nodded his smooth head up and down vigorously in agreement.

"Have you had your breakfast yet?"

Stardust nodded again and Brian knew he said no. He took an apple from a box he kept on a shelf and gave it to Stardust. Dinny told him that if he wanted animals to love him, he would have to give them something every time he saw them.

"Hey, there!"

Brian turned round quickly and saw Dinny looking at him the way he sometimes did when Brian was not sure if Dinny was mad or glad. Dinny Coleman was a man whose appearance was deceptive. To Brian he had at first seemed old, perhaps because he drank porter and moved and spoke slowly. The clothes he wore were not the kind to set off a man's figure: heavy army boots, trousers greasy and baggy, and a blue cap that was shiny from the pull of his swilly fingers. But Brian once saw Dinny at a party, and he had scarcely recognized the stalwart who had thumped him on the back by way of greeting.

Another time he had seen Dinny playing Gaelic football for the parish, and, although Dinny was not a fast player, he was a cool one and a rough one. The next time he had seen Dinny he had asked him why he worked on the farm, and Dinny had told him that he was looking for the crock of gold that was hidden on the Tracey farm, and that as soon as ever he found it, he was going to buy a farm of his own, find himself a girl that had money or good sense or both—"Although," he confided to Brian, "that was harder to find than the crock o' gold!"—and settle down. After this intimacy, Dinny and he had become the best of friends. Brian was very fond of Dinny, for Dinny treated him like a man and always said: "Since you're a man like one of ourselves, I can tell you this." And Dinny took Brian's advice and did not let the other children fool around with the animals, especially Stardust.

"What t'hell do you think you're doing?" called out Dinny. "Scaring the lights outta the baste?"

"The baste." That was the signal. When Dinny called Stardust "the baste" and not by his right name, Brian knew that Dinny's stomach was acting up because he had been out late the night before. Dinny always told Brian that the night air disagreed with him, but Brian had heard Uncle Jamie saying that Dinny and Tim Slattery, the other farm hand, often went out at night to get drunk together.

"I was just taking a look at Stardust, Mr. Coleman," Brian said. "Can I give him a little exercise this morning? I think he needs it, Mr. Coleman."

"It's *Mister* Coleman, ye humbug, when ye want anything!" said Dinny shortly. He walked away and left Brian wondering what to do. When he was about ten yards off, however, he stopped and turned round.

"Ye can go," he said. "But don't vex him an' "—there was a pause as if it was a bitter pill he had to swallow—"mebbe I'll let ye rub him down as well."

"Thank you, Mr. Coleman," said Brian politely. He felt like genuflecting the way he did while serving Father Quinn's quick Mass for the hunters. He knew Dinny knew he was only humbugging him, but Brian didn't care. All he cared about was that he was going to spend the whole morning alone with Stardust.

Stardust's stable had not yet been cleaned out and the dung lay around in small, dark-brown heaps. There was a pungent smell that the other children could not stand. It suited Brian all right. Anything that was around Stardust suited him. He gave Stardust another apple from the box on the shelf and loved the way Stardust's big velvety lips tickled the palm of his hand. While the horse crunched the apple between his long brown teeth, Brian ran his hands down the sleek, shining body. The muscles of the horse's legs and back twitched with pleasure, and his tail swished although there were no flies at him. Brian put his arms around him and hugged him and listened to his heart pumping the blood through his great body.

The only chance Brian ever got to ride Stardust was when Dinny let him exercise him and rub him down. For Stardust belonged to Uncle Jamie, who used him to follow the county hunt and to pull the trap on Sundays when the family went to chapel. The most Brian could hope for then was to be allowed to hold the reins when the trap was out on the open road.

Brian slipped the halter over the horse's long head. Stardust pretended he didn't like it and kept shaking his head and pulling away from Brian. But Brian knew that Stardust was humbugging, too, for when Brian got him out into the open air Stardust began to prance and dance like a race horse, which Brian knew he really was.

Brian walked him slowly and did not make too free, aware that Dinny, with his bad temper, might be watching. But when he had walked him for about fifteen minutes and had reached the Long Field that was over the crest of the hill where Dinny could not see him, he threw the reins over Stardust's neck and, mounting his bare, sleek back, slithered over the broad expanse until he got a firm grip with his legs.

"Com'on, Stardust!" he said.

Both horse and rider knew what they wanted—a good brisk ride. Stardust stretched his long legs and sailed over the ground, and Brian remembered the dream. The morning was still raw, and as they raced along Brian felt his clothes cold against his chest and knees. The sharp wind cut the tips of his ears and tingled his cheeks and made his eyes water when he locked ahead away from the ground that was flying underneath him in long, straight lines. Riding Stardust, Brian knew that all he would ever need to be happy would be a horse like Stardust to ride and a long field to ride him in. He rode him up and down the Long Field twice, shouting "Whooee!" at the top of his voice, and each time he shouted Stardust shook his head and whinnied.

But Brian was still afraid of Dinny's bad temper, and at the end of the ride he stopped Stardust and let him canter for a while to give him back his wind. When Stardust was breathing easily again, Brian slid off his smooth, swaying rump and led him to the farmyard, keeping his eyes on the ground all the time so that Dinny would see that he had been good and not up to any monkey business with Stardust.

About an hour later Brian had finished brushing down Stardust and was starting to brush him down all over again when he heard a clatter of machinery rattle past the stable.

"Anybody coming out to plow?" called out a voice.

That was Dinny, and Brian knew then that his bad temper had gone and he was in good humor again. Brian gave Stardust a pat on the head, threw the brush in a corner, emptied the basin quickly, and ran out of the stable. The two plow horses, Peg and Tom, were already pulling the three-blade plow out of the yard, for Dinny was too proud to stop for anyone. Brian ran after him and pulled himself up onto the connecting bar behind the seat. This was a dangerous trick and his mother had forbidden him time and again to do it, but Dinny had told him that if he, Brian, could already handle a plow by himself he was certainly able to stand up on one. "And anyway," he had concluded, "she's only a woman, and they're never right."

"Are ye there, Brian-og?" shouted Dinny.

"I'm here, Dinny!" said Brian. Dinny didn't want the *Mister* any more for he was in good humor again.

"We're going out to plow the new field your uncle bought from the Dorans," shouted Dinny again. After that there was no more talk, and Brian could give all his attention to the sights and sounds he loved.

Across the swaying brown-and-white rumps of Peg and Tom he examined the field that was covered with hard earth and the rotten stocks of the last corn crop. It was not so easy to stay up behind Dinny when the plow rolled over the uneven ground, but Brian held on and watched the curved blades turn up the slices of soil, sheer and polished by the blade, and twisting and crumbling under him. It smelt strong as rotten leaves when the stringy roots that looked like white worms half hidden in the dark, brown earth were uncovered. Two or three blue-black crows followed the plow and pecked at the seeds in the upturned soil. Dinny jerked his thumb back at them.

"They're the souls of farmers that paid poor wages to the help," he said. "God cursed them and condemned them to wander the earth in search of something to eat. That's what the farm help had to do when they were alive!"

"Are you hungry, Dinny?" Brian asked when they had been a long time plowing.

"Why wouldn't I be?" said Dinny. "But she won't be long now with the bread and butter and a good strong cup o' scald."

A few minutes later Brian saw Aunt Cathey, the sister of his father and the youngest of the three Traceys, come into the field by the top gate near the house. She was carrying a white enamel pot of tea and a plate of thick bread-and-butter sandwiches covered with a cloth.

Aunt Cathey wore a white apron over her long blue dress. She was, as Dinny had once described her, neither too small nor too tall. She kept her hair brushed back close across her head, tied at the nape of the neck, and then flowing loosely down her back. Her clear, fresh complexion gave her in Brian's eyes something of the nunlike quality of the Sisters at the convent school. Indeed, he always thought of her as a nun or a nurse, the way she had with her of never letting what was said or done around her disturb her overmuch, like the trout that would hover unperturbed as the brown waters of the brook bubbled noisily past them. Cathey had married an engineer years ago who had been lost at sea, and Cathey had been quiet ever since. But her smile was still there, and Brian loved to watch her lips separate and show her even white teeth when she smiled, for he always felt like smiling with her.

She now lived on the farm, working in the house and taking care of the children. They told Cathey more secrets than they told their parents and would as soon disobey the Sisters of the convent school as they would Aunt Cathey, with all her smiles and quiet.

"There ye have it, Brian," said Dinny when Aunt Cathey came within hearing. "The curse of Ireland. The beautiful girls that won't marry again because they're afraid they won't be able to kick up their heels any more at the dances."

"But, Dinny," Brian protested, "Aunt Cathey doesn't go out at all in the evening!"

"Oho!" said Dinny. "So she's hoarding her money to marry a somebody. Or mebbe it's for her dowry for the con . . ." Dinny stopped suddenly and for a moment Brian wondered why no one spoke. But he was glad Dinny had stopped, for it gave him the chance to speak up in defense of Cathey.

"But, Dinny, she gives all her money away!" Brian was indignant at the false accusations against Aunt Cathey.

"Hush, child dear," said Aunt Cathey. "Let the poor devil rave on if it does him any good. The girls don't marry now because the men don't want a wife. All they want is a woman who'll slave for them from morning till night for nothing."

After the sandwiches Brian brought buckets of water and corn in a box for Peg and Tom, and Cathey sat down on the axle of the plow and talked to Dinny, who kept plucking at the blades of grass by the side of the field. When the two horses had finished eating, they stood looking mutely at the ground, waiting for the work to begin again. After a while Aunt Cathey took up the pot and empty plate and went back up the hill toward the house. When she reached the crest of the hill she paused as if waiting, and a few moments later a second figure joined her from the other side. This was a young girl about ten years old. She had long dark, chestnut hair and a lean face. She wore a dress tucked in at the waist, black full-length woolen stockings, and high boots. Cathey spoke to her and patted her on the head and moved away. The little girl, however, stayed on and looked down at Dinny and Brian as if she were uncertain of her welcome.

Brian saw her and rose to his feet. "There's that Sheila Reilly again!" he said impatiently. "I warned her twice not to poke her nose in this farm!"

"Oh, what harm can little Sheila do?" said Dinny.

"What harm can she do?" echoed Brian. "She can annoy you and me and everybody, and I've seen her fooling about with the animals and even edge up to Stardust. You'd better be careful about Stardust, Dinny, with that skinnymalink hanging around!" He picked up a stone from the ground and threw it at the still standing figure.

The little girl provocatively stretched forward her head and shoulders, slowly and deliberately brought her right arm round in a wide, exaggerated arc, put her thumb to her nose, wagged her four fingers, and at the same time put out her tongue. She stayed like that until a flying stone came dangerously close. While Brian was groping in the soft earth to find another stone, she straightened up, placed her arms akimbo, and did one or two steps of the "Sailor's Hornpipe," a dance the Sisters up at the convent school were then teaching her, since dancing was one of the accomplishments of a young lady.

Brian ran a few steps up the hill toward her, and she suddenly stopped dancing, turned, and disappeared over the horizon, her hair streaming in the wind.

Picking up another stone, Brian threw it in her general direction. "You're a *woman!*" he called out after her. "That's what you are!"

"You really know how to handle them, Brian-og," said Dinny approvingly. He rose and stretched. "What are you going to be when you grow up?"

"A farmer," said Brian. "With pigs and chickens . . . and a horse like Stardust."

"Aye," said Dinny. He looked away toward the end of the field, and his bright blue eyes narrowed and the skin about them wrinkled up into small, smooth pieces like the back of an old leather glove. "It's a great life, Brian-og. At least the bastes and the land will never deceive ye. And you'll always have something when ye have the land." He dug his foot into the crumbly soil of a freshly plowed ridge. "But if ye stay long enough ye'll find yerself alone. Them that has to stay wants to go, and them that wants to go has to stay; and if them that goes would work half as hard at home as they did away, the country'd soon be rotten with rich men! And, anyway, what the blazes good is an Irishman without land?"

"But, Dinny," said Brian, "*I* won't leave the farm!"

"That's not the rumor that's flyin' around these parts," said Dinny. But before they could talk any more Dinny said something about the evening being short and having to finish before it got too dark. "I can't plow half as well without ye, Brian-og. So let's finish this bit of a field and head for home."

"I don't like school," said Brian when the plowing was over and Dinny sat down at the edge of the axle for a final smoke. "I like to take care of Stardust and plow."

"Aye," said Dinny, "but ye need book larnin' these days if ye want to get a job."

"I don't want to get a job; I want to be a farmer."

"But ye still need some book larnin'."

"I can read books—especially history books. I like *them.* But I don't like the history at school. I like to read books by myself."

"What history do ye like best?"

"Books about Red Hugh O'Neill, Patrick Sarsfield, Daniel O'Connell, and all."

"Oh, Irish history," said Dinny.

"Of course," said Brian. He wondered what other history Dinny could be thinking of.

"Hop on, Brian-og," said Dinny, rising. "And I'll let ye drive the plow home."

Brian jumped up at once into the cold iron seat, shaped like a pear leaf, and took up the reins. Dinny put his foot on the axle, laid his right hand with the broken and dirty fingernails on Brian's shoulder, and pulled himself up behind.

"Harrup!" said Dinny. Brian was going to tell him he should not have "harrupped" at the horses since he, Brian, was holding the reins. "Harrup!" he said louder than Dinny.

The horses tugged at the shafts and the heavy plow moved forward, and very soon they were out of the field onto the hard, dry road again and on their way back to the farm and supper and rest.

The sun was going down when they reached the farmyard. Brian helped Dinny unhitch Peg and Tom, and when they were unhitched Brian took hold of the rope bridles and led them into the stable for the night. He was so small in front of their huge bulk that he wondered what would happen to him if they squeezed him in between them.

"Stay there, Peg!" he said, and Peg stood waiting for him to tell her what to do next. Brian took the halter off Tom and put him into the stall. He did the same with Peg. The two horses began to chomp the hay from the manger, curling their upper lips and showing their long, brown teeth. Brian then brought them corn and water and left them for the night.

Dinny was still working in the machine shed, and Brian told him what he had done.

"Good lad," said Dinny. "Now run up and get something to eat. Ye have worked harder today than any kid brother of yours will ever do in a year."

"I can still do something else, Dinny," offered Brian.

"No, go on up now."

"If you want me to, Dinny," said Brian. He had been ready to work longer to show how much better he was than his brothers, but all the same he was glad that Dinny would not let him. He had a very empty feeling in his stomach.

He walked back up the lane toward the house, and when he reached the bend that would cut the farm out of sight he turned back to look. The sun had already gone down and had taken with it over the horizon all the rude noises of the day, and a soft purple glow was spreading among the branches of the trees on the hills beyond the glen.

Brian loved what he saw. He loved it fiercely, as if he had to show defiance to something or someone as proof of that love. He was so moved he slapped the trunk of a tree with his open palm, dug his hands deep into his trouser pockets the way Dinny did, and spat out mannishly.

"Begod!" he exclaimed. "When I grow up and get money I'll buy the biggest farm in Ireland! An' I'll live on it every day till I'm as old as Mattusalum Molloy!"

3

Brian did not take the long path he had taken in the morning that led from the farm to the little brick house standing on the north edge of the Tracey land on the Drumree Road. Instead he took the short cobblestone lane to the house where Uncle Jamie, his father's brother, who owned the farm, lived with his wife Meg, their two children, Patrick and Bridget, and Aunt Cathey. It was the custom for the two families to eat there together every Saturday evening and talk and play a little before Michael's children went home for the Saturday-night bath.

Once upon a time they had alternated houses every Sunday for the meal, although Cathey had always done the cooking. But Meg had changed all that. Now it was always at her house and on Saturdays, not Sundays. Brian had heard her saying something about being "at home" on Sunday, although he couldn't understand how her being at home should change things. She always had been at home when they went to eat there. Brian could not see much in eating at Uncle Jamie's any more. For, although he considered Aunt Cathey the best cook in the world, the parents now talked very little to each other and the children did not play together. Patrick went to his room after the meal and Bridget sat apart in a corner and read fashion magazines. It usually ended up with Brian, Paul, and Sean playing by themselves for a half hour or so with Patrick's and Bridget's old toys.

Another thing Brian could never understand was why his father should have to live in such a small house, while Uncle Jamie had such a large and comfortable home as the one Aunt Meg was trying to make everybody call a "residence." When he had asked his father to explain, his father had taken him up on his knee and kept him there despite Brian's struggles to wriggle free from this childish position.

"So you want to hear the facts of life, my lad," Michael had said. "Well, here we go. When *my* dad was alive he owned lots o' land round here and the two houses besides. Then one day he suddenly ups and dies on us without making a will, and his land and houses had to be divided among his three children: your uncle Jamie, your aunt Cathey, and myself. Uncle Jamie got the big house and most of the land he has today; your dad got a bit of land and the small house, and a third parcel of land was sold and the money given to Aunt Cathey when she married."

"But why did Uncle Jamie get so much, Da?" asked Brian.

"I'm not sure to this day," said Michael. The smile faded from his face when he said this: "But I can't help thinking that your aunt Meg had a finger in the pie. She's nobody's fool. Your dear aunt Cathey and I found out too late that the solicitor who handled the whole business was a cousin of hers.

"I was seeing a bit of the world then and trying to make my fortune, for there never was much in this country for a farmer's younger son. I asked them to sell my land and send on the money but keep the cottage for me in case I didn't come home with a crock o' gold. As a matter of fact, I came home broke—maybe I was a bit careless with my money—and got a job at the Drumree post office with a pay as tiny as the post office itself. After I married it was too little so I had to work in my spare time on the farm for my own brother. And that's not the easiest thing in the world, believe me!"

"But, Da," said Brian, "why should Aunt Meg have her finger in the pie? And anyway, she can't bake pies. She can't cook nothing as well as Aunt Cathey!"

"She can cook up things better than anyone I know," said Michael. "She has cooked up Jamie so that he'll hardly recognize his own, and since Aunt Meg went into business and opened the store in the village, he's beginning to believe he's the quare fella!

To think that at school we used to laugh at the dunderhead! I could'a twisted him round my little finger! But he's a good worker and she's a good manager, I suppose. Anyway, now she's trying to separate the two families, and I can't say but as usual she's succeeding in her intent. So I'm looking for a way out of it, my lad. Better to walk out decently while there's time than be thrown out later." At this point Michael was staring at the ground and was talking to himself more than to the child on his knee. He was brought back to reality as Brian, suddenly losing interest, slid from his arms to the ground and ran off.

Jamie and Meg lived in a two-and-a-half-story house that stood at the east end of the farm and was sheltered by an elbow of hill that curved round it protectingly and hid it from the Drumree Road. The building itself was not beautiful. It was of brick covered with white plaster and had a blue-gray slate roof. There were no shutters for the house did not need them, and the window frames were so flush with the wall they looked to Brian as if they had been painted on in blue. The white plaster on the walls always reminded him of the icing on the cakes his mother made, where the broad knife left little curved risings. At each end of the roof two skylights peeped out over the slates from the attics. The only thing that broke the slablike façade of the house was the little portico—a curious adjunct of fluted columns that had nothing to do with such a house other than to keep in the heat during the winter months and at the same time preserve a minimum of privacy, for the front door opened into the dining-sitting room. An earlier Tracey had, perhaps, found the columns in some elegant building about to be torn down and had seen how they could still be useful.

The house always gave Brian the impression that, although it was solid and compact and well able to withstand the raw winters of northern Ireland, it had, somehow, a smooth, chilly, uninviting exterior. It reminded him of the white-and-blue icebox at home where his mother kept things cold.

Tonight, however, the lamps were lit in the house, shedding around a soft glow of comfort, and, besides, he had a feeling of anticipation, for he was hungry and tired and the chill of the evening was entering his bones. He pushed open the outer door, closed it with a hind kick of his hobnail boot, rubbed his nose clean on the sleeve of his jersey, elbowed through the second door, and blinked as he entered the lighted room.

The two Tracey families were already seated around two tables when Brian came in. At one table sat the elders. Uncle Jamie was at the head; to his right sat Michael and Mary and to his left Meg and Cathey. Patrick and Bridie and then Brian, Paul, and Sean sat at the second table. Patrick, the oldest of the group, in the little contact his mother allowed him to have with Michael's children, imitated his father's air of master of the house and sat at the head of the second table. Brian sat at his right, but since Patrick rarely said a word Brian found it more interesting to listen to the conversation of the other table. Brian now went to his place, said a quick grace, and, putting his hand between his legs, pulled his chair close to the table. Cathey rose and brought over a large pot of meat stew and ladled out a generous portion for him. She stood behind his chair with her hands on his shoulders as she looked around the table. Brian did not like these little signs of affection to be given under the cold eye of Patrick, and he wriggled in his chair to free himself. But Cathey pretended not to notice. She cupped his chin and cheeks in her cool, soft hands for a while until the calls of the children disturbed her short reverie.

"Some more stew, Aunt Cathey!" pleaded Patrick.

"Brian's getting all the meat, Auntie!" called out Paul.

"You shut up, boy, or I'll give it to you!" retorted Brian.

"Hush children!" said Aunt Cathey. "You can't have any more meat and you can't have any more stew. Stuff yourselves the way you're doing and you won't have any room for the apple dumpling. If you're as hungry as all that, eat some bread and butter."

She left them and went into the kitchen for the apple dumpling.

There was a lot of noise from the younger ones at the table and a fairly continuous flow of conversation from the older people. At one point, however, the noise at Brian's table suddenly died before it rose again. In that momentary hush Brian noticed a silence at the elders' table, and instinct told him that something was amiss. He glanced sideways and saw Uncle Jamie and his father and mother looking down at the tablecloth. Aunt Meg was grimly staring straight ahead. Brian kept his eyes fixed in front of him but his ears cocked for any scrap of conversation that might come his way.

"I know it's hard, Michael," Uncle Jamie was saying, ". . . leave sooner or later . . ."

"I suppose so," said Brian's father. Brian watched him crumble a piece of bread between his finger and thumb and then with his forefinger bring the crumbs into a little heap. "But 't'isn't easy, when . . . flesh and blood . . ." He picked up the crumbs with his fingers, threw back his head, and dropped them into his open mouth.

Brian's mother and his aunt Cathey kept on eating with their heads lowered, but Brian saw Aunt Meg casting a sharp eye now and then at the two men. Aunt Meg was a great woman for business, and ever since his father had told him of the dividing of the property Brian never had any use for her. And from the day he had bitten her forearm to make her let go of him, Brian knew she was a little afraid of him, although his two younger brothers, Paul and Sean, were afraid of her.

". . . had to come some time." This was Meg, curtly, no-nonsenselike.

". . . your fair share, Michael, you know that . . . never quarreled about anything before . . ." That was Uncle Jamie.

". . . going to miss . . ."

"Sentimental rubbish!" said Aunt Meg. ". . . used to it."

Brian was very sad that evening after supper and his heart was full of misgivings. Without a word to anyone he slipped out of the house through the kitchen and down to the farm. It was always pleasanter, anyway, to sit around the farm when the animals were getting ready for sleep. When he went in to see the horses, even Stardust just turned sleepy eyes at him, closed them again, and dozed off; some of the cows were lying on their sides on the straw, ruminating and regurgitating contentedly; the hens were very quiet and stared at him indignantly for breaking in on their peace, the way Miss Lavin did when she suspected him of talking out of the side of his mouth. Only Turnip was still about and she was chasing rats, dashing from one hole in the floor of the barn to another and sniffing and scraping with her front paws. Occasionally she would look up at Brian for approval. When she got it she would start scraping with fresh vigor.

Brian went up to the little shanty that served as an office where the farm accounts, milk figures, and egg-laying rates were kept. It was also used as a sort of meeting house for the farm hands when they wanted a quiet smoke.

Dinny and Tim Slattery, the farm hand, a tall, angular man with weak eyes, uncombed red hair, and a general scrawny look about him, were sitting on two milking stools. Both men were sipping from glasses half filled with dark brown liquid. On the table between them stood a black bottle with a coffee-colored label: McCaffrey's Porter.

Brian sat down in front of them. He looked at them gloomily and they looked at him.

"Manalive!" said Dinny. "Look at that long face!"

"His mother-in-law must have died suddenly!" said Tim with a vacant grin that showed pale upper gums.

"What's wrong, Brian-og?" asked Dinny.

"Somebody's going to leave the farm," answered Brian slowly.

"Well, ye'll know who it is sooner or later!" said Dinny. "Ye can't have two roosters in one coop!"

"Oh, Dinny!" said Brian. "I'm so afraid it's gonna be me!"

"Cheer up, lad, cheer up!" said Dinny. "If ye was a man I'd give ye a belt o' this and it'd soon have ye leppin' like a hare and laughin' at your troubles!"

"What're you drinking?" asked Brian.

"Porter, lad, porter," said Dinny.

"What's porter made of?" asked Brian.

"Mornin' mist and Saxon's blood!" said Tim.

"Aye," said Dinny. "And it's the terrible stuff to get down!"

"Then why do you drink it?" asked Brian.

"It builds up your strength, and Tim and me needs to build up our strength with all the slaving we have on this farm. And it helps us drown our sorrows."

"If it drowns *my* sorrows can I have a sip?"

"No, ye can't. I told ye it was a man's drink," said Dinny. "It's not for kids." He looked across the big black bottle at Tim, who was just then sinking his cold blue nose into an inch of froth. Brian saw his underlip curl round the glass.

"I'm no kid!" he said.

"How was the flower show in the village this afternoon, Tim?" Dinny ignored Brian.

"There was a wheen o' nice chrysanthemums, Dinny," said Tim.

"I'm no kid, I tell you!" broke in Brian. "If I was a kid could I handle a plow alone? Could I comb Stardust better'n anybody?"

"Will ye hould yer whist, child?" protested Tim. "One sip o' that'd floor ye!"

"It wouldn't! I once gnucked some of Da's whisky, and that didn't floor me!"

"Well, just to show him that he's still a child in the cradle," said Tim to Dinny, "I'll give him a sip. But if it knocks him over I hope he won't open his mouth again when there's men talkin'."

"Aw, dry up, aul' Bluenose!" Brian was growing reckless in his sorrow. "You're always blowin'!"

"All right," said Tim good-naturedly. "Here! And begod if ye can't knock down a thimbleful like that, I hope ye'll have the good sense to knock off the yappin'!"

Brian raised the full glass to his lips and swallowed the liquid in a chewing motion.

"Oah!" He took the glass from his lips and gasped for breath. "There's half the glass down and am I floored?"

"Well . . . maybe I was wrong," said Tim. "If I find that I was ye'll see that I'll be the first one to admit my own mistake. Try another mouthful."

Brian tried another mouthful. He emptied the glass.

"Are ye boxed?" asked Tim. He reached down and took a fresh bottle from under the table. He refilled his glass and then rolled the empty bottle out of sight somewhere about his feet.

" 'Course I'm not boxed!" Brian put the glass down on the table and stared about him for a moment.

"Here," said Tim. "Now take a sip o' this. It'll kill the taste of the other." He drew a flat half-pint glass from his coat pocket and held it out to Brian.

Brian looked at the almost colorless liquid it contained. "What is it?" he asked.

"Mountain dew, lad," answered Tim.

"Mountain dew?" echoed Brian. "Where did you get it?"

"The fairies took it from the lips of the leaves early this morning before human hand or foot had time to contaminate the land."

"What a lot o' horse manure! Hic! Think I'm daft enough to take all that in!"

"Well, wherever it came from it's the one thing that'll kill the smell of liquor, so your Da won't know you've had a drop." Tim unscrewed the top and handed the bottle to Brian. Brian tipped the bottle to his lips and took one sip. The stuff was so strong it gathered up his tongue in a tight ball. He took another sip and the fiery liquid burned its way down the back of his mouth, down his throat.

"Whooaa!" he gasped. "There! That's down too. An' am I boxed? He, he, he, he, he! C'n down some more!" He was about to put the bottle to his lips again when Dinny, who had said nothing up to now, interfered.

"Take that away from him, Tim," he said. "He'll do himself harm with that poison." Tim rose and took the bottle from Brian. Brian stood in the center of the shanty looking vaguely from Tim to Dinny, seeing neither clearly. He felt odd, and to hide this he kept talking. "Could take another belt. Not bitter at all. Ha, ha, ha, ha! Aul' Bluenose said I was no man. Can I have another drop o' . . . Who's leavin' the farm? I'm not leavin' the far' . . . I ne'er . . . I'll ne'er leave. I'll . . ."

Slowly groping all the time as if he were searching for something to hold onto, Brian sat down on the earthen floor, stretched out his legs, joined his hands under a flushed cheek, and fell asleep.

He was on Stardust again but he was not riding him with his legs across the horse's broad back. He was lying across Stardust on his stomach, and the jogging pace of the horse was hurting him. . . . He opened his eyes and looked at the blackness beneath him; he turned his head and saw the low shadow of hedges.

"Hey, what's up?" he cried. "Where am I?"

The jogging stopped. Dinny set him on his feet again and held him by the arm.

"Are ye all right, Brian?" asked Dinny.

" 'Course I'm all right."

"We're taking you home."

"And get the lights knocked out o' me for drinkin' porter!" Brian stood looking around, undecided. Suddenly he broke away and ran behind the hedge. When he returned he shook himself like a dog coming out of water.

"I hope ye won't tell on me!" he said. There was a timid, almost querulous note in his voice. "Remember what you said, Dinny! One man doesn't tell on another."

"Of course not!" said Dinny stoutly. "One man never tells on another." He bent down, plucked a few blades of grass, and handed them to Brian.

"Here. Chew the cud on the way up. It'll kill the smell."

Brian stuffed the grass in his mouth and began to chew it, moving his head in time with his teeth. Then, without another word, he turned and ran all the way home.

4

The following Sunday night when Mother helped Brian and his two brothers to bed Brian decided to question her about the conversation at the table.

"Ma," he said, "what were they talking about leaving for last night? And who's leaving the farm, anyway? Are we?"

"Lie down, Brian darling, will you? There's a dear!" coaxed his mother.

"What's Brian want to know, Ma?" said Sean plaintively. "Can I know too?"

"Look, dears," said Mary, "I'll send Daddy in to you and he'll tell you everything and end up with a story. Isn't that nice?"

"Good!" chorused Paul and Sean.

"All right," said Brian noncommittally. When his mother left the room he sat up in bed and folded his arms across his knees. With his eyes fixed on the door he waited for his father to appear.

Brian was very proud of his father, Michael, who had a young-looking face capped by iron-gray hair. Brian's father was always first in the married-versus-single games in the parish and sang and danced at the parties. Sometimes something would happen outside, however, and his mother would have to soothe him and tell him that his temper was running away with him and he'd be sorry afterward. Then both his mother and father would sit quietly together holding each other's hands.

Brian's father could tell the most wonderful stories about the East and other places where he had worked and traveled. But he always ended up by saying that he had been glad to get away from the sweat and heat and the things that happened to men in those strange countries, back to the fresh air and the cool, green hills of Ireland. Brian boasted that his father was head of the post office at Drumree and even had another man to work under him for two weeks every Christmas.

"How's all the rebels tonight?" Michael called out cheerfully as he came in.

Walking over to the large bed where the three boys lay, he sat on the edge, put his right arm around Brian, and sank the fingers of his left hand into Sean's brown curls. Paul, who was next to the wall, struggled up to a sitting position, seized his father's large hand in both his small ones, and placed it on his own head.

Michael Tracey laughed and ruffled Paul's hair.

"Da," said Brian abruptly, "who's leaving the farm?"

"Well, now," said Michael, stroking an imaginary beard very wisely, "maybe it's the banshee that lives down the lane, or maybe it's the big stork that brought the three of you here and lives on top of the trees on Tara Hill."

"Oh, come on, Da, quit foolin'!" complained Brian. "Why don't you tell us? Who's leaving the farm?"

"Oho!" sighed Michael. "I suppose I'd better tell you, for Brian will give us no peace until he finds out. You're a stubborn little omadhaun!"

"So who's leaving the farm?" said Brian.

"We are, son," said his father. The bantering tone died in his voice, and the children sensed that something was wrong. Paul and Sean turned to Brian. They always turned to Brian when anything out of the ordinary happened. They saw Brian's eyes grow misty.

Michael Tracey saw this too.

"Come on, Brian," he coaxed, pressing the boy's warm body to him. "It's not so bad as all that! Listen. Daddy is leaving the small post office here for a very, very important job at a big post office in Belfast. He'll be a big boss with a post office for himself and plenty of money to spend! Besides, we were getting too big to live all together at Uncle Jamie's farm, and you wouldn't want to live in a place full of troublesome women and silly little girls like Bridie and that Sheila Reilly, would you? Of course not! Then . . . and then . . . Oh yes! Then Uncle Jamie says that we can all come up for the holidays to the farm or any time we want. So it's not really leaving, is it?"

Paul and Sean glanced at Brian again and saw him looking very glum. Their mouths drooped in sympathy.

Michael examined the faces of his three children for a moment with a feeling of dismay. More drastic tactics were called for, he decided. Seizing Brian's waist with a strong right arm, he fell back on the bed, ran his left arm under the necks of both Sean and Paul, and pulled them toward him. The three boys immediately understood and entered into the spirit of the fray. In a moment the bed was creaking dangerously under the weight of four squirming bodies and the room was filled with grunts from Michael and shrieks of delight from the boys.

"All right, boys!" said Michael finally. Brian knew that protests would soon be coming up from his mother. "All right! You don't have to kill me altogether, you know." He let them pin his arms down to the bed and waited, puffing, until he regained his breath. "What do I have to do?"

"Tell's a story!" they shouted.

"All right. What kind of story?" said Michael.

"A story about battles!" said Sean.

"A story about the prince who marries the princess and gets half the kingdom," said Paul.

"No," said Brian. "Tell us a story about Ireland."

"Very well, boys. Just let me up," said Michael.

"Wait!" shouted Brian. "Don't let him up until he promises. We let him up once and he ran away."

"I promise," said Michael.

"Cross my heart and cut my throat," said Brian.

"Cross my heart and cut my throat," repeated Michael, crossing his heart with his thumbnail and drawing a vicious forefinger across his throat.

He kicked off his slippers and pulled himself up to the head of the bed. The boys propped him up with pillows. Then they curled themselves about his feet, their eyes glistening with expectancy, for Michael was a good storyteller and had traveled much in his young days.

In a quiet voice that was only rarely sparked with undertones of anger, or enthusiasm, Michael told them of the conquest of Ireland by the Normans, who had invaded and conquered England, and of how the Irish were beaten by great odds in battle or surprised and murdered in treachery by the enemy until only the North held out under the O'Neills, the O'Connells, and the O'Donnells; and how, finally, after the disastrous battle of Kinsale that broke up Gaelic Ireland, the Irish leaders, rather than bow the knee to the invader, formed a plan to leave the country and find help in foreign shores and then to return with new forces; that this famous event, when Ireland was without leaders, was known as "The Flight of the Earls."

"And did they come back, Da?" asked Brian, breaking into the awed silence that followed Michael's story.

"No, son, they did not," replied Michael sadly. "They fought and died, like Patrick Sarsfield, on foreign battlefields and, like him, when they came to die, cried out: 'Oh, that this were for Ireland!'"

"If I'd been there," said Sean, "I'd have taken my sword and killed all the English dead!" He closed his chubby fists and compressed his small red lips fiercely. "When I grow up I'll fight and fight and fight!"

"Oh, dear me! Dear me!" Michael drew back from Sean in mock terror.

"Did they take all the princesses' crowns and jewels with them?" asked Paul.

"Go on with the story, Da," interrupted Brian. "What happened when they left?"

"Well," went on Michael, "when the country was left without leaders the people were beaten. Then Cromwell came and tried to make them accept the new religion. When he failed he chased them 'To hell or Connaught,' stole their land, and planted Scotch Protestants in their place. That was called 'the plantation,' and the very land you're living on now, my lad, had to be bought back acre by acre from their descendents. In time many of these foreigners came to love the country and the people and ended up by becoming more Irish than the Irish themselves!"

"Who were the foreigners, Da?" asked Brian.

"They were mostly Protestants from Scotland," said his father. "That's why in these parts we talk a wee bit like the Scotch."

"Is the trouble all over now, Da?" asked Brian again.

"No," said Michael. "Not yet. I suppose we'll always have a bit of trouble here until the land is ruled by men who love old Ireland."

"What kind of trouble, Da?" asked Sean drowsily. The story part was over, and he was losing interest.

"You're too young to have to bother your little head about that, Seaneen," said his father. He rose from the bed and rearranged the pillows. "Down you go!" he said.

The three boys lay back on the pillows, and Michael drew the bedclothes over them. "It'll soon be midnight, and I don't want the angels to see you awake when they come to close the doors and windows. Good night, boys!"

Paul had already turned to the wall and Sean did not speak. He half opened unseeing eyes and went off to sleep again.

"Good night, Da!" said Brian.

"Good night!" Michael turned down the lamp and closed the door softly behind him.

The next morning Brian complained of pains in his stomach and begged off school. His father came up, felt his pulse, touched his brow, and looked hard at him for a few moments. Brian met his cold stare unflinchingly. Then, without a word, he went downstairs again and left Brian wondering whether it was all right or not. Soon afterward his mother came up, and she felt his pulse and touched his brow and looked at him with her lips pursed, and Brian did not know what to make of her either until she smiled at him. He smiled back at her but only with the front of his mouth to show that he was weak.

"You seem to have a little fever," said his mother. "Stay in bed for a while and see how you feel." Brian allowed himself to smile weakly again. "I'll get you something for the pain."

In about fifteen minutes she came up again, carrying a teapot, cup, and saucer. She poured out a cupful of tealike liquid with a heavy, almost sickly smell.

"What's that muck?" asked Brian flatly.

"Camomile tea, dear," said his mother. "It'll settle your system."

Brian took the cup she handed him and gulped down its contents. "Bah!" he gasped. "More likely to kill me!"

He wiped his mouth with a corner of the bed sheet and did not look at his mother again. Instead, he turned away from her to the wall and pulled the clothes over his head. Mary looked at the bundle covered with the blue counterpane for a moment before she bent down and kissed the part where Brian's head was. She laughed softly at the answering wriggle that could have meant pleasure or protest and, taking up the teapot, cup, and saucer, went downstairs again.

Brian slept on for a couple of hours after that, and when he awoke he stared at the ceiling until he felt an appetite coming on.

"Ma!" he called down.

"Yes, dear?"

"Is Da home?"

"Of course not, dear."

"I think I'm cured," said Brian. "Maybe I could eat now. Not ordinary food but something . . . you know."

"I know, dear," said Mary.

She brought him up a bowl of hot chicken broth, three slices of buttered toast, and a currant bun and watched him as he gravely finished everything. When the meal was over she took away the empty bowl, sat on the edge of the bed, and looked at him. Brian looked back at her for a moment. Then he leaned forward, put his arms round her impetuously, and hugged her.

"You know, Mum," he said seriously. "You're the only real mother in the whole world!"

It rained that afternoon, and for a long time Brian sat staring out of the bedroom at the rain streaming across the windowpane. Suddenly he made up his mind to go out. But he had to wait until his mother went into the kitchen before he could go, for she would never let him leave the house in such weather, although it was just because the weather was like that that he wanted to go out. At the right moment he went downstairs, slipped into the tool shed, and took down his father's old tarry oilskin coat that smelled like stale fish. It was too long and too wide for him, and he had to tie it round his waist with a piece of hemp rope and pull it up over the rope until it was the right length. When he had finished the coat looked like the thick shiny carapace of a dung beetle. Next he donned the sou'wester and ran out of the shed into the strong, slanting rain, unafraid of the rattle against his coat and cap. He felt the rain run down the front of the coat and beat into the loose part of the uppers of his boots, and its cold wetness soon chilled his ankles.

He kept his head down so that the wind caught the upturned brim of his sou'wester and slapped it sharply down across his brow. He did not bother to turn it up again but now and then raised his head to see the stretch of field in front, and when he did this the rain splashed across his cheeks. He opened his mouth to let the heavy raindrops beat against his tongue and into his mouth as far down as his palate. He gurgled and laughed and once or twice shrieked aloud in open delight as he ran across the fields, his sturdy boots squelching in the plashy grass.

Finally he reached the place he was heading for, a knoll of leafy horse-chestnut, oak, and birch trees that stood on the slight raise of the land behind the house. The branches, like the long fingers of a lady, pointed delicately to the sky. From there on a clear day he could see the countryside in front and to both sides for miles. Today there were moments when all he saw was the rain rolling like gray smoke off the blue slates of his home, and it reminded him somehow of a ship in a storm at sea.

He felt well protected by his oilskins from the wind and rain as he stood in the half shelter of the thick foliage and looked through the visorlike opening between his sou'wester and the high collar of his coat. In front of him he saw the white houses on the slopes and in the valleys hug the earth as if they feared they would be lifted up by the fierce winds and blown out to the sea beyond the hills. The water was spilling over the hillsides in places in leaden strips; the trees were all bent away from him, and the dull-silver leaves trembled; the yellow water in the puddles of mud-ribbed roads and lanes leaped up to meet the heavy rain-drops pelting into it; and across the land the rain swept in great wide curves so thick it looked like mist.

For a long time Brian stood there, seeing and feeling and wondering, until, he knew not how, the mist swept over him and into him and he grew sad at the thought of how he was leaving all the people and things he was fond of, of events that had happened long ago, and even at the memory of how happy he had been. At last he shook himself from the cold and started back home, but his pace was slower this time and he kept his head down all the way.

5

By the early summer of that year Michael had made all the preparations for the change. Through relatives named Mooney he had been able to rent a house near the post office where he was to be in charge. The furniture had already been brought down to Belfast by horse and van, and the day had come for the departure of the Traceys for their new home.

Brian had worked until late the day before helping Uncle Jamie ready the trap that Stardust would be pulling, and now its woodwork shone and its brass fittings glinted in the early-morning light as it waited to begin the long trek to Belfast. Brian looked doubtfully at the gray sky and wondered if it would clear up when they got on the road. He wanted to see the new country he was going to pass through with the sun shining on it.

Uncle Jamie and Michael had already seated themselves in the trap and were smoking, rarely exchanging a word, for the mood was on them. Brian was the first of the boys to show up, and he ran behind the house and reappeared a moment later, leading an Irish terrier pup with a length of rope.

"What the blazes has he got now?" said Uncle Jamie, half impatient, half amused. Brian's activities always interested him, and he often protected Brian from Michael's wrath, especially where the boy's love of the farm and animals was concerned.

"Where did you get that pup?" asked Michael sternly.

"It's one of Turnip's pups," said Brian. "Dinny asked me to take care of him till he grows up."

"I didn't say you could take any animals," said Michael sharply.

"He's not an animal, Da," said Brian. There was an appeal in his voice. "He's only a pup!"

"We can't have dogs messing around," said Michael. Then he added, "Not for a while anyway." Brian sensed his father was well aware that he was in a bad mood but that he did not have to go visiting it on Brian. Brian was suffering enough already, for he, perhaps more than any of them, seemed to feel the separation from the farm.

"Can I just leave him here for a minute till I get something?" said Brian. He gathered the pup in his arms, letting it stretch its neck along his shoulder, brought him over to the trap, and placed him on the seat, pushing him very close to his father's thigh. The pup looked up at Michael, licked his hand sleepily once or twice, blinked at him, laid his chin across Michael's leg, and closed his eyes. He had been wakened early.

"Sly little devil!" said Uncle Jamie, laughing.

Michael chuckled despite himself. "All right," he said severely. "You can bring him down on trial. But one false move and back he goes to Dinny."

Brian took the pup on his lap and put his arms around him. He saw he did not have to pretend to go in for anything now.

"Is he baptized yet?" asked Uncle Jamie.

"Baptized? You can't baptize a dog, Uncle!"

"Not with holy water maybe, but I don't see why you can't use plain water. Anyway, what did you call him?"

"Rebel," said Brian.

Uncle Jamie slapped his thigh and laughed again, and Brian's father smiled. The pup turned to Brian. Brian bent down and let the rough wet tongue of the pup tickle his cheeks and ears.

"You're a clever pup!" said Brian. "You know your name already! Don't you, Rebel?" Again Rebel's tongue came out and after that he fell asleep.

Brian wondered how Uncle Jamie could be so happy or laugh so easily on such a sad occasion. Then he remembered that his uncle was leaving the house and the watchful eye of his wife Meg for a whole day. The only one of Brian's family who was not unhappy was Paul. But Paul, Brian reflected, had never liked the animals or the farm: the one was stinky and the other dirty. He was so openly pleased at the prospect of leaving the farm for the city Brian could have clouted him.

By this time Mary and the two boys appeared and they and the others came up the lane. When the kisses and good-bys were done, Cathey came to the trap, leaned over, and scratched Rebel's back. He opened his eyes, then closed them again. She kissed Brian on the cheek and he blushed.

"Good-by, Brian darling," she said. "Good-by, Aunt Cathey," answered Brian huskily. Impulsively he turned and kissed her determinedly but warmly. Then he swept round again and stared at the floor of the trap, his brows puckered up in a frown.

Uncle Jamie gave the reins a shake. "Com'on, Stardust!" he called out, and the Traceys moved down the lane, waving to those they were leaving behind. A heavy silence fell on the trap, and only Uncle Jamie and Michael spoke to each other occasionally in low tones.

Out on the main road Brian's attention left the pup and it suddenly came back to him that he was going away from the farm for good. Something dull and heavy began to press on his heart as the familiar sounds came up to him—the pigs squealing and grunting for food, the cows lowing to get out of the byre, the cocks crowing lustily, and above all, the sound of Dinny's voice urging on Peg and Tom on the high ridge.

Brian saw Dinny about the same time that Dinny saw him. Dinny stopped the plow, turned in his seat, and looked down from the high ridge at Brian. He took his short pipe out of his mouth, waved it stiffly, and held up his hand with the pipe in it in greeting. As the trap raced past he waved the pipe again at Brian and Brian waved back at him. Then he stuck the pipe back in his mouth and turned his face to the land.

It seemed a curt farewell to Brian for such a solemn time, and he wished that Dinny had done something more to show how much he felt the parting.

At that moment on the top of the ridge the figure of a little girl came into view, her hair done up in pigtails this time, with white bows flying at the ends. The sight of her somehow rather deepened Brian's pain, for in her appearance in his place beside Dinny so soon after his leaving he saw a kind of callousness on the part of Sheila and a shade of treachery on the part of his friend Dinny. All at once, however, he began to see everything in an entirely different light. Sheila must be there simply because she loved the very same things that he himself loved, the horses, the cows, Dinny, the plowing, the land. . . .

He raised his hand to wave good-by to her, but he did it very slowly and uncertainly, for he was not sure of her reaction. He had no reason to fear, however, for Sheila's right hand shot into the air and she waved both her arm and her head vigorously, and she kept it up until he was out of sight. Brian's feelings were oddly mixed as the trap raced briskly down the road.

At the cottage gate Turnip heard the noise, dashed out, and ran alongside Stardust, snapping at the horse's flying hoofs, but Stardust only shook his head scornfully at the dog. At the sound of Turnip's voice Rebel leaped in Brian's arms and Brian had to quiet him. After a few hundred yards Turnip gave up following them and all at once stopped, cocked her head to one side, and quizzically watched the trap roll away down the Drumree Road. Then she turned, lowered her head, and trotted back to the farm.

As Stardust cantered past the farmyard Brian's breath came in gulps, his throat tightened, the salt tears burned his eyes, the ache in his heart grew unbearable, and for one wild moment he thought of dashing out of the trap and racing back to the farm. But the trap kept moving away, and Brian's fleeting impulse resolved itself into tears and he hid his face in Rebel's soft, warm body. While he was shaking with sobs that he prayed would go unnoticed in the swaying trap, he felt a cool hand gently knead the nape of his neck, and he knew that someone understood. Yet that only made the tears flow faster, and he had to wait a long time before he could stop them and dry his eyes in Rebel's rough coat.

The sound of Uncle Jamie's voice calling him made him look up.

"Want to take a turn at handling Stardust?" said Jamie. "We men have got to share the driving between us."

Brian jumped up at once, put Rebel on the seat, and took the reins, standing while he drove.

Michael and Uncle Jamie sat on each side of him with their elbows resting on the rim of the trap. They looked ahead and talked without ever turning toward each other, and they talked about the troubles in the North. Brian knew that they did not want him to hear, for they spoke from the side of their mouths. He pretended to concentrate on driving but listened to every word they said, for Dinny had told him that he, Brian, was as good an Irishman as the best of them, and he wanted to know all about the quarrels between the Irish Catholics and the Irish Protestants up in Belfast.

"I see they're having more trouble in Derry," said Uncle Jamie. "I can't understand how under God they have so much religious trouble in the North. Up here they've everything tied in with religion."

"The Saxons keep the people fighting among themselves," said Michael. "You have to hand it to the buggers. They did a job with the plantation. Wonder how it's all going to end?"

"The day will come when old Ireland will be free," said Uncle Jamie, and to Brian's surprise he began to recite:

"I wish that in Munster they only knew,
The kind, kind neighbors I came unto,
Small hate or scorn would ever be
Between the South and the North countrie."

Michael nodded his head. "Yes," he said, "the plantation made a different race out of us in the North. When I was younger I traveled a lot more than I do now. I went to Scotland and heard for myself how the people in Glasgow talk just like the people in Drumree."

"Now we're in for it!" said Brian to himself. Any time his dad began, "When I was younger I traveled more than I do now," Dinny said it was a sign that "they were in for a big blow!"

"I don't think I'm very much like a Scotchman," huffed Uncle Jamie.

"You're like them and they're like you," said Michael. "I was traveling once to 'The Cobbler' near Loch Lomond, and a bunch of young fellows and girls on the bus sang and talked about freeing Scotland the way you'd hear the boys and girls talk at a *coelidhe* in Drumree! Oh, the Scotch, like ourselves, are Gaels all right. And they're terribly loyal, too, like all Gaels. But they're more concerned about being loyal than about what they're bein' loyal to. Do you follow me? I mind the time when . . ."

"They're a bit too pigheaded for my liking," interrupted Uncle Jamie. He wanted to stop Michael while there was still time. Brian had often heard him say that his father Michael got all the gab in the family.

"If Ireland's ever free, the North'll run the country all over again the way she did before the Saxons came," said Michael. "Look at all the great men that left the North to rule the world. Why, they tell me America's full of Irish Presidents!"

"Aye," said Uncle Jamie, "But why do they all have to leave the country to do big things? Why'n hell can't they stay at home and do something big here for a change? The bee in their backsides won't let them sit down for a while in their own country. If they worked as hard here as I've heard they do in Ameriky for their money, they wouldn't have to budge an inch." He took the long riding whip off Brian and flicked Stardust's hide crossly.

"As far as I can see," said Michael, who suspected that the remark might have been aimed at him, "if the spuds in Ireland were made of gold, you'd still have them crossing the water. The country's too damned small for a big man. Besides, they've got the bug for wandering, and you'll never keep them home. I remember when I was a chit not much bigger than Brian, telling myself that I would travel round the world."

Brian noticed that Uncle Jamie was not listening to his dad any longer but was keeping a sharp eye on the road ahead. He began to wonder what his uncle was looking for. They entered the main street of a small hilly town and he asked Uncle Jamie what town it was.

"Rusheen," said his uncle without taking his eyes off the road.

"How far is——"

"Here we are! Here we are!" said Uncle Jamie suddenly. He

half rose, seized one of the reins, and pulled the horse over to the side of the road. He whoa'd him to a stop in front of a public house. It had a swing sign over the door, and on the sign was painted "The Whistling Pig" and the head of a pig done up almost like the smooth fleshy face of a man with lips pursed. "I think," he said, looking at each of the family in turn, "that the boys would like a little treat—a glass of lemonade and a slice of fruitcake to take the hunger off them." He nodded toward The Whistling Pig. "You can get all you want in there."

They went through the door marked "Family Entrance," and the whole family wedged themselves into a booth with two little seats and a narrow table between them. Brian squeezed in between Mary and Michael and had to sit sideways to leave his right arm free for the treat. He held Rebel in his lap and his left arm was pressed so tightly against his side he was afraid it would go dead. The barman came over, looking as nice and clean as the barber who came to Drumree twice a week.

"What'll you have?" said Uncle Jamie to Mary.

"I'll have a wee half-un." Brian looked at his mother and she lowered her eyes immediately and added, "That is, if it's not too strong."

Michael said he would have a short one with something to kill the taste of it.

"You don't have to take it if you don't like the taste of it?" put in Sean, and Michael laughed. Uncle Jamie said he would like the usual.

"How does the barman know what 'the usual' is, Uncle?" asked Brian.

Uncle Jamie leaned over and ruffled Brian's hair. "How did you think Stardust handled himself along the road, Brian?" he asked.

"Stardust's too good a horse to be pulling a trap," said Brian stoutly. "He should be racing and winning a lot of money."

"What would you like, Brian?" asked Uncle Jamie quickly, before Brian had time to repeat his question about "the usual."

"A bottle of porter," said Brian without hesitation.

Uncle Jamie laughed and said that was a good one and ordered Brian a slice of fruitcake and a bottle of lemonade. When he asked the other two boys what they would like they blushed and began to fidget. Michael said he supposed they'd want the usual, and everybody laughed again, and Jamie ordered buns and lemonade for them. When the barman brought the orders and put the little glass with the whisky down in front of his mother, Brian saw her blush too. She sipped modestly at it once or twice, looked at Brian, and asked Michael to get some ginger ale to go with it.

"Mary," Michael said when they had finished, "take the children out for a breath of air, and, Brian, look after Stardust, will you? We want to sell a dog."

Mary and the boys went back to the trap and waited. Brian set down Rebel, took hold of the reins and tried to find out from his mother what sort of dog they were going to talk about. Were they going to sell Rebel to the man?

"You needn't worry about Rebel," said his mother dryly. "It's a very old dog they're trying to sell."

Finally the two men came out and they were both laughing.

"Did you see about the dog, Da?" Brian asked anxiously.

"Aye, son," said Uncle Jamie. "We just sold that fella a pup." Both men laughed at this louder than before. Uncle Jamie was still laughing when Michael helped him to the trap.

"Which road are you taking, Jamie?" asked Michael, as Uncle Jamie took the reins from Brian.

"We'll go through Seven Hogs and Toneroi, cut down by Ballycarry, and on to Belfast by White Abbey," said Uncle Jamie. "It's grand to come into Belfast by the Shore Road!"

"It may be all that," said Michael. "But it's still the land, and you'll find it hard to beat coming into Belfast by the sea!"

"Now, man dear," said Uncle Jamie, suddenly roused, "why would I want to come into Belfast by the sea?" He leaned back and sat down all at once on Brian's lap. Brian helped him to his feet again. "No Irishman has to go to the sea if it's real beauty he's looking for. Let him hug the land. Lookit there!" He waved the long whip across Stardust's rump. "The dark bosom of Mother Erin, the tideless waters of Lough Neagh, the Giant's Causeway, and Portrush, where the sea smashes itself in white fury against naked spurs of black rock! Oh man, if I was a poet or a painter

I could spend my life in County Antrim and make a million pounds! Lift them, Stardust! Lift them and they'll fall themselves! Da-da dum, dum, dum!" Uncle Jamie began to hum to himself.

Brian saw his mother smile at Uncle Jamie, and he thought that she, too, must like County Antrim very much.

Michael took out his pipe and crumpled the tobacco slowly between the palms of his hands, and the little shreds of tobacco kept falling out from between the edges of his palms, but he did not notice them. Brian thought he was listening too much to what Uncle Jamie was saying.

"It's everything you say, Jamie," said Michael at last, "but no one will ever convince me that the best way to come into Belfast isn't by way of the sea. When I was younger I traveled a lot more than I do now and——"

"There's the fine bit of land for you, Brian!" said Uncle Jamie, pointing over Brian's head to a large field ribbed with lines of straight furrows.

". . . I would be on deck when she sailed into Belfast Lough with the cold morning sun shining on the waters, and the foam of the surf edged with golden sand, and the whitewashed houses set in the dark green fields, and the blue turf smoke curling up from the chimneys, and I thinking to myself, for I was younger then and read more than I do now, that——"

"Man, Stardust's a rare baste!" said Uncle Jamie, turning to Brian again. "Dammit, you're right, Brian-og! I *will* put him in for the races."

". . . and you'd see the mauve-capped Divis Mountains and hear the rattle of cups and saucers and smell the breakfast toast and bacon. Then the hammers and the riveters of the shipyard would start to wake the damned in hell with their clatter! Oh, dear me, dear me! The tears of it!"

Brian thought his father was going to cry, and everybody was very quiet in the trap, and he heard the *clip-clop, clip-clop* of Stardust's hoofs clear and loud against the hard, white road.

"I can remember the rainbow oil stains in the harbor and the sea gulls screaming overhead, and they swooping down to snatch up food from the water and away over the ship again, crying like lost souls. We'd come up the Lough and see the tall cranes and the black crisscross of the gantries against the blue, and you'd wonder if you were glad or sorry to be back, for you loved the place, indeed, but there was always so much damn trouble and sorrow in it for Catholics!" Michael raised his voice as he recited:

> *"Was it for this the wild geese spread*
> *The gray wing on every tide?*
> *For this that all that blood was shed . . .*
> *All that delirium of the brave?"*

Brian was anxious to know when they would reach the city and he wanted to ask how much more they had to go, but he didn't know whom to ask, for his mother was dozing and his dad and Uncle Jamie didn't make sense any more. But he had to know.

"Hi, Da," he said impetuously. "When do we get into Belfast?"

"Son o' mine," said his father, staring at him from two red eyes, "if we never get there, it'll be soon enough for Michael Tracey!"

"Uncle Jamie," said Brian, "do *you* know how far more we have to go?"

"We shouldn't be too far off now, son," said Uncle Jamie. "But something tells me I'd better inquire to make sure. Let you and me, Michael, ask in that public house if they know how far we are from Belfast."

Brian noticed that they had to talk a long time to the barman to find the way, and, to his surprise, when Uncle Jamie came back he handed him the reins again, pointed up the road, and without another word he and Michael sat down, leaned on each other, and fell asleep, their heads swaying and jogging loosely with the movements of the trap.

On the outskirts of the city Brian saw a clock through a shop-window that said four, and Uncle Jamie awakened at this point, looked at him sharply, and almost snatched the reins from him as if Brian had been doing something wrong.

It was still very clear and Brian was glad. He was excited now and wanted to see what a city was like, for he had never been to one bigger than Ballymena. But Ballymena had no trams, and one of the boys at school who had been up to Belfast had talked about nothing else but the trams and how they ran like trains on tracks right through the streets. The trap turned onto a wide thoroughfare with houses and shops on each side and kept on that for some time. Brian had never seen such a long street before, and he and Sean invented a game of spotting the names of the side streets first. They crossed a tramway intersection where the shining rails reminded Brian of the river at home, and suddenly Michael shouted: "Here we come to the famous Falls Road!"

"What's it famous for, Da?" asked Sean.

"See up that little street?" said Michael, ignoring him. "That's St. Mary's Chapel, the first chapel built in Belfast, and it was built by—do you know who?—by good Protestant Irishmen who wanted to help their downtrodden countrymen of a different faith. Can you imagine them doing a thing like that nowadays, Jamie?"

"No," said Uncle Jamie crossly. "Nowadays they'd rather burn a chapel than build one."

Stardust slowed up as he climbed the winding road with tramlines and houses and shops.

"You've a great Fenian stronghold in the Falls ward," went on Michael, "and at the end of that street"—he pointed up a long side street lined with brick houses darkening with age—"lies the Shankill Road, center of the Shankill ward and stronghold of the Protestants. There's been many a bloody battle between the Shankill and the Falls, and the whole thing would be funny if plenty of good Irishmen on both sides hadn't lost their lives in the struggle. When I was younger I traveled more than I do now . . ." Brian thought that his dad must have been tired by the long ride, for he did not finish the sentence and his head slumped forward and he fell asleep again.

They drove past more houses and shops and side streets, trams and cars filled with people. Brian had never seen so many people together, not even on a fair day in Drumree. He tried not to be so excited as Paul and Sean—only kids acted like that—but his eyes betrayed him.

"Wake up, Michael!" Uncle Jamie shook Michael by the shoulder. "We must be near there now!"

Michael opened his eyes and looked lost for a moment.

"No," he said. "Keep going. It's up ahead!"

He pointed up the Falls Road where there were many dwelling houses, and they drove on for another five minutes.

"There it is!" said Michael suddenly, pointing to the left side of the road.

They all turned and looked to where he pointed.

"And down the street beside it, Lower Clonard Street, lives your aunt Kate Mooney," added Michael.

Brian marveled that his father could be so familiar with places so far away from home.

Uncle Jamie pulled up in front of a pair of two-story, red brick houses stuck together. A square of iron railing encircled the window, and planted in a hole in the few feet of concrete behind the railing was a stunted bush, ready to wither and die.

When Stardust pulled up, Brian looked around for a glimpse of a tree or a sod of green turf or a lump of brown earth, but all he saw was the dull, grim walls of houses and the dingy windows of shops; or a sign of birds and beasts, but all he saw was two or three slate-colored city pigeons settle on the pavement a few feet away, unconcerned with what was going on, and peck in the dusty gutter.

Perhaps it was because the sun was already going down and leaving the city chill and gray, and the shadows of the buildings opposite were reaching long black fingers across the road and creeping up the walls of his new home; perhaps it was because the people did not say when they saw him, "God bless the work!" or, " 'Tis a grand day, thanks be to God!"—they just stared and hurried past—but Brian shivered slightly as he stepped off the trap and walked up to the door of the red brick home on Falls Road.

6

When Brian accompanied his mother and Paul and Sean to St. Peter's National School in Raglan Street, his mother introduced him to the teacher. He was a very tall man who gave one glance at the black rim under Brian's nails and tsk-tsk-tsk'ed. Miss Lavin, for all her faults, had always called that "clean dirt," because it came from working with the land, and she used to talk so often to the boys about "honest toil" that they wondered what "dishonest toil" might be.

During the rest of the interview the teacher seemed to pick on Brian for most of his sharp looks, perhaps because he was the oldest. Brian did not mind. He enjoyed the teacher's evident misunderstanding. If the teacher thought he was going to have him under his thumb at school, Brian told himself, he was in for a "quare gunk." Brian was not going to school at all that year, for the family had arrived toward the end of the school year and Michael had decided to keep him home for the remainder to help Mary set the house in order. Brian was heartily glad of the arrangement when he looked over the surroundings of the new school. It had none of the compensations of the school at Drumree, for, although it was an early-summer day, when he looked out of the school window he could not see one green leaf, not one feathery wing, not even one ray of bright sunshine! All he saw were the dull brick walls, blackened at the top with city smoke, the dusty gray pavement below, and odd bits of refuse in the gutters.

At home the work with his mother was not real work. He had only to help her hang picture frames, hammer nails in the wall, and place crockery on shelves. Nor did it last long, and Brian was left with plenty of time on his hands. In one free period he tied a rope round Rebel's neck and took him out for a walk. In the beginning he had let Rebel run loose on the walks, but the pup with his playful nature got into too much trouble, and finally Brian had to use a leash.

This time he came up to a group of boys his own age, standing in a little circle in front of a fish-and-chip shop, and he made up his mind to speak to them. But he did not know how to break through the barrier of stares. Rebel, however, had no inhibitions and began sniffing at their boots and licking their hands.

"Get out o' here, you mutt!" one of them snapped.

Brian flared up at once. "Rebel's no mutt!" he retorted.

The two boys glared at each other for a moment until Rebel impatiently tugged at the leash and pulled Brian away from an atmosphere that had frozen into permanent animosity.

Brian went on looking around for something to amuse him and decided to go to Dunville Park where there was green grass and trees, to watch the men playing marbles, or admire the goldfish in the pond. A fruit shop where the fruits and vegetables were laid out in front of the shopwindow in boxes and trays caught his eye. They had russet apples—his favorites—oranges, lettuce, turnips, and, lined against the wall, burlap bags of potatoes ranging from small, blue-skinned skerries to the large Pride of Erins.

The colorful sight of the shop with its fruits and vegetables moved Brian as if he had been staring at the cinema screen and then had been carried through the screen and beyond it to the land. He stared right through the boxes of apples, through the lines of turnips and bags of potatoes, and saw the dark brown fields where they had been taken from. He saw again his friend Dinny pluck the potatoes off the plant, saw him tug up the turnips by the leaves, shake the earth from their tapering bodies, and toss them carelessly over his shoulder into the high-walled cart. . . .

The woman of the shop came out, looked up the street and down it. Then she looked at Brian. Brian walked over to talk to her about the potatoes and turnips and about the farm they came from. When he was closer he saw she had lusterless, stringy hair, a leathery face, and a body that was a shapeless bag of bulges.

"That's a fine crop of turnips you have, Missus," he said, looking at her hopefully.

"It is, is it?" said the woman.

"Where did they come from?" asked Brian.

"From the farm," said the woman. "Where did you think?"

"Whose farm was it, Missus?" said Brian.

"Whose farm was it?" echoed the woman. "How do I know? And anyway, what are you hanging round the shop for? Go on about your business, if you have any. Though by the looks of it, your business is going to land you into a heap o' trouble!"

Brian walked off with his ears burning, not so much at what she had said but because she had rebuffed his attempt to be friendly. He had thought that the products of the land would have formed a common bond between them. He looked behind and saw that she was still watching him. Only when he was well up the road did she leave the shop front.

Paul and Sean, he noticed, were quickly taken up with new interests and new companions, and he found himself alone even at home. He confided all his troubles to Rebel.

About a month after his arrival in Belfast he came home one day from the park and sat on the sofa for a moment. Then he turned to his mother.

"Where is he?" he asked.

"Where's who?"

"Rebel."

"I don't know. He followed you out to the park."

"No, he didn't."

"I'm sure he did, son," said his mother.

"He didn't!" said Brian.

"Lord, but you're the stubborn one!" said his mother.

Brian rose and went out of the house. He returned about an hour later without Rebel.

"Did you find him, Brian?" asked his mother. She had worried about Brian ever since they had come to the city, and she sensed how much the dog must mean to him.

"No," said Brian shortly. He walked aimlessly around the kitchen for a while.

"Do you want a slice of bread and jam?" asked his mother.

"No," said Brian again. He went upstairs, flung himself on the bed, and lay there with his mind a blank for some time until he heard the house door open.

"Ma," said Sean, "I'm hungry."

"Sean!" Brian shouted downstairs.

"Wha'?" said Sean.

"Did you see Rebel?"

"No, I didn't," said Sean. "Ma, can I have a slice of bread?"

Brian turned his face to the wall again.

Later he heard the door open a second time. Paul.

"Paul!" he shouted downstairs.

"What?" asked Paul.

"Did you see Rebel?"

"Think I'd bother my head about that mangy pup?" said Paul.

"If I go downstairs," said Brian, half rising in indignation, "I'll knock your mangy block off!"

Rebel did not show up that night, nor did a frantic search by Brian and Sean bring any clue as to what might have happened to him or where he might have gone.

The next morning Brian rose earlier than usual and ate a good breakfast. Mary was glad of this, although she noticed that he was very quiet. She put that down, however, to the fact that he had lost Rebel. When Michael left for work she went upstairs to wake the other two boys, and when she came downstairs again Brian was gone.

Around eleven o'clock he had not put in an appearance either to help Mary or to ask for the slice of bread and jam he invariably needed to tide him over to the midday meal. Mary felt this was rather odd. When he did not appear for dinner either she grew a little anxious. He was not in the habit of going off like the other two for long hikes with the boys of the neighborhood. She was aware that he had been keeping far too much to himself and several times had told him so. In the afternoon she sent Paul and Sean out to look for him, and they came home at suppertime with no news of him. Michael, when he came home, listened to what she had to say and then made light of the whole thing.

"He probably went to the pictures and forgot about the time," said Michael, and then buried himself in the *Belfast Telegraph*.

Perhaps for the first time since she had come to the house on the Falls Road Mary was aware of the *tick-tock, tick-tock* of the wag-at-the-wall they had brought up from the farm. At last the clock struck nine and she turned to Michael.

"Michael," she said gently.

"Yes?" said Michael, pretending he did not know what was coming.

"I'm getting nervous, dear," said Mary. "It's late."

Michael put down the *Telegraph*, folded his arms, and smoked his pipe for a while. "I wonder what the divil's keeping him out till this time?" he said. "Maybe he's staying at somebody's house. We'll have to find out. You take Sean and I'll take Paul and we'll try a few of the neighbors' houses."

It was almost eleven when the two parties came back. None of the neighbors had seen Brian all that day.

"I suppose I'd better go to the police," said Michael resignedly.

Michael went up to the police station and half an hour later came away with the unpleasant feeling that the police suspected him of having forced Brian to run away from home. They assured him, however, that if the boy had not been maltreated—again the suspicious look—the boy would soon turn up again when the hunger got him. That was when they all came home. Meantime, they would set up the usual machinery for a local search; if that did not bring him in they would make it a county alarm. One of the men accompanied Michael back to the house and asked Mary and the boys one or two questions. Michael was glad that he left convinced at least there was no evidence of the boy's having been forced to run away.

That night a noise in the next room wakened Paul, and he listened long enough to make sure that he was not just hearing things.

"Sean!" He nudged his brother who was sprawled across the bed. "Sean!" Paul shook his brother roughly this time and kept shaking him until he wakened. Sean sat up and stared blankly in front of him; he slithered over the side of the bed, sat on the edge, and began to pull off his nightshirt.

"What are you doin'?" asked Paul impatiently.

"Gettin' up," said Sean through half-closed eyes.

"You're cracked!" said Paul. "Listen. Do you hear anything?"

Sean stared bleakly at the foot of the bed for a moment.

"No," he said. "Can't hear nottin'!" He began to crawl back into bed.

Paul seized his arm and dragged him over to the wall that separated their room from the room of their parents. He put his ear to it and beckoned to Sean to do the same.

Shrugging his shoulders, Sean put his ear to the wall.

"What's Ma crying for?" he asked.

"Brian's lost," said Paul.

"Yah!" said Sean. "Brian can't get lost nowhere!" He listened for a little longer. Then he rubbed his eyes sleepily and climbed back into bed. Paul followed him.

The next day Michael kept in constant touch with the police, and after each call from the post office the desk sergeant answered wearily that there was no news yet. Finally he told Michael that as soon as anything turned up he would let him know, but Michael waited all day and no news came, and at last he had to make up his mind to go home and face Mary.

During the preparation of his supper and during the supper itself and when she was clearing the table after supper Mary cried. The crying was not loud but soft, something like a whimper, and it reminded Michael of a dog with a thorn in its paw.

"Look, Mary," he said at last, with a mixture of sympathy and impatience, "there's no use letting it eat your heart out. He'll turn up soon enough, and ten to one he'll be as right as rain."

"Michael," said Mary, "there's more to it than that."

"What more is there to it?" asked Michael, showing surprise.

"Och." Mary shrugged her shoulders.

"Now tell me, Mary," said Michael with a shade of annoyance. "What more can there be to it?"

"Brian isn't happy here, that's all," said Mary.

"Why isn't he happy here?"

"He doesn't like the city. He loved the farm."

"What the blazes can I do if he doesn't like the city?" exploded Michael. "Did I want to leave the farm? Was there anything else I could do? Tell me that! Was there anything else I could do?"

"No, Michael, there wasn't," answered Mary. "But Brian can't understand that. All Brian can understand is that we're not on the farm any more and he has no love for the city."

"The farm?" said Michael suddenly, half to himself. "The farm! That's where the bugger went! He went back to the farm. Ten to one that's it!"

"Oh, I hope to God it's true!" said Mary, her eyes lighting up. "If that's where he went, he'll have plenty to eat and a good warm bed."

Michael rose up and pulled on his coat.

"I'm going out to borrow a bike." He buttoned up his coat, pulled back his shoulders, and went out. Before he closed the door he called in: "Tell the post office not to expect me in tomorrow. And don't wait up for me. I'll stay over at the farm."

The following evening around dusk a prancing black horse and shining trap drew up outside the door of the red brick house at Falls Road. Dinny was driving, and Michael sat stiffly opposite him. In the back, one hand holding Michael's bicycle, the other around Rebel, sat Brian with his head bowed.

Mary ran out to the street and hardly let Brian step down from the trap before she smothered him in her arms. A group of children quickly collected round the trap to see the boy the police were searching for, but Mary was completely unaware of them. Still embracing Brian, who was holding on to Rebel, she brought him into the house and started preparing tea and toast and sausages for his supper.

Outside the men were talking to each other.

"Will you not stop the night, Dinny?" asked Michael.

"No, Michael," said Dinny. "Jamie wants me to get back to the farm. One of the sows has littered and I have to stay up with them."

"Well, come on in," said Michael, "and have something for the road before you go."

"I suppose I might as well," agreed Dinny, unconsciously drawing the back of his hand across his mouth. "Though to tell the truth, I promised Cathey I'd stay off it."

He came in and saluted Mary and the other two boys but did not say anything to Brian, who sat with his arms between his legs, staring into the fire.

The whole family sat down at the table, Dinny sitting in Brian's place, for Brian did not rise and his mother did not disturb him. She brought a second chair over beside Brian and placed his cup of tea and a plate with three sausages and several slices of buttered toast on it. Then she went back to the table and sat down with the others but every now and then glanced round at Brian or at his cup and plate.

After the meal Dinny rose and said that he had better make a quick cut for the road. Michael rose, too, and led him into the scullery where the two men stayed for a few minutes. When Dinny came out again he bade good-by to the family. Before he left he went over to where Brian still sat with his head bowed and pressed Brian's dark head to his stiff, work-stained trousers. "Never mind, Brian-og," he said. "Some day you'll make enough money to buy your own farm."

Brian heard the clip-clop of Stardust's hoofs stamping impatiently when Dinny reappeared on the street, and at a call from Dinny the horse set off at a fair clip down the Falls. In his mind he went with them until his father came back into the house and stood in front of him.

"I want to see you upstairs, young fella," he said at last.

Brian got up and Rebel followed him across the room.

"Put that damned mutt in the yard!" shouted Michael.

"Paul," said Mary, "tie up Rebel in the yard."

Reluctantly Paul rose and dragged Rebel by the collar across the floor so roughly the pup yelped. Brian was going to hit Paul, but his father stopped him. Then he turned to Paul. "You don't have to choke him, you know," he said.

"Get up them stairs," he ordered Brian sharply.

Mary rose quickly and went over to Brian. She hugged his listless body close to her.

"What are you going to do to the child?" she asked.

"Give him what he knows he damn well deserves," said Michael.

"You can leave him alone for once," said Mary. "He's had enough for this time."

"*He's* had enough?" shouted Michael. "I like that! *He's* had enough! And what about *me?* Maybe *I* didn't have enough all day yesterday and all day the day before, running up and down like a bloody idiot, trying to find out where he's hiding, and the whole neighborhood looking at me as if I'd driven my own child out o' the house!" Michael was trying to work himself into a rage. It would be easier that way to do what he had to do. "Maybe I'd better tell you what that boy of yours was up to when he did get down to the farm and found that bloody pup there with its mother. He snuck into the stable and without a cheep to anybody took out Stardust and nearly ran the lights out o' the poor defenseless animal, running him up and down the Long Field. And when Dinny spotted him he spun Dinny a yarn about being on the farm to do something for his sick father. *Me* sick, that never once! . . . Then he and that scrawny-legged imp o' Satan, Sheila Reilly, hang around Dinny all day, keeping that poor man from his honest toil"—here Brian, despite his fear of other things, began to fear a "big blow"—"and taking the very food out of his mouth at mealtimes. Come evening, he tells Dinny that he's going up to his uncle Jamie's, and what do you think really happens? You'll never believe it! That tomboy friend of his, Sheila Reilly again, if you please, goes home and steals—steals, mind you!—food and drink to make supper for the two of them, and they ate it together in the hayloft, and that's where she helps him to hide himself for the night. Poor Jamie wouldn't have known a thing about it if I hadn't gone down there myself. Now, under God, I ask you: What's going to become of that boy of yours if he'll go to them lengths? What'll become of a boy that'd do the likes of that to them that has saved and slaved all their lives for him?" Here Michael stretched out his arm to seize hold of Brian, but Mary fended him off.

"I don't care what he's done!" she cried. "You're not going to touch him!" She looked desperate and lost, as if she did not know how she was going to defend Brian if Michael insisted on punishing him.

At the sight of Mary's distress Michael felt his anger suddenly drain away from him. He stood baffled for a moment. Finally he looked at Brian.

"All right," he said. "If he wants to hide behind his mother's skirts, let him. But he's no longer any son of mine. Now make up your mind, my lad."

Brian struggled away from his mother's grasp. "I'm going upstairs," he said.

While Michael fumbled at the buckle of his belt, Mary stood looking on helplessly, wringing the ends of her apron. Then she put the apron to her face and ran into the scullery. Michael slowly followed Brian upstairs.

Up in Brian's room Michael slid his belt off his waist and wound the buckle end of it round his hand.

"Take down your trousers," he said. He had not been looking forward with any satisfaction to the task. Indeed, now that his temper had disappeared, his whole attitude began to change. Brian suspected that his mother's frightened visage stood before him and that he no longer had any heart in the matter.

"Lie across that bed," he said flatly.

Brian let his trousers fall in a limp bundle at his feet and he threw himself face downward on the bed. Folding his arms across his eyes, he waited.

Michael raised his right arm and brought down the belt across the boy's bare limbs. Brian's body quivered but he made no sound. Michael brought down the belt, once, twice more, and three ugly red welts broke out and spread over the white flesh.

Brian had no feelings about his father who was giving him the punishment, for somehow his father did not come into it. He accepted this punishment in the way he had accepted the punishment doled out at school for a misdemeanor. But he felt that somewhere an injustice was being done to him, and it angered him and he felt like striking back at somebody. But he didn't know who, because it was no particular person. Rather the city was to blame, and his anger changed into defiance. As each stroke burned into his flesh and hurt him so that he had a strange desire to vomit, he repeated fiercely to himself: "I'm going back! I'm going back! I'm going back!"

It was over. Breathing heavily, Michael straightened up, drew in his belly, and slipped the belt round his waist.

"Now get into bed and think over what you've done to your mother and me!" he said. It wasn't the right thing to say because it didn't cover the situation, but it was the only thing he could think of just then and he was glad it was all over.

Mary was not in the kitchen when he came downstairs, and Paul was still out in the yard. Sean stared at him as if he feared that his father was going to beat him too.

"What're you staring at?" said Michael angrily. "Dammit, I'm not a murderer!"

Paul came in. "Do you want me to beat Rebel as well?" he asked.

Michael looked up sharply. "Are you cracked?" he snapped. Then he threw himself into his chair, snatched up the *Telegraph*, spread it open in front of him, and glared at the printed pages.

7

For the remainder of the summer Brian depended mostly on the company of Rebel. His favorite pastime was to take the dog to a swampy area outside the town where a few bungalows had been erected on the higher ground. It went by the appropriate name of "the Huts." Here Brian and Rebel spent the time chasing rats from mounds of refuse, dumped there as fill, that were always burning and smelled of roast potatoes.

One afternoon while poking about with a stick he saw a fat gray body ripple along the ground toward the nearest hole.

"Cut him off!" he yelled to Rebel, and before the rat could reach the hole, he threw his stick at it, heading it off. The rat hesitated. This gave Rebel time to dart up with surprising swiftness, turn the rat first left, then right, and finally come up on him. With an angry growl and a snap of his head he seized the gray body between his teeth.

He ran off a safe distance and with a quick shake of his head tossed the rat into the air; when it came down he tossed it up again. Brian watched him do this until the rat finally dropped and lay still. Then to Brian's fascination and horror, Rebel, with his head at an odd, kittenish angle, began to devour the rat. He first crushed the rat's skull with the side of his jaws; then he attacked the entrails, an action which caused Brian almost to retch. The sight of Rebel, his jaws red with gore, coupled with the thought that a creature so friendly and so playful as Rebel could be so bestial and cruel, shocked him.

"You bloody cannibal!" he cried.

He threw a stone that made Rebel leave the remains of the rat and rise to his feet, undecided. He picked up another stone, held it poised threateningly, and walked up slowly to Rebel. When he was near enough he raised his foot and angrily kicked the dog in the hindquarters, sending him off howling.

Seizing the dead rat by the tip of the tail and aware that Rebel's eyes were fixed on him, he threw it into the shallow waters of the swamp. Rebel ran over, sniffed at the water's edge once or twice, turned to Brian, sniffed again at the water, gave up, and raced off after him.

It was the last time Brian ever took Rebel out to hunt rats at the Huts.

His only other diversion consisted of hoop trundling. He made a hoop from a circular steel bar and pushed it by means of an iron cleek, or rod, with an open hook. With this cleek he trundled the hoop along the ground and ran behind it. He had seen the other boys in Belfast do it and it appealed to him, partly because he and Rebel could do it alone, but mostly because it afforded both of them the chance to leave the city streets for the open country roads. In the evenings Brian took out his hoop and, with Rebel at his heels, ran for miles out into the country. He never seemed to grow tired behind the hoop, no matter how long or how fast he ran.

Summer came to an end, however, and one day his father brought him to school and introduced him to the headmaster. The headmaster looked like Mr. Pickwick with his kindly face, bald head fringed with white hair, and a large red nose which at the time Brian thought meant heavy drinking. He surprised Brian, however, by the affectionate manner in which he took hold of him and pressed his head against him. Years later Brian could still feel the rough hairs of the tweed coat press into his cheek. When Michael had answered all his questions and had said good-by, the headmaster led Brian down a corridor past partitions with doors and entered one of the doors at the north end of the building. Brian saw a desk on the floor close to the partition and to the right of that a blackboard with a wooden frame set on an easel. A tall young man, the same one who had disapproved of his nails some months ago, stood up at their entry. The headmaster called him Mr. Lawlor, introduced Brian to him, then left. The teacher pointed to a seat at the edge of the front row, and Brian dutifully sat down under forty curious and, he felt, unfriendly stares. He stayed there for the whole morning with nothing to do except look through some books that were handed to him at the beginning of each class.

These first days were dull for Brian with only one glimmer of relief. That was the singing lessons. For Brian those singing lessons began with the handing out of music sheets. After this the master tapped the desk with his tuning fork, something Brian had never seen before, put it to his ear, and hummed to himself for such a long time Brian thought he must be enjoying a little tune of his own. Once he dropped the fork, and when he stooped to pick it up Brian saw a sharp-pointed hump rise up suddenly on the master's back.

Brian nearly burst out laughing, but a warning nudge from the boy next to him, a stocky-shouldered youngster, stopped him.

"What in the name o' God is that?" asked Brian in a whisper.

"His cane," came the answer. "The school inspector must be coming, and 'Legs' Lawlor thinks that he can hide the cane up his back. They're not supposed to hit us."

Brian was holding up the music sheet in front of his face to hide himself from the master. He forgot that the sheet also hid the master from him. Later he also learned that, for the master, a sheet of music hiding any face was like a red flag to a bull.

"What sort of an egg is . . ." A stunning blow on the ear made lights burst before his eyes. A hundred sounds, among them the musical tones of a tuning fork, came closer and closer and louder and louder until they reached a high, piercing scream. This endured until at last the bursting lights dimmed and died away, and the sounds faded into silence. Brian opened his eyes.

"You weren't long learning Dwyer's bad habits, were you, Tracey?" The teacher was breathing heavily and looking down at him from the bench above to which he had quietly walked during Brian's conversation with his neighbor.

When class was over for the day, to Brian's surprise, he found that his adventure with the master had immediately made him popular. The boys also liked the way he pooh-poohed the idea that the blow had hurt him.

"You should see the way they hit us down in Drumree," he boasted, remembering with a twinge of conscience the harmlessness of "Spudface" Lavin.

The incident brought him the sympathy of his neighbor, the stocky boy whose name was Humphrey Dwyer, and with it the friendship of Dwyer's two companions, Downey and Finnegan. Their nicknames were Humpy, Curly, and the Mole.

Since Brian had proved himself such a good fellow, the Mole suggested that they should teach "Legs" a lesson for his insult to Brian.

The next time they had group singing all the boys gathered in the main hall and Lawlor took over. Brian saw Sean and Paul up in front with their classes. He was looking forward to the singing, especially since they were to sing Irish songs like "The Minstrel Boy"—a song that allowed him to open his lungs.

It was during the singing of "She Is Far from the Land" that Brian caught from somewhere in the mass of singers a soft but definite hum. Lawlor looked up. The humming ceased. Lawlor lowered his head, took up his tuning fork, and before he could strike it against the desk, the humming started again. He gave them a note to hold and then began a methodical search, bench by bench, for the hummer. But just as he had reached the source, the sound would cease in that particular spot and be taken up in another. What struck Brian was the fact that Lawlor refused to fly off into a rage but must have reached some sort of decision, for he deliberately walked back to the desk.

The humming went on.

"I shall now teach you one of our most beautiful songs," he said quietly. "Handel is supposed to have said he would rather have written this one song than all his works. It is 'The Last Rose of Summer,' by Tom Moore. No real Irishman would dare make fun of it."

When the master took in a deep breath Brian got ready to

laugh. But from the very first notes instinct warned him that a laugh was out of place. For the master had a pleasing tenor voice, and as he sang it was as if he had become another person. With the rest of the class Brian listened until the last notes of the song had died away and the singer had ceased to sing, although he still kept his gaze fixed far beyond the confines of the dusty classroom.

For a full minute there was not a single sound in the room. No one moved; no one spoke. Brian suddenly became aware that even the humming had ceased. Afraid that the emotion slowly building up inside him and loosening every inch of his body might be noticed, he glanced around furtively in the direction of the Mole. The Mole's head was bowed. Now he wondered why they had tried to torture Lawlor, and all at once he felt ashamed.

"All right," said the master, breaking a spell, "that's how we shall try to sing it. That's how we should try to sing all our native songs."

There was plenty of singing after that, but Brian did not hear the humming again that day or any other day, and his own feelings toward the master suffered a great change. That night, as he knelt down to say his prayers, he prayed, "God bless Mr. Lawlor. God bless me, too, so I can be as good as Mr. Lawlor."

As the school year progressed Brian gradually adjusted himself to his new life. Curly Downey, Humpy Dwyer, and Finnegan the Mole became his constant friends, and they fought together in the school battles between classes or between groups within their class. Sean and Paul belonged to lower classes, and at St. Peter's the classes never mingled.

Brian came home from school one afternoon full of a talk that Mr. Lawlor had given them on being Irishmen up to the hilt. He told Sean what the master had said but confessed that he didn't know what he should do to be an Irishman "up to the hilt."

"Why not get up a hurling team in the street?" suggested Sean. "Then we wouldn't have to play soccer."

"That's the idea," said Brian. "A hurling team."

Dwyer, Downey, and Finnegan, who were also under the influence of Lawlor's speech, agreed wholeheartedly. "We've got to be Irishmen up to the hilt," they said.

Brian asked Paul to join the team, but Paul said he preferred soccer. Only soccer players were important and got their names in the Belfast papers. After that Brian saw very little of Paul during the day. In the evenings he often heard his mother or father scold him for being out after nine o'clock, the hour set for the boys to come home. Paul invariably replied that he had been at a friend's house, giving names of friends that Brian did not know.

The next thing they discussed was how to raise funds to buy hurling sticks and the colored jerseys that were standard equipment for any team.

"We could sell potato skins," said Sean, "or, if that's too bad, we could sell papers."

For a moment there was silence. Selling newspapers in Belfast was a task left to ragged urchins. Selling skins meant borrowing a bucket and going from door to door to beg for skins or refuse. When a bucket of this had been collected, it was sold to a pig dealer.

"What do you fellows say?" asked Brian. He looked at Sean and said slowly: "I'd risk selling them if I was sure there were no spies around."

Sean said quickly: "I'll sell the first bucket."

When they had collected enough money they bought hurling sticks and jerseys with green and white stripes. They went to practice in one of the playing fields of the Falls Park, and when they were tired of practicing they pretended they were members of the secret Irish Republican Army, drilling with the sticks and attacking the English soldiers and the Specials. Brian had no qualms about attacking the English. That was all part, he supposed, of being an Irishman up to the hilt. But who were the Specials, and why should he shoot them?

"They're the police that fight the Catholics," explained Curly. Later from Mr. Lawlor, Brian learned that the Specials were auxiliary police who were called out in an emergency.

"Do they fight the Catholics?" Brian asked him.

"From my own experience," answered Mr. Lawlor, "I could not guarantee their utter impartiality in trouble between Catholics and Protestants. In fact," he added, "I have come to the conclusion that they are nothing more than Orangemen in uniform."

Brian eventually fielded his eleven "Clonard Stars" against the "Albert Stars" in a corner of the spacious Falls Park, using a new yellow pigskin ball which Sean could send from one end of the field to the other with a long "puck" or drive. Sean, too, seemed completely unaware of the danger from the hurleys the boys most of the time swung shoulder-high to clip the flying ball.

Two heaps of clothing served as goal posts, the imaginary crossbar being determined by the reach of the goalkeeper. Halfway through the game Sean sent in a shot. The goalkeeper reached for the ball with his stick, but it went past him. Sean shouted it was a goal because the goalkeeper did not jump his full height. The goalkeeper told him to go home and get his glasses. Brian took Sean's side and got into an argument with the referee. A moment later he glanced up and saw Sean struggling on the ground with the goalie. He rushed over and pulled the two boys apart, giving the goalie a cuff on the side of head for hitting Sean. Curly and the Mole intervened, but not before Brian had received a sharp, painful jab that peeled the skin off his cheek. The match was declared off and the boys took up their jackets and went home, Brian nursing his wound all the way. Before they were out of the park, however, he walked over to Sean and scolded him for getting into trouble the first time the team played. In a fit of temper he smacked Sean on the ear.

"That's for getting me into a fight," he said. But at once he was sorry he had raised his hand because of the quiet way Sean took the blow. It was only when they were near home that he learned from Curly the reason why Sean had got into the scrape. "The fellow he was fighting," explained Curly, "called you a bad name, and Sean went after him."

"Oh," said Brian.

For the rest of the way he tried to make up to Sean, but Sean still kept behind the wall of reserve he could sometimes build around himself. When they were near home and alone he tried again.

"Sean," he said, "if I take you to the pictures, will you come?" He felt a sudden gladness when Sean nodded his consent.

That night the two brothers sat in the Clonard Cinema watching the picture and eating caramels. Brian put his arm around Sean's shoulder and held it there until the lights went on again and it was time to go home.

One evening toward the end of the school year Brian and his three friends were standing idly at the Traceys' door wondering how they could spend their time when they heard a deep booming sound.

"A band!" said Brian excitedly.

"Band, my eye!" said Curly. "That's the big drums."

"The big drums?" asked Brian.

"Sure," said Humpy. "It's coming near the Twelfth, and the Orangemen are getting up their gander."

"They go away in the head at this time," said the Mole, "and beat hell outta the big drums."

"Let's go up and see them," suggested Brian.

"What?" cried Curly incredulously. "Go up amongst the Protestants in Shankill Road and get the lights knocked outta me?"

"You daren't go near them at this time of the year," agreed the Mole.

"If you're afraid to go, I'm not," boasted Brian. "I dare the rest of you to go up to Shankill Road."

There was some hesitation on the part of the other three, but finally they yielded. If nothing else it would provide a welcome diversion to a dull evening.

Rebel was preparing to follow them but Humpy objected.

"Why can't he go?" asked Brian.

"Because he's a Catholic dog," explained Humpy. "If they find out he's a Catholic dog they'll murder him, that's why."

Brian had some trouble chasing Rebel home, but after slapping him on the hindquarters, he sent the dog yelping with his tail between his legs and a look in his eyes that made Brian feel he had betrayed a lifelong friendship.

They reached the Shankill Road without mishap. From where he was Brian saw coming toward him a slow-moving group of men; in the center of the group were three drummers in shirt sleeves carrying huge lambeg drums on their chests and stomachs. They were using long canes to beat the drums, playing to their own rhythm and only rarely coming together on the beats. The sweat was pouring from them, and their shirts were darkened with perspiration under the armpits. Each drummer was surrounded by his particular friends and by one or two reliefs. But no one spoke: no one could speak while the drums thundered and the marchers kept their eyes fixed on the ground, reminding Brian of a funeral procession.

As the drums approached, the noise increased until it became almost unbearable. Brian heard the shopwindows near him singing with vibration; his feet and legs began to tingle, and a gooseflesh sensation crept up his spine. Remembering what the Mole had said about it's being so near the Twelfth, a time when Protestant tempers ran high, he was suddenly seized with panic, as if he were standing too near a rushing train and remembering that someone had told him that a rushing train could suck you in. He felt an almost uncontrollable desire to run. But with his whole body stiff and the goose pimples rising all over him, he stood frozen into immobility, while the huge drums boomed on past him.

At last they were gone and nothing remained of the sound except a singing noise in Brian's ears. The boys moved away and he followed them, still feeling dazed, taking side streets that would eventually lead them back to the Falls Road. Along the way they noticed on some of the end walls of the side streets life-size paintings of King William of Orange crossing the Boyne on a white charger and brandishing a sword. On top of the paintings in elaborate scrolls were written the words: *To hell with the Pope!*

In one deserted street the boys stopped and gazed up at the painting.

"Dare you to spit on it!" whispered Curly, although no one was within sight.

"They'd murder us!" said Brian.

"Let's do it," urged the other two.

They took a quick, fearful glance around to make sure they were alone. Then, elaborately working their tongues and cheeks to gather spittle, they spat on the painting. Frightened at what they had done, they ran down the street. Only when they were near enough to the Catholic section to feel safe did they stop to look back. The street was empty and silent and unaware of their dread escapade. As a last gesture of defiance at the Protestants, they stuck out their bellies and began to slap them in imitation of the drummers.

On the day following their visit to the Shankill Road the Mole passed the word around that he had a wonderful idea for the afternoon. When the bell rang, the four boys trooped into the street and were soon huddled together.

"What's the wonderful idea?" asked Brian.

"We're going to fight the Protestants," said the Mole.

"Fight the Protestants?" said Brian in surprise. "What for?"

The Mole explained. "You know how they get cocky around the Twelfth? Well, our boys always take them on in a stone fight in the brickfields. A fellow in our class says that he's going up and is looking for volunteers. Are you game?"

"I don't want to," said Brian. "Why should I go fighting Protestants?" There was a difference, he told himself, between fighting Protestants who, like himself, were Irishmen and spitting at any old picture of King Billy, who, after all, was a foreigner.

"Since we've nothing else to do today," suggested Humpy, "let's go up anyway and see what happens."

Curly and the Mole said they wanted to see the fun, too, and Brian finally agreed to go with them.

The brickfields lay outside the city, almost surrounded by the encroaching housing developments. A wide clay pit stretched between the Catholic and the Protestant localities. At the far end of the pit in the open country Brian saw two irregular lines of boys facing each other about two hundred yards apart. There was no attempt at organization, but stones were continually flying in the air, and sometimes they came over thick after a sporadic, concerted effort on the part of one or two small groups.

Slings were much in evidence, and Brian was amazed at the accuracy with which some of the boys could place a stone as big as his fist in a given area two hundred yards off. If one of these stones struck you, he figured, it would do considerable damage, but they were thrown from such a distance that only the careless or the bold would be hit by them. As far as he could see, the fight resolved itself into desultory stone-throwing or a name-calling contest. Sometimes, however, groups of boys would sally out into enemy territory and cause a moment of excitement.

Brian and his friends arrived just as a small group of Protestants sallied out and came around the edge of the pit. The unexpected appearance of Brian and the others cut them off. The boys saw their danger and decided to make a dash for it past Brian's group back to their own territory. There was a sudden flurry of stone-throwing and name-calling, and on an impulse Brian picked up a stone and threw it at one of the running boys. The boy put his hand quickly to his head, stumbled, and sank to the ground. It happened so suddenly Brian did not connect his stone-throwing with the wounded boy and continued to throw ineffectual stones at the boys who had kept on running. Only when these were out of range did he pay any attention to the boy on the ground. By the time Brian reached him, he was already surrounded by Curly, the Mole, Humpy, and several others. He was sitting on the ground holding a handkerchief to his cheek, and the handkerchief was stained bright red. Brian stared for a moment at the Protestant boy, trying to see how he was different. There was a period of embarrassed silence.

"You really hurt him," one boy said.

"You sure did," said another.

"You shouldn't have fired that stone so hard," said a third.

Brian was taken back at hearing them blame him for what they had all been doing moments before.

"How did I know I was going to hit him?" he protested.

"Better take him to the Royal," said someone else, mentioning the nearest hospital.

"Don't go, Brian," warned Curly. "They'll jail you for hitting a Prod."

There were a lot more comments, mostly against Brian.

"But you were all throwing stones as well as me." By now Brian was almost in tears.

"Aye, but you're the one that hit him."

"He was too near when you threw the stone."

After that the other boys withdrew, leaving Brian with Curly, the Mole, and Humpy to take care of the wounded boy. He was still sitting on the ground holding his bloodstained handkerchief to his cheek.

Brian felt that the next move was up to him.

"Feeling better?" he asked embarrassedly, bending over the boy.

The boy shook his head. Brian noticed that he had light auburn hair. "No," he answered.

Brian felt this was unfair. The boy should at least be co-operative. He straightened up again, baffled. "What'll we do with him?" he asked the others.

Curly knelt down on the grass on one knee and studied the wounded boy. "Brian," he said finally, "the only thing to do is take him home."

Brian bent over again. "Do you want us to take you home?" The boy shook his head negatively.

"Why not?" asked Brian in surprise.

"I'll get killed for throwing stones at Catholics," he said.

"Brian," said Curly again, "you've got to take him to your house then and fix him up. He might die or get blood poisoning or something . . ." He waved his hand vaguely.

"But why should I have to take him to our house?" wailed Brian.

"Well," said Curly judiciously, "you hurt him, didn't you?"

Brian was about to protest again but gave up.

"All right," he said reluctantly. "But I don't see why I should take all the blame."

He bent down and took hold of one of the boy's arms; Curly took hold of the other. Finnegan and Dwyer followed in the rear as they brought the boy down the Falls Road to the Tracey home. Brian's only consolation was that his mother was alone. His father had not yet returned from work, and Paul and Sean were still out playing. Nevertheless, Mary scolded the other three out of the house and was about to clout Brian for what he had done. He was saved only by the intervention of the Protestant boy, who gave his name as Charles Wilson. Charles's version was that they had only been playing and that it had been an accident.

Mary bathed the wound with a solution of boracic powder and covered it with lint fixed down with sticking plaster. She gave Charles a glass of lemonade and a bun and talked to him while he ate. Charles told her and Brian that his nickname was "Clute," as left-handed boys were usually called. When he had finished eating she asked him if he felt strong enough to walk. Clute said he was, but Mary said she doubted it after the blow her brute of a son had inflicted on him and warned Brian that "he would get it" when his father came home. As a first punishment she told Brian to accompany Clute right to his own door.

Brian felt embarrassed walking beside Clute, for neither of them had much to say. Occasionally he stole a glance at Clute, sensing that Clute was doing the same at him. Clute was a little shorter than himself and a little stouter. He was wearing the usual dress of any boy, jacket and short pants, golf stockings and brogues. His brogues were the same as Brian's, and this somehow pleased Brian. Clute's hair was auburn and was gathered up on the left side of his head in a solid mound of waves and curls. Brian remembered that Clute was left-handed. His brown eyes and freckles seemed to lend a curious orange tinge to his complexion. His mouth was relaxed and he smiled easily at the few remarks Brian made along the way.

When they reached Clute's home in Hamill Street, Clute's mother was standing at the door and she ran out, frightened, to meet her son. Reassured, however, that there was nothing to worry about, she brought the two boys into the house and heard the whole story. With her arms akimbo and her lips tightly pursed she looked hard at Brian. For a moment Brian thought he was in for it. She only shook her head, however, in a despairing sort of way. "I don't know under God what they teach their children on the Falls," she said. "To let them go off throwin' stones in that murderous way! . . ." She turned at this to Clute and scolded him for running with the riffraff that went up to the brickfields. She had warned him about it several times, she told Brian, and that he "would get it" when his father came home. She insisted that Brian should wait to see how Clute would be punished. The sight of Clute sitting in a corner wounded, dejected, and waiting to be punished was too much for Brian. He began to make excuses for him, saying that it had been only a kind of game and that Clute had not meant any harm. Clute's mother was taken rather by surprise at this, but in the end she relented and promised that she would not tell Clute's father the whole story. She still insisted, however, on Brian's staying for supper with Clute, just to show that there was no bad blood between decent Protestants and decent Catholics. Brian did not want to stay, but when Clute pleaded that he needed Brian for his defense Brian consented. Later he met Clute's father, a slow-speaking man who reminded Brian of the Dutchmen in the pictures, for he had a long, drooping mustache and smoked a pipe with a curved stem. Before Brian left that evening he had promised Clute he would return.

Brian did not see Clute after that until the Twelfth had come and gone, for Mary was nervous about letting him go into the Protestant quarter at a time when feeling there against the Catholics was running high. But as soon as she thought it safe she let him go, and Brian was glad to visit Clute again and they began to exchange things and Clute eventually came to Brian's home. They also began to confide their secrets quietly while the two of them sat together in a corner of the room working on Clute's meccano set.

On his first visit to the Wilson home everything had seemed somehow "Protestant." There was a print of King William crossing the Boyne River—again he remembered the spit—and an orange sash with symbols of the Orange Order on it. Clute's father had been a member of the order but had allowed his membership to die. There was a cross in the house, all right, but it was no good in Brian's eyes for it had no figure on it. They did not have any pictures of Our Lady or the saints, or holy water, and Brian's mother always said that these things were necessary to keep away temptation. Every room in the Tracey home had something in it to keep away temptation. Brian's father one day had lost his temper and asked his mother if she was trying to turn the house into a bloody convent. But his mother had paid no attention to him, and his father went on taking holy water to bless himself with every time he left the house and every night always said his prayers before one of the holy pictures.

"Why do you Prods pray to King Billy?" Brian once asked Clute. "He's no saint."

"Who says we pray to King William?" was Clute's sharp response. "You're the ones that pray to everybody, even to sticks and stones! Our King William won the Battle of the Boyne and raised the siege of Derry, and King James's Catholics kept the Protestants for one hundred days without food and made them eat dogs and rats. If our King William had lost the war we'd all have to be Catholics. Boy, imagine the Orangemen all blessin' themselves and drinkin' holy water!—That's why we celebrate the Twelfth of July."

"Why do you Protestants hate us?"

"We don't hate you!" said Clute. "We just don't want to be like you."

"Why not?" insisted Brian.

"Mean to say you don't know?" Clute was incredulous. "Protestants be like Catholics? Oh, don't let us argue about that, Brian," said Clute finally. "You'll only get angry and then you won't come back here any more."

"If I promise you I won't get angry?" said Brian pugnaciously. Then he relented and again became genuinely curious. It had never struck him before that such fundamental differences existed between people. His early contacts with Protestantism had been confined to seeing Protestant families going off every Sunday evening with their Bibles under their arms to their church. In his mind the sum of the differences between Catholics and Protestants had been lumped together in this simple formula: Catholics went to chapel; Protestants went to church. But in Belfast the difference was played up by each side. Now he wanted to know exactly what that difference was as far as he could understand it. "Go on, Clute," he pleaded. "I won't mind. Solemn promise."

"Well," began Clute, "you have to do everything the Pope tells you, like not eating meat on Fridays, going to Mass, and spitting on the picture of King William."

"Yah!" said Brian hotly. "You're away in the head! Who says we spit . . . ?"—he suddenly remembered the escapade of a few nights ago—"I mean *have* to spit at Billy o' the Boyne or believe everything the Pope tells us? You Protestants think——"

"What did I tell you?" said Clute. "Now you're getting waxy at me!"

"I'm not, indeed!" shouted Brian. He quickly calmed down again. "All right, go ahead; I forgot."

"You Catholics pay the priest in confession and he forgives your sins. My Da says you can even buy a permit to commit sins, called an indulgence."

"That's not an indulgence!" interrupted Brian again.

"What *is* an indulgence then?" asked Clute.

"An indulgence means you don't have to stay in hell or purgatory."

"That's what I said."

"No, it doesn't mean exactly that either. It means . . . Och, I'll ask a priest what it means for you."

They brought up many horrible things in each other's religion, and Clute spoke of the monks and nuns who lived together, and the Black Mass said by the devil, and priests who mumbled-jumbled in Latin because they didn't want the people to hear them praying to Satan. Clute had often heard his mother and father say that the Catholics would be decent people if only the priests would leave them alone.

"Have you ever met a priest?" asked Brian.

"No."

"You see!" said Brian triumphantly. "What did I tell you? You're just prejudiced, that's what you are! You blah, blah, blah about the priests, but you've never met one—I mean a real one," he added rather nervously, "one that plays hurley and soccer."

"I don't have to meet aul' Nick to know what he's like, do I?" objected Clute.

"Well, you oughtta meet some of the priests I know, that's all," was Brian's crushing reply.

As he came home that evening the stars were out and the air was warm. He had been a little annoyed at first for being unable to give Clute clearer answers, but the annoyance quickly passed and he again soon felt in a pleasant frame of mind. Of late the city had seemed more agreeable to him than before—especially at night. For the night hid the gray monotony of the streets and quieted the city's harsher sounds. Perhaps at night, life in the city might even be better than life in the country. There was so much more to do. At night in the country . . .

Suddenly it struck him that he had not thought about the country for a long time. The realization made him anxious, for deep down within him he still felt a distrust of the city. He was afraid that the city might try to get a hold on him; and he remembered the day Aunt Meg had tried to make up to him. He had suspected she wanted help in something her son Patrick had refused. She had at first tried to embrace him and he had struggled to get free. But she had held on to him, and in the end he had sunk his teeth into her arm. She had wanted to clout him then, but he had easily eluded her.

Now he wondered if the city, too, were trying to make up to him like Aunt Meg, trying to wean his affection from the land. That was one thing he did not want to happen to him. He had no wish to belong to the city or to become one of the city people. The people of the city seemed subdued, cowed, closed up, and anxious, as if they had something to hide. They did not have the upright ways of Dinny, his own father, or even Uncle Jamie. Besides, in the city people rarely talked about Ireland, about her history, her heroes, poets, and martyrs. Mr. Lawlor, their schoolmaster, was a rare exception. Half the while they did not seem to be Irishmen at all!

He would have to be careful not to let the city hold him as Aunt

Meg had tried to do. The best way was to get down to the farm again and live the free and open life of the land. As if shuffling off the discussion with himself, he shrugged his shoulders, and since the urge came on him, began to run. Carelessly he struck the tip of his shoe against the ground, but there was no ring, no sparks flew out, for there was no iron on his shoe now and the pavement was too soft.

II The Trouble

8

Oh! the old turf fire and the hearth swept clean.
There is no one half so happy as myself and Paddy Keane;
With the baby in the cradle you can hear her mammy say,
Wouldn't you go to sleep, alanna, till I wet your Daddy's tay?
I have got a little house and a tidy bit of lan';
You would never see a better on the side of Knocknacran;
I've no piano in the corner and no pictures on the wall,
But I'm somehow quite contented in my little marble hall.

Brian listened to his mother singing softly to herself as he came in from the yard, where he had been tinkering with his motorcycle, to wash his hands at the sink. At twenty-two years of age he still thought that Sunday afternoon at home was something to look forward to, and on that mild June afternoon it was even pleasanter than usual. The house had a well-scrubbed look after its usual Saturday cleaning that extended even beyond the limits of the house to a well-scrubbed arc on the pavement outside. The house smelled sweet, and a cool breeze blew in through the open windows, bellying the fresh parlor curtains. They always used the parlor on Sundays, both for the sake of change and because people dropped in for a visit and a cup of tea.

At that particular moment the appetizing smell of a fry his mother was preparing pervaded the house and mingled with the savory smell of newly-baked potato "farls," very thin, triangular cakes of potato bread. His taste had changed as he had grown older, from sausages and bread fried in gravy to sausages and boiled potatoes. When eating alone he loved to mash his potatoes and sausages together, and using his knife as a bricklayer uses his trowel, turn them into a smooth round mass. Out of this he cut a small square, slid the knife under it, popped it into his mouth, and drew out the knife as clean as a whistle. When his mother caught him at this she would exclaim, half annoyed and half amused: "In the name o' God, will the Traceys ever grow up?"

Brian watched his mother slide the pot of tea off the hob and put it aside to draw. He knew she would not bring out sausages or potato farls or toast or tea until everything was ready. She hated to see the four of them, without waiting for the table to be laid, peck at this and that, trying to keep their eyes away from the food. Dad could be every bit as aggravating to her as the boys. Sometimes Brian thought his father did it just for the fun of it, but most of the time it seemed that he could not help playing his transparent little tricks on her. It wasn't so bad when he did it at home, but he also did it when they were out with other people, and often went too far, and Mother had to go into a huff to bring Dad back to his senses.

Mother said the boys took after him. Especially Sean, who was still so much of a kid despite his muscles and his eighteen years. He was the smallest and best-proportioned of the three. And Sean got along well with people outside. When you thought of Sean you thought of his friendly smile with the beautifully formed lips—he had the "singer's mouth," people said—and the healthy, red cheeks. Remember the time they thought he had a notion for the priesthood? Although there were only four years separating him, Brian, from Sean, with Paul in between, Brian had begun to feel much older than Sean. He still referred to Sean as "my kid brother." With Paul, who was now twenty, and two years younger than Brian, although a few inches taller, it was a horse of a different color. Paul sometimes tried to act as if he were superior in years and ways to Brian, and Brian then had to put him in his place. Paul was of a make altogether different from Sean. Paul's slim dark looks made him a favorite at the dances. Brian never liked to go to dances or parties with Paul. Paul always looked so smooth and attractive and at his ease while Brian just felt uncomfortable. On the other hand, Paul never seemed to be at ease with his own family, and Brian was sure that once Paul left home he would never come back again. Paul could get forward and cheeky at times even with his father, but he had never tried to do it with Brian.

Paul now worked in a large downtown store and was being trained in the different departments with every hope of being given a good job when his training was finished. Brian thought that Paul was in the right spot for one of his kind. He looked more and more every day like a smooth—well, like a floorwalker.

Sean, on the other hand, was more the intellectual type. He worked in a branch of the Hibernian Bank in a Protestant quarter. Sean was crazy on improving his mind and was forever attending evening classes for this and that, was a great Irish speaker, and had even been to one of the Gaeltacht schools in Galway where they spoke nothing but Gaelic. People were always calling for Sean, for he was a good organizer and usually had one affair or another on his hands.

And yet Mother still treated them like children. Was that just a mother's failing? Brian wondered. Maybe not, for now, although they were so grown up and looked like men when they were dressed up on Sundays, they still lost things, quarreled over trifles, complained of unfair treatment, and huffed when she scolded them.

Brian rolled up the sleeves of the white Sunday shirt that he knew made him look so much broader across the chest, worked up a lather with his hands, and scrubbed his nails with the nail brush. He was sensitive now about dirt under his fingernails. He remembered the day Mr. Lawlor at St. Peter's had cleaned them for him with a nail brush. Brian had tried to explain that it was clean dirt, but his new teacher would not listen, and Brian had been sensitive ever since about his nails—his nails and the deep-V hairline. He gazed into the mirror. Not bad at all when he was cleaned up, he concluded, and if the point of the deep V of hair on his forehead could only be shaved . . . He had good teeth, good complexion, reddish with a slight tan around the edges of the red. Thank the trips to the farm for that. When he had saved up enough, it wouldn't be weekends only at the farm. No, sir. And now that he was finishing his apprenticeship as a steam-fitter the money would come in faster.

"Brian, will you give over admiring that mug of yours and go in for your tea!"

Brian blushed at being caught staring into the mirror. He dried his hands quickly and threw the towel absent-mindedly in a corner. His mother glared at him. He picked it up again, draped it across a rack, kissed his mother's cheek, making her smile, and went into the parlor.

Inside the cool parlor Michael, Paul, and Sean were talking in a desultory manner, waiting for the meal.

"What are you boys doing this evening?" said Michael suddenly. He looked at Sean. "What's the Gael going to do, for one?"

"I'd planned to go to St. Mary's Hall for the *coelidhe,*" said Sean. With the edge of his sleeve he rubbed the little gold circle or *fainne* in his buttonhole, a trick of his to show that he was a Gaelic speaker. "But since the weather is so fine I think I'd as leave go up the Glen Road and have a bit of fun at the crossroads. But whatever dancing I do you can be sure it'll be Irish or nothing." He glanced across at Paul.

Brian knew his father had asked Sean where he was going in order to get Paul to admit that he was going to the Plaza, where they had only English dancing. He waited for his father's next move.

"And where are you going, Paul, might I ask?" said Michael.

"I'm only going down to the Lavertys'," said Paul casually. "That's why I might be a little late." He walked out to the kitchen as if to fetch something.

"That's what you'd like us to believe, Mr. Smart," called out Michael after him. "As if we didn't know you're heading for the swanks at the Plaza. And as if the price wasn't enough to keep them penniless. They have to beg or borrow dickies and dress suits, and the half of them not able to pay for a package of fags!"

Paul came in again and sat down as far away from his father as he could. He seized the newspaper and spread it defiantly in front of him.

"Paul," said Michael.

"What?" Paul looked up for a moment and then returned to the paper.

"Is it true that you're blowing to them mashers at the Plaza about your father's property and our home in the country—wherever the hell you got that notion from? Home in the country! And you a pound-a-week apprentice!"

"I dunno what you're talking about!" blustered Paul.

"Maybe you do have a home in the country. You must spend most of your time in it, for we don't see much of you here; and maybe, also, this house isn't good enough for your lordship."

"Is there any harm in trying to be clean and decent and . . . better?" Brian sensed that Paul was searching unsuccessfully for the right words.

Michael almost jumped out of his chair. "Maybe we're dirty and indecent!" he shouted. "For two pins I'd give you a slap across the mouth, you cheeky ba—brat! Watch your step, my lad! I'm not as soft as the mother, you know!"

"You're always at me, anyway!" complained Paul.

"And why shouldn't I always be at you?" said Michael. "The way you're carrying on now, God only knows how you'll turn out later on! You're out till all hours and nobody knows where you get the money to keep up with your great friends. You certainly don't get it here, and I hope no son of mine is sponging on them good-for-nothings. None of them ever poke their noses inside this door. It's not good enough for them. Well, let me tell your lordship that if we're not good enough for them they shouldn't be good enough for you! Them and their dickies and dress shirts!"

"Getting worked up for the Orangemen and the Twelfth of July, Dad?" said Brian. He smiled at his father, and when he smiled he showed a contrast of black hair and white teeth.

"Of course I'm not," grumbled Michael, settling back to his chair. "It's Master Paul here. If somebody doesn't do something with that boy pretty soon, I don't know where he'll end up."

"You're right there, Dad," said Brian. He drew down his shirt sleeves and buttoned them. "Mother tells me that you saved me just before I went to the dogs altogether with that Dinny Coleman down at the farm . . ."

"Now quit it, Brian," said Michael gruffly. "I'm in no mood for coddin' around. You did make your mother and myself sweat blood in them days, more than the other two put together. But that was different. A lad isn't dangerous at that age, and a belt or two where he feels it will soon quiet him. The dangerous ones are them that gets wilder as they grow older, when they should be getting more sense. But forget about it—where are you off to this evening? To Clute's?"

"No. I think I'll take a quick run down to the farm on the motor-bike." Brian worked unconcernedly at his fingernails with the blade of his penknife.

"Boys o' boys!" said Michael. "You certainly love that farm!"

"What if I do?" said Brian a little defiantly. "It's a sight better than working in the shipyards. Shipyards and machine shops and oil and dirt and dust in the air . . ."

"Oh, you can get just as dirty on the farm as anywhere else," said Michael.

"Of course you can," said Brian. "But that's clean dirt! And the farm'll never make you as foulmouthed or filthy as I have seen it make the young fellas in the shipyards in the four years I've been there."

He recalled the first morning four years ago when he had pushed his bicycle out into the quiet street on his way to the Queen's Island shipyard. His parents had decided that he was to learn a trade, and through the influence of Nat Wilson, Clute's father, he had been accepted as an apprentice steam-fitter.

It was also through Clute's father that he had been put to work with the squad Clute himself was in. Brian had been glad of Clute's company in the beginning, for the rest of the squad were Protestants, as were the vast majority of workmen on the Island—a fact that made the Island a sore spot with the Catholics.

He remembered, too, that the next morning he had taken his first ride on the bicycle to the Island down past the Castle Junction where the crisscrossing, shining tramlines had confused him and the thin tires of his bicycle had skidded and sent him sprawling the length of the junction. Later, when he had reached the Island, he had been strangely saddened by the long, subdued lines of workmen, lines of ants making their blind way to their holes, thin steady streams of humanity pouring into a mold.

His first assignment had been to help Sam Dickson mark the points where the fitters would first bore, then thread holes in the bulkhead for screws for the ship's piping. It had frightened him at first to stand on a shaky plank over a yawning hold, raise both arms above his head, and mark a girder or a plate, but he had been too proud to ask for a change. It had been interesting during lunch hour to visit the ships in for repairs—once or twice, when work was slack, Sam had let him off to see a launching—or to stand thrilled underneath the bulging hull of a liner in dry dock and wonder what would happen if the forest of blocks gave way under her twenty thousand tons.

But he had soon tired of walking through inches of dust red with rust from the steel plates; and he felt uncomfortable at the dirty talk of the men during the lunch hour. In the end he made up his mind to spend as much time as he could down on the farm, and every Sunday afternoon he left on the bike. But it was a long ride and a sore one on a bicycle, and as soon as he had been able he had bought a secondhand motorcycle that took him there inside the hour.

"But, Brian," Michael was saying slyly, "surely there can't be that much to do on the farm on a Sunday afternoon?"

"I have to . . . I want to give the bike a tryout," said Brian. "There's something wrong with the fuel system."

"I see. I see," said Michael. He said this slowly, as if he were tasting a well-aged dram of Bushmills. "Would you do me a little favor when you're down that way?"

"Sure I will."

"Drop in on Paddy Reilly and ask him for the flies he was supposed to send me weeks ago. And . . . ah . . . ahem!" Michael grew heavily subtle. "If young Sheila happens to be around, tell her to finish them socks she's knitting for me very soon, or she'll have to pull up my shroud to put them on! Either that or else she'll have to pass them on to somebody much younger. You might tell her, too, that now that she's grown up into a purty young hussy, she'd better be more careful of them slick city fellas dashin' up and down the country on their motor-bikes."

All the time Michael had been talking he had held a cool, innocent eye on Brian, and Brian's face, despite himself, had gradually reddened, until he turned away from his father with his cheeks and ears aflame.

The incident set Michael back into good humor. He always felt in good humor on Sundays. He could have a long lie-in every Sunday and get to a late Mass; he enjoyed the leisurely breakfast, followed by a stroll up the road with one or two of his cronies, a good dinner, a long nap, and then a good tea. He and Mary later went to "devotions" at the Monastery, the popular name of the nearby Redemptorist Church, and then paid a call on some friends or, if Mary felt like it, dropped in at the pictures. The only displeasure, the tiniest fly in the family ointment, was the fact that he loved to top off the day with a bottle of Guinness's stout and Mary did not hold with that. She detested its heavy smell and obliged Michael himself to put away the empty bottle and wash the glass. But Michael insisted on that bottle of stout before he went to bed, for Sunday was a special day, he said, and it was fitting to drink its health in Guinness's before bidding it good-by for another week.

At that moment Mary appeared carrying a plate of buttered toast. Michael smiled broadly at her. She frowned back at him, marched across the parlor, and set the plate on the linen tablecloth. She could tell by her husband's look that he was in a playful mood, and she wanted to forestall any attempt at what she called his "antics."

"Woman dear," said Michael, "this is the one time I don't regret having jilted the lovely Eileen O'Donnell."

"She wouldn't have had you with a crock o' gold!" said Mary shortly.

"A woman's secret is locked forever in my heart," said Michael. "Nothing you say will ever overshadow the charm, heavenly grace, and good sense of that girl."

"Whoever she is she must have had more sense than me not to fall for that old guff!" said Mary, unruffled. "Say the prayer and quit the nonsense! The boys want to have their tea and get out."

"I will, my love, my dove, my beautiful one, I will." Michael put his arms around the protesting Mary and raised his eyes romantically to the ceiling. "The lovely lady's slightest wish is my command!"

"Did you ever hear such . . ." Mary looked at Brian who was laughing at her discomfiture. She slapped and pulled at her husband's hands with an odd mixture of pleasure and impatience. Finally Michael released his wife and touched his forehead with two fingers. "In the name of the Father . . ."

"I see the Orangemen are getting the big drums ready for the Twelfth." Michael sipped noisily at his mug and with his underlip supped up the spread of tea that clung to the lower part of the mustache he had grown in the past year. It still seemed a little in the way at mealtimes.

"Wonder will they start anything?" asked Brian, thinking of his first contact with the religious strife for which Belfast was notorious. That was when he had dared Curly to go up to the Shankill Road and listen to the Orangemen practicing on the big drums.

"There hasn't been any trouble since we've been here," said Michael.

"There wasn't all this fuss and talk the past years," objected Mary. "There wasn't this early show of bad feeling."

"Aye," admitted Michael. "There's something in that. The big bugs are givin' off more this year than ever I remember. Makes you think they'd like something to start."

"The Catholics aren't doing anything to help," said Brian.

"How can you say that?" said Sean. "We've as good a right as the Protestants to make ourselves heard! We can't be cowed all our lives! The Catholics don't write 'To Hell with the Archbishop of Canterbury!' on the walls."

"What about 'Up the Republic?'" responded Brian. "And don't we burn King Billy?"

"There was a butcher on the Shankill," said Paul, "who hung up a side of bacon and stuck a label on it saying 'Cured at Lourdes.'"

"All I can say," interrupted Michael, "is that I'll feel a lot easier this year when the Twelfth has come and gone. They are a bitter lot, them Orangemen, and they hate the Catholics. I suppose they think that if ever we're united to the South we'll make them all turn."

"If you're finished," said Mary, "you can move back and let me rid the table."

"Aye, my lady," answered Michael, rising. "Anyway, it's time we were making for devotions. And after the devotions I think we'll drop in on the Wilsons, before the Twelfth comes. I don't feel easy in that quarter around that time of the year."

He rose up, glanced out of the parlor window at the passers-by, and worked his lips and teeth contentedly for a moment. Brian watched him with amused interest as he came back to his chair and pulled off his slippers with a grunt for each. As he drew on his boots and bent over to lace them, his ears grew red and the back of his neck bulged.

"Glory be to God!" he gasped as he stood up. He went to the dresser, brushed back his evenly parted white hair, and smoothed down his neat gray mustache.

"The coat, Mary," he said.

"The man would need a servant!" said Mary to Brian.

She helped her husband into his coat, tugging at the ends, pulling down the sleeves, and smoothing the shoulders free of creases.

"Where did you leave the hat?" asked Mary.

Michael with his chin nodded toward the cupboard, and Mary brought a black homburg and brushed it before she handed it to him.

"Here it is, Lord Tracey," she said dryly.

Michael smiled good-humoredly. "What do you think I married you for, darling?" he said as he turned and again surveyed himself seriously in the mirror for a moment.

"Tsk! Tsk! Tsk!" clicked Mary, looking at him and shaking her head. "And they talk about the women!"

"Are you ready, woman dear, for the devotions?" asked Michael. "Father McGuire keeps telling the women it's their job to get the men out early."

"And me all the time dressin' you!" Mary turned on him indignantly.

"Well, hurry up now, like a good girl," said Michael blandly. "We haven't all night. And don't forget the coppers for the plate. With three workingmen around you can't expect me to keep this house going and keep up the chapel as well. I'm still quoting Father McGuire."

Brian knew that his mother and father were fond of listening to Father McGuire. The people who had spent their lifetime in the neighborhood remembered Father McGuire twenty years ago as an errand boy for Sorley's grocery on the Falls before he had gone abroad to study for the priesthood. He had returned to the Monastery to take charge of the sodalities. He was rather tall and wiry, walked with a springy step, and at forty still handled a fair stick in the sodality hurling matches. He was so dark his clean-shaven chin had a curious blue tinge to it; his high cheekbones offset the deep eye sockets and had always a line of black hair on them beyond which evidently Father McGuire did not allow his razor to go. Otherwise, as Sean had once remarked, he would have ended up shaving off his bushy eyebrows. Mary had scolded Sean for making such familiar remarks about one of God's priests. Brian had also heard it said with something of awe that Father McGuire had written books, although he had never taken the trouble to find out what those books were. Michael said he liked Father McGuire because there was no blether about the man and he was as straight as a die; Mary said she liked him because he was a wonderful preacher and a grand wee man to talk to in any trouble.

Brian had liked him since the days of the boys' sodality that had devotions once a week attended by as many as two thousand boys. Devotions for the boys' sodality consisted of hymns—great roaring affairs helped on by the booming organ—a story, and benediction. The Tracey brothers had sat in the same bench and snuggled up together to listen to the story by Father McGuire. The most hair-raising and most interesting stories were always those about hell and the tricks of the devil to drag people into it. And the night the boy skipped the sodality to go for a swim in the

Falls Park pond and was drowned! For months afterward Father McGuire had kept them frightened with that one example.

The boys believed the priest had extraordinary powers. He had once stopped in the middle of the story and pointed to the farthest corner of the large church. "There is a boy down there not listening to me," he had cried. "He's whispering to his companion instead and paying no attention to what I'm telling him to save his immortal soul from being dragged down to the pit of hell!"

A thousand necks had craned to get a glimpse of the boy who was disturbing, and a thousand young minds wondered how Father McGuire had been able to hear a whisper at such a distance.

Brian had never seen Father McGuire so mad as the night the boys had left the Monastery grounds singing songs against the Protestants until the singing was stopped by police and plainclothes men. At the next meeting he had lashed into the boys, but somehow Brian had come away with the idea that he had not been so mad at them for singing patriotic songs as for singing songs against the Protestants, who, he had made it very clear, were Irishmen like themselves.

Michael now tamped tobacco down into the bowl of his pipe, lit it, and with his head in the air, like a hen drinking water, puffed on it once or twice. When it was drawing well, he rubbed his hands clean and clasped them behind his back, spread out his legs, and swayed contentedly back and forth on his heels.

When Mary was ready, he followed her out and waited while she pulled the door closed behind them. When she threaded her arm in his he pressed it comfortably to his side, and they walked away together in the direction of the Monastery.

9

Brian raised himself up off the seat of the motorcycle and kicked down on the starter. After a quick initial sputter the engine died down to a quieter purr and he settled back comfortably on the broad seat, threw it into gear, and slid away from the pavement. When he was clear of the city traffic he opened the throttle and let the machine roar along the Shore Road on the way to Drumree.

It was a summer afternoon, but with his speed the wind was cool as it swept across his face, though at times he felt it come in warmer puffs. He smelled the tang and tasted the salt of the sea breezes blowing in from Belfast Lough, and he remembered the first time he had traveled over this road in the trap and a world had ended for him. It had broken his heart to leave the farm, and Dinny and Stardust and Turnip! He smiled. Everything had not died that day. He had outlived that sad period, had finished at the very school he had detested in the beginning, and had resigned himself to becoming an apprentice at the shipyards. "There was more money in it." He had sunk his early despair in machines and to his surprise had come up with a liking for them. And he was doing well at the Island, for they had invited him to take courses in draftsmanship, an invitation reserved for their best men.

Another month now and he'd finish at the Island and go on for an engineer's certificate. Not that he intended to give up the idea of the farm. Oh no! Nothing was going to take him away from the farm! They could think all they liked at home and make all the plans for him they wanted. *His* plans for the future included a farm even if he had to work for it every minute off the job. Lots of the fellows in their spare time were building bungalows in the country and traveling to work. Only he wouldn't build any useless little bungalow. He'd buy a farm and sink every penny in it and borrow to build it up, and when it was a going concern he'd leave Belfast and move into it.

He swung down the Drumree Road past the high ridge of his uncle's farm and pulled out his watch. Forty-five minutes; five minutes faster than any time so far. That was because a lot of young blood had passed him on the road and he had tailed them for a while. But he never did like pitting himself against anybody. He preferred to go along with them and enjoy their friendship. He also preferred to hear his machine run smoothly, and when he felt the urge for speed he waited until he found a level stretch of road and then eased her up to her limit. But as soon as he heard her miss or show any sign of strain he slowed her down again. A machine was like a horse or a dog or a body. You had no right to hurt them; you treated them well and they gave their best.

He braked slowly, turned a sharp right into the farmyard gate, and crawled up the uneven, pitted cobblestone road stained with and smelling of cow dung. He stopped opposite the milking house and let the engine *put-put* quietly to see if anyone came out. No one came, so he shut off the engine, swung his leg free of the machine, and when he put it down again he nearly stepped on a dog that had come up without barking. It was an old Irish terrier, big with a litter of pups, that growled at him in a careless, sleepy way.

"Hello, Turnip," said Brian. He bent down and patted Turnip's head. Turnip licked his hand but kept on growling.

"So it's more Irishmen, Turnip, is it?"

He moved on toward the milking house, and Turnip trotted after him, her heavy belly scraping some of the high cobblestones. He spent some time examining the milking machines in the airy milkshed where the concrete floor was still wet from the scouring of the cans and then went on to the machine shed where the farm equipment was kept. All the machines were out except the heavy plow he had often driven as a boy with Dinny. It now lay in a corner, rusty from months of nonuse. From there he made his way up to the Long Field, leaned on the low gate, raised his head as if scenting the air, and whistled: a moment later the head of a jet-black horse broke over the crest of the hill and looked down in his direction.

"Stardust!"

Stardust shook his head once or twice, stood still for a second or two, and then trotted down to the gate. By the time he reached the gate Brian was already on the other side waiting for him. He seized the horse by the mane and ran his cheek along the warm, smooth neck. Stardust struggled to free himself, and Brian leaped onto his bare back and grasped two fistfuls of his mane.

"Come on, Stardust," he said. "Show 'em you've still got speed in you!" He dug his heels into the horse's soft flanks and galloped to the far end of the Long Field. Turning the horse quickly, he held him tightly between his thighs. "Ready?" he said. "Go!" He jerked his body, and at the word both horse and man moved ahead as one. Stardust stretched his neck and elongated his body as he raced. Brian stretched his body, too, lying flat across the bare back of the horse with his cheek against that smooth neck now hard with muscle and the hair of the horse's mane blowing across his face. They raced to the other end of the field. Here Brian drew up his slackened thighs, felt Stardust quiver under him, and as he listened to the heavy *dum-dum* of his pumping heart, he knew that Stardust was growing old. He felt sorry for him. He turned the horse's head toward the ridge and rode over it. On the other side Dinny was gathering potatoes at the top of the potato field, and Tom and a hired man were working the field with him. Brian knew that Dinny saw him as soon as he came over the ridge but was pretending not to, and Brian decided to humor him.

"Hello, Dinny," he called out when he was close enough. He pulled Stardust up short.

"So it's you, Brian-og!" said Dinny. He still kept his head down and shook the soil from the potato plant he held in his hand. "How did ye come down?"

"I came down on the motor-bike."

"You're getting on in the world with your motor-bike!" said Dinny. "I mind the time I would have walked it. How's things in Belfast?" Brian smiled at Dinny's country way of saying Bel*faast*.

"Oh, dry and dirty as usual," said Brian. He did not dare say anything good about the city in Dinny's presence. "It's grand to leave it and come back to the country. And if I didn't have the bike I could never make it at all, Dinny."

"Aye, mebbe you're right, Brian-og," said Dinny. "There must be some use in all these newfangled doodas. Mebbe it's me that's wrong. Mebbe I'm just getting old." He straightened up and looked at Brian, and only his eyes returned Brian's smile. "Have ye seen your uncle?"

"No, not yet."

"He says that there's a job to do on Miser Donaghy's thresher. They want to get it ready for the threshing."

"I'll take all the jobs they give me, Dinny," said Brian. "They'll help me to get my own farm all the sooner. I'll run up and see Uncle Jamie."

"I don't think ye need bother," said Dinny, bending down again. Brian watched him curl his hand round the green stalk of a potato plant and wrench it violently from the grip of the soil that had nourished it until now. The earth that dropped from the straggling roots looked to Brian like blood dripping off a limb torn from the body of a man.

"Speak o' the divil . . ." said Dinny. He jerked his thumb toward the ridge.

"Well, well, well!" Uncle Jamie greeted Brian cordially. "So the city folk is down here again! And you're still fond of Stardust, I see."

"I used to think that Stardust was the only horse in the world!" said Brian, looking at Stardust nosing the brown earth in search of food. "But he's getting old now. Aren't you, Stardust?" He leaned over and rubbed his hand up and down the long muscles of the horse's flanks. Stardust's muscles flicked in answer.

"I suppose you came down on the bike?"

"I did, Uncle Jamie," said Brian. "I couldn't do without it."

"I think he'll marry that motor-bike," put in Dinny. "And throw Sheila Reilly out the window."

"Sheila Reilly is no concern of mine," huffed Brian.

"It's always the way, Dinny," said Uncle Jamie. "A city fella could never be satisfied with a simple country girl like Sheila Reilly."

"Don't kid yourself, Jamie," said Dinny with his head still down. "She's not as simple as she looks, that one."

"You may be right, Dinny," said Uncle Jamie, nodding wisely. "Come to think of it, I have heard one or two things about the lassie. Never expected it from a Reilly. But today's youngsters . . . there's no tethering them!"

"What did you hear against her?" asked Brian. "I wish to God some of these old blatherers in Drumree would say something against her to me! I'd—" The silence warned him. Too late he tried to recover. "I hear there's a thresher to be fixed," he said shortly.

"Who's talking about a thresher?" said Uncle Jamie.

"Can I see it?"

"Well, Dinny," said Uncle Jamie, "if he doesn't want to hear certain things mentioned again for his own good, that's up to him." Uncle Jamie gave a short nod of his head to Dinny as if to say that he had done his part to put matters right. "But before we see the thresher we'll have a bit of supper. Nobody's home but Cathey and myself. The wife and young Bridie went out to a party, and with Patrick now at college the house is overquiet."

"Dinny," said Brian before he left, "have you anything for Stardust?" He slid off the horse to walk with Uncle Jamie.

Dinny went over to the haycart and opened a wooden box under the seat. He took out an apple and threw it toward Brian. Brian caught the apple and held it out to the horse, and Stardust's velvet lips swept up the apple from Brian's palm; and as he crunched it between his teeth, still looking at Brian, Brian saw that he had the indefinable splayfooted stance of a horse that was growing old. He moved down the field toward the house with Uncle Jamie and watched Stardust out of the corner of his eye.

Stardust looked after him for a moment in doubt, shook his mane, and followed Brian to the gate. Brian passed through the gate and closed it behind Uncle Jamie. Stardust came up and looked mournfully at him.

"The old put-on!" said Uncle Jamie, shaking his fist at the horse. "You'd think you hadn't a friend in the world, and there's not man or baste gets more attention than yourself! You're worse than a woman, dammit!"

After a good supper prepared by Cathey, Brian and Uncle Jamie sat down before the fire of logs that was always set during the summer months but never lit.

"What's the latest in Belfast?" asked Uncle Jamie. "I hear there's trouble brewing?"

"Trouble?" asked Brian.

"Trouble between the Protestants and the Catholics. Sean was down and told us all about it. He says the Orangemen are arming and drilling again."

"I don't know anything about it," said Brian. "Sean has his head stuffed with shooting and drilling and the I.R.A."

"Maybe so," said Uncle Jamie. "But Sean has it that the Orangemen are afraid the Catholics are getting too strong for them and are beginning to take away all the good jobs. He says, too, that the shipyards are in the thick of it."

"I work with Orangemen on the Island and I haven't noticed anything amiss. If there's any trouble anywhere, Sean's the boy to find it."

"Down here in the country," said Uncle Jamie, "things like that never bother us, and I hope they never will. But it's strange what different times will do to the same people."

"Let's take a race down to Miser Donaghy's and look at the thresher," said Brian, rising.

"All right, Brian," said Uncle Jamie, rising with him. "If you're not worried and you work on the Island . . ."

On the way down to Miser Donaghy's farm Uncle Jamie stopped by the side of the road and pointed his stick over a whitethorn hedge. "Brian," he said, "if you look across that hayfield of ours, you'll see the Widow Dooley's fifteen acres. Tickle that land with a hoe and I guarantee it'll laugh with a harvest. She's ready to sell it dirt cheap."

"Where would I get the money, Uncle Jamie?"

"I'll tell you where you'll get it and without being beholding to outsiders. Me and Dinny have been talking it over with Fiddler Reilly. We all like you, son, and we know you're fond of the land, and, God knows, we want to see you back to where you belong. We could put up something and you could borrow the rest on your wages as a journeyman."

"I don't know what to say, Uncle Jamie . . ."

"You don't have to say anything." Jamie lowered his voice to a whisper. He looked at a staring thrush as if the bird were listening in to what he said. "And if you do say anything, we're sunk! Let Kate know I'm lending you money, or even that I had any money to lend you, and there'd be hell to pay! Besides, me and Dinny and the Fiddler have been thinking hard these past few weeks, and here's our thoughts: Every day the country's turning more and more to machines, and they tell me you're the quare hand at fixing them. Suppose we was to start up a little business to rent and repair farming machinery? You could handle it for us and we'd all share—ah, hum"—Jamie spat on the grass—"in the profits. Eh?" He cast a furtive glance around the field they were crossing, but the only living things within sight were the Widow Dooley's four cows with their necks stretched to the ground and the setting sun growing redder in the low sky, so that to Brian the four cows looked like cut-outs on a sheet of orange paper.

" 'T'would be the dream of my life come true!" breathed Brian. "But——"

"But what, man?" interrupted Uncle Jamie.

"But what makes you so sure Fiddler Reilly will put up his share? He may be great shakes at a wake with his fiddle, but he's not a great hand for throwing the ha'pence around."

"What?" said Uncle Jamie. "And you and Sheila planning to get married? Could he do less?"

"Uncle Jamie," said Brian impatiently. He felt like stamping his foot the way Sheila did when she was mad. "How do you know

I'm going to marry Sheila? I never said so and I'm sure she didn't either!"

"Quit coddin', man!" said Uncle Jamie. "It's as plain as the purty wee head on her shoulders. Everybody in Drumree is sure of it. They're only hoping it'll be after the harvest and not before, so they can stay drunk all night at the wedding!"

"Uncle," said Brian, straightening up, "I don't like forcing any young lady into an embarrassing situation."

"Hold your whisht, man!" said Uncle Jamie, unimpressed. "You forcing her? The vixen's just letting on you're forcing her! Wait till you're married, Sir Gallyhad!"

The two men marched on in gloomy silence for another while, and Brian watched the sun swell into a huge ball of fire, trembling and turning with the heat as it set over the tip of Tara Hill, and he could see the very leaves of the distant trees turn black in the blaze of the setting sun. A lone curlew complained as she winged her way home, at the sight of the sun going down, and as the purple rim of dusk peeked over the east the crows, the rowdies of the woods, that had bullied the noonday world with their raucous cawing grew still and afraid and perched silently on the tops of the high trees. A canopy of quiet settled over the land, and all the sounds that during the strife of the day had come up clear and defined had now a hush on them, a blur that dulled their sharp edges, making even the far cries of children or the barking of a dog seem touched with melancholy . . . From another world the voice of Uncle Jamie broke into Brian's ken.

"I don't see how such a thing could fail. And when we talk it over with the Fiddler——"

"How can I talk it over with Mr. Reilly if I don't know whether I'm going to marry his daughter, if I don't know whether I'm going to marry at all?"

"Look, Brian," said Uncle Jamie. "If you don't talk it over with *him*, he's going to talk it over with *you!* That's how! We've already fixed everything between us and Sheila, and for God's sake, man, don't you go messing it up with any daft notions of your own!"

They reached the Reilly farm and found the outside light on and a model-T Ford standing in the lane in front of the house.

"Who's the visitors?" Uncle Jamie asked himself aloud as he pushed open the door and walked into the dim hallway. "Are you there, Fiddler?" he called out before he stepped into the brightly-lit room. There was an answering call from inside.

Brian followed Uncle Jamie into the lighted room and saw three guests with the Reillys. Sheila was not there. Brian shook hands with Mrs. Reilly, a buxom woman with apple cheeks and red lips, and remembered the stories his father had told about the help she had given the boys "on the run" in earlier troubles and how she had once carried half a dozen rifles all the way from Drumree to Belfast at a time when it was a crime to be found with a bullet.

Fiddler Reilly was a wiry little fellow with brown skin drawn tightly across his cheekbones and two tiny slanted, sloe-black eyes. The Fiddler rarely smiled, and when he was told a joke he merely nodded his head. The three other people in the house were the Widow Dooley, a fresh-faced, spry little woman who owned the land that they had just inspected; Parnell Gilroy—"Parnell" because of his stately bearing and heavy mustache—a local teacher and reputedly a very clever man; and Paddy Dugan, an only son with a good farm waiting for him when his father died. "If he can slip out of the mother's clutches!" the neighbors always added. All three wore riding breeches, and the wind-blown look on their faces told Brian they had just come in from a day's hard riding. Dugan cut a handsome, strapping figure in his breeches and tweed riding jacket, and suddenly Brian began to wonder if he had dropped in at the Reillys' by accident or by design. The men were drinking stout and the women had whisky and water in front of them. Brian and Uncle Jamie had stout, too.

"Paddy," said the widow, addressing Dugan, "is it true you're soon to take the jump?"

"Will you leave me be!" said Paddy angrily. "Time enough to think of taking the jump when I get the farm. Right now I'd rather hunt a fox than a woman!"

"Come now, Paddy," insisted the widow. "If you found a girl with a long sock full of money, a tender disposition, and looks to match, would you not then take the jump?"

"Mrs. Dooley," said Paddy. He eyed the widow coldly although his head swayed slightly. "If she had any money, I'd be so busy spending it there wouldn't be any time to enjoy her looks; and as for the tender disposition . . . She'd have one by the time I'd finished with her! Wouldn't be half as hard to break her in as to break in a young colt. Now does that answer your question? And now will you leave me be?" Paddy always grew cross in his cups.

"Fiddler," said Uncle Jamie in the lull that followed, "could I see you a minute?" Uncle Jamie nodded his head to Brian, and Brian rose up and followed the two men out to the scullery. Here Uncle Jamie lowered his voice to a conspiratorial whisper and told the Fiddler that he and Brian had talked about their plan on the way up. The Fiddler's sloe-black eyes darted from one to the other as they spoke, but he himself kept silent.

"What do you think, Fiddler?" said Uncle Jamie when he had finished.

Brian felt the Fiddler's little black eyes gimlet through him. Then the Fiddler offered his hand and Brian took it. "You're a good lad, Brian," said the Fiddler. "And I'd love to have you as a . . . friend."

The three men trooped back to the kitchen where the others had kept up the conversation to cover the absence of the conspirators.

Just as Brian sat down again he heard the tinkle of a bell and the scraping sound of a bicycle being leaned against the wall.

"Here's Sheila," said Mrs. Reilly. Brian coughed and shuffled his feet and everybody kept their eyes away from him.

"I think . . ." he said, making a move as if to rise and then sitting down again. To his surprise no one was looking at him at that particular moment, and he felt relieved.

There were footsteps in the hallway and a slim young woman of about eighteen stepped into the kitchen. She had a fresh complexion that was heightened by her ride on the bicycle and she wore her dark brown hair halfway down her back. Her eyes were not sloe-black like her father's but brown and large like those of her mother, who was a kindly, easygoing woman. Brian saw that she was dressed in a long green skirt with something very attractive like a black waistcoat, and she wore low-heeled brogues. Brian watched her shake hands with the visitors. With the tail of his eye he saw that Paddy Dugan was watching her, too.

"Hello, Brian," she said, at once composed and shy when she came to him.

"He—hello, Sheila," said Brian. He stood up, shook her hand, turned away quickly, and sat down again.

"Mother," said Sheila, "why don't you give these poor people something to eat? They must be starving!"

"I was waiting for you to come home, dear," said Mrs. Reilly, "to fix up something for them. Brian, will you give her a hand in the kitchen? She needs a little help, poor child!"

Brian straightened up, knocked over his bottle of stout but quickly righted it again, and walked across the floor, holding his arms stiffly against his sides. The others kept on talking.

About half an hour later he came out of the scullery with a platter of split soda farls, a flat triangular cake baked with flour, buttermilk, and soda, in one hand and a platter of fried sausages and ham in the other. He set both down on the table and pulled out of his pockets a fistful of knives, forks, and spoons. He dropped a spoon and in picking it up dropped a knife.

"In the name o' God!" blurted out Uncle Jamie. "Have you been tippin' the bottle out there?"

Brian's ears and neck flushed a deep red but he said nothing.

"Who wants a cup of good strong tea?" Sheila appeared at that moment, serene and cool. Brian was relieved at her appearance, for she immediately drew attention to herself. She set the pot of tea primly on the table and began to hand out the cups and saucers. Some took the cup and saucer in their hands; others balanced them on their knees. The Fiddler and Uncle Jamie placed theirs on the floor between their feet.

When they had all been served, Sheila took a plate, put two portions of sausages and ham at the side, and covered them with a soda farl each. Then she picked up two spoons and two forks and walked over to the far end of the sofa.

"Brian," she said, "bring over two cups of tea." She sat down on the sofa, leaving a place for Brian.

Brian coughed and went to the table. He poured out two cups of strong tea, emptied some sugar from the bowl into the cups, added milk, and brought them over to the sofa. He sat down beside Sheila and the two of them ate out of the one plate and spoke to each other in low tones.

Brian was the first to leave, for he had a long way to go. Sheila and her mother came to the door to see him and Uncle Jamie off the farm.

Ten minutes later he kicked the starter of his machine and sent it roaring into life. He switched on the headlight and a white beam of light seared the darkness. The edges of the bushes and trees and the corners of the outhouse etched sharply on the black canvas.

Brian's thoughts were pleasant on the road home. His talk with Uncle Jamie about the farm and the little business was the best thing that had ever happened to a man. Imagine Dinny, the old fox, having so much money saved up!—and offering to loan it to him! When he was a kid he had always thought old Uncle Jamie a bit of a skinflint, but Uncle Jamie was a lot like Michael, his father, by nature, although he was kept in check by his wife. And Sheila . . . How kind Sheila could be! She was always thinking how she could help . . .

The motorcycle cracked staccato in the high levels of the road and deepened to thunder in the covered quiet of the glens. Now and then his headlight caught the flash of frightened eyes that shone like brilliants from the hedges, and he felt a twinge of remorse for shattering the wall of silence nature had built around her creatures for the night.

How healthy he felt after a day on the land! A pleasant fatigue that a good night's sleep completely dissolved. Not the lassitude, the nervousness, the dust and the dirt of the shipyard that dried up the soul the way it dried up the nostrils and the throat and kept a man from breathing freely. It had begun to worry him that he might be drifting unwittingly into a groove that would bind him up with machines and city life instead of with animals and life on the land. And now this offer of the farm had come up. It suited him down to the elbows. Sheila, the farm, the rent-and-repair shop . . .

That night Brian folded his long nightshirt across his chest and stood staring out of the window at the Falls Road below. How dark and deserted the city looked at night compared to the country! Everything seemed not to sleep but to die. Outside there were none of the night sounds of the countryside that told you nature was still breathing, still alive. Here everything was quiet, dead, and if there was a sound at all, it was harsh and discordant and not in harmony with nature.

A car roared its way up the Falls. The light from Sirocco's fish-and-chip shop lay in a white streak across the pavement. The loud voices of a few late strollers drew only a careless glance from the two night policemen in capes and spiked helmets.

Down below him Brian saw a figure cross the road quickly, stop and knock at their door, softly at first, but getting no response, knock again, louder the second time. The door opened quietly; the figure entered, and the door closed behind him. He heard the sound of a bolt softly slide home. Now he knew that it was Paul. Mother had evidently been waiting up for him. Paul and Mother must have gone into the kitchen, for the next thing he heard was the rattle of teacups. Voices came up to him.

"What kept you out so late, Paul?" said Mary. "You know he doesn't like it at all."

There was a noise upstairs close by Brian.

"Was that Paul who just came in?" Michael shouted downstairs.

"What d'ye think?" Mary answered shortly.

"Nice time to come home, dammit! Wonder he came home at all!"

Brian could imagine Paul eating in silence, his mother sitting beside him and watching him anxiously. She suffered with all of them. He could hear what they were saying.

"Sean and Brian home?" Paul asked.

"Hours ago, son. Why do *you* always stay out so late?"

"The others stay out later than me!"

"What others, Paul?"

"All the . . . all the fellows I go with!"

"Why don't you leave them earlier and avoid trouble?"

"Well, I . . . I had to see somebody home."

"Are you still going out with that girl?"

"What's wrong with her?"

"She's a Protestant, Paul."

"And what's wrong with that, may I ask? Doesn't Brian go with Clute Wilson?"

"The Wilsons are fine people. And anyway, Clute's a boy. There's no danger there. You're going out with a Protestant girl."

"Look, Mother! If you're going to——"

Brian heard Paul pacing up and down the kitchen.

"All right, son. Only I hope you're not doing anything wrong in that company. But there is one thing I'd like to ask you, Paul. Where do you get all the money to keep up with these people?"

"Oh, I earn a little extra on the side."

"Where, son?"

"Here and there."

"Paul, why don't you tell me the truth?"

"Don't you start on me next, Mother! If you turn against me, I'll leave the house and you'll never see me again! So help me God!"

"I'm not turning against you, dear. I'm only trying to help you. I'm trying to—— Well, maybe we can talk about it some other time. Go to bed now, darling, and get a good night's rest. You haven't been getting much rest lately."

Paul came upstairs quietly. Brian heard him pass his father's room on the landing and the heartless boards creaked a betrayal.

Inside the room, his father turned in bed and grunted. As Paul walked past the door, Brian heard him curse. Brian went back to bed.

10

Brian sat on the packing case by the ship's rail and threw another scrap of bread down into the waters below. Before the bread hit the water a squawking sea gull, curving from the sky, caught it in mid-air and settled on the waves in front of Brian. Brian's eyes stayed on the rippling water, and as he watched he had the sensation, as the waves slipped past the unpainted hull of the ship, that the ship was moving.

It was lunch hour, and he and Clute Wilson had lined up with the rest of the men at the boiling-water faucet to fill the tea cans, laughing at the jokes they had made. He marveled at the way some men could tell jokes. He always lost the humor of his own jokes somewhere in the telling and halfway through regretted having started. Even when the men told dirty jokes they told them so well he had to laugh, although at the same time he felt embarrassed.

He finished his lunch of two meat sandwiches and a banana, exhausted all the scraps he could spare for the sea gulls, and turned to look down the River Lagan, toward the broad expanse of Belfast Lough, beyond which lay the sea. It was a gorgeous day. There was not the feather of a cloud in the sky and the sea reflected the blue. The fresh breeze coming in from the sea was a welcome stranger and Brian let it blow around him, cooling his armpits and drying his sweaty undervest. But his feet were hot and swollen from walking the rusty iron decks, and he longed to take off his boots and wade with his bare feet in the waves lapping at the unpainted hull.

His gaze crossed the waters and went out past the broad mouth of the river, on out to the open sea. He felt a vague yearning stir within him, looking at the line where the gray rim of the sea and the blue sky met, and all at once he felt a strange urge to sail down the lough and away to lands his father used to mention in his stories.

Three months ago he had been chosen to go with the S.S. *Bermuda,* a ship built for the South American fruit trade, on a trial run. It was the practice for the shipbuilders to man the instruments while the ship was on trial runs before signing it over to the owners. The run had lasted three days, and the ship had been put through its paces with the owner's agents on board. Brian had seen neither agent nor owner but had enjoyed his spells of duty in the engine room where everything was shining new and the oil still smelled fresh. The squad had been told to call it a "watch" but had fought shy of the word. At first Brian had dutifully entered into the spirit of the thing and had insisted on calling it his "watch." But when the men had begun to answer his questions with "Aye, aye, sir," he had blushed and called it what the rest of the squad called it, a "spell."

At midnight he had to go down to the engine room for his spell among the massive diesels that throbbed through the night with smooth power. Afterward he had come up on deck to look at the late stars, feeling the gentle rising of the deck press under him, and opening his mouth now and then to let the warm wind whistle through his cupped lips. Then he went below and ordered corned-beef sandwiches and tea and slept in a comfortable bunk on the lower deck.

He chuckled to himself as he remembered the trick the squad had played on him. He had gone in search of a bathroom and had found one in the first-class quarters, a new and dazzling thing in enamel and white marble. Lying back with his head on the rim of the bath and luxuriating in a soft enveloping mass of warm water that flattered his body with a million fingers, he remembered the muddy rivers of Drumree and the stone-cold mountain ponds outside Belfast. He shivered deliciously in the warmth as he thought of the wintry bathing in the Falls Park and the dressing under a hedge while his body trembled and turned blue from the sharp winds of the Divis Mountain.

Suddenly he heard a short, quick knocking on the bathroom door. He started guiltily. He had no right to be in a first-class bathroom.

"I say there!" said a voice haughtily.

"Yes?" Half timidly.

"Who are you?" asked the voice. "And what on earth are you doing in the owner's bathroom?"

The owner's bathroom! "I'm sorry," said Brian. "I can explain, sir."

"I'm afraid, my man, you'll have to do a deuced lot of explaining. Would you mind coming out at once, sir?"

"Very good, sir. Very good, sir." Brian lifted his body out of the bath so hastily the water swirled over the smooth sides.

"Come, come, sir! Señor Bubbalupo has something more important to do than wait for you all day."

"I'm coming out as fast as I can, sir!" Señor Bubba . . . That must be the South American owner! What a fix he'd got himself into! Why did he have to go fishing in the first-class section for a bath? Now there'd be the divil to pay all round! He pulled his shirt over his wet body, worked his trousers up his dripping legs, seized the door, and threw it wide open, an apology on his lips.

There was no one there.

During that trip they had gone into the North Sea and up the River Clyde. Not that he had had the faintest notion where they had been. He had learned it from the sailors who came to have tea and sandwiches with the men. The yarns the seamen had told them, the strange things they had seen and done, had made Brian feel a twinge of envy. The world they were familiar with, the world beyond, was a world of strangeness and adventure.

But it was a passing envy. He knew all the time that he loved his own land more than he could ever love anywhere else. To him the land was the pivot around which all things revolved. And even the sailors with all their lives at sea and in strange countries, after a mug or two of Guinness's, had moved aside this façade of the romantic like a stage setting and had confided to him that what they, too, dreamed of was to own a patch of land in Ireland on which to build a home.

Brian now rose and went toward the unfinished first-class saloon, the messroom of the squad, and put his tea can on the rusty deck below where his coat hung. Then he strolled down to the lumberyards where the men were playing cricket in a clearing. He had no love for cricket. Cricket made him think of elegant men in white clothes who spoke in a way that awed ordinary people. It was too foreign for him.

He moved on ground that was dirty with rust and spiraled slivers of steel, sheered off the plates, across the clearing among the piles of ships' plates. Here they were playing soccer. Soccer, like cricket, was English, too, but at least everybody played soccer. He thought of the players on a Saturday afternoon, away from the rust and dirt, dribbling a ball along a trim, green field under an open sky.

As the horns blew and the men reluctantly moved back to the shops and docks, Brian made his way to the S.S. *Manipur,* climbed the gangway, and crossed the deck to the first-class saloon.

Three men in the squad, Randy, Speed, and Boots, came over to him, and although they kept straight faces, Brian had to laugh at them. They were three wags who often enlivened the work with impromptu sketches. Brian hoped he wasn't going to be the butt of one of their practical jokes.

"Brother Tracey," began Randy nasally. "While you were out we brothers were talking about you and we think that you're worthy to bear witness to the Light."

"We think you ought to be baptized," said Boots.

"Before the Twelfth of July," added Speed piously. "So you can share in the glories of the resurrection of King William of Orange."

Brian knew now that he was to be the victim of the joke, and in spite of himself he smiled.

"What's all this about?" he asked, assuming a nonchalance he did not feel.

The three men approached Brian, encouraged by the laughs of

the squad. They knew Brian took it all good-naturedly. That was why they were fond of him, the only Catholic in the squad.

As the three men came closer Brian looked round for something with which to defend himself. In the corner of the messroom he spotted a can of white-lead paint with a heavy brush in it. He seized the brush and brandished it threateningly.

"All right," he said with humorous grimness. "You baptize me with water and I'll confirm you with white lead!"

But the three men still advanced on him, and Brian's confidence began to wane. He hesitated for a moment, then before the men could jump on him he threw the brush with its flying drops of paint at Randy. Without waiting to see the results of his action, he turned and ran for the door.

He found it blocked by half a dozen strangers.

"Can I get by you, please?" he said.

"No, you can't," said a stocky young man who stood in front of the others. "You're a Mickey, aren't you?" Mickey was the shipyard nickname for a Catholic.

Brian was taken completely by surprise. "What do you want to know for?" he asked, bristling.

"Get to hell out o' here . . . fast!"

"What do you mean, 'get to hell out o' here'?" said Brian angrily. "I work here."

"Listen. If you don't skite, we'll bash your head in!"

The men of Brian's squad started to argue with the stocky man, but he told them that anyone who sided with a Mickey would get what the Mickey got. What followed after that had such a dread and unreal quality about it that Brian wondered if he were not still sleeping during lunch hour and living through a dream. First the stocky man stepped up to Brian and without warning slapped him on the face. Then the rest of the gang moved up behind him. One of them hit him on the forehead with a short stick he carried. Brian got mad and, dashing over to his toolbox, seized a hammer and came back to face the strangers. But this time his own squad got in between him and them and hustled him through the door out onto the deck. They told him to run for it. He protested at first but then took their advice and ran across the deck toward the gangway. At the bottom of the gangway he looked up and saw some of the strangers leaning over the rail, throwing rivets after him but making no attempt to follow him.

He ran on out of the dockyard gates to the first-aid station, still confused at what had happened. Outside the gates he noticed a man in dungarees sitting with his back against the wall. He was moaning and held his head down, drooling blood and spittle. Brian then knew that what had happened to him just now was happening to other Catholics in the shipyard. Men were standing along Island Road in little groups talking excitedly, but nobody made any move to stop him. He could not figure out who the gangs were who were causing the trouble. An ambulance flew past and he heard a shot from somewhere; then one by one the hammers and the riveting machines ceased their clatter, and all of a sudden it was like Sunday.

The first-aid attendant bandaged Brian's bleeding head and kept him in the station until a lorry came past. He told the driver to ask no questions but to get Brian off the Island at once. Brian climbed on board and stayed there until he was outside the main gate. Then he took a tram home.

As the tram rumbled and swayed up the Falls Road that quiet, sunny afternoon, Brian saw the children playing in the streets and smacking their bare feet on the warm, dusty pavement, a scene so utterly removed from the world of violence he had just left, it made him again wonder if he had not after all been living through a nightmare. He got down from the tram opposite his home, and when the tram had gone it left a quiet disturbed only by the children's cries and strange for that time of day.

When he walked inside the house he looked out into the yard and saw his mother take the last clothespin, gray with age, from her mouth and pin the arm of a striped shirt on the line. She came into the scullery, took a small saucepan off a nail, entered the kitchen, and caught sight of Brian. He was leaning with one elbow against the mantelpiece, examining in the mirror the scarlet stain that clashed with the snow-white folds of the bandage round his head.

The saucepan clattered noisily to the floor.

"Jesus, Mary, and Joseph!" whispered Mary. "What happened, son?" She touched the bandage gingerly. Her hand shook.

"The Protestants hunted us from the Island."

"Christ save us!" she exclaimed. "Have the troubles begun all over again? Oh, thank God you're safe! Do you know if anything happened to Sean? He works in a Protestant quarter."

"I don't know," said Brian. "The trouble hasn't spread yet. Although by the time I reached the junction to catch a tram, everything was quiet. I haven't the faintest notion how they heard of the trouble so soon, but the people certainly were clearing off the streets!"

At this point a neighbor hurried in. She was nervous and upset. "Did ye hear about the Island? My John has just come home and he tells me . . ." She saw Brian and stepping back, clapped her hands to her cheeks, her mouth and eyes wide with fright. "Oh, dear God!" she cried. "What's going to happen to us at all, at all? I always said they were a bad lot on that Island!"

"They'll never have a day's luck for this! Mark my words!" said Mary.

Before the horns blew at five o'clock that day more men appeared in the streets with clean, white bandages showing up against their soiled working clothes. The sight of these men and the tales they told of what had happened when the Protestants had attacked them in the shipyards and workshops and factories all over Belfast, struck terror into the hearts of the Catholics, and like a dank, heavy mist an air of foreboding settled over the Falls.

That evening the Traceys sat down to supper without Sean. Paul had made a detour of the Protestant area and had come home a little later than usual. Sean had not yet showed up.

"Telegraph!"

The sound of the newspaper boy's voice startled them. Michael jumped to his feet, hurried to the door before anyone else could rise, and snatched the paper out of the boy's hand. Tucking it securely under his arm, he took his round-framed spectacles from the mantelpiece and adjusted them. As he peered at the headlines his mouth grew very small. This evening he did not, as was the custom, separate the sheets and hand them round, and the others waited impatiently.

"They're playin' down the whole rotten business, the Protestant . . . !" He stopped short and read aloud, mincing the words in mockery. "'There has been some disturbance in the shipyards and in a few other places around the city. No one knows what sparked the incidents, but religious differences are believed to be the cause. Those not favorable to the reactions of the Protestant majority during the historic Orange festival of the Battle of the Boyne might with profit exercise a little patience during this period!' . . . The divil take them!" he burst out indignantly. "They know damn well how it started and by who, and for why, but they're not man enough to pin the blame on them professional bigots, the Orange Lodges!"

Brian began to wonder if he would get back to work on the Island the next day. It did not look like it. In that case he had better ask Clute to bring out his tools for him before they were lost or stolen. Although it was not a prudent thing, perhaps, to do just then, he decided to go at once to the Wilsons' in Hamill Street. He also wanted to hear from Clute what had happened after he had left. He could slip out without letting on to his mother or father. After supper he left the house, pulling the peak and sides of his cap well down to cover the bandage on his head. He was going near the Shankill Road and did not want to attract attention. As he hurried along the Falls Road past the little groups of people excitedly discussing the outbreak in the shipyard, he turned over in his mind the things he had just seen. He remembered the conversations he had heard as a boy on the farm about the "troubles" in Belfast and the scenes of terror they had conjured up in his imagination. Now he was observing them at close quarters. The thought crossed his mind that he had better get out of the city before he was dragged into "troubles" of which he wanted no part. Let those who were interested in fighting stay behind and fight. It was not for him.

A tall man in a cloth cap rode a small bicycle past him down the street. He was holding his arms close to his sides, and when he pedaled he spread his knees out grotesquely to prevent knocking them against the handle bars.

"The military's out!" he kept shouting, like a town crier announcing disaster. "The military's out and the Catholics are stoning the Prods in Thompson's Mill!"

Brian guessed that the military had been called from the English garrison at Balmoral outside Belfast. They were permanently stationed there for emergencies such as these. The soldiers themselves, being English, had little or no interest as individuals in the "troubles." They considered them squabbles among the Irishry. For the first time Brian saw how incongruous it was to call in Englishmen to settle a quarrel among Irishmen.

He ran about a hundred yards down the Falls and saw a crowd surging round the mill door and the windows. On the roof, however, he also saw a score of khaki figures in steel helmets take up positions along the parapet and then sprawl upon their bellies, spread-eagling their legs. He saw the rifles sliding up and hiding their faces and was seized with a sudden, sickening fear. Good God! he asked himself, were they taking aim? Surely they weren't going to . . . !

A thundering roar split the sky. It was followed by a hush as if the whole city were waiting for the echo. The rifles roared again. The mob turned and, bending down, ran in all directions. Brian saw a woman stumble and fall, but she picked herself up again and ran on with the rest. Brian ran, too, and the rifles roared again. Now it seemed to him that they were firing in his direction, and for a moment he thought that the next volley would sear into the small of his back. Panic seized him. A man and a woman in front of him turned into an open doorway. He dashed in after them. Someone slammed the door behind him. He stood inside the hallway for a moment, trembling and trying to get a grip on himself.

Inside the house he could feel the atmosphere of terror that had frozen the household into immobility. The rifles cracked again, and, hardly knowing what he was doing, he threw himself on his knees under the stairway of the house and joined in the prayers of desperation the women had begun. He prayed against this new and unknown terror, volubly, incoherently. . . . The sweat poured out of him.

"Hail Mary, full of grace . . . Hail Mary, full of grace . . . Hail Mary . . ."

The sound of firing ceased, and as the silence drew out longer and longer the fright of the people slowly dissolved.

"Sarah," said a man's voice, and to Brian the voice seemed to come from a distant shore where the quiet sea washed up against the sand, "make these poor souls a cup of tea to settle their nerves."

"I declare to God," said a woman's voice this time, "when the soldiers let off them rifles I thought the end of the world was come!"

"What's going to happen to us at all, at all?" This voice was tearful and muffled by a shawl.

"Aye. You can well say that. They've started now, and God knows when they'll stop!" This was an old voice, and somehow Brian read into it hopelessness, resignation, and the wish for death that would bring peace.

He took the mug of strong tea in both hands to hide the trembling and tasted the tea's sweetness and bitter tang. Slowly his calm returned and he gathered his scattered thoughts, and all the time the stout woman of the house called Sarah, who had risen and asserted herself again, kept talking and asking questions she herself answered. Brian's mind went back to the farm and suddenly he felt a stranger among these people. That's where he should be, he told himself; on the farm. He began to wonder whether he should go down to Drumree at once or wait until this frenzy of religious rioting blew over. He would not be leaving his family in any danger. The Protestants would no more think of attacking the Falls Road, that stronghold of Catholicism, than the Catholics would think of attacking the Shankill Road. The ones in danger were those who lived on the wrong side of the fence or in the fringe areas. Then there was the danger run by those who took an active part in the fighting. On one side the Protestants and Orange Lodges, who, being backed up by the English, held the whip hand; and on the other side the Catholics, supported by the

I.R.A., who were against the domination of Ireland by the English.

There was little danger in all this for the Traceys excepting, perhaps, Sean. Brian wondered about Sean.

There was a loud knocking at the door. The room grew hushed.

"Who's there?" asked Sarah, frightened.

"It's only me, Sarah," said a woman's voice. "You can come out now. The soldiers have gone. Nobody's hit. They only fired over the people's heads to scare them."

There were sounds of relief in the room, and one by one the people thanked the man and the woman of the house and began to leave.

"Thank you, ma'am," said Brian to the stout woman as he handed her the empty mug. "That was a grand mouthful o' tea."

"And you were welcome to it," said the woman. "And it's only hoping to the Mother o' God that the trouble won't last. If it stops the work I don't know what we'll do. You can't keep a house and four children on fresh air."

Along the deserted streets between the Shankill and the Falls Brian was stopped by a military patrol of about twenty men. They were holding their rifles in front of their chests at the ready. The lieutenant in charge looked very young and spoke with an English accent.

"Where are *you* going, sir?" The young man had a light strip of blond hair on his upper lip, and the strap of his helmet deepened the dimple in his chin. Brian could see him coming down the steps of his home with a scarf around his neck and a pair of leather gloves in his hand.

"To the Shankill Road," said Brian.

"The Shankill Road?" The young lieutenant's eyes narrowed. The name had been entered in his instructions. He turned to the sergeant behind him.

"Sergeant," he said, "isn't that the Protestant part of the town?"

"Yes, sir."

Brian explained that he had been chased off the Island—"The Island?"—the dimple deepened again—and was going to see if a Protestant friend of his in Hamill Street would pick up his tools for him.

The lieutenant stared coldly at Brian; Brian stared coldly at the lieutenant.

"You'd better go back to where you came from," said the lieutenant.

Brian held the lieutenant's gaze a moment longer. It was on the tip of his tongue to utter a tart rejoinder about foreigners ordering people around in their own country, but out of the corner of his eye he saw the sergeant tighten his hold on his rifle and take a step forward. Without another word Brian turned and walked down the street again. When he reached another side street, however, he simply doubled back up a second parallel street and made his way to the Wilsons'.

11

"Burn him out!"

"Aye, burn him out! Burn him out!"

"You can't do that," shouted someone above the clamor. "You'll set fire to the whole street."

"Throw out the furniture then and we'll burn that!"

"The furniture!" cried the mob. "The furniture!"

There was the sound of smashing glass and breaking wood, and a heavy stool flew out of the gaping hole that had been a window and crumpled against the ground. It was followed by a dressing table. The table hit the ground with two legs that gave way and then sank down like a tired animal resting on its haunches.

Brian had made a detour to avoid one or two danger points and had spent an embarrassed half hour with Clute's family, outdoing them in taking the blame for what had happened between Protestants and Catholics. It was dark by the time he had come away. To get back to the Falls he and Clute, whose father had insisted that Clute accompany Brian back to the Catholic section, had cut through Cooper Street, which connected the Shankill to the Falls. In a side street in the Catholic section he had seen a crowd collected at the door of a house. At first there had been only a few men standing at the door shouting up at a lighted window. The crowd had quickly grown, however, and the shouting had become louder and more threatening.

Clute had wanted to go on but Brian had held him back.

"Like all the rest of them, he's afraid to show his clock at the door!" said someone in the crowd.

"He'd better get out in a hurry!" added another. "We want no dirty Protestants here!"

"He can take King Billy and the Boyne with him!"

"He's lucky he's getting out alive. Our fellas didn't get the same chance when the Prods burnt them out."

The anger of the crowd rose, egged on by men who kept crying out that the Protestants had stoned or kicked their Catholic comrades in the shipyards. Somebody struck up a popular party tune. The mob seized on it and it soon swelled into the fierce earnestness of a battle hymn.

"If he's afeered to come down and face us, let's go up and chuck him out!"

"Aye," roared the crowd. "What're we waiting for? Let's chuck him out! Come on!"

A few men moved out of the crowd, banded together, and charged at the door. The door took the first charge with a sickening thud, but at the second charge it flew open with a report like the crack of a gun. The men ran through the hallway up to the lighted room. One of them pulled up the window and poked out his head.

"He got away! Bad scran to 'im!"

"Booo!"

"Yahoo!"

The wrecking was now shared by anyone strong enough to elbow his way into the house past those who, burdened with articles of furniture, were trying to get into the street. Some raced to the entry behind the house and attacked the kitchen before going inside, scurrying back and forth like ants that had discovered carrion. Those waiting outside seized the articles of furniture as they came out and piled them up in a rough mound in the center of the street. When the mound was about as high as a man, calls were made for lights. One or two men touched matches to the ends of rolled-up newspapers and with these prepared to set fire in several spots to the pile.

Up to that moment Brian had been a spectator, one who had

watched the actions of the mob, the way he had watched the actions of Rebel that day at the Huts when Rebel had caught the rat and had begun to devour it.

Now with the same kind of horrified fascination he saw one of the men approach the pile of furniture with a lighted newspaper.

It was hardly anger that moved Brian; rather it was disgust that the man was about to do something as foul and repugnant as Rebel's devouring of the entrails of the rat. It was unnatural for one man to do this to another. Even before he started toward the man a slight shiver of disgust ran through him.

It was this slight shiver that warned Clute. He seized Brian's arm.

"Stay where you are, you idiot!" he whispered. "Want to get killed?"

But Brian would not be stayed. With a jerk of his arm he freed himself and dashed across the open space that separated him from the man who had stooped to set fire to the furniture. With a sweeping blow of his clenched fist he struck the man behind the ear. The man staggered a few paces from the fire, toppled over, and lay still. Brian hardly even glanced at him. Instead, white-faced and tense, he turned to the crowd.

"People!" he cried. "Have you gone mad? Have you suddenly become wolves that prey upon each other? Have you ceased to be Irishmen and suddenly turned savages that burn and kill your fellows because they live on another hill? You wild dogs, you jackals, feeding on the bowels of your brother!"

His rage at this point shook him and bending toward the fire, he seized a burning stool by the leg and raised it aloft like a flaming sword. The mob, cowed for the moment, drew back, and it was well they did so, for Brian recklessly hurled the burning stool full at them. They shouted in hoarse terror at the sight of the burning stool flying through the air, leaving in its wake a trail of smoke and sparks. Brian saw it strike a fleeing woman in the back and she screamed; then it fell and burned where it lay.

The terror that Brian's strange conduct had at first created in the mob now spent itself and there was an unconscious rallying of forces. Their fury broke loose.

"He's away in the head!"

"He's off his nut!"

"He's a filthy Protestant. That's what he is. We should burn him too!"

Like a bull pawing at the ground and lowering his head before he attacks, the mob stamped its feet and shook its head and prepared to rush forward and gore.

Brian glared at them defiantly. The elation of the moment had killed fear. He crossed his arms and waited.

"Look at that, for God's sake!" cried a woman suddenly. "Look!"

The mob looked where she pointed. In the dimly lit opening of the wrecked house stood a little girl. One hand hung by her side; the other dug into tear-filled eyes. She was crying and looking at the fire, not in terror, thought Brian, but as a child will do when someone has destroyed its toy.

"It's his wee girl," said the woman, an odd hush in her voice.

"Where's the mother?"

"Dead these three years."

The sight of the child confused the mob, and for a moment they were uncertain what to do.

Before they had time to think of attacking Brian again, a tall wiry figure in clerical garb appeared in the dancing light of the bonfire, coming from the direction of the Falls Road. He had been walking quickly and was out of breath.

Brian saw his mouth and nose outlined sharply in the red light of the fire.

"Good evening, Father McGuire," called out one of the women.

"Good evening? Good evening?" echoed the priest. He peered at Brian. "It's you, Tracey," he said. Then he peered at the mob. Brian saw his mouth tighten into a thin straight line and his nose grow even sharper.

"Good evening? Good evening nothing, my friend! As a minister of God I'd say a bad evening, a very bad evening! Yet you all look very pleased with yourselves." He paused. He looked again at Brian. He looked again at the mob.

"I'm sure Almighty God is pleased with you too. I'm sure he'll bless you all for this night's work." Father McGuire spoke with heavy sarcasm. His tone changed suddenly. "Who started this . . . this work of the devil?" he asked.

The crowd was silent.

"He's a Prod," growled one man. Brian recognized him as the one who had first tried to set the furniture on fire before Brian had felled him.

"Aye," said the priest. "Aye, he's a Protestant and you're a Catholic, I suppose, though I've never seen you in chapel or around these parts before. But you're a Catholic and must know the Ten Commandments. Well, tell me, my Catholic friend, did God ever command you there to seek out a defenseless man, and because he's not one of us, threaten his life and destroy his home? Did he?" He glared at the man. He glared at the crowd. "Did any of you read that?" Silence. "Did any of you read that?" He raised his tone almost to a scream. "Did any of you read that?" Brian was afraid that he had roused himself to such a pitch of anger he would strike the nearest man or woman.

Those among them whom Brian suspected were best known to the priest edged to the rear of the crowd and disappeared. The rest stood there uncomfortably, clearly wishing they were out of the priest's presence.

Only then did Father McGuire see the child. He walked over to where, totally uncomprehending, she stood in the gaping doorway.

"Whose child is this?" he asked.

A woman came forward and told him she lived in the next house. "It's his wee girl, Father," she said timidly. Then, moved by the sight of the helpless child, she pleaded tearfully:

"Let me take her into our house, God help 'er! Let me give 'er somethin' to eat."

"No," said the priest roughly. "No, you will not. You are not worthy to serve Christ tonight. Not one of you is worthy. I'll take care of her myself. Won't I, child dear?" He knelt down on one knee and snuggled the child to his breast, and because the recent emotional outburst had shaken him, too, he wept unashamedly at the child's innocence and sorrow. After a while he turned again to the remainder of the crowd around the fire.

"Are you still there?" He glared angrily at them through the iridescence of his tears. "Are you not so ashamed of this devilry that you want to run away and hide yourselves? Though how you'll hide from the face of Christ I don't know. Go home, you blackguards! Go home and beg Him to forgive you!"

The crowd broke up quickly after that and only a few spectators were left standing in the doorways of their homes. Some of the women covered their faces with their aprons, but whether it was because they were crying or wanted to hide themselves from the priest's wrath Brian did not know.

The priest bent down and with his handkerchief wiped clean the nose and face of the child and with the same handkerchief wiped his own eyes. He stood up and dug his hand into his pocket.

"Stop crying, darling," he said, holding up two pennies, "and I'll take you to Daddy and give you a penny for each hand."

The child looked up at him with red-rimmed eyes, examined the two pennies in his hand, and then looked back at the priest who was now smiling. Gravely she reached out two chubby palms and took hold of the two pennies. She was still examining the two pennies when the priest caught her up in his arms, almost squeezing the breath out of her, and carried her up the Falls Road toward the Monastery.

Before going he turned to Brian.

"Walk ahead of me, Tracey," he said. "Until you're out of danger."

When Brian and Clute, who had come with him, were in the shadows and out of the mob's reach Brian thanked the priest and left him. Before he left, however, he kissed the child good-by and she looked at him in wonder.

When he was out of sight of the priest and had said good night to Clute he stopped. A reaction now set in, and a great heaving sob rose from the deepest part of him and shook his whole frame. So strong was the effect of the moment on him he could not go on and had to lean against a lamppost and press his hot cheeks and throbbing temples to the cold iron.

"Oh, I'm glad you got back safe!" said Mary when he reached home. "Did you run into Sean?"

"No, hasn't he come in?"

"He hasn't been in all day and me nearly out of my mind, worrying about him. What under God could be keeping him out till this hour on such a day?"

"Will you stop worrying about him, Ma!" said Brian irritably. "Maybe he went into some friend's house and they told him to stay for the night."

"I hope to God you're right, son!" said Mary.

But Sean did not come home that night, and Brian lay awake in bed wondering about him and listening to the strange, secretive sounds on the streets, men running on tiptoe or scurrying for cover at the hum of an approaching vehicle, muffled conversation coming from his parents' room, for his mother was still worrying about Sean. Finally he heard an exclamation of impatience from his father, and the conversation ceased.

He thought of the day he had cycled to Saintfield, a green and sunlit village with clean tar-macadam roads and a steep hill. He tasted again the dinner of boiled beef, potatoes, and parsnips. After dinner he had been talking outside the door with two pretty cousins, and to show off he had jumped onto the seat of his bicycle without touching the pedals and had raced down the hill. He felt again the swift wind press into his ears, caught again the glimpse of a man waving his arms. Too late he had realized that he was rushing toward the main road to Belfast. He heard the screeching of metal and the shouting of men and a high-pitched whistle in his ears. . . . The next thing he realized was that he was dancing round the edge of a crowd trying to get a look at the victim of an accident who was now lying on the ground. When he saw that it was himself lying there, moving his head slowly from side to side in pain, he said: "God help him!" He remembered, too, the ride back to Belfast in the sidecar of a motorcycle, and the Royal Victoria Hospital, and the ache in his bones from shock, and the strangeness of passing Sirocco's ice-cream parlor and not being able to call out to his friends standing in the doorway. At the hospital he was afraid that the blow on his head might have knocked him crazy and he had counted to himself, two and two is four, four and four is eight, to make sure he wasn't away in the head.

Now once again he was standing on the edge of a crowd and looking down at himself after he had been in an accident. Everything today had been an accident, and he felt as helpless now as he had felt the day they had picked him up and put him in the sidecar and driven off with him to the hospital.

Suddenly it came to him that he was witnessing a burst of the violence he had always suspected that the city hid behind its walls ever since the day his family had driven up from the farm. He remembered now having noticed that, where the sounds of the country had been gentle and soft and never harsh, the sounds of the city had been so rasping, high-pitched, and cruel they had frightened him.

Even as he fell asleep in bed that night his dreams were filled with figures, strange and violent, and dangerous moments from which he escaped only through the odd powers a man possesses in his dreams. And through it all he saw Father McGuire, his blue-black face staring hideously from the leaping flames of the bonfire, pointing his finger accusingly at him and screaming, "Work of the devil! Work of the devil!" But after Clute Wilson had thrown him off the shipyard dock into the water he began to suffocate and there was no saving him; and his struggles awoke him and he found himself in a sweat, trembling. For a long time afterward he could not sleep but kept staring at the shadows and at the streaks of cold, blue light cast into the room by the rising moon.

12

"The Orangemen are going to burn down the Monastery tonight for reprisals," announced Sean, as he came in for supper a few days after the riots in the shipyards.

"They'd never attempt the likes o' that!" exclaimed Michael.

"Wouldn't they?" said Sean. "It's the chapel nearest the Prod section. Our boys are looking for volunteers to picket it. Will you come up, Brian?"

"What do you want *me* for, Sean?"

"You're a Catholic, Brian, aren't you?"

"Yes, but I still don't want to get into this fight, or, for that matter, any other fight."

"And they firing shots at the Monastery?" Sean was shocked. "They say Father McGuire himself escaped a bullet by the skin of his teeth. Somebody'll have to defend our own priests!"

"Did you ask Paul?"

"No, I didn't. Why waste time?"

"Brian." Michael took up the discussion. "This is a fight to defend ourselves, and I don't see how a Catholic can help going up. Not going up tonight to protect the Monastery is something like . . . well, like denying the Faith."

"I'm still not convinced, Dad, that they're going to—" Brian read his father's face, stopped short, and blushed.

"*We* know what their intention is," said Sean. "To chase us off the Falls. Would you like to be chased off the Falls?"

"Of course I wouldn't, but—"

"Then come on, man!"

Brian hesitated. "But what'll I do when I get there?"

"Never mind. We'll show you."

A week after the outbreak on the Island the fighting had already spread to other areas in the city where Catholics and Protestants came together, and in those few days Brian was made fully aware of the importance of the religious problem agitating Belfast. It made little sense to him. He could not understand why one Irishman should want to *fight* another because of his religion. Each side talked of oppression, the Catholics of oppression by the Protestants in Belfast, and the Protestants of oppression by the Catholics in the rest of Ireland. Yet the country's greatest patriots had been Catholic and Protestant. . . . It was all very confusing to him. One thing, however, was not; one thing stood out very clearly in his mind: he was not going to let himself become involved in a senseless struggle that would only widen the gap between Irish Catholic and Irish Protestant.

With great reluctance he followed Sean out of the house that summer evening, walking up Clonard Street for about ten minutes until they came to the Monastery. Already in the railed-off square in front of the church little knots of men stood talking. Others were converging on the spot as Brian and Sean came up. On the side of the Monastery away from the Falls Road stretched a long street that led into the Protestant quarter. It was from this direction, Sean told Brian, that the Protestants were expected to attack the Monastery.

A man with a sandy mustache whom Sean addressed as "Sandy" but whom Brian had never seen before approached Sean and spoke to him in low tones. Not wanting to overhear, Brian stood back a little and his eyes wandered over the groups of men gathered on the streets and inside the square. In the strained quiet he made out faintly the sound of the big drums booming on the Shankill Road. The sound stirred him uneasily and brought back to him the idle afternoon years ago when Humpy Dwyer had suggested that he and Curly Downey and the Mole should go up to the brickfields to fight the Protestants and he had hurt Clute Wilson.

A priest appeared from the residence at the back of the church.

It was Father McGuire, and his black robes twirled about his thin ankles as he walked. He pushed his collar down before he spoke.

"Now, now, men!" he said in a businesslike manner. "What's this all about, I'd like to know?" He looked around him and then fixed his attention on Brian. "You seem to be getting into a lot of trouble recently, Tracey," he said. "What are you doing here?"

"They say they're going to attack the Monastery," said Brian. He felt he was making an apology.

"Stuff and nonsense!" said Father McGuire. "What on earth would they do that for? There's nothing to be gained by it. All rumors. Probably spread by troublemakers. What might happen, however, is that the Protestants will see this crowd and think that *you* are going to attack *them*."

Even as he spoke there was a sharp crack and a sudden, wild scurry for cover. Brian ran with the rest and found himself pressing into the doorway of a public house with Sean, the man who had spoken to Sean, and two others he had never seen before. The man with the sandy mustache came over to Brian.

"You Sean's brother?"

"Yes," said Brian.

"Then take this," said Sandy. He drew a heavy object out of his pocket and slipped it to Brian. "Keep pinking an odd one up at them to keep them indoors."

"But who are you fellows, anyway?" said Brian.

"Who do you think?" said the man. "We're here to see that you don't get run out of Belfast."

Brian's right hand closed over a cool metal object that fitted perfectly into the mold of his closed fist, and for a moment he stared at the pistol he held in his hand. On the right side of the barrel he read *Esperanza y Unceta, Quernica* (*Spain*). Spanish, he repeated to himself, and he wondered why this should appear so important to him. Below the name there was the number 76439, and all at once he knew that never again would he forget that number. Like the number on the garments of a convict, that number would be stamped forever on his soul. There was something snakelike, too, in the smooth barrel, so fascinating to him that for a moment he was not aware that the men were crouching and peering around the edge of the wall and firing shots at the Protestant section.

"Going to use it?" asked Sandy crisply.

"Some of these blerts," said one of the men, using a Belfast expression, "want to sit on their backsides and let us die fighting for them."

Sandy and the other two men stared at Brian. So did Sean, and Brian saw in his brother's eyes a hard expression he had never seen in them before. He felt a cloud of hostility rising up and surrounding him, making him shiver. Forced by their looks, he moved over to the wall and peered with his right eye down the long street where he could see that the windows had been shuttered. The men still stared at him as he raised the cold revolver to his hot cheek, and he prayed they would not notice the scraping sound the revolver made as it shook against the wall.

He raised the revolver higher until it was level with his eye and he looked down the black barrel and saw the tiny pyramid of the sight tremble from side to side in front of him . . .

"When are you going to fire?" There was anger in Sandy's voice this time.

. . . and he earnestly wished for the courage to throw the revolver away and tell his instigators he would not fire, for that would make him one with those who threw stones in the faces of people like Clute, but his courage failed him before those staring eyes, and he turned again to the trembling sight and his hand slowly tightened about the moist stock of the revolver. It kept on tightening, and he felt that it was pressing an aching band of steel about his soul. All of a sudden there was a roar in his face, the revolver jumped in his hand, and the acrid smell of burning sulphur parched the back of his nostrils.

His mind sped on with the bullet toward the Protestants whom he could almost see crouching in fear in their homes, and he felt now the way he had felt when he had struck Clute Wilson with the stone in the brickfield, and Clute's face now rose before him and he saw the bullet smash into Clute's face, jerking his head back, hideously, and Brian groaned in an agony of horror and shame. He brought the back of his shaking hand to his forehead to wipe off the sweat, and as he did so it seemed to him that the cold metal of the revolver drew a line across his brow that was the mark of Cain. A wave of revulsion for what he had done seized him and he retched.

With that one shot he knew he had stepped into the land of Cain where Abel lay murdered and where no love was; and he lived again on the mountains at home in November with the bleak mist swirling about him, sucking the warmth out of him. He remembered the feeling that suddenly would come over him then and he wouldn't want to be there any longer but back with his mother and father and brothers in the snugness of his home. Now all this was receding from him the way it did in the cinema at the change of scenes, and he wanted to run after it, but Sean and the men were standing between him and escape, staring at him, their eyes full of the suspicion of cowardice, of disloyalty, of he did not know what. He would have cried at what was happening to him, but Sean, this new Sean with the hard look in his eyes, and the others would see him cry and they wouldn't understand, and he could never hope to make them understand, for he wasn't sure that he could explain it even to himself. But what was happening to him, what had happened to Sean, was a terrifying thing, and it was changing him so that he was not himself any more. He heaved a great, sobbing sigh and shook with tears at the thought that, like Cain, he would wander about that cold, misty world of hate, suspicion, and distrust for the rest of his life. . . . It was not he, it was an alien body, cold and senseless, that raised the revolver to the level of his eyes and fired again. . . .

He did not know how long he had been there and he had not yet emptied the revolver when a new sound struck his ears. It was the hum of a motor and it was coming up behind them from the Falls Road. All of a sudden glass smashed somewhere near him, and then he saw a gray police lorry with high steel plates round the sides and rifles peeping out from small oblong holes in the plates. He heard another burst of firing, heard more glass smashing, and then one of the men crouching for protection in a corner of the doorway sagged to a sitting position, his head sinking between his knees. All four rushed into the shelter of the public house, dragging with them the wounded man, who looked as if he were falling asleep. There was one more burst of firing as the lorry again raked the streets, and then there was silence. Brian noted that, curiously enough, no one had cried out.

The wounded man's companions quickly examined him and found that the bullet had entered the body under the armpit. Not a dangerous wound, but one that drew a lot of blood. They made preparations to get him to the hospital, about fifteen minutes away, and called up for a taxi.

"Why did the police open fire like that?" asked Brian dully, staring at the wounded man lying on the ground.

"They weren't the police," answered Sean. "They were the Specials."

"All right," insisted Brian. "But why did they have to shoot us?"

"They hate Catholics, that's why."

"But we were only protecting the Monastery," said Brian. "That's what they should have been doing."

"Stop bletherin' like a wee girl!" said Sandy impatiently.

A few minutes later the taxi ground to a stop outside. When the driver saw what had happened he at first objected to taking the wounded man.

"The police'll want to know if I had a hand in this shooting and they'll take away my license," he complained. But he was finally persuaded and, still complaining, drove off with the wounded man and one of his friends.

A little later Brian saw the men who had gathered round the Monastery emerge from their hiding places and make their way home one by one, keeping close to the walls. Brian left the public house alone. Sean and the man called Sandy had gone off together without him, and when he reached home he went at once up to his room. He did not want to talk to anyone for he was confused and his mind was filled with strange thoughts and unanswered questions. He had still a clear image of the man who had been shot, and in the man's eyes he had seen the same look he had seen in the eyes of the first rabbit he had ever killed. It had nearly escaped, and he had hit it on the head with a stick and it had sunk quietly to the ground, looking sideways from eyes half closed in pain at its killer. At the sight of it Brian's heart had nearly burst and he had cried at the cruelty within himself; and the memory of the rabbit sinking to the ground and looking at him sideways had stayed with him for days.

"Forgive me, Father, for I have sinned. It's been two weeks since my last confession."

"Yes, my son?"

"Father, I fired a gun at people."

"With intent to kill?"

"No, Father, not exactly."

"Or maim?"

"I don't know, Father."

"Was it in self-defense? Were these people attacking you?"

"I don't know, Father. You see it was like this . . ." Brian explained.

"I see. Then these people were not attacking you?"

"I suppose not, Father. Is that a mortal sin?"

"Is it a light matter to endanger the life or limb of another, my son?"

"But, Father, we can't wait till they mow us down before we start shooting back!" It sounded so unlike himself, Brian knew he was just repeating what he had heard Sean say.

"All I can do, my son, is to point out to you the teaching of the Church and help you to apply it to your particular case."

"What does the Church say, Father?"

"The Church says that civil war is the cause of very grave evils, physical, moral, and social. It requires a just cause, the certainty that all peaceful means have been tried and found unavailing, that the matter at issue outweigh the havoc that civil war brings, and that it be reasonably certain that it will not make things worse. The Church teaches us that no private individual has any authority to judge these issues or to involve the people, from whom he has received no mandate, in the serious losses inevitable in such hostilities. The bishops, therefore, have declared that it is sinful for a Catholic to belong to any private society that arrogates to itself this right to bear arms and use them. It is also sinful to encourage or co-operate with them."

"And you think that I committed a mortal sin?"

"No. You might still have been confused about your intentions. In that case there would be a lessening of guilt. But the material sin would be present just the same."

"But, Father! . . ." Brian checked himself. "I'm sorry, Father," he said. "I see now that I did a terrible thing."

"Do you firmly resolve here and now that you will not commit this sin again?"

"Yes, Father, I do."

"Say five *Our Fathers* in honor of the passion and death of our Lord who died for all of us. *Ego te absolvo . . .*"

Brian stepped out of the confessional and went up to the altar rail where a flickering red lamp hung from the vaulted ceiling. He knelt down and recited the five *Our Fathers* the priest had given him as penance. When he had finished them he did not get up at once but stayed on praying, and after he had prayed for a long time in the echoing quiet of the church, he vowed never again to take up arms against his brother. The price in sorrow and remorse for hatred was too great. Humbly asking God to give him strength to keep his vow, he rose and left the church.

13

Brian came home that evening from confession in a peaceful frame of mind and stood outside the door observing with a sense of deep enjoyment. He had seen the sun set over the city, transmuting the walls of the houses into solid masses of yellow gold that melted at the windows into warm, shimmering pools. Inch by inch the line of gold had climbed upward until it had cleared the chimney tops and scattered itself prodigally over the clouds; there it had burst into flame, setting the heavens afire, and great billows of smoke had risen from the flames, betokening, pall-like, the fire's approaching end; and the end had come as the sky-long tongues of flame grew shorter and shorter until they disappeared and the fire burned itself out on the horizon, leaving nothing but the green-gray ashes of the spent day.

But dusk followed quickly, and he noticed that with the fading of the light the streets grew quiet, children were called in from the doorsteps, and idlers hurried homeward, so that by the time the darkness deepened and the curfew came, the streets were stilled and empty of people. There was no moon that evening, though Mars stood out prominently from his fellows, red and blinking angrily.

At one end of the block the light from Sirocco's café shed a clear white patch on the pavement as the lights from the other houses were extinguished, and a pungent, appetizing odor of fried fish and chips hung about the door. At the opposite street corner, beside the Hibernian Club, the light from O'Kane's pub was a brilliant rectangle on the road and the air around O'Kane's pub was heavy with the smell of whisky and stale stout. These two remaining lights, however, like two pieces of white cloth, suddenly slid toward the windows and disappeared behind the drawn blinds, and then everything was dark. Brian went indoors.

After supper Mary cleared the table and Brian sat down with Michael and Paul by the fireside, reading. Later Mary came in again and sat down with her knitting, and the smooth click of her needles was the only sound in the room except for the occasional sough of the caked, black coals as they caved into the red heart of the fire.

An hour or so later Michael put his paper down on his knees, unhooked his spectacles, first off one ear, then off the other, and reached up to the mantelpiece for his pipe. As he dug his little finger into the bowl he glanced at the others, pausing momentarily on each of them.

"Did Sean say if he'd be home?" he asked. He rolled a taper to light his pipe.

"He said he didn't think he'd be home tonight," said Mary. She did not take her eyes off her knitting. "But he had a good rest during the day. I made sure of that much."

"He'll kill himself," said Michael with something of impatience. "If the Specials don't do it first."

"Don't say those things, Michael!" she pleaded. She put her knitting down on her lap and looked at Michael. "Oh!" she sighed. "I wish to God we were a thousand miles away! At least until things settle down again. We had none of this in the country."

"The Twelfth has come and gone," said Michael. "And things are getting worse instead of better. More trouble and more shooting. The Specials that they recruited so fast to put down the trouble are no help."

"They're the ones that are doing this terrible night raiding," said Mary. "So that our boys have to sleep away from home for fear they'll be arrested or worse in their beds."

"Does that surprise you?" asked Michael. "And them recruiting only Orangemen? Decent Protestants wouldn't be seen dead with that riffraff! It's like calling in a cat to protect the mice. At first they were supposed to help the regular police only. Now they are taking over the whole damn shooting match!"

"To think that our young men can't stay in their own homes at night," repeated Mary.

"At least it's a good thing we have the pickets to give us some kind of protection."

Mary was referring to something that was causing a reign of terror in the Falls Road area—the raids carried out in the dead of night by the Specials with the purpose of making surprise arrests of men suspected of being members of the I.R.A. or of uncovering caches of forbidden arms. That was why most young men, whether they belonged to the I.R.A. or not, did not dare sleep at home but had to find lodgings with friends. There was great suspicion that informers were at work with the Specials, for once or twice the people had noticed crosses chalked on the doors of houses that had been raided. At first these raids had taken everybody by surprise, but a picketing system had been quickly organized and volunteers now stayed up all night on guard. At the first sign of a raid the picket would let off a few revolver shots and other volunteers would gather to beat off the raiders in a gun battle, or at least give the wanted men time to escape. The women, too, when they saw an armored car or a police lorry drive up to any house at night, would start screaming *Murder! Murder!*—and beat the lids of the garbage bins to warn the pickets or scare off the raiders.

Brian listened distractedly to the conversation between his father and mother. He was thinking of what had happened in the house since the riots had broken out. He had not been able to start again at the Island for work there had been cut down to a minimum. Besides, to get there he would have had to pass through one or two "black Protestant" quarters.

To the surprise of everybody in the house Paul had been kept on at his old job, although the owner was an active Orangist.

Sean's time seemed to be well taken up, for Brian saw little of him. He was absent most of the day and all of the night. It was now an open secret that he was some sort of officer in the I.R.A. He had tried to interest Brian and Paul in joining, but Paul had answered him with a surly look and Brian had told him that he saw no reason why he, Brian, should join. He had no taste for shooting anyone, especially other Irishmen.

"Well, Brian," Sean had responded, "I can't accuse *you* of being a coward. I suppose all I can say is that you just don't understand. You just don't understand."

Michael was now taking his final puff before going to bed and Mary was gathering up some of the articles carelessly left around by the others. Brian picked up the newspaper Michael had thrown on the sofa and began to read when he heard a noise like the patter of light rain against the window. He listened. The fingernails kept drumming on the glass, louder than before. He ran quickly to the door and opened it. A figure brushed past him and hurried into the kitchen.

"What brought you back, Sean?" asked Brian in surprise.

"Och!" Sean shrugged his shoulders. "I'd finished picketing and was on my way to the Devlins' for the night when I thought I'd come home just for once. After all, I live here, don't I?"

"But, Sean——" began his mother.

"I know. I know," said Sean impatiently, "but I have the devil of a cold coming on and I thought I'd come home and sweat it out of me."

"You shouldn't have come home, Sean," said Brian. He knew that Sean sometimes acted impetuously. "You know what happened in the raid on the Toners. All four of them."

"Och!" said Sean again. "Will you leave me alone! Surely I'll be safe for one night. Besides, the Specials have been fairly quiet of late. Stop blethering, Brian, and give me something to eat!"

Brian looked at his father for support.

"Leave him alone," said Michael. "He does look tired. Give him a bite to eat before he goes to bed."

Paul, Brian noticed, was the only one who did not show any pleasure over the appearance of his brother. Paul even began to show signs of discomfort and Brian wondered why. Then he shrugged his shoulders. Either Paul was nervous, thinking that Sean's presence might draw danger, or else he was just allowing his dislike for Sean to show. He certainly looked ill at ease. Finally he stood up.

"Paul, dear," said his mother, "wouldn't you like to have a cup of tea before you go?"

"I don't think so, Mother," said Paul. "I can get some at the house where I'll be staying."

"Who are you staying with anyway?" asked his father.

"Oh," answered Paul vaguely, "it's not with anyone you'd know."

Brian watched Paul go upstairs and heard the muffled footsteps in the room, and the clock ticked loudly in the kitchen. A little later Paul came down fully dressed in a soft hat and an ulster that hung loosely about his hips. A glance at the mirror, a slight tug at the brim of his hat, and he moved into the hall.

"Good night, all," he said.

"Good night." Michael did not lift his eyes from the newspaper.

Mary went with Paul to the door and with her fingers lightly brushed the shoulders of his coat. Brian rose and followed them.

"God keep you out of harm's way," said Mary. Brian felt that it was all she dared to say in such a moment.

"Don't worry," Paul said. He made no move to kiss his mother.

Brian opened the door . . . and quickly closed it again as one of the Specials' lorries with steel walls rumbled down the road. The lorries now carried triangular-shaped wire covering against hand grenades being dropped into them from the housetops. Moments later there was a sudden burst of machine-gun fire. The Specials always fired an occasional volley down the streets to keep them clear after curfew. The shots echoed and re-echoed through the deserted streets and slowly died away. Brian opened the door again. Paul slipped past him out of the doorway and, keeping close to the wall, melted into the pitch-black darkness of the night. The street lamps had been shot to pieces.

When Brian came back into the house Michael scratched his head violently and went upstairs, and Brian heard his stockinged feet pounding heavily on the ceiling as he moved about the bedroom. A little later Mary came in with a teapot and two thick slices of currant cake for Sean. She sat down beside Sean and kept talking to him while he ate. Brian returned to the newspaper.

The clock chimed ten musical notes and Brian tossed the newspaper onto the sofa. Still sitting down, he yawned, stretched out his legs, then stood up.

"Think I'll blow off," he said.

There was no response. But Brian caught his mother looking at him with pained eyes which he pretended not to notice as he climbed the stairs to the room. As he passed by his father's room, he saw him kneeling by the bed, his head bowed. Brian was dressed for the road when he came downstairs. Sean was now reading the newspaper and his mother was knitting vigorously. "I'm off," he said very casually.

"Where'll you sleep tonight, dear?" his mother asked. She put down her knitting.

"I'll stay down at Aunt Kate's, Mum," said Brian. "It's only down the street, but the Specials are not very fond of going down streets at night."

She rose and followed him to the door. "Don't get into any trouble, darling. Please."

"Don't worry, Mum," he said brightly. "Night, Mum. Night, Sean."

"Good night, love," said his mother.

"Night, Brian," said Sean.

The soft-running engine of one of the new type of patrol cars, nicknamed a "whippet," hummed along the Falls Road. Swift and dangerous.

"A 'whippet,'" said Mary in a whisper. "If they saw you now they'd mow you down!"

"Don't worry, Mum," called out Sean cheerfully from the kitchen. "They daren't go down the side streets, whippet and all. Wouldn't we love to meet them there!"

Brian insisted with his mother on getting Sean up to bed at least for one good night's rest. Then he quietly pulled the door of the hallway closed behind him.

"Murder!"

Brian stirred uneasily in his sleep.

"Murder! Murder!"

He sat up in bed, still half asleep, but beginning to be aware. Then he started. *Murder! Murder!* That was what the pickets had told the women to shout if the Specials raided a house at night.

Brian debated with himself what he should do. What *could* he do? He had no weapons, for he had given back the gun forced upon him that night at the Monastery. He could not go up and, like a woman, start screaming at the Specials. They'd shoot him. But he had to do something. He couldn't just lie there and do nothing during the raid.

The raids offended his sense of justice, for they were carried out under cover of darkness and not in the light of day by the men responsible for upholding the law. He was becoming more and more convinced that his father was right when he accused the Specials of being less concerned about upholding the law than in wreaking vengeance on their opponents. If men like that held the whip hand, if men like that *were* the law, what chance had those who opposed them?

For the first time since the riots had begun in the shipyards Brian had doubts about the rightness of his own attitude. For what were the pickets doing, after all, but trying to defend those who had no one else to defend them?

By this time he had dressed and had decided to go up and see what he could do. In any case, he could stay idle no longer, for the first woman's screams had been taken up by other women farther down the road. To their screams had been added the horrendous clamor of pokers rattling on bins, and the din frightened the air.

He ran up the street toward the Falls Road where the noise came from and he knew that the people in the houses he passed heard him but would scarcely hazard even a glance out of the window. For if it were the Specials they were peeping at, the Specials might let them have a precautionary burst from their machine guns, and, on the other hand, if it were the I.R.A., they might wonder whether someone were not checking on their movements and would make inquiries later.

Brian was halfway up the street when he heard the sound of

the first shots, and the shots seemed very near. The pickets were moving in. It must be near his own home, too. He wondered on which side of the street it might be, and for the first time since the woman's screams had wakened him he felt uneasy. But he dismissed the thought at once and kept on running, and when the presentiment returned he tried to keep calm although his breath, despite himself, came quicker. He told himself impatiently it was from the running and he listened to the shots increase in number. That meant the pickets were gathering forces for a united attack on the raiders. Now he was almost at the top of the street and near enough to the scene of the raid to make out the voices of the people who were screaming. It was then that he heard one woman's voice and the sound stopped him like a sudden blow in the chest.

"Sean! Sean! My God, they've murdered him! Sean! Sean! My Sean! My Sean! My Sean! . . ." The voice trailed off into a moan.

Brian's knees weakened; the pit of his bowels melted with fear, and the saliva dried up in his mouth. He staggered on to the top of the street but could go no farther. He leaned against the wall and vomited something that tasted bitter. He ran across the street to the doorway of the Hibernian Hall. As always, it was open to provide cover for some harassed picket. He climbed the stairs. His legs almost buckled under him before he got to the top. Once in the hall, he crouched under a window that overlooked the Falls Road, threw it open, and stuck his head out, insensible to fear. A full-scale street battle was on, and the angry twang of rifles had now mingled with the snap and crack of pistols. Two cages were halted outside his own home and their Lewis guns kept swirling round and round with a sense of panic, trying to silence the pickets. He drew his head back into the room, now aware of the danger from flying bullets.

At the thought of the injustice of this murderous action Brian felt himself being possessed by a rage such as he had never experienced before. He actually shivered from its intensity. In that moment he flung aside every idea he had had of standing aloof in the struggle. This was what Sean had seen and had found no solution for, but to meet violence with violence. If that was so, then he, Brian, had been wrong, not Sean. But he should be *doing* something. Where could he get a gun? Oh, how he regretted having returned that revolver! He'd give his heart's blood, he'd give the rest of his life to have it now! He stood up and in his agitation crushed his moist palms helplessly together. Maybe if he went down to the street he could get a gun from the pickets. Before he left the hall he pressed his hot, sweaty cheek against the cold brick wall and again peered out of the window.

The raid must have been swiftly executed, for even as he looked the first cage swung out into the middle of the road, veered around, and backed up to eliminate the perilous open space between it and the door of the house. But by the time it reached the door the left rear tire blew out, settled down, and flattened out over the wheel rim. The Specials in the hallway scrambled into the cage, the engine roared, and the cage bumped back onto the road, turned right, and raced off in an ungainly fashion down the Falls Road, its guns blazing. Watching it leave, Brian wanted to follow it, cling to its sides, and tear down the wire netting with his bare hands to reach at the throats of the men who had killed Sean. But they were getting away! They were getting away! . . .

Immediately afterward the second cage began to repeat the maneuver of the first. Brian caught the glint of a round object flying out of a nearby window. It struck the wire of the cage with a chink, rolled lazily off the wire to the ground, and burst into a red-white roar that jolted him back with shock and surprise. The Specials hastily clambered aboard and the steel door clanged shut behind them. The cage lurched forward, but before it reached the roadway another round object came flying out of the same window. Like the first it clinked against the wire, rolled lazily down part of the way, but stopped with a slight jerk as the hooks tied to it with cords caught in the strands. Brian's fingers and toes curled up in horror at the thought of what was about to happen.

The men inside the cage were instantly alert to the danger. They jabbed frantically with their rifles at the hand grenade to dislodge it; they cried out hoarsely and banged the rifle butts furiously against the sides of the cage in desperation as the cage jolted off the pavement. They were too late. In a nightmarish scene a second roar lit up with eerie yellow the interior of the cage, and Brian saw the figures of the men stand out in stark relief, grotesquely gesticulating in wild panic. But the cage sped on, followed by a few stray shots, until its engine droned away to silence.

Stunned and sickened by what he had seen, Brian's rage drained out of him. He turned away from the window and for a long time did not move, his mind numb and his body cold.

Outside the people in the nearby houses waited until the drone of engines had faded away. Then Brian heard the window sashes creak again and muffled voices speaking in unlit rooms. But after a little while even these sounds ceased and once more everything grew quiet.

He shivered, rose, and made his way home across the street. It was only then he realized that in one house alone did any sound persist and that was in the Traceys, and the sound was that of a woman sobbing with the subdued resignation of hopelessness, because she knew that no matter what she did she could not call back the dead.

The events of the next hour or so were to Brian like the scenes of a sad play, like a mummery in which the silent actors were his father and mother and himself. There was no word spoken as they played their parts. He took up Sean's body from the floor of the room where he had been cornered and shot and laid it on the bed, covering it with a white sheet. Then he moved about the room arranging things. Michael brought in two candlesticks, one in each hand, and two candles under his arm. He set down the candlesticks on a little table by the side of the bed, screwed in the candles, and lit them. Both he and Brian led Mary out of the room, and Brian felt his mother was leaving only because she was too dazed with sorrow to understand.

When the body had been laid out and Mary had left, Michael took the time to tell Brian how his son had died. As he told the story his quiet, subdued manner recalled to Brian the days when his father used to tell the three brothers of the deaths of Ireland's heroes. Now he told this story in the same subdued, almost flat, voice, that depended on no device for its effect other than the death of another hero, this time his own son.

The Specials had broken in without warning, he said, and, using flash lamps, had headed for the different rooms. Two of them had tried to climb the stairs, but Sean had reached the landing first and had fired three shots of white flame, and the world must have exploded in front of the first man, said Michael, as he fell. The second man had tumbled backward downstairs and the oath on his lips had been choked when his mouth had struck the wall.

Then the windows had rattled up all around the house and the cry of *Murder!* together with the noise of the bins, had gone out to warn the pickets.

Sean had been cornered in his own room when the Specials had rushed the landing, and had been shot. When his mother had heard them shooting him, said Michael, she had nearly gone out of her mind.

"It was a horrible night, Brian," said Michael dully. "And what hurts me most of all—maybe I shouldn't say it—but not one of his brothers was there to help him. Poor Sean! He had nobody to help him, Brian. His own brothers were all safe and sound somewhere else while he was being shot. I don't like to say it, Brian, but while he was being killed, neither you nor Paul was there to lift a hand to save him. Maybe I shouldn't say it, Brian, but there was not one of his———" Michael's voice was rising.

"Stop it, for God's sake!" burst out Brian. "Do you think I don't feel the weight of it on me? Do you think I'm made of stone? Do you think I didn't love Sean? Do you think I won't be haunted by this for the rest of my life? But what's a man to do? Can you tell me that? What's the right thing to do? Will one killing wipe out another?"

"Oh, aye," said Michael, with a frightening, detached calm. "You've been asking yourself those questions for a long time, Brian. I could see that. But your brother Sean was killed here tonight, Brian, and while he was being killed—maybe I shouldn't say this, Brian." Michael's voice began to rise again. "Brian, not one of his brothers was here to lift a finger to help him. Where were you? And Paul? Where's Paul now? Is he dead, too?"

Brian seized his father by the shoulders and shook him roughly, unfeelingly, brutally, and Michael took it quietly. Then his head drooped and he burst into tears. On Brian's harsh order he rose and climbed the stairs slowly, wearily, to his room.

When he had gone Brian drew a chair up by the bedside and gazed at Sean. In the light of the flickering candles there were moments when he fancied he could see the muscles twitching slightly on Sean's face. He tried to make himself think that the nightmare had not happened and that tomorrow he would awaken and everything would be as before. It wasn't the first time something horrible had taken place in his dreams, had seemed so real at the time he had even pinched himself to prove that it was not a dream, and yet he had awakened next morning to find that the frightening thing was gone with the coming of the day.

Sean did not breathe. Sean did not move. Brian took up Sean's right arm but the flesh was already cold and had a strange powdery feel, a strange dryness to it. He let Sean's arm drop again by his side. Sean did not even open his eyes. . . . That was when the whole night's happenings rushed upon Brian and he fell across the bed and sobbed. But in his tears there was no lightening of the weight, no lessening of the bitterness in his soul. He was conscious of this and it deepened his misery. He wondered how he could have slept while they were killing Sean.

"God! God! God!" he cried out. "Did You sleep, too, when they were killing my brother Sean?"

The light pouring into the room next morning awoke Brian and he raised his head from the crook of his arm. The two candles Michael had lit had burned out meanwhile, but two fresh ones had been stuck on top of them. He rose stiffly and went to his own room and was surprised to see the hands of his old alarm clock with the bell on top point to nine. As he cleaned up he noticed that there was an odd quiet to the house, as if everything were edged with velvet, and when he went downstairs his father was sitting smoking by the side of the fire. He had already prepared a pot of tea and a plate of buttered toast for Brian.

"I made her stay in bed a few hours longer, Brian," he said.

"Oh," said Brian. "Is Paul——" He stopped suddenly, remembering what his father had kept repeating the night before. He could find nothing else to say, however, and sat brooding over his breakfast. The toast he could not eat, but he was glad of the cup of strong, sweet tea. He asked for a second cup, and his father rose and poured it out for him. Brian felt he could go on sitting there and drinking the strong, sweet tea forever. But when he thought that, he knew that he was only seeking an excuse for not carrying out a resolution that had been forming in his mind. Later he put down the third cup of tea so heavily he almost broke the saucer and glanced up guiltily at his father. Michael turned away quickly but not before Brian caught the odd look in his eyes. Brian rose and walked toward the door.

"Where are you going, Brian?" asked Michael.

"Not very far," said Brian, reaching for his hat on the dresser.

"Look, son," Michael pleaded, "don't go. Your mother and I need you to . . . to . . . well, to arrange things with the undertaker."

"What's the use of all that? Sean's dead. Will the undertaker bring him back to life?"

"Now look here, Brian," said Michael. "Don't go out. Forget what I said last night. Maybe I just wasn't in my right mind. Forget it. You owe it to your mother. If anything happens to you at this point, it'd kill her. Don't go."

"Leave me alone!" said Brian coldly. "I wasn't thinking of what you said last night."

It was a bright, sunny morning when he left the house, and he felt the warm breeze bearing the summer heat of the day caress his cheeks. The morning traffic had begun to increase, but Brian did not notice it. He did not notice the bow of black-and-white crepe tied to the door knocker; he did not recognize anyone among the little knots of people who stared at the house; he did not see them point out to their friends the cross traced in white chalk on the lintel of the door.

He walked down the Falls Road and turned right at Albert Street and kept on walking until he came in sight of the barracks that had recently been taken over from the regular police by the Specials. The Specials had wrought several changes since their coming. A semicircle of sandbags the height of a man had been erected in front of the door; other sandbags were piled halfway up the windows, and the top of the yard wall to the right was covered with interwoven strands of barbed wire. Nobody came out and nobody went in, and Brian got the impression of a building under siege.

Squaring his shoulders, he walked up to the barracks and glared at the round muzzle of a rifle poked out at him from a slit between the sandbags. He could see several flat police caps moving about just above the sandbags as if they were floating on top of a tankful of water.

"Where are you going?" asked an upcountry accent from behind the sandbags.

"I want to see the officer in charge," said Brian.

"What for?"

"Important information."

"Put up your hands and come in."

Brian stretched his arms into the air and walked behind the sandbags. It was dark behind them after the bright sunlight of the street. A uniformed Special first ran his hands along Brian's body and then escorted him into the charge room. Several other Specials in uniform and a few men in plain clothes were in the room and Brian was aware of their sharp scrutiny. He felt a coldness creep over him and he knew that it was fear. But he also knew that neither fear nor any other thing would stop him now from doing what he had to do.

The guard led him before a sergeant sitting on a raised desk behind a grill of polished brass rods. The guard went up to the sergeant and whispered something to him and then stepped down.

"Well?" said the sergeant bluntly. "What information have you?"

The moment Brian stood alone before the sergeant fear dropped from him and in its stead rose a strange sense of elation that lifted him oddly out of himself. This must be what dedicated assassins felt, he thought, when they drew the knife or fired the shots, knowing that they could not escape.

"I have no information to give you," he said steadily. "But you have information to give me."

The sergeant eyed him dubiously. "What information are you talking about?" he asked.

"I want to know who murdered Sean?"

"Sean? Sean who?"

"My brother Sean, Sean Tracey."

"Oh! Sean Tracey." The sergeant's eyes now left Brian and casually searched the charge room. He must have had it thoroughly drummed into him, thought Brian, that he was not safe even inside the barracks, behind a high desk. He must know by now that the activities of the Specials had made men desperate. Brian knew that the sergeant had already realized that something was happening that was out of the ordinary, knew that he would call for help. Before Brian had time even to repeat his demand the door to the barrack room flung open and a dozen men in various stages of undress with pistols in their hands stormed into the charge room. When they saw only one unarmed man standing in the middle of the floor they were nonplussed.

With a swift intake of breath Brian turned and pointed an accusing finger at them.

"So you are the men who were out last night?" he said. He had worked himself up emotionally and he was glad. It would make his task easier. "So you are the men who killed my brother," he went on, "and now, like snakes, are sleeping off your glut of blood!" They stared at him. "Why did you not shoot him in the light of day, for that's when God will judge you? You sought the darkness to hide your deed from the eyes of men but not from the eyes of God, who will one day punish you for your crime."

"You're mad!" roared the sergeant. "Mad!"

"Yes, I'm mad!" roared Brian back at him. "Mad at the injustice of it! Mad at the futility of hoping for justice. I want the whole world to know what you have done, you, the upholders of the law, the protectors of our rights. And it will be known, for I will shout it from the housetops!" Brian's voice rose to a high pitch. Some part of him vaguely sensed that he was growing hysterical, but he was not concerned about that or about anything else in the world except to make these men endure for once the torment of their guilt. "Now you hide yourselves," he went on. "You fear you'll be marked out for death by friends of my dead brother. But I tell you that God has already marked you. Even those of you who escape the avenger's bullets will be hounded to your graves by your own conscience!"

Brian's voice faltered at this point. He stopped and burst into tears of weakness and frustration. In that moment his power left him, the spell of his lashing tongue which had bound these men dissolved, and when he recovered he knew that he no longer spoke to men who stood alone, each facing his own conscience, but to a mob with the collective courage and insensibility of a mob.

"Shut him up, somebody!" cried the sergeant in a rage.

A burly Special stepped over and jabbed his revolver into Brian's ribs. "Close your trap!" he said.

Brian did not even turn to look at him. "Go ahead!" he shouted contemptuously. "You double traitor, first to your country and then to your God. Go ahead! Do you think I care? You don't care either, for I'll just be one more number on your list of blood!"

At that moment a gray-mustached inspector came in to find out what was happening. Without any more ado he curtly ordered two men to throw Brian out of the barracks. Brian felt himself suddenly raised off his feet and ignominiously half walked, half hoisted out past the door, past the sandbags, and then pushed forward so violently he fell and landed in the gutter. White with fury, he picked himself up and, flinging his arms wide open, turned and offered his breast to them.

"Shoot!" he taunted. "Shoot now while you have the chance. Shoot this new enemy you've made, for, as God's my judge, I shall avenge my brother's death on more than one of you!" For one breathless moment he stood with his arms outstretched. In that age of time nothing happened. He lowered his arms again and then, slowly and deliberately spat upon the sandbags.

The warm sun shone brightly across the white pavement at Brian's feet, everything was still, and the muzzle of the rifle that poked out from between the sandbags glinted wickedly in the sun's rays as it moved into line with Brian's heart. Brian waited defiantly but again nothing happened. Finally he shrugged his coat back into place, beat the dust off his clothes, and placing his hat squarely on his head, walked back up the sun-drenched street.

14

He had not walked a hundred yards from the barracks when a man stepped out of a doorway. It was Sandy.

"Hello, Tracey," said Sandy.

"Hello," said Brian absently.

At first he was too confused to realize the coincidence it was to meet Sandy just after his encounter with the Specials.

"How did you know I'd be here?" he asked.

"I didn't," said Sandy blandly. "I just happen to be keeping an eye on the barracks. We have something in mind for them."

"I know what I have in mind for them!" exploded Brian. "I'd blow them and their blasted barracks sky-high! They murdered Sean. Do you know that? They murdered Sean!"

"I know all about it," said Sandy.

"How do you know all about it?" asked Brian.

"I was up there shootin'," said Sandy. "When we heard he was dead I didn't go into the house. We had other work to do. By the way," went on Sandy, "where was brother Paul last night?"

"I don't know," said Brian. "Like me, he left the house a little while after Sean came home."

"Did anybody—did Paul ask Sean to come home or maybe stay at home last night?"

"Sean came home because he complained that his cold was getting the better of him."

"Well," said Sandy, "I suppose it doesn't really matter much now anyway. Come on in here and have a belt or two. It's what the doctor ordered for a fellow that's had a tough night like the one you had. This pub is as good as any." Sandy took Brian's arm and led him through the doors of a public house they were passing at the moment. Except for an occasional bottle of stout or a glass of punch with friends, Brian was not accustomed to drinking, and, in the ordinary way, he would have thought twice before drinking with Sandy. It was Sandy who had forced him into the shooting match that evening at the Monastery, and since then he had never cared much for the man. But with the recent encounter on his mind he was in the mood to agree that he needed "a belt or two" to quiet him.

Inside the public house it was dark and cool but the air was heavy with the smell of spirits. A smooth-cheeked, deep-jowled barman, prematurely bald, swabbed the polished counter in front of Brian and with head bowed listened to Sandy's order for two Bushmills and two pints of stout to wash it down. Sandy took up the small, thick-walled glass filled beyond the white line with deep amber liquid that the barman placed before him. Brian followed his example.

"Sleante," said Sandy. With a quick arching movement of head and elbow he downed the glass. "Bwah!" he gasped. Then he belched contentedly and looked at Brian.

"Sleante," said Brian, and he raised his glass to his lips and let the liquid pour across the tip and cradle of his tongue, stinging it almost painfully. It flowed past his palate and down his throat and there it seemed to take fire, but along the digestive tract the fire left it and instead it radiated a glow so pleasurable that when Brian set down the empty glass he continued to stare at it, enjoying the invigorating warmth that spread all over his body, even to the tips of his toes. It was like stepping out of the cold into a warm bath. He nodded to Sandy in approval.

"Same again, Willie," ordered Sandy.

After the first "belt" or two it was easy for Brian to open his heart to a man who had the same feelings as himself about the Specials. Besides, he was glad of something to shake off the weight of despondency that had descended on him again at the thought of having to return to a cold and cheerless house. The brush with the Specials at least had made him forget for a while. Now he dreaded having to face reality or having to assume responsibility at home. He was also in the mood for agreeing with Sandy that he should give some thought to the possibility of joining forces with other men whose aim was to curb the power of the Specials and protect the Catholics. It would make him feel less helpless and less alone. He stayed a long time drinking with Sandy and two other men who joined them later.

At one point in their drinking Brian set down his whisky glass with such force it slipped from his loose fingers and rolled off the bar. Then, with a haughty gesture of his hand, he dismissed both the glass and the incident. He still kept staring, nevertheless, at the spot where he had last seen the glass.

Finally he looked up. "That's the only way to handle it," he said.

"Don't worry," said Sandy, "the barman will pick it up."

"Pick what up?" said Brian with a certain truculence in his voice. "I was referring to my irre–irr–irrevocab' decision." He glowered at Sandy. He glowered at each of the other two men in turn. "I shall go up and shoot my way through. At least I'll nab a couple o' the blerts before they get me. Two, meb' three, to one! Good odds. But I need a 'volver. Anybody got a—"

"Look, Brian . . ." Sandy tried to interrupt.

"Look, Brian, nothing!" shouted Brian. The other men in the bar turned to see what it was all about. "Look, Brian, nothing! Brian's been looking too damned long! 'Bout time Brian stop looking and start *doing* something for a change. And"–he glared at Sandy–"don't you try to hinder me." He glared at the second man. "Nor you." He glared in turn at the men gathered at both ends of the bar. "Anybody in this pub got a gun?"

All conversation stopped at the bar, and in the interval the barman's eye caught Sandy's and pleaded with him. Sandy's raised palm answered, "All right, we're going now." Brian saw all this but did not understand it.

"If you want a gun, Brian," said Sandy, "I know where to get one. Let's take a ride up the Falls and see if we can't pick it up before it gets too dark and the Specials hole up for the night. The air will clear your head and you'll shoot straighter."

"Whad'ya mean? Clear my head?" said Brian suspiciously. "My head's clear. You see anything wrong with my head?" He took his glass jug, half filled with porter, and drank deeply from it. With his legs outspread he stood squarely in front of Sandy as if challenging him, and all the while his body rocked gently to and fro.

"If you don't stop swaying you'll spill over," remarked one of the men. The others at the bar began to laugh.

Sandy stepped back a little as if to appraise Brian's condition. "No," he said, "not a whit wrong with you. As sound as a barrel!"

For a moment Brian continued to look insolently at Sandy and the man who had made the remark then, patting Sandy on the shoulder, he suddenly burst out laughing. "An' as tight as a tick!" he said. "As tight as a tick!" Putting down the jug, he tried to embrace Sandy, but Sandy deftly moved aside.

"Knock off the rest of that, Brian," he said, "and let's go." With a flick of his forefinger he called the barman over and paid the bill. Then he and one of the other men took Brian by the arm and led him outside.

After a drive in a taxi they reached a low hedge broken here and there by people taking short cuts to the bungalows that lay scattered in the stretch of marshy fields below. Brian recognized the place confusedly. It was the Huts. Sandy led him to a bungalow painted dark green, too large to be a dwelling place, that had evidently not been taken too much care of.

"Brian Tracey," Sandy announced to a thin little white-haired man in shirt sleeves who opened the door to his knock.

"Brian Tracey," echoed the white-haired man into the hall.

"See," said Brian to Sandy, "know me already." He smiled benignly at the little man and hiccuped.

Following Sandy unsteadily, he came into the hall of a workingmen's club furnished with dart boards, checkers, cards, and a pool table. At the moment, however, the tables had been pushed back against the walls to leave as much space as possible. At the front end of the hall a group of young men, stripped to the waist, were going through drill movements under an instructor in gymnasium dress. At the far end about forty men were seated around a table and a blackboard, and on the table were strewn the parts of a rifle, a cheap alarm clock with a bell on top, a flashlight battery, and some strands of wire. Brian tried to see some connection between these items, found it too difficult, and gave up. Sandy led him down the hall and placed a chair for him at the edge of the group. Brian sat down on it and tried to concentrate.

"Most effective of our weapons is the time bomb . . . certain principles of electricity . . ." In the close room the heady fumes of the liquor clouded Brian's mind and he began to nod. Finally he fell asleep.

A loud voice startled him into bewildered wakefulness. He turned toward the door with the rest.

The door opened and a tall, confident-looking man with smooth, raven-black hair entered the hall. He was followed by a short gray-haired man in a brown suit who seemed rather diffident in contrast to his companion.

"Up, boys! Brigadier Seamus McKenna!"

Everybody in the hall hurriedly rose to their feet. Brian tried to follow them but nearly overbalanced. He sat down again.

"All right, all right," said the tall man good-humoredly as he covered the length of the hall in a few long strides and turned to face the men. "You can put everything away. Pat Doran is here from Dublin to give you a talk on the history of our struggle for independence." He nodded toward his companion and sat down. The short man rose, smoothed back his sparse gray hair with his palms, adjusted his thick-lensed spectacles, and pulled at the hem of his coat all the way around. Brian watched him examine the ceiling carefully and then heard him begin in a very high-pitched voice. This sounded so funny to Brian that he chuckled at first and then laughed out loud. He felt a sudden painful jab in the ribs, stopped laughing at once, and tried to concentrate on what the man was squeaking about. But the effort was too much for him and he fell asleep again.

The scuffle of feet as the lecture ended awakened him, and this time he succeeded in standing up straight. He was feeling proud of this achievement when Sandy roughly pulled him down again. He heard McKenna call the men of Company "C" to the pool table. Sandy nodded at Brian and reached out to help him to his feet, but, scorning him, Brian dragged his chair along the floor to the pool table, sat down, and struck up a conversation with the man to his right. He had the Kerry rise and fall to his speech, and Brian asked him if he had come up to live in Belfast.

"Me live in Belfast?" repeated the man. He had beautiful strong teeth and a small, lively red tongue like a kitten's. "I wouldn't live long! Would I, Terry?" he said to his companion. They both laughed. This laugh irritated Brian and he loudly asked what the hell was wrong with Belfast anyway. The two men turned away from him at that, but several others looked around and stared. Sandy shushed him into silence.

"We all know," said McKenna, who was on his feet again, "that the Specials have planned a campaign of terror for the Catholics of Belfast, and we've been watching for a chance to pay them back in their own coin . . ."

McKenna's voice came to Brian from a long way off, stayed for a while, and then floated away again into silence. Brian closed his eyes to concentrate and at once felt his whole body rise up from the floor and spin round dizzily. He had the odd, ridiculous sensation that his body had gone off in search of McKenna's voice.

He giggled at the idea and looked around, ready to apologize. But no one was paying any attention to him. They were listening too intently to what the tall dark man was saying. For the tall dark man was no longer smiling; he was tense, and the light above his head accentuated his temples and cheekbones, and his mouth was grim each time he snapped it shut.

Some part of Brian whispered in his ear that he was drunk, but the very suggestion spurred him to reaction. He shook his head indignantly at himself and with a supreme effort stretched his eyebrows high up on his forehead and opened his eyes. He would have to stay awake, he warned himself. Or else the others would catch on. He must concentrate on what McKenna was saying.

". . . information that they intend mass raids . . . area which they consider a nest of ammunition dumps, and we have planned . . . as secret as possible, each group only know what part they have to play . . . You all heard . . . Violations could mean court-martial . . . Last meeting of G.H.G. sentence of death discussed . . . Use if that's only way we can protect . . . Finally . . . That's all. Meeting dismissed."

McKenna and his aides moved away down the hall and the others began to rise. Brian sat where he was. It would be better to wait, he decided, until the rest were out of the way. When he did try to rise he felt someone seize his arm, but he disdainfully shrugged off the hold, stood up, and gazed possessively around the swaying hall. He walked a few steps and bumped into one of the men but in compensation gave the man a warm, ingratiating smile. He wanted him to be his friend; he wanted everybody to be his friend. The man smiled back and Brian swept him a low bow —he was really making an impression on these people! And only his first time here! Imagine what he would do after a few visits! Strong, bony fingers seized his arm again, and at first he was inclined to protest. Then in a wave of comradely feeling he decided to let it pass. After all, he told himself, the fellow means well. Besides, this time, no matter how he tried, he could not shake off the grip.

Once outside the hall he felt the cool night air press like a damp cloth against his face. One moment he was walking between Sandy and another man; the next moment he was sitting, still between them, on the long and smooth wooden bench of the tram. When the tram pulled up he felt the rough cloth of Sandy's sleeve press against his cheek.

As he stepped down from the tram the conductor reached out his hand to help him. Brian took the man's hand in his own, pressed it to his heart, and gave the man a deep and searching look.

"Do you kick with the right foot, mate?" he asked solemnly.

"Would I be on the Falls Road run if I didn't?" the man answered.

At this Brian's manner changed suddenly and he smiled broadly. "Up the I.R.A.!" he cried. With the palm of his hand he planted a resounding smack on the rear of the tram. "Keep her on the tracks, mate!" he called out cheerily, "And never let her bottom trail the ground!" He gave a friendly wave to the conductor as the tram rumbled on down the road.

With the men on either side of him he crossed over to his home. He was surprised to see the lights of the house still on despite the curfew. Then he remembered, and when Sandy remarked that it was the only house on the Falls Road still lighted he said quite casually: "They killed Sean, you know. Won't bother us for a long time now that he's out of the way."

A neighbor opened the door for him. Without bothering to thank her he turned to his two companions. "Come on in, fellas," he said. "Plenty of booze for the wake."

Sandy and the other man, however, waited until Mary came out. They handed Brian over to her.

Brian put his two hands on his mother's shoulders and leaned his head on her breast.

"Michael," called out Mary above the din of the loud conversation inside.

"What is it, Mary?" asked Michael anxiously as he came out. He saw Brian. "So he's home," he said.

They had neither reproach nor resignation. They simply took Brian from the two men who followed them into the brightly lit kitchen. The people already gathered for the first night of the wake stood up at their approach. There was some whispering among them. Brian's dull senses were roused a little by the realization that he was approaching Sean's corpse, and he overheard what some of them were saying.

"Nice thing to come home footless and the brother lying stiff as a poker."

"Aw, God help him, he's had only a sip or two taken."

"After what he went through last night, poor crattur . . ."

"They'll be plantin' him instead o' the brother."

Brian turned to them. "Don't be afraid to speak up," he said thickly. "Say what you have to say, take as much booze as you can hold, then clear out." He began to shout. "Do ye hear? Clear out!"

Frightened, the little knot of people edged away from him.

Mary and Michael led him to the door of the back room to

which Sean's body had been brought by the undertaker and some of the neighbors. The room had been rid of the odd bits of furniture usually stored there and now held a dresser covered with a white cloth on which stood two brass candlesticks, each with a lighted, thick brown candle. A dark wooden cross stood between them. Then there was the bed. Brian saw an expanse of white sheet that made the bed seem disproportionately large in that small room. The sheet sloped upward toward the center of the body and brought Brian's attention at once to the top of the bed where, on two white pillows, lay the head and shoulders of his brother. Sean was dressed in a brown shroud that made Brian think of the time he and his brother had been altar boys at the Monastery. For no reason at all he remembered the day they had been surprised by the sacristan drinking the leavings of the wine. They both had laughed at the incident afterward. Now he did not want to laugh. He wanted to cry.

Sean's two arms were encased in long brown sleeves with frills at the wrists like the dress of an old woman. His hands held in a tight grip a small black cross with a white metal figure, and in the center of the right hand Brian saw a small dark spot almost disguised by the flesh-colored powder of the undertaker. The forehead, nose, and temples of the dead man had a transparent quality about them that was accentuated by the undertaker's efforts on the cheeks and chin to give the features a lifelike look. On the right temple and below the chin were two tiny round spots of flesh-colored sticking plaster. Sean's lips and nose had a thinness about them that gave the face a grim look so alien to his brother's open and friendly nature. To Brian the room had a stuffy air and smelled of faded flowers.

He stood between his father and mother for a moment. Then he could no longer bear to look at Sean. His head dropped and he turned away, pressing his eyelids so tightly together the tears started from them. Mary cried, too, and with the edge of her apron gently wiped dry his eyes and her own. Without a word the three of them left the room and walked back toward the stairway in the hall. Sandy and the other man took Brian from his parents and helped him up the stairs.

Dazedly Brian watched them turn up the gaslight, set him down on the edge of the bed, and take off his clothes. He found himself in bed, the light turned low. Two dark hazy figures waved at him from the door. After that he closed his eyes and the bed rose from under him and spiraled giddily to the ceiling, and giant hands seized him painfully by the temples and pulled him wildly hither and thither among the dark recesses of his troubled dreams.

The next morning he awoke, conscious of a sickness in his stomach. Later the sickness went away. Not so the pain in his head, or his dry, furry mouth and swollen tongue, or the hum he heard in his ears every time there was quiet in the house.

He went downstairs for a breakfast of tea and toast and in the scullery saw all the preparations for the evening wake: trays of cakes and buns and sandwiches, packages of cigarettes, long rolls of Gallagher's tobacco, lemonade and ginger ale. At the rear of the table on which his breakfast had been set stood a row of squat bottles with coffee-colored labels: McCaffery's Stout.

Brian glared at them sullenly throughout the meal. When he had finished eating he rose, walked over to the rear of the table, and without warning swept the back of his hand across the line of bottles, knocking them off the table onto the floor. They fell on a pile of wastepaper and did not break.

Hearing the noise, Mary came running out to the scullery.

"What do they think they're doing?" Brian asked her. "Making a mockery of my brother's death?"

She did not answer him, and Brian, finding that he had nothing to struggle against, walked out of the scullery, through the kitchen, without even a glance at the death room, and climbed the stairs. Once in his room he threw himself on the bed again—he was still tired—and fell asleep. He did not wake until noon and he must have been roused by the noise of many people below. Shivering slightly, although it was quite warm, he brushed his hair back with his fingers and went downstairs, blinking as he entered the bright kitchen. Again he noticed that the people lowered their voices when he came in. He did not greet anyone, nor did he respond to those who greeted him, but walked directly over to the room where his brother lay.

It irritated him to hear the three or four people mumbling *Hail Mary's* as they knelt beside the bed. He felt they were doing it as a chore to have the right to share afterward in the drinking. The people at prayer acted self-consciously when they saw him, and Brian was well aware that they were watching him while they prayed.

He did not go inside the room or kneel down, or take part in the prayers. With folded arms he stared fixedly at the body, his face settling into a scowl. He stood there brooding for a long time, not moving or showing any sign of life other than the rise and fall of his heavy breathing. Slowly the attention, first of those nearest him, then even of those farthest away, centered on him. Brian was well aware of this but he continued to stand there, rooted to the spot, disdainful and aloof. At a certain moment he turned on his heel abruptly, crossed to the hall, and snatched his hat off the rack.

Mary had been watching him all the time and now she asked him rather fearfully: "Where are you going, son, and you without your supper?"

Brian did not look at her. "I'm eating at the Mooneys'," he said. "After that I'm going up to the Huts. And let me tell you it's only for your sake I allow these food-and-drink vultures to feed upon the body of my brother; it's only for your sake I didn't rise up and drive that scum from the deathbed they're desecrating!"

Just as Brian was about to leave the door opened and Paul walked in. He brushed past Brian without a word, slipped off his coat and hat, hung them on the hall stand, and went on into the house. Slowly and reluctantly Brian took off his own hat again and followed Paul inside.

Paul stood for a moment at the door of the kitchen surveying the scene and nodding—rather primly, Brian thought—to his parents and the rest of the people. Then he moved slowly toward the death room. Brian followed him. At the door of the room Paul stopped again and, folding his arms, shaded his eyes with his hand like a man who was thinking hard. Brian began to suspect that Paul was putting on a little act, for Paul had never shown any great liking for Sean or his ways. Who did Paul think he was fooling? He must have picked up these little dodges from the smart company he keeps. Paul continued to stand there without showing any sign of life. Finally Brian gave him a light, impatient jab in the ribs to rouse him, and to Brian's surprise it was as if he had set in motion a mechanical toy. Paul's whole body sagged, his head drooped, and, covering his face with his hands, he hurried forward and fell down by the bedside. At this moment Michael and Mary appeared and Mary was about to go to Paul's assistance, but Michael seized her by the arm and prevented her.

Paul buried his face in the bed; clasped and unclasped the sheet, and all the time kept mumbling words that Brian only half understood.

"Oh, Sean, Sean, Sean! . . . Hate me! Why? Why? Why? My own brother! . . . Judas, Judas, Judas . . . Forgiveness . . . My own brother . . ."

Finally the mumbling and the movement of the hands ceased, reminding Brian of a man who had passed from pain into restful sleep. In that brief moment of silence Brian reflected on his brother's strange conduct. For a while he suspected that Paul might be drunk, but there had been not the slightest smell of liquor from him. He had never imagined that Paul had felt any great liking for Sean until this disturbing display of emotion. It was more than he could fathom.

The death room was still hushed and stayed so for what seemed a long time to Brian. At last Paul stirred. He gave a slight shiver, rose to his feet, and turned to look about him with red-rimmed eyes. Brian took his arm and shook it lightly to rouse him. Paul ran his hands up and down his flushed cheeks. Then he saw his mother and went over to her and kissed her. He nodded to his father who returned the nod.

Brian now faced the people in the room. "Clear the way," he said roughly. "Clear the way for my brother!"

The people hastily obeyed, and Brian led Paul out of the room into the hall. It was only then that Paul seemed to recover fully. He shook his ruffled coat into place and with the palms of his hands swept his hair back across his head.

"Why did they have to shoot him?" he asked dully. "Why did they not just arrest him? And why did he not let them arrest him. He'd be alive now."

"Sean was a real Irishman," said Brian somewhat stiffly. "And they don't give up."

"I see," said Paul heavily. "I see."

"What do you see, Paul?" said Brian.

"Oh, I don't know," said Paul wearily. "I don't know. I . . . I wonder where it will all end?"

Suddenly, disappointingly, thought Brian, the old Paul reasserted himself. "Did I say anything over there . . . queer, or out of place?" he asked, eying Brian warily.

"Not that I know of," said Brian, coldly now. "I couldn't make head or tail of what you were mumbling."

"Well," said Paul, briskly this time. "I don't know about you, but I'm off. I just can't stand these people who prey on the corpse. You're the eldest brother and it's up to you to handle things. I'll be up again tomorrow for the funeral."

To Brian it was impersonal talk of the kind that Paul might hand out to a customer, and Brian did not like it. But he refrained from comment as Paul put on his stylish gray overcoat and carefully set at an angle his brown trilby.

"So long, elder brother!" Paul said almost gaily as he closed the hall door behind him.

Brian ate his dinner that night with the Mooneys and to pass the time paid a visit to the Huts. Here he received a warm welcome, for they sympathized with him for the death of his brother. Besides, they told him that they valued highly his knowledge of engineering. It would come in very handy for the project they had in mind. Someone also suggested that it would be a grand chance to pay the Specials back for what they had done to Sean.

When he came home from the Huts Brian stood in silence before the body of his brother. A resolve formed in his mind grew stronger and, in the end, took possession of him so that he could think of nothing else. He had found a mission: he would avenge the murder of his brother. He was never calm when he looked upon the face of Sean. Instead there swelled up inside of him a rage that surged and surged until it shook him. Looking at Sean, he wanted to cry out at the top of his voice: "I'll have their blood for yours!"

Back in his room brooding, he saw how providential had been his chance encounter with Sandy outside the barracks. It had provided him with the means of revenge, without which he might have had to vent his fury on the winds. He had no desire whatsoever to help the organization. It was only a means to an end. When he had had his revenge he would leave the organization, leave Belfast, and hide out on the farm.

In the afternoon he heard his mother climb the stairs. She opened the door.

"What's up?" he asked.

"Uncle Jamie has just arrived," she said. "Sheila came up with him." The look in Brian's eyes encouraged her. "Wouldn't you like to go down and speak to her? They have to be back in Drumree before curfew."

For the moment Brian was elated. The thought that Sheila was in the house gave him an unexpected joy. With Sheila near . . . But wait, he told himself. Mother has certainly asked Sheila to try to talk me out of doing what she thinks I intend to do. Therefore, he decided suddenly, I must not see her. One word, one look from her, and I would find myself giving in to what she asks.

"Very well," he said aloud, a plan already forming in his mind.

He went downstairs and saw the familiar girlish figure waiting for him. He had intended to rush out of the house before he had time even to look upon her face, before his eyes met hers. But Sheila was standing at the entrance to the hall. He took a deep breath and, before she could utter the greeting on her lips, with his right arm attempted to brush her aside. But she seized his arm and held him, understanding.

"Brian," she cried. "Look at me. Don't run away from me like that. Look at me."

But Brian stubbornly refused to turn his head. He jerked his arm free. "Let me go," he said roughly. "Don't try to stop me from doing what I want to do more than anything else in the world."

"More than—" began Sheila. But Brian had already fled into the street.

He wandered aimlessly about the streets for the next hour or so. As the afternoon wore on, however, it became clear to him how wrong he had been to rebuff Sheila. She was the one person in the world, he saw now, who could help him, and only his black mood had blinded him to that. Two hours later he suddenly decided to return and began to hope against hope that she would still be at the house. But when he reached home his mother told him she was gone. She and Jamie had stayed as long as they had dared and then had taken the trap back to Drumree.

At this Brian retreated once more to the solitude of his room and sat there alone in the growing dusk until he realized that it was nearing suppertime. He was on the point of leaving for the Mooneys' when he heard his mother call up to him: "Father McGuire has just come in and wants to talk to you."

Brian did not answer. He could almost see Father McGuire nudge his mother to make her repeat the request.

"Do you hear me, Brian? Father McGuire would like to see you."

"He knows where I am," answered Brian coldly.

There was a moment's pause. Footsteps climbed the stairs up to the landing. There was another pause, and then the door of Brian's room opened and a slight, wiry figure stepped inside. Brian was sitting on the edge of the bed at the time, and Father McGuire sank into a chair in front of the window. The shadow made his face look darker than usual and his eyes and teeth flashed white in contrast.

"I came up to the house several times to see you since your . . . since the raid, but each time you were out."

Brian frowned but did not venture any information. He felt no obligation to supply it to Father McGuire or to anyone else.

"I can easily understand how it must have hurt you, Brian," went on Father McGuire. "And I . . ." The priest's voice droned on.

How could he easily understand how much it hurt to see your brother dying in his own blood? Did he think that he was taking me in with that pious blether?

"It's all over now, of course. Nothing can undo the past. I can only ask that you try to accept it as God's holy will."

God's holy will! They were always dishing out that! God's holy will! Was it God's holy will that sent into the house a gang of cutthroats? Was it God's holy will to see Sean slaughtered? God must have had the grand time that night chucking around His holy will! This was one he would always remember: God's holy will!

"No use closing up over it. No use brooding over it. Offer up our own suffering in this terrible tragedy for Sean's soul. It will obtain God's mercy for him and make him more ready for heaven."

In case you don't know, Father, my brother Sean was as ready for heaven as you'll *ever be. What he did he always did for some-one else's good. Though what he got from that, nobody can tell. Wouldn't you like to hear the plans I have for God's holy will in a week or so!*

"I am well aware that this is hardly the best time to talk of forgiving one's enemies, Brian, but we have to try. I know how difficult, how bitter that is, but we must try to put away all thoughts of hate and revenge. And yet, to tell you frankly, you look like a man who had revenge in mind. That would not be like the old Brian Tracey I used to know. Right?"

Right or wrong, you'll go on talking. That's your business. Talk. Talk. Talk. Talk. Blast you, man! Why don't you get out of here and leave me alone? Can't you see I don't want to talk? Can't you see I want to be left alone?

" 'Vengeance is mine, saith the Lord.' If you look for vengeance now with a gun in your hand you won't be one whit better than the Specials. In fact, you'd be just another Special. You'd even be worse, for you've been brought up in the Faith and you know where your duty lies. They don't. You'd be a traitor to the very cause you think you'd be defending."

So the old fox has smelled out something! You don't miss much, do you? But if you think you can change me with all your blether! . . .

"Dammit, Brian, I'm talking to you! Say something! You sit there like a stubborn mule! You look like a different man! What has happened to the old Brian I used to know? You make me feel like taking you in my bare hands and shaking the life out of you! Oh, you needn't glare at me. I could and would do it if I thought it would do any good!"

Hold yourself in a little longer, Brian. He'll be going soon. That's also part of God's holy will!

"If you won't say anything there's nothing I can do about it. Only I warn you, Brian. If you do seek revenge, you're the one that will pay the heaviest price for it. So long, now, and God bless you! If you need me my hours these days are from twelve to twelve." Father McGuire traced a circle with his forefinger and smiled.

Brian watched the tall silhouette rise and leave the room. He heard him go down the stairs lightly and quickly and waited until the people chorused a "Good night, Father!" Then he, too, rose and went downstairs. Uncaring of the curious glances of the people, he walked over to the door of the death room and for a long time stood with his arms folded, staring at the corpse. Then he turned abruptly on his heel and left the house.

15

Brian roughly pulled his hat down tighter as he hurried along for it was a wild, blowy night. He scarcely noticed the clouds scudding across the moon and polishing the stars so that they shone brilliant and clear against the opal wasteland of the sky. When the moon was covered he could not see the other side of the street, for it was now two hours past curfew. The people had withdrawn from their front rooms, not a glimmer of light showed anywhere, and the houses seemed asleep.

No movement was expected on the streets so long after curfew, but from the position Brian took up in an open doorway at the top of Raglan Street, he heard a bicycle wheel past, not on the smooth surface of the roadway, but on the cobbled footpath, and its tires ribbed softly over the stones. It would turn into St. Peter's School yard at the corner of Raglan Street, he knew, where Raglan Street ended and split up into two other streets.

That was the signal for him and several other men to go round to the entries separating one row of houses from another and tap the backdoors of the houses that gave into Raglan Street. Some of the people answered at once, some tardily, but all answered. They knew who the tapping on the window would be from. No one else would dare go into those entries.

Brian found no satisfaction in rousing these scared people out of their beds in the dead of night. He was no Special, no gunman anticipating the night of shooting that lay ahead. He was carrying out a personal mission: to avenge his brother's death. All through the weeks of preparation since the days when he had first gone to the Huts he had neither swerved nor let himself be swerved from his intent. He was not taking whatever risks the night might hold for him for the "cause." He was settling a personal account with the Specials. So coldly bent was he on this there had been moments when he honestly felt he could face death itself to settle it. It mattered not who else might be involved or what their intentions were. He was in this for one purpose only. He was even oddly unconcerned about the fate of his comrades in the coming battle.

"I'm sorry, Granny," he apologized to the old woman who opened the first door. He held his hand over a flashlight and it glowed through his fingers and showed the red of the flesh and the dark outlines of the bones. "Going to be trouble here tonight. You'd better move across the way. They're waiting for you with a nice hot mug of tea and a bun."

The old woman before him was crooked with age and there was a pungent, sweet smell of snuff about her. She sniffed and seized Brian's arm so tightly he felt the sharp points of the fingers and thumb claw into his arm.

"God bless ye, child," she croaked. "It must be hard on ye to leave your home on nights like these. But it's all for aul' Ireland! I'll do whatever ye want, but I suppose the best thing an aul' body like me can do is to get out o' your way and pray."

She called sharply over her shoulder into the lighted house: "Come on down, the lot o' ye!"

Brian went past her into the house and all at once felt foolish brandishing a pistol in front of the young couple and the small boy and girl who came downstairs, hurriedly dressed. The little girl had jet-black curly hair and soft, dark, wondering eyes. At the sight of her something stirred within him. He drew a deep breath.

Mother of God, he thought, how I'd love to have a child like that! I'd spend the rest of my life taking care of her! . . . Oh, why was everything so wrong? Why? Why? Why? In subdued fury he slapped the barrel of his revolver against the palm of his hand. At this the child's soft eyes opened wide and she backed away, and the movement twisted the sword in Brian's soul. Impulsively he reached forward, drew the child to him, and wrapped his arms around her.

"I didn't mean to upset you, darling," he said.

The soft, warm little body trembled in his arms as he crushed it to him. Frightened, the child struggled to free herself and, when Brian released her, ran lightly cross the entry after her brother. Brian's eyes did not leave her until she disappeared into the house where the family was to pass the night. Then he turned to the parents.

"Put out that light," he said brusquely. "Nobody will bother the place while you're away."

The man went inside again, turned out the kitchen light, and jerked his thumb inquiringly at the kitchen door. Brian shook his head. An open door meant a friendly door. The man hurried across the entry and disappeared.

One of the houses in his section was completely dark. Brian's fingernails drummed on the window.

"Whozzat?" whispered someone.

"As if you didn't know," said Brian dryly.

"Who is it?" the voice insisted.

"Brian Tracey."

"Password?"

"Sarsfield's the word." The name and the phrase of the historic Irish hero, Patrick Sarsfield, had come to the men spontaneously as the ideal password for their undertaking.

"They trained you well, Mole," said Brian as he moved past the man who held open the door and went inside. He dimmed his flashlight to light himself upstairs.

"Who's that?" said another voice when he was halfway up.

"Och, it's me," said Brain, impatiently this time. "If I got past the Mole, *you* needn't be afraid."

"The Mole's doin' all right," said the voice in the dark.

"Can't be too careful with this baby in the house," added another voice.

"I hope it works," said Brian.

"If anybody can make it work"—Curly Downey moved into

view—"it's yourself, Brian. I hear you read a British Army Manual on how to handle it."

Brian flashed his lamp once on the subject of their attention. In a corner of the room a dark blanket covered something the shape of a large telescope, and one foot of a heavy metal tripod stuck out beneath the trailing ends of the blanket.

He sat down on the floor and leaned against the wall. The other two began to talk in low tones, but Brian did not join them. He did not want to talk. He wanted to be with himself. Since Sean's death three weeks ago he had had little time to think out things for himself, and it was only now that the strangeness of his position struck him. Was this a dream? Was he really in this? Were Curly Downey, Mole Finnegan, and Humpy Dwyer in it? He had played with the three of them for years. As late as last week they had gone to the pictures together, and until recently there had been very little out of the ordinary in their lives. Now they were tense and waiting to ambush a convoy of Specials in Raglan Street. They were waiting to shower death on their victims and to face, in turn, a hail of bullets that could smash the life out of themselves. It was fantastic. One of them might be killed. Killed? *One* of them. Would *he* be the one to feel the red-hot bullet sear into him, burst inside him, and shatter his whole being? He cringed within himself. God! How he feared to be hit! How he feared to die! . . . Even after the ambush, if nothing happened to him, would he be a marked man? If he left Belfast would the Specials follow him?

At home Mum and Dad would be in bed. There was nobody else at home now except Mum and Dad. He had told them that he would be out picketing and that did not worry them any more. They felt even less anxious then than when he or Paul slept at home. He wondered where Paul was at this moment. Paul never said anything about where he went when he left the house. Brian had asked him where he had been the night Sean had died.

"On the job," Paul had answered.

"What job?" Brian had insisted.

"You mind your business," had replied Paul, "and I'll mind mine!"

He might be picketing at night or he might just be getting out of the house. But Sean . . . Ah! If Sean were alive! He'd be in the thick of tonight's business. Unlike himself, however, Sean would find zest in the adventure, would enter into the fray with the mind and heart and arm of a crusader. And he would have closely guarded the secret. Oh! Sean was always the great one for guarding secrets! Brian recalled how one day he had casually asked Sean about his activities in the I.R.A.

"I'm not supposed to talk about this," Sean had replied very seriously despite Brian's smile. "Not even to my own brother." Sean was a great kid altogether! But now Sean was dead.

Brian began to think back to the day the trouble had started in the shipyards. A long while before that he and Clute Wilson had been talking during lunch hour about the fighting in the South.

"Brian," Clute had told him, "I read in the paper that if the Catholics in the South win they'll come up and start persecuting the Protestants in the North. We're scared about the Catholics, not of fellows like you, but of the bitter ones. Some nights I stay awake and listen to the sounds in the street and wonder if anything will happen to any of my family. Believe me, Brian, I don't hate anybody, but the man that touches my family is a dead duck!"

"All right! All right!" Brian had said with friendly impatience. "Nobody is going to touch nobody! You and our Sean give me the willies! He tells me what the Protestants are going to do to us; now you're telling me what the Catholics are going to do to you. Wave one flag in front of you and another in front of him and whoops!—off you go! Why don't both of you grow up?"

Brian had always thought that way. He had never had any wish to see men at each other's throats, to see blood spilled. Even in the country when he went to hunt, before starting out he had always felt a slight qualm about killing, which soon left him, however, in the excitement of the chase. When he had been caught up in the senseless riots in the shipyard, he had been averse to taking sides. He had had some doubt as to the justice of the Protestant cause, and this doubt had increased in the events that followed, but he had persevered in his hope that the better elements on each side would eventually make themselves felt and the riots would die down. He had discussed this over and over again with Clute who saw things exactly the way Brian did and was equally convinced that both sides would soon come to their senses. Then the Specials had stepped in; then they had killed his brother Sean; Sean, his Sean. And the horrible way they had killed him. He'd never forgive them for that. He'd . . .

Suddenly the moon wrested free of the heavy clouds which held her captive, and as she raced away from them, Brian saw her sad, sad face, and across her brow still clung the veil-like remnant of a cloud. It made him think of the face of a widow in mourning. A widow in mourning . . . Sheila . . . Sheila would mourn for him. The knot on his forehead that gathered there often nowadays dissolved at this reflection and his lips softened into a smile. After this night's work, he promised himself, he'd go back to the farm and never put his foot on city soil again. . . . A widow in mourning . . . All at once his daydreaming ceased and he sat up, his body taut. Like the flash of blue-white light the moon now shed on him through the framework of the window, he saw clearly what he was about to do. He was about to attack a convoy in which might be some man like Clute, and that man would be thinking of *his* plans for the future, *his* plans for his home. Suppose he killed that man tonight . . . he'd be a murderer! He sucked in his breath. A murderer! Could he ever live in peace again with himself if he killed such a man?

The night after Sean's funeral, when his brother's friends had marched four abreast behind the hearse in open defiance of the police, he had sat brooding before the fire. For a moment he had worried for having allowed himself to be persuaded while half drunk to join the I.R.A. But this momentary anxiety had not shaken him in his resolve to avenge Sean's death, and the only way he had been able to see of carrying out that resolve had lain through the I.R.A. Tired and dispirited, he had risen from the cold, dying fire and climbed the stairs to bed. On the way up he had tiptoed past Sean's empty room.

The remembrance of the scene at Sean's bedside called up before him the white face and wounded body of his brother lying still and cold on the bed, and he saw himself again weeping beside it on the night of the murder. The face of his brother disappeared and in its place appeared the indistinguishable features of a stranger. Brian's conscience told him it was the man he would kill tonight. Instead of himself sitting by the bed, he saw a second stranger who was weeping over the second corpse as he had wept at the thought of what had been done to one he loved.

In agitation Brian now stood up, determined to rush out into the night and disappear, leaving the I.R.A. and the Specials to carry on their struggle without him. Their world of violence and hate was not for him. They would not drag him into it. He now understood—oh, so clearly!—that the pit dug by Cain was yawning at his feet and he was falling headlong into it. Vengeance only called for further vengeance; blood only spilled more blood! But how could he stand aloof and see these sons of Satan, the Specials, go unpunished for their crime? God's curse upon them for having sped him along a course of anger, hate, and blood! He would run away and leave them all, Catholics, Protestants, I.R.A., and Specials, to save or damn themselves, help or destroy each other! He moved as quickly across the room as the darkness would allow and seized the handle of the door . . . and at that moment a shot rang out, shattering the silence of the street and cutting off instantaneously the flood stream of his jumbled thoughts and emotions. He stopped, trembling and expectant. Stray shots in the night were common, and it could mean merely that somewhere a picket was alert. A second shot split the echo of the first.

"That's it!" he said, not knowing whether he had said it to himself or to the others. He was almost glad that the night's work had begun and taken off his shoulders the necessity of making a decision. That part of him that was turmoil closed itself off from the world. He assumed a brisk exterior.

The men, too, had waited nearly a week for this moment, and all during that time tension had been mounting. Indeed, some of them had begun to drink, adding to the danger of disclosure. They also were anxious to start the night's work and get it over with.

"Two shots means they're leaving the barracks," said Brian.

"What we have to worry about is whether they'll come up Albert Street and along Raglan Street as we were told they would."

"And if they get wind of the ambush?"

"Then my plan, all our plans go up in smoke," said Brian. "Listen!"

Bicycle wheels whirred past the door again, and as they went the cyclist blew softly and sweetly on a bird warbler, and the sound of the warbler grew fainter and fainter as the cyclist went up the street until it finally ceased.

"They're coming this way."

"Not a move until we get the final signal," warned Brian. "After that we're on our own."

A faint droning sound crept into his ken more and more distinctly, the quiet and unmistakable sound of an engine. It was followed by the rattle of a cage.

"They're here!" said Humpy. Up to now Brian noticed that Humpy had been the least conspicuous member of the crew, sitting with his oversized shoulders hunched up against the wall and his head sunk on his chest. Brian suspected he had been nursing his fears. Now he began to hop around the room like a boy.

Brian kept his eyes glued to the corner of Raglan and Albert streets, and when the moon shed its intermittent light he made out the dark and indistinct form of a vehicle turning left into Raglan Street. When it came near enough for him to recognize it, he saw it, black, squat, dangerous, crawling noiselessly up on its prey. It looked as mean as a panther and its headlights were yellow slits that glinted wickedly. At the sight of it Brian was so stricken with fear he scarcely heard the rasping sound of changing gears as one vehicle after another ended the climb of Albert Street and wheeled onto the level ground of Raglan Street: a whippet, two cages, another whippet, three more cages, and a third whippet in the rear. The plan of the Specials, Brian had been told, was to seal off Raglan Street for an all-night house-to-house search for suspects and arms, in their biggest raid so far.

Brian's skin tightened at the top of his scalp and tingled down his back and from there down to his toes. Waves of hot and cold passed up and down him, oddly reminding him of the winds that played about his body when he stripped for a swim in the river at Drumree. As the convoy moved up the street, he drew a deep breath or two and his taut skin slowly loosened again and his fright began to dissolve. And as the fear left him, a totally unexpected wave of exultation swept over him. How odd, he told himself, that this should happen to him in the midst of danger. Something his father had once told him as a boy now came back to him, to the effect that an Irishman always drowned fear in drink or the rapture of battle. Whatever had happened to him, he was no longer afraid.

"I'm ready for anything now!" he said, as he thought to himself. But he saw his companions turn to look at him and he was glad that the darkness hid his blush.

By now the convoy had reached about one third of the long street. Suddenly the street lamps, always kept turned off by the pickets, lit up, and Brian had the impression that he was witnessing some eerie fireworks display. The lamps enveloped the convoy in a yellow aura that had a ghostlike quality, since it was the only lighted area in the neighborhood. For one brief moment everything stood still and was imprinted forever in Brian's memory. Then the lamps went out.

16

A burst of fire smashed against the sides of the vehicles, and two heavy detonations roared above the sound of the shots, shaking the floor under Brian's feet and rattling the windows in front of him. That was the mines going up. He wondered how they could have laid them in the street and kept it a secret. A second burst, machine-gun fire this time, made some part of his dazed self suppose this came from the convoy.

"When do we start, Brian?"

Surprised that anyone else was near, he turned and saw Curly's silhouette.

"Hold on, Curly." The words were his but not the voice. "The convoy can't go forward now because of the mines, and the mines in the side streets'll go up, too, if they try that way out. They can only wheel round and back down Raglan Street. That's where we come in. Listen to those gears! They're trying to get out in a hurry!"

The gunfire was continuous now and frequent explosions lighted up for an instant patches of the total scene. There was also at first a crisscrossing play of searchlights from the vehicles. But one by one Brian heard them being smashed out of existence, and the sound of the breaking lenses mingled with the leisurely, musical tinkle of glass falling from broken windows.

"Ready!" said Brian.

He took out his flash lamp and flashed it down on the street. The weak beam of white light struck the whippet at the head of the convoy which by this time had turned round and was moving back toward Albert Street.

Brian knew that the moment had come to bring into play his closely guarded secret. In the light of his torch he crossed over to a corner of the room and with the others' help dragged the blanket-draped, heavy tripod rumblingly to the center of the floor. With an upward flourish he swept off the blanket, revealing a small fieldpiece. The house they now occupied had been left empty for weeks while he and the others had carried the gun there part by part and reassembled it in the room. They had replaced the gun carriage with a tripod and extension of steel piping.

Under his directions they now placed the gun at the open window with the muzzle facing the street. "Direct fire," he said, using self-consciously a term he had learned from the manual.

The gun reminded Brian of some sort of scrawny three-legged bird, and looking at it, he remembered the one task for which he had come, for which he had joined the I.R.A. He had thought of doing many things, even of stepping out and throwing a grenade at the first whippet to halt the convoy: certain death, he had been told curtly, and a useless sacrifice. He had volunteered to set off the land mines: they were already in expert hands. Finally one night as he lay in bed thinking of what he could do he had hit upon the idea of the fieldpiece.

He had explained his plan to the men in charge of the ambush and they had agreed to let him try. The next task had been to find the gun. The I.R.A had been unable to help. Brian had thought of raiding some armory, but things were now too well guarded. He had almost given up the idea, until one day, passing the headquarters of the British Legion, he had seen standing on the square patch of lawn in front of the house a war trophy, an old two-pounder, the breech-block of which had been removed and the muzzle plugged. A few nights later he and his three friends had unscrewed the gun from the wheel base and had made off with it in a borrowed car.

For the next week Brian had been so completely absorbed in repairing the gun he had almost lost sight of his original intention.

But each time he passed Sean's empty room and stood over the spot where he had seen Sean lying dead in his own blood, the brooding fury burned anew. Some vintage shells had been supplied by the organization, and one night in the hills back of the Glen Road they had tried out the gun. After a quick, successful trial they had hurriedly packed it off in a car again before the Specials could have time to explore. The moment had now come to use it. It was the moment of his vengeance on the Specials for having killed his brother Sean, and he gloried in the destruction he was about to cause.

"Get the ammo," he said, handing the flash lamp to Humpy.

Humpy shone his torch while Curly knelt down, put his arm under a dresser, and pulled out a shallow, oblong box with rope handles. He dragged this over to the gun, lifted off the lid, and Brian saw six smooth, pointed shells glinting dully. He watched Curly take up one shell very gingerly in both hands and pass it on to Humpy, who took it from him nonchalantly and slid it easily into the breech. Brian slammed home the breech-block and knelt down behind the gun to aim, with Humpy and Curly on either side.

"Grab the lanyard, Humpy," said Brian. "And when I tell you, pull quick and pull hard. Stand clear, everybody." Humpy slid the cord along his palm until the ball of his hand stopped at the knot on the end. Brian set his sights on the slow-moving whippet in the lead.

"Fire!" he cried, jumping away and jabbing his fingers quickly to his ears.

Humpy closed his eyes and gave the cord a strong tug. A blinding scarlet flash, a roar, and the gun recoiled past him several feet. Opening his eyes an instant later—he was anxious to miss nothing—he rushed to the window ledge, peered over, and saw the whippet lift on its side, right itself, move on for a few more yards, and grind finally to a stop.

Humpy's shadow danced grotesquely in front of the window. Brian guessed he was shouting something, but the roar of the gun in the small room had deafened him.

Seconds later there was a crashing, spattering sound, and a burst of machine-gun bullets sprayed the brickwork and the window and the ceiling of the room above their heads. In the brief silence that followed Brian heard the plaster dropping to the floor like the murmur of a quiet waterfall. Peering again over the window ledge, he realized that had the cage behind not crashed headlong into the suddenly halted whippet, upsetting the gunner's aim, the hail of bullets would not have sprayed the ceiling above their heads.

From where he was Brian guessed he could easily have fired almost directly into the cage. But he motioned the others not to rise from the floor. Only after what seemed a long time did he signal them to set up the gun again. They dragged it back to the window.

"The machine gun," he said, no longer in a whisper. There was no danger of his voice rising above the din of the gun battle now being fought the length of Raglan Street.

The same preparations as before; a moment of suspense; a sudden tug. For the second time a scarlet flash, a roar, the gun recoiled to the back of the room, and for the second time there was a wild burst of machine-gun fire from the whippet. After the third shell there was no reply from the machine gun. He hazarded another glance over the chipped window ledge to see why.

The third shell had struck the turret of the whippet, jamming it. From the jerky movements of the machine gun, Brian guessed that the gunner was trying to pull the turret around but in desperation was also squeezing the trigger and shooting a stream of bullets high over the roof. They wouldn't do much harm in that direction, he reflected.

They fired two more of the remaining three shells without, as far as Brian could see, causing any damage. The other vehicles were now too far away, Brian said, for "direct fire" to be effective. Either that or the shock of the firing had shaken the gun loose, impairing its efficiency. Brian did not know.

While he was wondering what to do next, there was another deafening roar that he judged to be somewhere near the school. The battle went on between the men trapped in the vehicles and the ambushers hidden in the houses or on the roof tops. He took another peek up the road and saw, about twenty yards farther on, a cage and a whippet pitched forward oddly to one side. Again he marveled how the I.R.A. could have mined the middle of the road and still have kept it secret.

"They're making a run for it!" said Curly suddenly. Brian looked down at one cage as the iron door at the back swung open with a loud clang. A dark figure dropped to the ground, dashed to the opposite side of the street, and flung himself on his face, hugging the wall. He was followed by three or four others, and a burst of shots was fired in their direction. The side door of the disabled whippet now creaked open. To Brian there was something tragic in the lone figure that emerged and half limped, half ran to the sidewalk, where, like the others, he threw himself on the ground.

The Specials who had reached the far side of the road had begun to fire into the houses. Brian guessed they were trying to cover their escape up the side streets. The Special from the whippet rose to his feet and limped a few paces up the side street. A single shot snapped out from somewhere and, like a man met by a strong wind, the Special retreated backward a step or two and fell.

The lights went on in the street.

"You haven't a chance," a voice called out through a megaphone from the direction of the school. It sounded like Seamus McKenna, the man who had spoken at the Huts. "Put down your arms."

The lights went off again. A long silence followed.

Finally someone answered from the convoy: "All right. What do we do?"

"Get out of the cars and stand face to the wall with your hands above your heads."

Brian heard the dull thuds of the wooden butts of rifles and the sharper clanks of revolvers as they fell on the floor of the cages and lorries. The lights went on again and this time they stayed on. The Specials began to line up against the wall, their hands raised. Ambushers now poured out of the houses and collected the arms. They also separated four or five Specials wearing Sam Browne belts from the rest and led them up toward the school.

"What's that for?" said Brian.

"Hostages," said Curly.

After that one group of men on the street packed the rest of the Specials inside two or three of the cages and another set to work methodically smashing the guns they could not take away and the engines of the vehicles with sledge hammers.

While this was going on, Brian and the other two dismantled the fieldpiece and loaded it into a car that had been sent from the school for it.

The lights then went out for the last time; the ambushers disappeared in twos and threes, and quiet once more descended on Raglan Street, leaving it, thought Brian, as he and Curly walked away, a thing jagged and torn, like the body of a fox cornered in the hunt, wounded in many places.

That night he did not go home. He went instead to a friend's house far removed from Raglan Street where he knew he would be safe. He was made welcome and comfortable but he did not fall asleep for a long time. When late the next morning he awoke, the bedclothes were lying in a crumpled heap on the floor. He rose, dressed, and had breakfast with the man and his wife. Outside of the usual courtesies there was no conversation. They sensed his mood and he was glad of it.

When he came out of the house he saw that it had rained. The pavement was shining with a dull, steely glitter like the blade of a sword. Everything else was the color of ashes and lead, even the sky. On his way to the center of the city he passed by a newspaper shop and saw a poster leaning against the wall announcing: *Police Smash Belfast's Bloodiest Ambush.*

He did not buy a paper. He had no heart for reconjuring up the horrors he had seen with his own eyes. Besides, he had the feeling that the shopkeeper might recognize him as one of the ambushers. Indeed, half expecting someone to cry out after him, he lowered his head and walked on.

Along the way vivid scenes of the night's battle kept impinging on his memory: the whippet rearing itself on its side after being hit by the shell, the driver of the whippet limping up the side street but being felled by that single shot; the gashed street, and the jagged chassis of the vehicles, their engines smashed, lying like trapped rats with the bowels torn out of them.

Remembering all this, he kept reflecting to himself that he had had his revenge and should feel satisfied. Ever since he had stood in front of his dead brother and made his resolve he had looked forward to this day. Now it had come—and gone. He should feel lighter, he knew; he should even be rejoicing. Yet the only feeling he had now was the heaviness of guilt. He had spent his passion and was empty, and there was no joy in him. He would have liked to have been able to go apart somewhere and grieve over what his enemies had done to him. Tears, he felt, might have afforded him some relief. But he could not weep; he was too dry, and dull, and spent. He had used up too much of himself, building up the fires of hate and urging himself on, before and during the battle, to the fulfillment of his revenge. Now he had nothing left, nothing but the weight of guilt.

By this time he had reached the bottom of the Falls Road and he turned up Chapel Lane, taking a short cut to North Street where the bus depot lay. On the way he had to pass St. Mary's. The sight of the little church with its blackened-brick, Romanesque façade brought back to him the day he had arrived in Belfast. His father then had told him how it had been built by the United Irishmen, a group of Protestant patriots who had helped their Catholic countrymen toward emancipation. It was doubly sad for him to remember now those early days, when it had broken his heart to leave the farm, and at the same time to reflect on how few Irish Protestants today would fight for Catholic Irishmen. They would rather burn a Catholic chapel—he remembered what his uncle Jamie had said that day—than build one.

As he approached St. Mary's he saw the people passing in and out for visits. The thought struck him that if he went to confession the mere routine might afford him some relief, the mere motions of the sacrament might somehow clear his conscience. At least it would give him consolation. He would be thankful even for that.

Inside the church he debated with himself for an instant if the emptiness in him were not, after all, the sorrow that was required for absolution. But he brushed aside the thought. The emptiness he felt was emptiness, nothing more. Perhaps sorrow would come later. It would at least be easy for him *now* to promise "never to do it again." He would never need to do it again.

Even at that early hour a dull light glowed over one of the confessionals. He walked up to it and drew aside the heavy curtain.

"Forgive me, Father, for I have sinned. It's been about a month since my last confession and since then I . . ." He finished his ordinary confession and paused.

"Anything else, my son?"

"I was in the ambush last night. We ambushed the Specials."

"Was anybody injured in this action, this ambush?"

"I suppose so, Father."

"Were these men attacking you unjustly so that your own life was in danger?"

"Well . . . not exactly, Father. But we can't wait till they knock us off one by one. The Specials may dress in police uniforms but they're just out to kill the Catholics, to destroy the Faith."

"My child, the Faith has never been destroyed by violence. As for defending it with violence, that's hardly, say, how the early Christians of Rome defended it. They preferred martyrdom."

"Father, it was hundreds of years before *they* got anywhere and thousands of lives were lost! You don't want us to . . ." Brian did not know how to finish adequately. By breaking off, he thought he would be more convincing.

"No, my son, yet look at the value of their sacrifice. God repaid it with the conversion of the Roman Empire and the known world. Perhaps Ireland has a vocation no less grand than that given to Rome—the task of spreading the Faith across the earth. And for such a great vocation do you not think God will ask a great price?"

"Father," said Brian shortly, "I don't want to argue with you, but my brother was a Catholic and they killed him . . ."

Pause.

"Revenge is never self-defense," said the priest quietly. "And only in self-defense can we endanger another's life. Am I to take it that you were in this attack from motives of revenge?"

"You can take it any way you want it!" Brian had to force himself to keep his voice low. He was breathing hard. "You don't seem to know what's going on. If you did you wouldn't be scolding me for fighting the enemies of the Church."

"I'm not scolding you, my son. I'm trying to put before you a thought that may never have occurred to you. Do you believe there is a God?"

"Of course I do, Father."

"Very well, then. You explain to me why a nation as holy as Ireland should be called upon to suffer the way she does."

"Father," Brian said, "give me absolution and let me get out of here."

"Are you sorry for any sins you may have committed against the Fifth Commandment?"

There was no reply.

"You're making it very difficult for me, my son," said the priest gently. "You know I can't give you absolution unless you express sorrow for your sins."

There was another moment of silence on Brian's part.

"Well, listen to this," he finally burst out. "I'm not a damn bit sorry! There you are! They killed my brother and I hope I killed some of them! They're responsible for the trouble I'm in today! And if you want to know the truth, you can keep your absolution. I won't drop dead for the want of it!"

Brian jumped to his feet, gripped the little board in front of the grill, and pressed his fingernails into the wood. He wanted to scream out defiance at the top of his lungs; he wanted to do something desperate against this world that was torturing him, that had plunged its sword into his bowels and was letting the life drain out of him, slowly, calmly, twisting the blade to make sure that every drop of blood was spilled. He wanted to curse, rave, blaspheme, kill. He wanted to annihilate with one vicious, murderous blow this enemy, the world.

Seizing the heavy curtain with both his hands, he pressed it tightly to his temples and, moving it slowly back and forth, wiped the sweat off his brow. Then, in cold, trembling fury, he gathered his strength and rent the curtain from top to bottom. Without waiting to see the effect of what he had done, he hurried drunkenly out of church. Once outside, he walked, walked, walked, until some semblance of calm returned to him. Finally his eye caught a sign pointing to the bus depot, and almost unconsciously he headed for it.

At the bus depot he boarded a bus for Drumree, taking one of the rear seats so that he could see everyone in front. The people who boarded the bus after him were mostly of the farming type, and as Brian calmed down and began to take stock of where he was he noticed that they had an undefinable air of being at peace with themselves. One of them, an old farmer with the brilliant blue eyes of a child, stared at Brian from under a crumpled brown hat, making Brian lower his own gaze self-consciously and wonder if the man had recognized him. He felt easier when the bus moved out of its bay into the city streets and ripped along the wet main road.

He was in no pleasant frame of mind as a gray line of buildings streamed past the window. He had calmed down now and was angry with himself for his recent outburst. It had deprived him of something he now longed for—a lessening of the weight of guilt that lay heavy on him. He shrugged his shoulders uncomfortably. With the revenge he had obtained in the ambush he felt he had cut himself off from the friendship of man, and now, with his rejection of forgiveness, he had cut himself off from the love of God.

The buildings, mostly houses by now, began to thin out, and patches of open field appeared at intervals, as if the earth's fresh, green body were showing through holes in its robes of tattered gray. The streets disappeared and he saw homes standing in lawns; these, too, ended and before him lay long, wide stretches of plowed fields and fields of grain, their emerald green set off by the dark brown earth enriched in color by the rain. For the moment he forgot himself, immersed in admiration of the neat, well-tended farms, and his tired spirit revived at the sight of the patchwork quilts created out of the fields of barley, cabbage, and mangel-wurzels they were growing for cattle feed. He noted the varying shades of green from one field to another and began unconsciously to name the type of grass seed used. A delicate pearl-gray sheen lay over these fields from the raindrops, making the hedges and trees seem darker by contrast, and the gold-and-white cattle stood motionless under the shelter of the trees.

As if in answer to his unspoken wish, the rain stopped and the sun broke through, shaking itself free of hampering clouds that were reluctant to relinquish their hold over the sodden earth. He followed the broad line of sunshine that raced across the face of the land, over homes and farms, rivers and woods, hills and valleys, and his spirits rose as the sun scattered its rays lavishly on the scene, transforming the whole world with its magic, turning the barley and oats to gold, the dark soil to deep amber, and the wet leaves on the trees to pure, shining silver. Even the moisture rose from its damp couch in the valley, and in clouds of mist, like another Salome, danced sensuously in the warm rays of the sun.

Two children dashed out of a house followed by a white collie barking excitedly. Ha, said Brian to himself, the sun has come out again!

How happy children in the country were! he thought. How far away from the world of trouble that marred life in the city! How happy they were to have no understanding of the tragic thing it was to be outside the brotherhood of man and outside the friendship of God. *They* would never plunge themselves into depths of violence or cross into the wasteland of hate. It was a world they would never know; it was a world that he himself wished he had never known.

He was surprised to see so soon places he recognized, and with a start he realized that he was nearing Drumree. A certain uneasiness crept over him, much akin to the uneasiness he had felt as a boy when, for one reason or another, he had failed to prepare for an examination, or when "Spudface" Lavin was in one of her black moods. That apprehension used to lie like a cold stone in the bottom of his stomach and had always killed any pleasure he would have had at accidentally rising, on his way to school, a cocky, rainbow-colored pheasant or startling a squirrel sitting upright on its haunches, its hands joined in prayer. So now the thought that he was approaching the end of a journey that for a brief moment had taken him out of the world of reality into the fairyland of nature dissipated the joy he had just experienced at the sight of the sun breaking through and lighting up the countryside. His somber mood settled on him again when he stopped the bus about half a mile beyond the farm. Retracing his steps across the fields away from the road, so as to enter the farm unobserved, he walked up to the house with the white walls and the blue window frames. When he opened the door Aunt Cathey was there to greet him.

III The Flight

17

"If this isn't a wonderful surprise!" said Cathey. She hugged him so tightly he wondered why. For the first time he noticed that her hair was streaked with gray.

"Anybody home?" he asked.

"Only myself. Meg went to the village and Uncle Jamie is down at the farm. Have you eaten yet?"

"Don't bother about me, Cathey. I'm not hungry."

"Nonsense, Brian darling, you look starved. Sit down and I'll warm up something for you before Meg . . . in half a jiffy."

She went out and Brian sat down on the sofa with hunched shoulders and his hands joined between his thighs. He was like that when she returned with a saucepan of hot meat stew. She prepared the little table and laid out a blue cup and saucer and plate.

When he had topped off his meal with a helping of apple dumpling laced with cloves, he drew back from the table and sucked his teeth in satisfaction. He volunteered to help Cathey put away the dishes, but Cathey insisted that he should take a good rest on the sofa. He sat down on the sofa again, and while she cleared the table he caught her glancing at him from time to time. She took care not to make noise with her work. Finally he stretched out full-length on the sofa and dozed off to sleep.

He was awakened later when Aunt Meg came in. He moved back into a sitting position but did not rise.

"Hello, Aunt Meg," he said.

"What brought you down? Shipyards not started yet?"

"No," said Brian. "Not yet." He lifted the cushion under him and found an old picture magazine. He concentrated on it and she went upstairs.

Jamie came in next. "Well, well!" he greeted Brian cheerfully. "What good wind brought you? You must've smelt the harvest, you aul' divil! Man, she's going to be a bully! If that damned weather doesn't act up like a woman, we'll be sitting on the pig's back. How's things in Belfast?"

"What do you mean?" asked Brian guardedly.

"Has the trouble blown over yet?"

"I don't think so," said Brian.

Meg came downstairs again. "Will you be staying for long?"

"I don't know," said Brian.

"The troubles in the shipyards have upset him," said Cathey. "He needs a rest."

"I'd give my right arm to have you help with the harvest, Brian," said Uncle Jamie. He rubbed his hands briskly together. "Man-alive! She's going to be a bully!"

"I'll think it over," said Brian. The conversation dropped. "I'll take a race down to the farm and see Dinny." He stood up.

"Won't you have a bite first?" asked Jamie. "Cathey is putting on the pot this very minute."

"Oh, I've had something already," said Brian. He caught the quick glance Meg threw at Cathey. "See you down there, Uncle."

He found Dinny in the machine shed where he and Tim were tinkering with the thresher.

"An' if it isn't me bold expert from the city!" Dinny threw his arm around Brian. "You're just in time! We can't get her to run for love nor money. See what you can do with her."

"What's wrong with her?"

"She just won't start. We've been cranking her till our arms bloody well fell off and she just won't start."

"Maybe the plugs need scraping or she may just be flooded. You go up and get something to eat and I'll have her running like a Derby winner by the time you're back."

"You're a clever lad, Brian," said Dinny. "And I hope the little business we have in mind goes through." Pause. "Sheila's been up a coupla times." This remark was casual, but by now Brian had learned to be aware of Dinny's casual remarks. He pretended not to hear. "Where do you keep the toolbox?" he asked, hoping his voice sounded as casual as Dinny's. He bent over the engine of the thresher, aware that Dinny was eying him with curiosity.

Dinny continued unperturbed. "Last time she came I asked her if she was looking for anybody. She tossed her head and for a while said nothing, then it bust out of her: 'There's better fish in the sea,' she said, 'than ever came out of it!' 'What made you think I had him in mind?' I asked her, and boys o' boys! You never saw a prettier blush this side of Drumree!

"'I came down with a message from my father,' she said." Dinny winked at Brian. "She was trying to find her feet again, you see, but the fight was gone out of her. A man or a woman in love never deceived anyone. Well, I'll be after going, Brian. God bless the work." He was about to leave when he stopped and turned around. "Oh, Brian," he said. A deeper red suffused his features and, aware of Brian's searching gaze, he bent down and slapped the dust off the cuffs of his trousers. "Cathey and me has fixed things up for good." He straightened up again. "I've finally made her change her mind about going into the convent. I hated to do it, for she's very good-living and the Sisters had nearly turned her head."

"Congratulations, Dinny," said Brian. "When is it going to be?"

"Oh," said Dinny. "Come Easter time, next year."

"Where are you setting up house?"

"We're buying the wee brick house you used to live in. And my farm will be on the other side of Jamie's land."

"Your farm?" Brian was genuinely surprised. "Then you won't be working for Jamie any more?" He had never imagined Dinny anywhere else except on the Tracey farm. Dinny, Stardust, Turnip . . . all these things went together.

"No," said Dinny slowly. "An' I don't mind telling you, Brian, for you're a grown man now, but I'm more glad than sorry to be leavin' even after all these years. It never was easy to work for a woman like Meg Tracey. Jamie wouldn't be half so bad if she left him alone, but she's a born meddler, and a nasty one at that.

Now it's getting so I just can't take any more aul' guff from her."

"The farm won't be the same without you," said Brian regretfully.

"Mebbe you're right there," Dinny agreed. "Although it's me that says so. Many's the long and hard day I put in on this farm—and loved every minute of it, by God! But things isn't the same any more. Jamie seems to be growin' very bitter about the way Pat and Bridie turned out. They won't lift a finger to help him on the farm. He blames Meg for it all. Now he's saying that if they're not worried about the farm why should he be? He's getting a bit careless about things, and . . ." Here Dinny glanced over his shoulder to see if anyone was watching them. Reassured that no one was, he bent his right elbow and jerked both arm and head back in one quick movement. He lowered his arm again and looked hard at Brian. "Somebody, someone in the family," he said, "will have to do something fast or else the farm will go to blazes."

Brian looked at Dinny, but Dinny changed the subject. "How's you and Sheila coming along anyhow?"

"Oh," said Brian vaguely. "I don't know. I haven't time to bother about that." He saw Dinny watching him closely. "Show me where the toolbox is and I'll get started on your thresher."

That evening at sundown, when he could stay no longer on the farm, Brian had to come in and have supper with the rest of the family. Unlike the meals of other times, this one was rather strained. Brian wondered what had been said about him in his absence, particularly by Meg. After supper he wanted to go to his room, but it had not been readied yet, and while Cathey went upstairs to prepare it he sat reading with the others. Meanwhile the boy arrived with the morning edition of the Belfast newspaper. As was the custom, Uncle Jamie took it first and began to read out the headlines.

He glanced at the first page. "Goddamighty!" he burst out. "Listen to this! 'The bloodiest ambush in Belfast's history!'" He read on, "'Hundreds of armed rebels ambush police convoy in Catholic section of city. Armored vehicles shelled and mined. Gunmen repulsed with heavy losses. Terrorists escape in darkness. Suspects rounded up and scores of arrests made.'" He went on to read the details, and Brian felt a cold sweat breaking out all over him. He tried to steady the book he was holding. He stole a glance, first at Cathey—she kept on knitting—then at Meg. She sat staring into the fire as if she saw something written on the coals.

When Jamie had finished, Cathey put down her knitting and crossed herself. Jamie laid aside the newspaper, went over to the mantelpiece, and began to wind up the clock with jerky, agitated twists of his arm. Brian remembered that they went to bed early in the country. Meg rose, and on the way upstairs she stopped and turned around.

"I hope they won't bring the trouble down here with them from the city," she said pointedly.

The sound of the cuckoo wakened Brian early next morning. At first he marveled at the airy brightness of the room and lay wondering how high the cuckoo's call was. As a boy he had often tried to imitate it, but it had always seemed too high for him. When he went downstairs he was glad that only Cathey was about. She had breakfast waiting for him.

It was a fine, fresh day when he went out and he knew by the warm, early mist clinging to the trees and hedges that they were in for a scorcher, and all at once his heart lightened at the thought of a full day in the fields.

Two young cocks were in the yard a few feet apart, their necks straight out, squaring up. They flew at each other and the force of the impact sent them both straight up into the air in a flurry of feathers and fierce squawks. After one or two of these flights Brian stepped in and shooed them apart. But they still kept eying each other and strutting, Brian thought, like two small boys in a fight.

He rubbed his hands briskly together once or twice, threw back his head to take in a few deep breaths, and then, almost to his own surprise, began to run; and the dull, red sparks flashed from the toe of his boot as it struck the cobblestones, and the noise sent a couple of foraging rabbits scuttling back to their burrows. No matter what, it was good to be back on the farm.

He was brought up suddenly by the sight of a cock pheasant

with a breastful of rainbow feathers, a white neck, and black cap cautiously leaving the shelter of a hedge. The pheasant was crossing the brown ridges of a plowed field when Brian made a sucking noise with his mouth. The pheasant ran a short distance, stopped again, and looked around. Instinct warned him not to rise—a fatal move if there should be a gun. Brian *crock-crocked* loudly this time, and the bird stretched his whole body in a low crouch and, with his feet working like a toy machine, raced with the speed of a hare along the ground to cover.

For the rest of the week Brian lived a busy life and loved it. After a day in the sun he luxuriated in the feeling of tired muscles at night and ran his palms and finger tips together to rouse the dull, pleasurable sting in them from the thistles he had picked up binding sheaves.

During the threshing the machine encircled some field mice, closing them into an ever-tightening circle. The mice finally made a race for life outside the circle. The men who had come to help with the threshing made great sport of killing them, a sport in which Brian did not join. One of the men with a wide sweep of a scythe uncovered a nest of little mice which were still blind. They squeaked in terror. Brian was affected by the sight of the tiny naked creatures lying at the mercy of the reaper. To his horror the man deliberately swept the scythe across the nest and sliced through three or four of the mice, dragging the upper part of their tiny bodies along with it and reddening the golden straw with their blood. The man burst out laughing. Horrified at such callousness, Brian stepped up to the man, drew back his hand, and caught him a resounding blow on the cheek. At first the man was so surprised he did not know where the blow came from. When he recovered he turned around, threw down the scythe, and squared up to Brian. A fight would have started had not the other workers interfered.

The country in summer was filled with pleasant experiences for him. He delighted, for instance, in watching the swallows. To him the essence of all summer days was the sight of a swallow skimming over a sunlit lawn. In the evening a flight of them usually landed on the edge of the brook at the bottom of the Long Field to drink. After dipping their beaks delicately into the water, they took to the wing again and dived about him, for they were used to his presence. The flight of the swallows was always soothing to him after the noisy street-corner sparrows; where the sparrows were garrulous and bold, the swallows were quiet and well mannered. He never tired of hearing the swallows call, as they brushed past him, what sounded like a polite: "Do you want some tea? Do you want some tea?" Their hushed chirping reminded him of the quiet laughter of nuns.

Before he went to bed he would walk up and down his room, stretching luxuriously, throw himself on the bed, and pass his hands over the warm flesh and taut muscles of his calves and thighs, abundantly aware of the current of life coursing through his body. It made him think of the hum of shipyard generators. Turning out the lamp, and with barely a sheet to cover him, he would watch the beams of moonlight move across the room. He never had to wait long for sleep but had only to lie on his back and he would soon catch himself in a snore: then he would turn over on his right side—he had a childish fear of pressing on his heart—and fall asleep. In a way, that was the part he did not like, for the pattern of his dreams rarely changed: crowds, noises, great disorder, and sharp explosions from the bursting of tires or the roar of motorcycle exhausts. . . . His fight was not so much against the noises as against the crowd. In one of many ways he would be with Sheila and the crowd would get between them and they would struggle to be united again, but they would be helpless against the surging masses of people. He would find himself borne farther and farther from her until her face would disappear and only her soft voice would be left whispering in his ear, a voice without a body.

About the middle of the following week he was sitting with the rest of the men at his midday meal of sandwiches and tea when Cathey, who had brought away the utensils, reappeared soon afterward at the gate of the field.

"Brian," she called out, "will you come down here a minute?"

"What's wrong?" he asked as casually as he could, while an uneasy feeling crept over him.

"Your father's here."

"I'll be down right away."

When he reached the house he saw a bicycle leaning against the wall outside the door. Inside Meg and Jamie were talking to his father who was sitting on the sofa. Michael rose to greet him.

"Is this any way to treat your father and mother?" he began abruptly. "It wasn't right to run off like that and leave us so we didn't know what to think. You shouldn't have done it. We thought you might be . . . we didn't know what . . ." He threw his arms around Brian, his hands clutching at him, passing over him, as if he were feeling for signs of a wound. Finally his head sank on Brian's chest.

Meg walked out into the scullery; Jamie dug his thumbs into his vest pockets and stared glumly at the unlit fire. Cathey turned away and shaded her eyes with her hand.

"Maybe you're right, Dad," said Brian slowly, trying to keep a hold on himself. "But I thought that if I didn't tell you you wouldn't have anything to hide if they questioned you."

"Aye, I suppose it was the best thing to do, son," said Michael, steadily now. "But what with Sean . . . your mother and me thought . . ." He groped for his pipe, lit it, and looked out of the window. "Well, never mind that now," he said, taking a deep breath. "Did you get hit?"

"Not a scratch. The papers were all blow."

"How're you doin' down here?"

"Never felt better. I'm putting on weight."

"Thank God and your mother's prayers for that! She doesn't stop praying from morning till night for you . . . and Paul, too."

Meg returned from the scullery and began to pick up the cushions from the chairs. She shook them peevishly. "Maybe I should say this and maybe I shouldn't," she began. "But I don't think it's fair for people to come down here when they're in trouble with the police."

Brian and Michael said nothing. After a short silence Jamie spoke. "There's not much danger in it. Nobody around here knows about his part in the trouble."

"They'll find out sooner or later," said Meg.

"And if they do?" Jamie burst out suddenly. They all looked at him in surprise, but, uncaring, he went on. "Dammit all, woman! He's one of our own flesh and blood! An' now that I am talking I might as well say my piece. I'd like you to know that Brian is a Tracey who loves the farm. There's no better worker than Brian, and God knows, with our own two children faldelahin' in the streets of Dublin, I'd give my right arm to keep him on the farm just now."

Brian knew that if Cathey, his father, and he had not been present, Jamie would never have dared to let himself go in front of Meg. Nevertheless, he was pleased at the outburst for more than one reason. Meg's way of bringing up her two children, Patrick and Bridie, had always been a heartburn to Jamie and the rest of them. She had trained them up so elegantly, Jamie often complained, that now they were too good for the land. And that was no more than the truth, thought Brian, for when Patrick and Bridie had finished school both of them had taken jobs in Dublin and rarely came near the farm. The two of them had not spent more than a week at home that summer, and even then they had not done a stroke of work, but had passed the day telling anybody who had time to listen about the fun they had in the city. They were simply living the life for which she had trained them.

In a way this disappointment in her children was a just punishment on Meg. Moreover, she was now worried, Brian suspected, about the future of the farm, for Jamie was drinking more than he had ever done before and in his less sober moments had sworn he would not let the farm fall out of Tracey hands. Perhaps she was afraid that, if ever anything happened to Jamie, he might see fit to leave the farm to "a Tracey who loved the land." Her dislike of himself, concluded Brian, and her distrust of the growing intimacy between Jamie and himself stemmed from that fear.

"Oh, I don't want you to get the idea that he's not welcome among his own." Meg retrieved herself. It was not the moment to bring up certain objections. She had the four of them against her. "He's very, very welcome," she went on, "but we have a farm and a shop to take care of, and if the Specials ever find out that he's staying here——"

"If they ever do," said Brian, "I won't be here when they come."

18

Two weeks later the harvesting was done, and after that Brian kept himself busy for a while overhauling the machinery on the farm. Finally, however, that, too, came to an end and the burden of idleness began to lie heavy on him. Also, with his usefulness at the farm diminished, Meg's attitude toward him underwent a change. Her animosity to him became more pronounced. Brian felt she did not show her hand too openly only because she knew the others would range against her.

Nevertheless, it was her spirit that predominated in the house, and the thought that she was against him depressed Brian and made him want to keep out of the house as much as possible. On the other hand, there was little left for him to do on the farm, for the regular help was more than sufficient to take care of the few early-autumn chores such as storing the potatoes, repairing roofs and outhouses, clearing drains for the winter, and the like. Even the farm hands noticed he was just hanging around. "Swingin' the lead," Dinny put it jokingly.

He could not seek diversion elsewhere for he did not care to expose himself beyond the limits of the farm. He was anxious to keep his presence in Drumree as little known as possible.

Over and above all this, slowly, imperceptively, to his deep regret, the life and warmth and color of summer withdrew. The quiet of the autumn evening was like the quiet of a summer evening, only it came earlier. Once he had gone out late in the day when the air grew chilly, to gaze upon a whole countryside bursting into autumn fire, noting the smoldering, tinted woods and the trees along the brook that were already aflame and reaching toward the rushing waters. It would not be long now, Brian knew, before these fires would die out and strew over the countryside the gray ashes of dead winter, with only here and there a scattered patch of maple, its leaves stained in blood, until the blood drained from them, leaving them the ivory color of death.

Later the air grew cold and he saw the leaves fall, wild leaves that on a sudden impulse flew earthward from the tall trees like flocks of startled geese winging their way to lands where all was bleak, where everything died. He felt no sympathy for the fainthearted leaves which lost hope at once and fell while they were still green; he did for the braver ones which resisted the sharpening air and the buffeting of the winds until at last they, too, dry and sere, let go their hold on life and were swirled pitilessly about the fields and paths until the rains trapped and pressed them into a sodden, ugly mass. That was when the gaunt, bare figures of the trees, robbed of their thousand tongues, were silent to the invitation of the wind.

All his life autumn had appealed to Brian as much as any of the seasons for its peculiar joys. With this new feeling of unwelcome about the house, however, he now understood that plodding across a field baked hard with the first frost, or walking over rainswept hills, or having a gnawing appetite edged by the cold were pleasant things only when set against the background of the warmth and comfort of a home. For when the wind and the rain in earlier days lost their companionable character and slowly penetrated through him, he could anticipate the cheerful fireside, the tasty food, and the being together again with friends. But now that background was gone and with it that anticipation. On bleak days when he did work outside in the wet and cold there was nothing he could look forward to besides a bite to eat at a table where, despite the comfort of Cathey's presence and Jamie's gruff attempts to make him feel at home, he felt he was an unwanted guest . . . a bite at table and his bed at night with its aloneness and the shelter of the dark.

One raw, gusty day, having no work to do, he covered himself well and went out to watch the wild fowl fly in. They appealed to him, these lonely birds that sought the deserted marshland. On the walk across the country he paused at the top of a hill and, looking down, saw, close to the shelter of a hedge, two wild duck, squatting in a little pool of water the rains had made. They looked so forlorn they made him think of an old couple dressed in drab brown clothes that had been evicted and were without a home.

To his delighted yet sad surprise he noticed that the gale had blown the gulls in from the coast. He had something in common with the gulls and he told himself they were the same ones he had often fed in the shipyards. He found endless pleasure in watching them make fun of the gale. Despite the mighty fury of the wind the gulls played with it, using its very strength to mock it, to soar and swoop and twist and turn against it. Even in the wind's worst rage they sometimes poised in mid-air with insolent calm. Yet to Brian there was nothing comic now about those sea gulls or their battle with the elements, for it somehow reflected his own struggle. Their loneliness in sea and sky and their sad, sad cry strangely affected him that day. As a boy he had believed the legend that the sea gulls were the souls of brave men lost in battle or at sea. He smiled to himself and indulged for a moment in the childish fancy that the soul of Sean could be among them. He waved his arms at them and they called back to him. He sensed the plaintive, human quality in their call, like the cry of a child or a woman in pain, or of someone mourning the death of a loved one. He never could observe sea gulls for any length of time without coming away a little sadder.

That night, in this somber and somewhat bitter mood, before he went to sleep he knelt down without thinking by the bedside and began to say the prayers he had said at night since childhood: the Our Father, the Hail Mary, and what his mother always called the "Glory Be."

"Our Father," he began, "Who art in heaven, hallowed be Thy Name, Thy kingdom come, Thy will be done on earth as it is in Heaven. Give us this day our daily bread and forgive us our trespasses as we forgive those who . . . forgive us our trespasses as we forgive those . . . who . . . as–we–for–give–those–who . . ." He pressed the tips of his fingers into his eyeballs until they hurt; he felt a coolness on his brow as it grew moist; his jaws locked but he forced the words through his teeth: ". . . as–we–for–give–those–who . . ." He jumped to his feet. "I can't ask for forgiveness, until I forgive!" he cried, "And I can never forgive them! I'll always hate them! I'll die hating them!" He paced up and down the room for a while in agitation. Then slowly there grew upon him the suspicion that what he had suffered since Sean's death, that what he was suffering now, was but the punishment of his hating and merely part of God's plan to bring him back. He raised his clenched fist and shook it angrily at the ceiling. But he did not dare utter the blasphemy that had formed on his lips.

The next day Jamie asked him to take a look at the drainage in the lower fields before the heavy rains set in. Glad of the chance to be useful and occupied, he saddled Stardust and rode him at an ambling pace around the limits of the farm, including two new fields that Meg had bought some distance off. While he was out alone with Stardust he began to reflect moodily on his sorry state out of which he could see no escape. His thoughts turned to Sheila. She had not written a word or communicated with him in any way since he had brushed past her at the wake.

He thought he knew why. Sheila could never approve of his attitude. She was of strong convictions, religious and patriotic. He could see her despising him for going into a patriotic action like the ambush in Raglan Street, urged on by the unpatriotic motives of revenge and hate. He could see her avoiding him entirely if she ever found out that he had given up the Faith. The Reillys, father, mother, and daughter, were not ones who knew how to compromise. Despite all this, however, he confessed to himself that he needed her. He needed someone close enough, kind enough, understanding enough, to help him bear this dread loneliness that was overtaking him. And in this no one could take Sheila's place. No one else could understand him even if she disapproved of his motives; no one else could comfort him like her; no one else could drag him from the edge of this pit of despair into which he had a vague fear he was falling. Even now when he thought of her face in repose, of her lovely smile, her gentle, soothing manner, her quiet confidence, his own face softened and the harsher lines that had begun to etch into his features smoothed away. He would not feel so lonely if she were near. He must not let neglect and time raise up a barrier between them, he decided. Later it might become insurmountable. He must not lose her, for if he lost *her!* . . . He would write her a letter tomorrow telling her that he was sorry for all that had happened, beg her forgiveness, and ask if he could see her again for he needed her desperately; he needed her more than anything else in the—— No. He had better not write things like that, because he would have to send the letter up to her through Dinny and he wouldn't put it past Dinny to peek into the letter and read it. He blushed at the possible effect of such a note on Dinny. Instead, he would write a simple note, asking if he could see her again. Dinny couldn't make much out of that, and Sheila would read the rest into it.

When he had finished his ambling tour of inspection and was returning home, Brian saw Dinny halfway up one of the fields doing what he called "some quiet plowing." He decided to broach the subject of Sheila with him. It had been a cold day and the morning frost had crusted the wet earth, whitening the edges of the ponds, but Dinny still wore the same coat, trousers, and greasy, peaked cap he had worn all summer. His only concession to the weather had been to button up his shirt front.

"Man, but you're the tough one, Dinny!" said Brian admiringly. He knew Dinny took pride in his hardiness. "How under God can you stand it?"

"Phff!" Dinny dismissed the matter. "I mind the time I could go without even a coat winter an' summer. But what are you doing around here? You and that aul' fraud?" He stroked Stardust's long muzzle and put his hand in his coat pocket. Stardust's dull eyes lighted up and watched his hand closely. Dinny did not draw it out again, however, but held it there tantalizingly, pretending to talk to Brian. Stardust stretched out his head and nuzzled at the coat pocket. Dinny drew out his hand and showed that it was empty. He tried to stroke Stardust's head with it, but the horse pulled back and shook his mane in disappointment. Dinny laughed. "Niver disappoint a horse or a woman, Brian," he said. "They can't abide it."

This was the moment to bring up the question of Sheila, Brian thought. "Dinny," he began embarrassedly and stopped, distracted for the moment by the sound of a machine groaning faintly in the distance.

"A tractor?" said Dinny, turning his head. "Somebody come into the money?"

Brian turned his head, too, but for a while neither of them could see anything and the sound became more and more distinct, as if the wind were now carrying it in their direction.

"Beyond the ridge," said Dinny suddenly. He pointed north where the Drumree Road branched off the main road. Brian looked and saw a red tractor, like a huge May fly, crawling up a gray-brown field. He kept looking at it, wondering as to its make and power, until his eye caught something else. Three vehicles were moving along the road at what seemed from that distance a very slow pace. The one in front was squat; the other two had high sides, and above the sides Brian thought he could make out the net wire of a cage. The three vehicles raced along the white road until the hedges hid them and the sound of them faded away.

"Specials!" he whispered, half to himself.

"Them must be the new recruits," said Dinny. "Now that the harvesting is over, the Orangemen around will have plenty o' time for that sort o' nonsense."

Brian left Dinny at once and rode back, but the air had become dank and cheerless and he did not have the heart to take the horse for a canter across the Long Field. Instead he brought him to the stable, fed and bedded him, and walked up to the house.

At supper, with the rest, there was not much conversation. Jamie usually had little to say now that life on the farm had slowed down; Meg always confined herself to generalities, as if she were afraid of compromising herself, and it would have been strange to hear Cathey say much in her gentle voice at the table.

"Man, but there was a great to-do at the village today," volunteered Jamie. He waited for someone to ask more.

"What about?" asked Meg, as if she begrudged having to ask.

"A bunch o' young fellas were in the fields and shooting like mad things with rifles and generally arsin' about like scalded hogs. Sergeant Butler says they've started to recruit Specials. They're afraid the trouble in Belfast is going to spill over and spread itself."

"Were there many?" asked Brian.

"I'd say forty or fifty. Butler tells me that a bunch of smart alecs are coming down from Belfast to teach them—"

"That's the way it always is," interrupted Meg. "When the city people come down to the country they bring trouble."

". . . how to handle the whippets and armied cars." Jamie went on as if he had not been interrupted. "But he says they have a . . . that . . . a"—Jamie's reluctance to finish what he was saying caused the others to focus their attention on him. Brian found it difficult to control his breathing—"says that they're on the lookout for fellas on the run."

Brian fell asleep that night and dreamed he was on his motorcycle, letting the engine throb quietly through his whole body. He awoke and the noise of the engine persisted so that he had the odd sensation of thinking that he was still asleep. Suddenly instinct warned him and he sprang out of bed. It was a real engine and it sounded very close. Probably on the road. He heard voices too. They carried farther at night. He stood at the window, tense and listening, until he heard a second engine splutter, burst into a roar that was followed by a rasping of gears, amateurly handled. Then he knew that it was a patrol of some sort and one of the cars had stalled. The two cars drove off again, their engines finally dying away in a protesting whine.

Next morning as soon as he went down to the farm Dinny came over to him.

"Something to tell you, Brian," he whispered.

"You're getting very mysterious, Dinny," said Brian, forcing a smile. "What is it?"

"Do you know the Nelson family that lives on the other side of the river?"

"I've never met them."

"Well, they're Protestants, but fine, brave people. Pete come up to see me this morning. He told me he had heard that the Specials was getting ready to raid the Catholic farmhouses and if we had anything in the way of guns about the house, we were best to hide them. He says, too, you'd better sleep somewhere else the night."

"You're taking good care I won't get caught, Dinny." It was all Brian could say just then for his mouth had suddenly gone dry.

"Don't worry, Brian," said Dinny encouragingly. "You can sleep in the hayloft. Just get a couple of blankets, without letting anybody up there"—he nodded toward the house—"know you're doing it, and I'll fix ye up snug."

After supper that evening Brian dropped two blankets out of his room window, went downstairs, picked them up, and brought them to the farmyard. He climbed the ladder up to the hayloft and, in the light of a stable lamp, found Dinny on his knees in the far corner near the hayloft's only window, spreading a deep layer of hay. He took a blanket from Brian, threw it over the hay, and at the head of the blanket placed a stuffed sack.

"There y'are, me boy!" he said. "If the fleas find out how snug ye are, they'll bite the bottom off ye!" Laying himself down on the hay, he sank deep into it and uttered a loud snore. He opened one eye. "And if the sound of a snortin' horse don't annoy ye," he commented, "ye won't wake up till the loft burns down!"

They both clambered awkwardly down the ladder again; Dinny bade Brian good night and left.

Brian went back to the house and stayed up, reading, until bedtime. He retired a little before the others, put out the lamp in his room, and sat up to wait until they went to bed. When the house was quiet he went downstairs again and slipped out by the back door.

Up in the hayloft he undressed and was placing his revolver under his pillow when he heard a scraping sound on the ladder. A few moments later Turnip's head appeared above the opening.

She cocked her head puppylike at him for a moment, then, with an effort, pulled herself up the ladder all the way and loped over to him, licking his hand and his face with her wet tongue as he lay down, making him laugh. She curled herself up contentedly at the foot of the bed and closed her eyes.

"You were always the great girl for sleep, Turnip," said Brian. "And I suppose you need more now than before." Turnip paid no attention to him and Brian eased himself down into the depths of the hay. A few minutes later he was buried in the warm nest, listening to the rustle of the hay every time he shifted his position and the sound of the horses' labored breathing from the stables below.

Almost immediately afterward, or so it seemed to him, he was awakened by a growl from Turnip. He listened. Nothing. Turnip growled again.

"What the hell's wrong with her?" he asked in annoyance. "Is she having a nightmare or is it more pups?" He pushed his feet down the full length of the bed to feel for her. She wasn't there. Brian rose and hastily pulled on his clothes. He was taking no chances.

Creeaak! The sound immobilized him for a moment. Someone was in the creamery opposite the hayloft. The hinges of the door, rusted by the steam when they scoured the milk cans, had always creaked loudly. "Nobody's looking just for milk at this time," he remarked without humor. Stuffing the revolver in his pocket, he crossed to the little window, pulled it up quietly, eased his legs out first, then his body, and dropped. His feet made only a soft plash on the muddy ground beneath and he felt the bite of icy water penetrate almost immediately to his feet.

Cutting through a hedge, he kept climbing and stumbling up the wooded slope behind the stables until he reached a spot where he thought it was safe to pause. Only then did he stop to look back.

The farmyard was lit up. The Specials—he had no doubts as to who it was—were now searching for him openly. Standing on the road about a hundred yards from the farm gate were a whippet and two tenders. The raiders had left the cars there and had entered the farm on foot to surprise him. They moved from one place to another and he heard the clatter of feet on the cobblestones and a lot of voices. A light danced in the hayloft. They knew now he had escaped.

Turnip suddenly ran out of the stable in a trundling sort of way because of her weight and age and dashed at the legs of the nearest Special. The Special saw her coming and, before she could reach him, pointed his gun at her and fired. Turnip halted in her tracks and lowered her head the way she did when Brian squirted warm milk from the cow's smooth teat in her face. Then she staggered about the yard blindly until the Special strode over, slid his heavy boot under her soft belly, and half kicked, half hoisted her against the whitewashed wall of the creamery, where she lay twitching.

"You didn't have to shoot the beast," Brian heard one Special say.

"I couldn't let her eat me alive, could I?" the other answered.

Brian gripped the handle of his revolver so tightly he could feel each one of the little triangles embossed on the stock. Determined to shoot the man on the spot, he stumbled and slipped down the hillside. But before he was halfway he stopped, realizing that before he even got near the man he would be riddled.

The light in the hayloft went out. A little later it went on again. It was not so bright this time, however. It was a dull light that increased in brightness and suddenly flared up, and it was only then Brian knew that the hayloft was on fire.

All at once he was startled by the neighing of Stardust and the other two frightened horses in the stable below the hayloft where he had slept. He heard the heavy thudding of their hoofs against the doors as they tried to escape the terrifying smoke and flames. The Specials knew what was happening now and he heard them shouting hoarsely. A few minutes later he heard another sound that gladdened him. It was the clatter of horses' hoofs on the cobblestones of the yard. The horses had been freed.

His gladness was soon cut short, however, for the neighing in the stable continued. So did the wild pounding of the hoofs. Someone shouted, "There's another one there!" Brian stiffened.

"A black stallion." Stardust, whispered Brian to himself. "His hoof's caught in the manger and he can't get out. He's going wild with terror! What the hell should we do?"

"Let 'im roast," said another voice calmly.

"If only I had my hands around your throat!" thought Brian.

"Listen," said the first voice. "We'll handle the guns your way, but we'll handle the beasts our way."

"Do what you want," said the calm voice. "Shoot him if it makes you happy."

"If I can get through the smoke, I will. God forgive me if I'd let a dumb beast die like that!"

With a sickening feeling Brian waited. One—two shots. The neighing and pounding ceased. Another shot. And another.

"Why doesn't he stop shooting?" he moaned.

The flames coming from the hayloft, dark at first, changed quickly to bright red, even white at the center. They reached up eagerly, leaping over each other until they pyramided high into the air. At the sight of the leaping flames and the thought of Stardust's violent death something snapped in Brian. Waiting until he saw the Special come out from the stable, he raised a hand that shook with rage, took aim, and fired at him. He must have missed him, for the man kept on walking. He fired again, and this time the Special instantly grasped his left side at his abdomen with both his hands as if he were trying to pull something away from it. Doubling up with pain, he swung round and round, moved over to the wall, leaning his head against it, and then lowered himself to the ground and lay there writhing beside the dead dog.

It was only when the man lay on the ground that the others seemed to awake to what was happening. Brian reflected grimly that it must be a new and startling experience for them to be shot at. In their brief training for their special task they had assumed as if by right the role of conqueror, of hunter, of attacker. To be shot at was something new, unexpected, and not within their scheme of things. They scuttled at once for cover. As they ran Brian fired at them out of sheer defiance, and when they were already under cover he fired again.

Once under cover, however, the Specials had time to gain a

semblance of discipline. Brian heard orders being shouted, and then all at once a volley of shots burst out and he heard the whine of bullets flying overhead and the light zip of bullets imbedding themselves in the trees near him. He ducked and ran through the woods and, now that his rage had subsided, marveled how he had not been riddled as a result of his angry gesture. He debated with himself what he should do and decided that his best chance of escape lay away from the road, across the brook and deeper into the country.

It was then that the top of his left shoulder began to burn. Putting his hand up quickly, with his fingers he felt gingerly around a little tear of his coat. The spot was also damp. "So I've been shot," he told himself, surprised at his own calm. He had often heard men describe the effects of being shot and in the hours before the ambush had cringed at the thought of its happening to him. Now he had been shot and he hadn't even known it at the time. It was not a serious wound, evidently, but he was aware that it could give him trouble if not seen to.

In a matter of minutes, he guessed, the Specials would be fanning out to search for him. This was the sport they loved, the hunt, with scores of them in full cry after one lone man. They would expect him to bear away from the farm toward the east, for that was the direction from which he had shot at them. He decided, therefore, to head west at once and cut behind them. It was difficult to make any sort of progress in the dark through the woods and undergrowth, and every time a branch or twig snapped under his foot he expected the sound to be followed by a hail of bullets. At last the ground began to slope toward the brook, and when he saw the dark reflection of the water he felt he had got behind the Specials safely. The drop from the bank into the brook looked frightening in the dark. He jumped, and in landing—he knew it was only a foot or two—his foot slipped and he fell shivering into the icy water. But almost unheeding of the cold, he crossed the brook and, keeping close to the hedges, pushed on as fast as he could across the fields.

Still walking as quickly as the darkness and the rough ground would allow, he began to wonder what had happened to the others up at the house. The Specials certainly had gone there first to look for him and, not finding him, had guessed he was hiding somewhere on the farm. Turnip's warning had saved him. Poor old Turnip! She had saved his life and then lost her own in a feeble protest against his enemies. He had an impulse to try to get back to the house by a roundabout way to find out what had happened, but decided against it. The Specials would be guarding it at least during the raid. He fervently hoped that his presence at the house would not give the Specials an excuse to wreak their vengeance on the other three. Cathey and Jamie, he knew, would accept whatever befell them at the hands of the Specials with a fortitude born out of their love for him and a sympathy for the cause. But Meg? How would she take whatever damage the Specials had done to the farm? Never having had much love for him, she would hate him now for this. And if anything had happened to her house! . . . In his heart Brian could not feel anything but sympathy for her. Always an ambitious woman, she had spent her whole life in building up her possessions. Her possessions were to her the tangible proofs of her success. He could picture her screaming at him, reviling him for having brought his troubles on her. The thought that he had been the cause of such disaster to his uncle's home lay heavy on him. He sighed wearily, then he turned his attention to finding a place where he could dry his clothes and see to the wound in his shoulder.

19

The first name that came to him was Sheila and her family; the Reillys would certainly be willing to shelter him. But on second thought he decided against that. The Specials might know that the Reillys were more than friends and, if so, would be sure to look there for him. He had brought enough trouble, God knows, on one home already and had no wish to spread the sore. He considered one or two other Catholic families but dismissed them, too, always on account of the danger he might bring on them. But, given the state he was in, he had to go somewhere. In desperation he finally decided to try the Nelsons. Pete Nelson, a Protestant, was the one who had warned him about the Specials. Brian knew him only as a tall, neighborly man with a small, nervous, but good-natured wife and a houseful of children. Since their house was not too near and they were Protestants, Brian reasoned that the Specials would never think of looking for him there. He set out for the Nelsons', fervently hoping that his stay would bring no harm on them if they took him in. A ten-minute trudge over sodden fields brought him to the farmhouse, and somewhere at the back of the house a dog began to bark at his arrival.

Fearing to knock at the door in case the noise might give him away, he took up a handful of gravel and threw it at one of the windows. There was no response to the first quiet swish of the gravel on the glass. On the second try, however, he heard the sound of muffled voices; a light went on, the window was pulled up, and a tall silhouette showed at the window. Pete Nelson peered down and, seeing nothing in the dark, called out: "Who's there?"

"It's one of the Traceys, Mr. Nelson," said Brian. "Brian Tracey, Dinny's friend," he added.

"Oh," said Pete. "Are they after you already?"

"Yes. But I got away," said Brian. "Think I could stay somewhere around here for the night only? My clothes are wringing wet and I've hurt my shoulder. If I go anywhere else they're sure to find me."

Pete turned to someone in the room and a muffled conversation went on. This time the window was open and Brian heard the woman say: "But it'll scare the children to death if they know there's a Catholic in the house!" The woman's words hurt Brian. They made him aware that the city poison, like the huge black, bilious mouthfuls of smoke the chimneys coughed up from pouted lips to pollute the sky, had drifted out to the land. Pete protested. Then: "All right," the woman answered. "But don't let the children see him." Nelson turned round again. "I'm coming down," he said.

Minutes later Brian was out of the rain and the cold and sat in the comfortable kitchen of the house drinking the sweet, hot cocoa Pete pressed on him. Pete started the kitchen fire again and in front of it hung Brian's clothes on chairs to dry. He also bathed the wound, calling it a nasty gash, and covered it with a rough lump of cotton wool held down by sticking plaster—the same things, Brian noted, that his mother years ago had put on Clute's cheek. After that he showed Brian an empty spare room and a cot which he quickly arranged and set up for him.

"Don't get up till I call you," he told Brian. "I don't want any of the children to see you. They'd either get scared or start talking. Besides, I want to make sure the road is clear before you leave. Good night, now, son, and God bless you."

With a troubled heart Brian lay down to rest on that strange bed, listening to the Nelsons taking up again the muffled conversation before they settled back to sleep, and the barking of their dog that was answered by another dog somewhere in the night. At last, however, the sound of conversation died away and the barking of the dogs came at longer intervals, until it ceased altogether and Brian slipped into oblivion.

The house was astir next morning when he awoke, and the first thing he was conscious of was the ache in his left shoulder. He remembered Nelson's advice and did not rise but lay on, looking out at a gray sky swollen with rain clouds and wondering what he would do that day. There seemed to be nothing ahead of him now but to keep moving away from the Specials. But keep moving to where?

When later Nelson knocked at the door he rose and was soon sitting down to a stout breakfast prepared for him by Mrs. Nelson. Once the children were off to school and out of danger, observed Brian wryly to himself, thinking of the woman's remark of the night before, the nervous little woman showered him with sympathy and attention. Meanwhile Pete Nelson went out to explore. He was gone for almost an hour, and when he returned his long, bony face was set and grim. He told Brian that he had found the Tracey house still guarded by a group of Specials and a tender standing in the yard. The Specials had raised no objection when he had gone inside. But before going in he had noticed that one of the door panels had been smashed. He had entered the house and had been shaken by what he had seen. The place was a shambles, he said, uprooted floor boards . . . broken crockery . . . slashed wallpaper . . . ripped-up mattresses. . . .

Jamie had told him what had happened. He had been wakened by the headlights of the whippet and the Crosley tender as the cars swung off the Drumree Road down the lane to the house. Even before the cars had stopped the men had jumped out, with hardly any sound, and had surrounded the house.

A rifle butt had hammered against the door until he had pulled on his trousers and opened it. The men had brushed past him and gone inside.

Cathey had been with them when they had searched Brian's room.

"Who sleeps here?"

"Nobody," she had told them.

"What do you mean, 'nobody'? This room has been slept in recently. Who was it?"

"One of the boys who helps on the farm."

"What's he like?"

"Tall and thin with blond hair," Cathey had told them. "With glasses."

They had called her names and then, angered by Brian's escape, had taken their revenge on the house. Meg had acted like hell let loose, Pete said, when they had started, screaming and cursing them and tearing at them with her nails until they had grabbed her and locked her in her room. When the Specials had left, Meg had cried most of the night, Cathey had gone upstairs to pray, and Jamie himself had stayed up, staring into the smoldering embers of the fire.

When Meg had learned that Pete had just come from Brian she had acted up again, Pete said, abusing Brian and blaming him for what had happened.

"Don't let him dare put his foot in this house again," she had shouted. "For if he does I will go right up to the Specials myself and tell them where he is!"

Pete said that when he had come out of the house the tender had gone but one or two Specials were still on guard. He had seen no other Specials anywhere else.

Brian got ready to leave.

"Where will you go?" said Pete.

"Oh," said Brian vaguely, "I'll go to a friend's house a few miles off."

As he was leaving Mrs. Nelson asked him where his overcoat was and Brian told her that he didn't have one. Telling him to wait, she hurried into one of the rooms and returned with a used overcoat of her husband's, insisting that Brian wear it. Brian thanked her, and as he left the tears started to her eyes.

Nelson accompanied him for a short distance across the fields, and when it came time to leave he pressed something into Brian's hand. Brian looked at it: two crumpled pound notes. He refused to accept them. It was a deal of money, he said, and the Nelsons needed all they had.

"Take them, son," urged Nelson. "God knows you'll need them more than we do. You can pay me back some other time. And . . . and . . . try not to think so hard of us Protestants. We have good ones and bad ones, like everybody else."

Since he could not go south, for the border, he imagined, would be thick with Specials, Brian decided to head for the coast. There, he told himself vaguely, he might get a job on one of the boats. He would have to do it on foot, for he was afraid to ask for a lift. He might ask the wrong person, and besides, he would have to keep off the roads, away from the patrolling tenders and whippets. Twice that day he stopped at eating places, and to nurse the two pounds Nelson had given him he took as much of the free bread and butter as he could and ordered a cheap, filling dish. When he left the second eating place, it was already dark and he made his way across open country, intending to sneak into the first hayloft.

The rain came down soon afterward and caught him while he was crossing a wide stretch of farm land that offered no shelter other than the low hedges. It began at first with a slight drizzle, and Brian smelled the dust rising from the dry earth. Then it increased until it became a heavy downpour. In the beginning it made no sound, but soon it had beaten the earth flat and smooth and Brian could hear the heavy raindrops smacking against the wet face of the clay. The winds rose, causing the rain to slant against him, making him turn his face sideways.

The wet clay made slippery going on the sloping ground near the hedges and forced him away from the meager shelter of the hedge out to the center of the field in spite of the rain. A streak of wetness seeped in between his shoulders and spread over his shoulder blades, and he gave up all hope of reaching shelter before he would get soaked. It was not long before the rain had penetrated the rest of his clothing and he was wet to the skin. He plodded on in the dark, he did not know where, slipping and sliding over the drenched fields. Once his feet shot from under him and sent him tumbling headlong to the muddy ground. It was more than he could stand. Rising slowly, he turned his face upward to the heavens. "Pile it on!" he cried. "Pile it on!"

He had barely spoken the words when a wriggling flash of blue-white brilliance lit up the dripping countryside. He remembered how the explosions during the ambush in Raglan Street had lit up the scene in the same eerie way. Followed an earthquaking peal of thunder, and rumbles that shook the ground beneath him.

Defiantly Brian raised his face to the rain and let it beat down on him, run into his eyes, across his cheeks, into his mouth. He spat it out contemptuously. There were more rumbles, more crashing peals, but now they only gave him a sense of pride to know that he was defying in some way the power of the Almighty. A sudden crack and roar sent him reeling backward so forcefully he lost his balance and sat down in the sodden fields. Angry and humiliated, he struggled to his feet and in one of the flashes caught sight of a huge oak about ten yards ahead that had been rent right down the middle, exposing its white, torn flesh. The smell he smelt had something in it of the smoking gun and the smoking candle, and deep down in the depths of him he knew the two were one.

He pressed on until finally he came in sight of a farmhouse. Skirting the buildings, he crept up to the barn. In a few minutes he was undressing in a far corner of the loft where he made himself a deep nest in the hay. Taking off his soaking clothes, he wrung as much water out of them as he could. Then he shook them out and laid them on top of the hay to dry. There was nothing to do after that but cover himself with hay and try to sleep. Even covering himself so, however, it was still too cold for him. Finally he sat up and, cuddling his knees in his arms, with drooping head, he dozed off and on for the rest of the night.

The next morning the rain had ceased, and as soon as the gray morning light appeared he inspected his clothes. They were still wet and cold to the touch and it was all he could do to put them on again. He consoled himself thinking that once they were on they would dry quickly. He coughed when he told himself this and he noticed that his cough had a hard, dry sound his mother used to call a "bark." It was only when she heard the children "bark" that she began to worry.

As he came away from the barn that bleak November morning before the farm hands rose, he saw a flock of stiff-necked geese stretching to the wind and heard their wings whistle as they passed him heading for the coast. He also saw two men in red coats waiting across the marshes for them. After a blast from the guns one of the geese quietly, meekly, withdrew from the rest of the flight, then plummeted to the ground. The sight angered Brian and he felt like emptying his revolver at the two men in red coats.

For four days he traveled over the country, avoiding all the roads and eating where he could. It was slow going, but it was safe that way. One cold, starry night he stopped by the side of a lonely road to stare enviously at the warm, yellow blinds of a small cozy-looking brick house. Uncertain whether he would be received or rejected, he approached the house and crouched beneath the window lest he should be seen.

At the side of the window blind was a space through which he could peer into the room. Sitting in a deep armchair in front of the fire, reading a newspaper, was a young man about Brian's age; his wife sat near him sewing. She was trying to thread a needle at the moment and she turned her head and moved her lips in speech, and Brian was struck with the strong resemblance she bore to Sheila.

His eyes moved across the room. The long pendulum and brass disc of a wag-at-the-wall clock swung back and forth until suddenly its springs rasped and wheezed and it boomed out nine musical strokes. Finally his eyes found what he had been looking for: a framed print hung in the center of the wall. If the print were of our Lord, or our Lady, or of the saints, the family would be Catholic and inclined to help him; if not, if instead it had a Bible quotation or a picture of King William, then he could expect neither food nor drink, nor warmth for his freezing body, nor sympathy for his flight.

The picture he was looking at was the picture of a man brandishing a sword and riding a white charger.

Slowly Brian edged away from the window and was soon back

on the lonely road, and the thought that he was shut out from so much warmth and comfort was made more poignant by the other thought that the woman by the fire might have been Sheila and the man beside her himself.

Six days after he had left the farm he came within sight of the Irish Sea. The days before had been drab ones, rainy and cold, and the whole countryside had looked like a scene painted in charcoal gray. But this was a bright morning and the air was keen and he was still fasting when he saw it. From the hilltop where he stood his gaze swept across a long stretch of dark, green land strewn with fields, woods, and streams reaching to the white sand of the shore and the black, doom-laden rocks of jutting promontories; and beyond that lay the sea with its wide-open arms and limitless bosom of blue, a blue so deep and mysterious that it stirred strange emotions within him. Every detail was so sharp and clear that field, wood, and stream, houses, and sea were etched on a plate of polished silver. The whole panorama had an ethereal, other-worldly atmosphere about it. The air had a new freshness for him and he smelt the wracky smell of the sea and tasted the salt under his tongue, and he walked along a cowpath where the ridges made by the farm carts were solid and white with frost and made hard walking. He heard the breakers coming in with the tide, faint at first, then rising to the sound of rushing wind and increasing to the roar of a man in a drunken rage. As he walked on, the grass beneath his feet grew sparser and there was sand among the blades and the wind now never ceased to blow in his face.

At last before him lay the broken coast line where the waves in mad, unavailing fury kept mustering forces and smashing them against the jagged, imperturbable rock. In the background, in full sympathy with the struggle of the waves against the headland, glowered the angered sea. It was a moving sight, and Brian looked for a long time before he pressed on toward a promontory that abruptly from the beach soared heavenward. Although the waves in their wildest leaps could never hope to reach half its heights, the promontory was damp and slippery, and Brian picked his way up carefully, stumbling sometimes and sometimes bruising his ankles against sharp stones.

When he reached the top he did not dare approach too near the edge but contented himself with looking upward from where he could see only the blue sky fringed with wisps of pure white cotton. The strong winds caught his dark hair above the V of his brow, flattening it against his head. He stood like that until, accustomed to the height, he dared farther up the rock, and the wind buffeted him in protest, billowing out his clothes and pressing him backward. Unexpectedly the wind dropped, his clothes went limp, and his body, released of a sudden from the force of the wind, fell forward dangerously near the edge, startling him. After that, placing his right foot on the rise of rock as a precaution, he put his arms behind his neck and held them there, sucking the salt air through his teeth and blowing it out noisily. He turned his head to let the wind stroke his cheeks and play about his ears and neck, and out of the corner of his eye he saw his body in that position throw on the rocks behind him the shadow of a cross.

He stood there feeling as if he could touch heaven with his hands and slowly felt himself become part of the grandeur of the scene. Then, unexpectedly, as if it came from the skies themselves, he heard the plaintive, appealing sound of the pipes. There was a strange softness about the pipes that held him. Never before had he suspected they could be so sweet, so mystical. Their shrill chanting in closed places had always offended him, and only now he realized that the music of the pipes had been created for airy, open spaces to lift the feet of marching men, or stir their souls to melancholy. Now distance lent them a haunting quality that conjured up in him the voices of those whose lives had shriveled in the blaze of civil war. He thought of Sean.

A few moments later he carefully moved back down the face of the rock a step or two out of the rushing wind and the roar of the waves the better to hear the pipes. The music seemed to come from the sea now, but that was impossible; not a living soul was in sight.

Suddenly and unaccountably his melancholy thoughts were swept aside by a fierce desire: he would speak with the piper.

This time he hurried down the face of the rock, stumbling and sliding, uncaring of pain or danger. He must reach the piper before he returned to the mists of time. On reaching the sandy grasslands of the level ground again, Brian dashed to the right, from whence the sound came. The pipes were nearer now, but to his surprise the sound still came from the sea! At the edge of the rocks he looked down upon a quiet cove sheltered from the noisy breakers, but as yet he saw no piper. Following the narrow, uneven pathway of pebbles onto a lonely strip of beach overshadowed by masses of black rock, at last on a ledge to his left he found him.

He was sitting on a tuft of grass, holding the pipes on his knees and looking out to sea. About Brian's own age, there was no spare flesh on him, and Brian compared him to a hundred other lean and hardy young men that competed on the hurling field. Beneath the piper, on a lower ledge of rock, Brian saw something else that surprised him. A dark-haired young woman sat nursing a child. She paid no attention to the piper but was smilingly absorbed with downcast eyes in breast-feeding her little one.

The woman was pale, though her pale face made a pleasing contrast with the dark brown hair. When Brian approached she looked up directly at him and her eyes sparkled with fire as if her whole strength was gathered up in them. The child, on the other hand, was healthy and vigorous; he bounced about joyously in his mother's lap, and his restless fingers grasped at airy nothings.

As Brian clambered down the sheltered cove, the piper moved his eyes toward him, nodded in recognition, but kept on playing. Only when he had played out his sad theme did he remove the yellow-stained, ivory mouthpiece from his lips and wipe it dry with his fingers.

"That's the fine music you're making," said Brian.

"Thanks," said the man. "And God be with the listener."

The woman smiled at Brian again and kept on feeding her child.

"Why do you come down here to play?" asked Brian.

"Och! The people up there don't like the pipes or the songs," said the man. "I come down here where the pipes have to struggle only with the waves for a hearing. The wife comes down with me to listen for she's the crazy one about things Irish."

"She doesn't play the pipes, too?" asked Brian.

"No, then," said the man, a little woefully, it seemed to Brian. "But she's quite the singer, and in the tongue at that." He smiled proudly at the woman. "Sing to us, Moira . . . in the tongue."

"It's lucky the stranger came!" said Moira, pouting. "Or I wouldn't get a chance all morning to hear the sound of my own voice." She smiled again. "What'll it be then?"

"How about 'Mise Eire, I am Ireland,'" said Brian quickly. He was pleased with himself at this happy suggestion. It was a song he had heard Sean sing. Sean, yes, dear, dear Sean. The glad feeling drained from Brian and he grew sad again.

"Whatever the stranger says," said the woman in her soft tones.

She stopped feeding her baby and arranged it more comfortably on her lap. Tossing her dark locks and pinning them behind her ears with a quick gesture of her hand, she cast a shy yet challenging glance at her husband and began to sing. But her song she addressed to her baby, as if crooning him to sleep, and as she sang Brian felt he was assisting at some strange drama, with the rocks and the seas for stage and the sound of the distant, crashing waves for music. Slowly the three figures before him grew to the stature of the gods.

> "*I am Ireland* [sang the woman, in the tongue].
> *I am older than the Old Woman of Beare.*
> *Great my glory:*
> *That I bore Cuchullain the Valiant.*
> *Great my shame:*
> *My own children that sold their mother.*
> *I am Ireland;*
> *I am lonelier than the Old Woman of Beare.*"

When the sound of the song rolled out to sea and mingled with the sound of the waves the woman stopped. Without any prompting from either of the men she began again:

> "*I do not grudge them: Lord, I do not grudge*
> *My two strong sons that I have seen go out*

To break their strength and die, they and a few,
In bloody protest for a glorious thing . . .
Lord, Thou art hard on mothers:
We suffer in their coming and going:
And though I grudge them not, I weary, weary
Of the long sorrow—and I yet I have my joy:
My sons were faithful and they fought."

When the song was ended the woman looked up and her eyes met Brian's, deep blue eyes that blended with the sea, and held him. At last she turned to give attention once more to her child, smiling at him with her young, fresh lips, and the spell was broken. Brian rose and thanked her for her song and the young man for his playing.

"God go with you," they said to him.

"May the luck remain with you," answered Brian. He longed to stay but he was afraid that, if he stayed, in their purity they would see the wounds in his own soul, and he had no wish to spoil their happiness by visiting his troubles on them.

Wearily he climbed back up the uneven pathway and, like the closing curtain in a play, the rocks closed out the sight of the three from him and he felt he had wakened from a dream, the meaning of which he could not fathom.

All the way up the path he kept turning the event over and over in his mind, trying to unravel the message he knew it held for him, until finally he shook his head, vexed at his failure. But it had done something for him, he admitted. It had spelled out for him in some indefinite way his love for Ireland, the permanency of her ways, her people, and her destiny. The longer he meditated on what he had seen in this light the more he saw the meaning of the man, the woman, and the child in their strange setting.

The whole thing finally led him, he did not know why, into an odd train of thought. Like the cryptic words of the old songs that once sang of Spanish ale bringing hope to Ireland, referring to the aid the rebels asked from Spain, the scene he had just witnessed had a double meaning. Maybe, he mused, these people, in telling him that Ireland was forever, were also telling him that all that was now happening to Ireland was part of a divine plan. If that were so, the plan could not, then, be for Ireland alone, for although Ireland had never sinned, yet she had suffered far beyond what was needed for redemption. Why then had Ireland been called to so much suffering?

How like God to choose the Irish for such a task! Had He not chosen an oppressed race, the Jews, to confound the great and to bear the seed of the world's salvation? Had He chosen this way to prepare Ireland to fulfill the sublime dignity of being, not a nation of priests, but a priest-nation that would as a nation suffer for the sins of other nations, even as a priest is called to suffer for the sins of other men.

At this point he caught himself up suddenly, shook his head, and called himself a blundering fool for letting his imagination lead him so far away from pain-filled reality. He shouldn't be thinking of God, not after the way God had let Sean be murdered, not after the way God had sought to punish him for taking revenge on Sean's murderers.

Nevertheless, forever afterward the incident preserved its dreamlike quality for him, and there were times when he even wondered if it had been real and not something a tired mind, a wounded shoulder, and an empty stomach had fashioned out of air.

He walked on for another hour that morning before he found a harbor. But it was too small for steamers, the type of boat he was looking for. After that it was impossible for him to keep to the coast line. It was too rugged, and he was forced to take the road that led inland toward the north. Before he left the coast line, however, he passed through a village where he saw a small restaurant. He stopped at the window to study the menu scribbled in pencil on a well-used sheet of paper. His eye caught one item: sausages and bacon; fried bread; one shilling. The price was cheap compared with the prices in Belfast, but the thought of having to spend even a little of his money irritated him. He turned to walk into the restaurant but before going in glanced around to see if anyone was watching. It was then his eye caught the figure in the window.

Up to this moment he had looked at himself negligently and mostly in tiny mirrors. He had already noted that his hair was too long and that his beard had been shaved properly only twice since he had escaped from the farm. The beard he was looking at was two days old. On his head was a rumpled hat. But it was the rest of him that caused his dismay. He had dressed that morning without a mirror and had not even washed. He had simply swept his long hair back with his comb and fingers. When he was at home his mother saw to it with irritating insistence that he did not go outside the house unkempt; at the farm it was always Cathey who gently insisted. Now he stared at a figure wearing an overcoat too large for him, which drooped at the shoulders; beneath the ends of the coat hung a pair of bulgy trousers; the cuff of the left leg was frayed and fell over the heel of his boot; the boots themselves were caked with dried mud and were starting to give between the insole and the uppers. Brian stared at the figure for a moment in amazement. Then he darted into the restaurant and was relieved to find that it was empty. He ordered a meal hastily and gulped it down so fast he hardly tasted it. He paid the bill, seized his hat and coat, and hurried out of the restaurant and out of the village.

During the day his cough returned with the bark more pronounced than before, and a sudden fear seized him. For a while his imagination ran riot about diseases of the lungs, and he put his hand on his brow: it was quite warm. He fervently hoped it was nothing serious. He was also taken with colic, either from a chill or from the poor food he had been eating, and this weakened him still further. The festering wound in his shoulder had not been dressed since he had left the Nelsons', and it throbbed painfully. It began to dawn on him that if he stayed much longer under these circumstances his health might break.

He had been on the run for the last six days, he reflected. On the run. How often he had heard the phrase! How romantic it had sounded! To dash from one hiding place to another, escaping in the nick of time—that was the life! But that was the storybook version. That version did not mention the leaden feeling that lay on the heart at the thought of being hunted by Specials, eager, dedicated, and ruthless young men who had turned his land into a police state, who exulted in the new power thrust upon them, placing them above the law. The hunt for a man on the run was a fierce sport to them and a feather in their cap when they cornered their prey. And he, Brian reminded himself bitterly, was their prey. He was a lone wolf, too, because he had made no attempt to keep in contact with the I.R.A. He had joined the organization for his own ends, and once these ends had been attained he had left.

There was no mention, either, in the storybooks, of the numbing chill that crept into his hands and feet, spread to his shoulders, and finally covered his whole body, making him so painfully cold he did not want to move. When there was no food in his belly he could not warm up again no matter how much he moved, nor could he sleep at night when he was cold and hungry. When he woke up in the morning most of the cramps went away after a little movement, all except the feverish cramp in his left shoulder.

Yet the cold was nothing to the rain. There were no dry spots in the fields when it rained, and he had to avoid the roads as much as possible for fear of the patrols. The rain always got in through his clothing and made his shoulder ache. His boots, too, had been sturdy enough in the beginning, but the long treks had worn them, and after splashing across a wet field in search of a hayloft or barn for the night, the water in them made the raw inside of his toes rub painfully against each other, at times crippling him.

How much longer could he stand it, he asked himself gloomily as he leaned against the long, narrow gate of a field. How much longer could he stand it?

An engine droned somewhere down the road. Quickly he swung over the gate and disappeared behind the cover of a hedge.

A military-gray whippet swept past.

"Damned lucky for once in my life!" he commented wryly.

The countryside was becoming more and more unsafe to hide in, he realized. Hardly a day passed now but he did not see a patrol or convoy of Specials on the roads, stopping travelers to search and question them. Until then he had always thought that the safest place to hide in was the countryside, away from the busy city. Now he saw that the very openness of the country presented a special danger to a fugitive.

He was alone here, too, terribly alone; and he was sick. If he were back in Belfast he would not be alone. He would have friends, plenty of them, to take care of him. There was safety in crowds, too. And there would be no call to endanger his parents by living at home. If he found it was too risky to live at home he could always stay with friends and the Specials would never catch up on him. In any case, in Belfast by now they would probably have forgotten the ambush in Raglan Street. The memory of it would have been urged out by more recent events. Finally, he was not a big gun in the movement and had been in the I.R.A. only for a short while, and the Specials would not be aware of his return to Belfast for some time. When they did he could start moving around. He should have seen all this before! There was probably no connection whatsoever, he told himself, between the searches at the farm and the ambush in Belfast. At Drumree the new Specials were simply raw recruits trying out their new cars and new weapons: they had wanted to arrest him because he was a stranger and a Catholic.

"Yes, I will go back to Belfast!" he told himself defiantly, adding, "At least for a while." At least until he had shaken off this fever and had a long, long rest.

20

Brian lay in bed half awake, glancing with sleepy eyes at the brightness of the winter sunshine on the blinds. The pale, distant sun would now be rising over Tara, sending its long rays down the deep furrows and making the young wheat grass cast fledgling shadows across the rich, dark earth. Everybody on the farm would already be up and about and Dinny would be feeding swill to the squealing pigs, smacking their smooth, pink rumps the way he always did when Brian was around for he knew it made Brian laugh. But if everybody was up and about what was he doing in bed? He should have been out hours ago and down with the horses, he thought drowsily.

A shot rang out, a long, mournful shot that clanged through the empty streets. Brian realized then that he was back in Belfast and listening to a warning shot some picket had fired from a street corner or roof top before ending his all-night vigil. As the horned snail, roughly touched, withdraws itself back into its shell, Brian instinctively withdrew into himself, pulling the bedclothes over him and trying to make himself smaller and smaller, as if he were pressing his body into the shelter of a doorway to avoid the flying bullets. From this place of retreat he watched the events of the previous night unfold themselves again before his eyes.

He had slipped into the house during curfew, and his mother and father had made a great fuss about his home-coming. They had been careful, too careful, in their attempts to hide their shock at the raw, ugly wound in his shoulder and at his unkempt state.

He had washed and changed, then had eaten greedily the hot supper his mother had prepared for him, listening meanwhile to the accounts they gave him of what had happened since his flight.

"Where's Paul?" he had asked suddenly.

"Oh," his mother had said brightly, "we haven't heard from him for two days now. I was worried sick at first, until your father found out that he was safe but had been sent away on a secret mission and was doing something very important for the cause."

Brian had wondered what the secret mission could have been when his father had leaned across the table and, reaching for the sugar bowl, had turned his face toward Brian and away from Mary. Slowly and deliberately Michael had closed his left eye so tightly he had pulled up the whole side of his face. Only when his mother had gone into the scullery to fetch something had Brian learned the truth. Paul had disappeared from the house without a word of warning. That was all that Michael knew. The rest had been a fairy tale to put Mary at her ease.

"That's mighty odd," Brian had said. "Any other news?"

"Yes, son," Michael had told him. "But it isn't too good."

"Let's hear it."

"A lot of people have been arrested while you were away. Only yesterday they lifted two of your friends."

"Who?"

"Mole Finnegan and Humpy Dwyer."

When his mother had returned Brian had finished his supper and his father had risen, saying that the rest of the news would keep and that Brian should go off to bed at once for a good night's sleep, he looked so tired and worn. His mother had been about to go upstairs to prepare his room when his father had stopped her. "I'll go up and do it myself," he had said, and Brian had felt glad he had come home.

But now he wondered how safe it would be for him to stay in Belfast. If the Specials had already lifted Humpy and the Mole, it meant that the net was closing in and that he could not risk another night at home. From tonight on he would sleep at the houses of friends, beginning with the Mooneys.

Someone was already moving about below in the kitchen, probably his mother. She had always risen first to get them out to work. Rising, Brian sat on the edge of the bed, staring dully at the checkered pattern of the cold linoleum for a moment before he pulled on his trousers and drew his boots over his stockinged feet. He had gone to bed half dressed in case the Specials made a chance raid on the house. If Sean had done the same that night, he thought, he might still be alive. The pain in his right shoulder caught him; he massaged the area of the wound gently, and the flesh of his body was soft and warm to the touch, as it always was after rising.

"Are you up, Brian?" His mother must have heard him.

"I am, Mum."

"All right, son. I'll get your breakfast ready."

Brian came down, and while he washed in the scullery an appetizing smell came in from the kitchen. On the table he saw three or four pieces of bread fried brown and crisp covering sausages and bacon.

"Things seem to be letting up a little now," his mother said, as he sat down to eat. "At least there isn't so much shooting. And about time. They've been at it now for months, and I'm sure the Protestants must be feeling the pinch as badly as ourselves. It's hitting everybody hard this winter."

"Can't last too long, Mum," said Brian. "I don't think the Catholics have the heart to carry on. The other side has everything; the Catholics have nothing."

"What do you intend to do these days?" asked his mother.

"First I'll have to arrange to sleep somewhere," said Brian. "Then I'll see if I can get a job in one of the mills."

"Will that not be too dangerous?"

"I'll have to take the chance," said Brian. "Besides, I can give the Mooneys' name and address."

He rose to go out, and as he walked down the hallway out of the house, he stopped short at the picture of a young man wearing a Sam Browne belt over civilian clothes. He read the inscription beneath the frame:

SEAN TRACEY

Captain "C" Company, Falls Road Division

Killed in action

He was taken by surprise; he had not noticed the picture when he had come in last night in the dark. Sean, smiling Sean, so full of youthful warmth and charm. Sean, Sean, Sean, why did you die? Why did they have to kill you? Tears started to his eyes as he noted all the pleasing features of his brother's face. He felt so drawn to him he could have reached out and embraced the picture. But he abruptly checked the tears and once again his hatred of the men who had killed Sean welled up in him. He was not one whit sorry, he told himself, that he had avenged his brother's death.

There was a holy-water stoup below the picture which the family used to bless themselves as they came in and out of the house. Brian ignored it.

Keeping away from the Falls Road, he walked down a side street and saw a sandbag shelter the English soldiers had thrown up at the intersection. Since his absence, Michael had told him last night, the Specials had become so ruthless they had forced the Catholics to appeal for protection to the garrisons of English troops. To Brian this was a sad irony: Irishmen appealing to the foreigner for protection against brother Irishmen! It was also a bitter reminder of the lessening strength and influence of the I.R.A., for the shelter was in a spot the Specials had never dared to patrol in the beginning, and when the military had first come even they had stayed there only during the day. Now they stayed there day and night; the children played around the shelter, and he saw the women bring out hot tea for the sentries. On his way to the Mooneys' to make arrangements for the night, he saw little Malcolm Mooney, his cousin, playing with a young redheaded soldier who was showing Malcolm how to shoulder his heavy rifle. He called the boy around a corner, cuffed him on the ear, and told him that he was no Irishman if he played with an English soldier.

He dropped in on the Finnegans and they brought him up to date on what had happened during his absence. The Mole's brother, Pat, pushed a newspaper at him. "See this?" he asked, pointing to a front-page insert in heavy type.

> It has become known to this organization that certain prominent citizens of Belfast are responsible for the deaths of many innocent people by their continued fomenting of religious strife. These people will receive one warning. After that, if they continue their work of separating one Irishman from another, they will be tried by a duly-established court of the Republic of Ireland. If found guilty by this court, they will be sentenced to death, the death sentence to be carried out at the first available opportunity.
>
> SIGNED:
>
> The Commanding Officer
> Northern Area, I.R.A.

To Brian this was only another hopeless attempt to make the people realize that their struggle was not a religious struggle but a patriotic one. But in this, too, they were fighting a losing battle. Distrust and hatred between Catholic and Protestant had been too well planted in the North. It ran too deep to be uprooted in one generation. New generations, perhaps, brought up in understanding and love . . . But, he asked himself sadly, who was there to bring up in this way these new generations?

Groups of idle, discontented men were lounging at the street corners. He watched a whippet drive up and order them to disperse. The men moved away, glaring sullenly at the whippet. But as soon as the whippet drove off again they returned to the street corner.

Toward the center of the city he was shocked at the number of shops that had been looted. In the side streets military patrols were searching the houses and loading onto lorries as much obviously looted property as they could discover: articles of furniture stridently out of keeping with the rest of the household; tins of biscuits; bags of flour and salt; cases of candles. . . .

For Brian this was a painful disillusion. The I.R.A., he knew, had held up places to get funds and supplies for the cause. They were the government of the people, they had declared, and had a right to commandeer what they needed. But they had opened up a wound, and with the growing shortage of food and clothing and money, the holdups and the looting had spread like a cancer. In the beginning the I.R.A. had checked this by meting out severe penalties, but with the gradual weakening of their organization they had been unable to prevent it. Brian felt almost glad the English garrison troops had stepped in.

He came home that evening just as his father and mother were sitting down to supper.

"Any luck, son?" asked his mother.

"Not a thing," said Brian. "I tried Barker's and the manager asked for my qualifications. He even wanted to know if I'd be willing to travel. Then he asked me where I lived. When I told him the Falls Road district he gave me the glass eye and said he'd let me know if anything turned up. Then I—"

"It's no good, son!" broke in Michael impatiently. "We Catholics have always been beaten. We're cursed in our own country!"

"I've a good mind to clear out of this dump and try to get to the States!" said Brian in frustration. "What's the use of rotting away in this Godforsaken hole!" He was sorry he made the remark, however, for his father and mother lowered their heads and ate the rest of the meal in silence.

The following day was Sunday, and he came up to the house from the Mooneys' to put on his Sunday clothes. While he was there his mother took it for granted that he was going with his father to the Monastery for Mass. Brian decided to go, for he did not have the heart to disillusion either of them by telling them that he did not believe in going to Mass any more. He would go to Mass and sit it out.

As they neared the Monastery, a taxi passed them up Clonard Street and drew to a sudden, screeching stop in front of the church railing. Instinctively Brian and his father slowed up to see what would happen. Things happened so often in these times one became skilled at reading the signs.

A man in a dun-colored ulster backed out of the taxi, pulling at something on a chain as one would pull at a dog. A few more tugs, a muttered curse or two, and an ungainly, ambling figure, like a huge pantomime cat, its hands tied in front, stumbled out onto the pavement. Another man followed, and the two men led the monstrosity across the pavement, hooking the chain to a spike on top of the railing. The first man knelt down on one knee and began to write; the second man kept looking up and down the road. When the first man stood up, he and his companion hurried back to the taxi which swung round and shot back down the road.

Other men on their way to Mass reached the chained figure before Brian and Michael and stopped to look. Brian heard some click their tongues in sympathy, but most of them, he noticed, grimly tightened their mouths. Meanwhile, the figure at the railing kept turning his head dejectedly from side to side in a vain attempt to hide his face. He might have spared himself that anxiety, thought Brian, for no one would have recognized in that crouching shape the semblance of anyone they knew.

As Brian came closer he saw that the man had been stripped of his garments and soft tar had been poured over his body. Feathers had been thrown over the tar and stuck unevenly on him, leaving some parts black and featherless, reminding Brian of old Turnip when she had been troubled with the itch. The soft tar dripped slowly off the man's body, and already his feet were making tarry footprints above the writing on the pavement.

"Poor buggar!" said Michael sympathetically as they came up. "Isn't he a sight!"

Brian looked at the man so shamefully disfigured and wagging his head from side to side. A wave of compassion passed over him and he stooped to read the writing on the pavement. The man had tried to stamp it out with his dripping feet, but most of it was out of his reach and he had succeeded in only partially covering with tarry footprints the one word: *INFORMER*. Still untouched were the two lines of writing below. Full of curiosity, Brian read:

Paul Tracey
Falls Road

Like a white-hot branding iron the words seared their way into his brain. *Paul Tracey, Paul Tracey, Paul Tracey*. As he whispered them to himself in utter disbelief, they sounded like the hiss of the branding iron on his flesh.

Shaking his head, he straightened up and turned to his father.

In that moment if he could have prayed he would have dropped on his knees and prayed for just one favor: to have his father spared this awful moment, even if that had meant taking away his own life. The look in his father's eyes at that moment had in it something of the look Christ must have given Judas after the betrayal. Then to Brian's horror a different look crept into those troubled eyes, and Brian could have cried out to prevent it as he would have cried out to warn his father were a rushing car bearing down on him. For the look in Michael Tracey's eyes was changing to a look of loathing and hate.

The few other spectators had already left the scene to go to Mass, and Brian stirred himself into action. He quickly decided that the best thing to do would be to get Paul to the Mooneys', where they could clean him and hide him for the time being.

"Get a taxi," he said to his father, almost forcibly turning him away from his son. In a dull, obedient manner Michael walked to the edge of the pavement and looked up and down the road. Occasionally he would glance over his shoulder at the railing.

In the meantime Brian spat on the writing and with the toe of his shoe made it indecipherable. "Move to the side," he said to the figure, which smelt heavily of tar. Paul slumped to the left, and Brian reached up and unhooked the chain from the spike.

"Cab coming," said Michael.

Brian walked up to the corner, from where the driver of the taxi could not see Paul, and flagged the taxi. The taxi pulled up in front of him.

"Know where Lower Clonard Street is?" he asked the driver.

"Sure. Hop in."

Brian turned around. "Bring him over," he called out to Michael.

"Hey!" protested the cab driver when he saw Paul. "What's the matter with you? Think I'm taking that circus ape in my cab?"

Brian slid his hand into his coat pocket and poked his forefinger against the cloth. The forefinger stuck out like the muzzle of a gun. "You'll do what you're told," he said coldly. "This is an I.R.A. job." His face, still white and tense from his recent experience, convinced the driver he was a determined man. "Besides," he said, eying the Sunday newspaper on the seat near the driver, "I'll see that he doesn't mess up your cab. You'll also get double fare." With his hand still in his coat pocket, and wondering what he would do if a whippet were to appear, he stood guard over the driver. Michael came up, spread the newspaper on the seat and floor, and settled Paul in the taxi. Brian guessed that his father's emotions had been pushed into the background for the moment by the difficulties of trying to keep the taxi and himself from being covered with soft tar. He got in beside the driver. "Let's go," he said curtly. The driver threw the car into gear and drove off.

As far as he could see, thought Brian, Paul had been guilty of some betrayal and the organization had caught up with him. What could possibly have been that betrayal? It certainly was serious if they had tarred and feathered him.

As if to find the reason, he turned and looked at Paul. Paul was sitting a little removed from the corner of the seat, his attention concentrated on keeping the rustling newspapers about his naked, shivering body. His head swung from side to side with the movements of the cab, and to Brian he looked like a weary, beaten fighter waiting in his corner for the verdict.

Michael Tracey was sitting forward on the seat and leaning against the side. His arms were folded tightly across his chest and his head was turned away from Paul.

Brian did not feel like speaking to either of them; not to the figure covered with the newspapers, for Paul seemed incapable of speech; not to his father, for fear of releasing all the dangerous emotions tormenting that brooding face. He wondered if his father had had time enough to overcome those first reactions to the terrible discovery that his own son was an informer, was one of those whose names were always mentioned in tones suggesting an evil that is past all understanding.

Only once did his father turn his face to Brian, and Brian saw that it was writhed up like a dried pear. "What he must be going through!" Brian said to himself. Then he thought: "And Paul? God, but he must be suffering, too, shivering there in that garb of shame!" In that moment, and for the first time, perhaps, in all his life, Brian felt a deep, shaking sympathy for his brother Paul. For now he wondered if Paul had not, like himself, been dragged to the pit, had not been urged, pressed, forced against his will into the land of Cain.

By this time they had reached the Mooneys at the bottom of Lower Clonard Street, and to Brian there was something unreal about the scene that followed, something that had in it the same unreal quality that linked it up with the night Sean had been murdered. When the taxi stopped Brian told the driver to wait, went into the house alone, and hurriedly explained what had happened. Coming out again, he looked up and down the street, but at that hour on Sunday morning there was no one about.

He opened the taxi door and Paul stepped out like some grotesque, yet comic, Dixie minstrel and ambled into the house. For years afterward Brian could recall in detail the cartoons of Mutt and Jeff and even some of the sports headlines from the pages of the newspaper that covered Paul's back.

"It's a lot o' dough, for dirtying a newspaper," he grudgingly told the driver. While he was paying the fare his father was following Paul into the house, but Brian hurried in and caught his father by the arm.

"Take it easy, Dad," he said.

Michael Tracey brusquely pulled his arm free and turned two smoldering eyes on Brian.

"I know. God, don't I know how you feel!" said Brian. "But you've got a job to do."

Michael brought his hand up to his brow with a stiffness that betrayed his inner tenseness. His eyelids pressed together until they were almost closed, a film of moisture glazed over them, and his mouth was drawn out into a thin straight line. Brian felt that this was one of those moments when his father needed the quieting touch of his mother's hand.

"Brian," said Michael without emotion, "why did they not shoot him? Shooting is a good way to die; so is hanging in this country. That's the way an Irishman dies. But to tar and feather him! That's for traitors and informers. He can't be an informer. He's a Tracey. Do they know that, the men who tarred and feathered him?"

He sat down on the chair beside the hall stand and looked up at Brian. "I thought Sean's death was the end," he said, shaking his head. "But how good that was compared to this! I know you won't believe me, Brian, but I always knew that one day Paul would disgrace us. I knew the day would come when we would sorrow over him. But I didn't know it would be this way. Brian, son . . . son. Yes, you're the only son I have now. Two of them have gone, one right and one wrong. Sounds even. One right and one wrong. But it's not even. Nothing will ever even up the way that he was wrong!"

Brian patted him on the shoulder. "Dad," he said, "why don't you go on home and take care of Mum. Tell her you heard that Paul was being hidden by the organization." Michael looked up sharply in disbelief. "I mean it," went on Brian. "Tell her he'll write as soon as he thinks it's safe; tell her that for the time being he has to lie low; tell her anything you want, but, for God's sake, don't tell her the truth! Sean's death was one thing, but this! . . ."

"I suppose you're right," said Michael after a pause. "She couldn't stand it. It'd break her heart. I'll build him up in her eyes, all right, although I'd rather . . . oh, what's the use!"

"And, Dad," said Brian as Michael rose to go, "don't forget to tell her that I went to the Monastery. She might get worried about that." It was a double deception of the mother, Brian knew, but he thought it was the only way to spare her.

Brian spent the morning taking the bulk of the soft tar off Paul with repeated washings of paraffin oil. Then he left the Mooneys' and made his way up to the Huts.

When he entered the clubhouse the floor was occupied by a group of young Fainna Faille, a junior offshoot of the I.R.A. They were going through drill formations with a listless air very different, thought Brian, from the enthusiasm he had seen in his earlier visits.

At the other end of the hall a small group of men were talking among themselves while an instructor in front of a blackboard filled with rough designs strove to hold their attention. In a far corner a few others were seated round a table playing cards.

Brian could see no one that could answer the questions he wanted to ask, and he sat down to wait. Gradually other men began to stroll in. Coming in from Mass, he thought. Suddenly he heard Sandy's loud voice, and the next moment Sandy appeared in the doorway. Brian rose at once and went up to him.

"How's things with my old engineering genius?" he greeted Brian cordially. "Haven't seen you for quite a while. You been in jail?"

Brian did not respond to his geniality. "Sandy," he said shortly, "can I have a word with you?"

"Sure," said Sandy. "You can have all morning if you like. Pity it's Sunday, though, and the pubs are closed, or we could have a belt or two to celebrate that night in Raglan Street. Let's sit down here. Now, what do you want to know?"

"Sandy," said Brian, "why did they tar and feather Paul?"

Sandy rubbed his chin for a moment. Then he looked challengingly at Brian.

"You don't know?" he said. "And if you don't, are you sure you want me to tell you?"

"Sandy," said Brian evenly, "I want to know why my brother was tarred and feathered."

"Well, you asked for it." Sandy leaned forward, joined the tips of his fingers into an arch, and through the arch examined a knot in one of the floor boards. "Where did your brother Paul go the night Sean was murdered?" he said.

"I don't know."

"Do any of you know?"

"I don't think so."

"Then I suppose I'll have to tell you. He went straight up to the barracks in Albert Street to inform the Specials that Sean had just come home and that they could lift him if they went up there at once."

There was a long silence. In the end Brian drew in a deep, deep breath that was more of a painful sigh. Sandy closed the arch and rubbed his hands together uncomfortably.

"So that's what Paul did the night Sean died," said Brian.

"Yes, Brian boy," said Sandy. "Paul did exactly that."

"How do you know?"

"We've someone keeping an eye on who goes in and out of the barracks."

"You may be just guessing when you accuse Paul of informing on Sean."

"We also have someone who tells us most of what goes on inside the barracks. Paul told them that Sean was at home. That's not the only thing we have against Paul, but it's the most important."

"But why under God should Paul? . . ."

"Can't you guess?" asked Sandy. "You ought to know more about your own brother than we do."

"If I knew I wouldn't ask you," said Brian dully.

"Well, your brother Paul has always been the great one for hitting the high life. You can't do that for long unless you have a rich uncle, or a bank manager's job. Paul had neither. So to keep pace he started sampling the firm's dough. The Specials got wind of it. So they saw a chance to nab Sean through his brother. So they blackmail Paul. So Paul informs on Sean and Sean gets killed. Paul admitted everything to us. But he says the Specials told him they only wanted to arrest Sean, and according to Paul, it would have been a good thing for Sean to be arrested, for if Sean were left free he'd end up being shot. We didn't know how to take that one."

"His own brother!"

"I know it's tough, Brian boy, but the best thing you can do with brother Paul is get him out of the country, pronto. We didn't bump him off simply because he was Sean's brother and yours. Otherwise . . . ping, ping." Sandy stuck out his forefinger and fired an imaginary revolver. "But some of the boys still feel they have a score to settle with brother Paul. They might decide to take the law into their own hands. Can you blame them? They were very fond of Sean."

Brian rose. Sandy rose with him.

"The only thing I can do for you, Brian boy," said Sandy, "is to stop the men from interfering if you want to get Paul out of the country. And you should have no difficulty from the other side. He's done so much for them already they'll be dying to help him."

Sandy accompanied him to the door. "Tough goin' for you, I know, son," he said. "But these days it's tough for all of us."

It was as Sandy had said about the other side helping Paul. When Michael, through friends at the post office, contacted the District Inspector of the Specials, that official agreed to ease Paul's escape to England.

On Wednesday evening of that same week, about two hours before the cross-channel boats set sail, a taxi drove up the Falls Road and stopped in front of the Traceys'. Brian and his father and mother were there, for Paul had let them know that he was coming to say good-by. Michael had already warned Paul that his mother did not know the truth and that the best thing Paul could do now would be to keep the truth from her. Brian heard the door open and Paul stepped into the room where the three of them were waiting.

He was dressed in new clothes; his features looked sharper and a little haggard. He did not raise his eyes to look at Brian or his father but walked straight over to his mother who hugged him repeatedly. "My son, my son!" she said. "I'm so glad you're safe and that you've turned out such a fine, brave man! Sometimes your father and me worried about you. But now we're proud of you. I'm not saying I hold with any of this terrible fighting, but I can't blame you, son, for doing what you think is right. God bless you." She kissed him on each cheek; she hugged him again and held him close.

Brian and Michael edged out of the kitchen into the hall. Paul saw this and, breaking away from his mother, followed them.

"Don't come out, Mum," he said to her. "I want to see them alone."

Out in the hall he saw the two men standing with their hands clasped behind their backs underneath the picture of Sean. He looked first at his father. Michael lowered his gaze and studied the floor at his feet. He looked at Brian. Brian stubbornly refused to look up.

"Will you shake hands with me, Dad, before I go?" Paul's

voice quavered. He held out his hand timidly to his father. His father did not raise his eyes from the floor.

"Will you, Brian, *please?*" Paul was openly pleading now.

Brian did not raise his eyes. He supposed he was presenting an outward appearance of calm. But he wondered how long he could hold himself in, how long it would be before the icy shell about him dissolved in the fierce, hot pounding of his heart. He felt that any moment he might break down and embrace his brother, forgiving him and asking forgiveness for him, no matter what he had done; declaring that the awful past was the past; that the family had suffered enough, and that they should try to build up a new happiness on the ruins of the old; that they should face whatever sorrow the future held for them together. . . . But Sean was dead; he had loved Sean, and Paul had murdered Sean. Brian held his gaze fixed stonily on the floor. There was a long pause.

"All right," he heard Paul say hoarsely, keeping his voice low so that his mother would not hear. "I tried to tell you I'm sorry for what I've done. I asked for your forgiveness but you refused it. Well, then, listen to this: with or without your handshake I'll go, and be damned to the lot of you! Stay on the Falls Road till you rot. Fight, fight, fight until, like two Kilkenny cats, you and the Protestants destroy each other. It'll be a damned good riddance for at last we'll have some peace!"

Then he was out of the house and slamming the door behind him. Brian heard the car go into gear and move away.

21

The events of the week had made time pass quickly for Brian and he was surprised when it was again Saturday. It was brought abruptly to his notice when he returned home that evening and his mother asked him if he had been to confession.

"Now isn't that an odd question?" he bantered warily, wondering why his mother should ask it. "As if I didn't know my duty!"

"Good, son," said his mother. "I'm glad you remembered that tomorrow is the monthly Communion for the Sodality. You need the grace of God to protect you these hard times."

Brian sighed. This meant that he would have to go out with his father again to Mass and that this time, moreover, he would have to avoid receiving Communion. He would find a way to do that, too, however, and for the Sundays after that, if there were any, he would make better arrangements.

Next morning he left with Michael for the Monastery.

"Brian," were Mary's parting words, "don't forget to pray for your brother Paul in England. With the danger he's in he'll need all our prayers."

In a short while Brian was kneeling beside his father in the same section of the Sodality he had been in since he had come to Belfast.

As the Mass went on Brian deliberately looked around the church to distract himself. He noticed four or five men seated at the mahogany confessionals with the heavy plush curtains. Then he remembered the day he had rent the curtain in the confessional at St. Mary's. And he let his thoughts wander back to the times when, as boys, he and Sean and Paul had snuggled together on those benches, listening to the evening story. He recalled the day he had hit Sean for getting him into the fight at Falls Park. Who'd ever have thought that the time would come when Sean would be lying dead in his grave, that Paul would have betrayed him, and he, Brian, would have turned against the Faith?

Suddenly it was Communion time. Brian's bench was well down the middle aisle and one of the first to go to the altar rail. An usher was already moving the men out seat by seat. It was only then that Brian realized his predicament. In a dozen pews ahead of him not a single man stayed behind. Naturally, he told himself, they had come here precisely to receive Communion. In a few seconds, he realized, with something akin to panic, it would be his turn to approach the altar rail.

It was in that moment that he began to understand what he was about to do. Ever since the day he had refused absolution he had kept away from the sacraments, away from the Church. He was in sin. On the other hand, all his life he had been brought up with a deep reverence for "receiving." As a boy the importance of receiving Communion in a state of grace had been drummed into him and impressed upon him by stories of the dreadful fate of those who dared to receive Communion in sin. He could not receive this morning. He did not belong to the Faith any more; he did not believe in God. But he could not receive this morning.

By now, however, his father was making his way down the aisle. Still thinking of how he could escape, Brian mechanically moved with the other men and knelt beside his father at the altar rail. He thought of running away from the rail, but a line of men quickly formed behind him, blocking his escape.

The priest edged along the rail, distributing Communion. Brian watched him come nearer, raise the white wafer, and place it on each man's tongue. He saw the priest's lips move as he did this and remembered the words of the prayer:

Corpus Domini Nostri Jesu Christi custodiat animam tuam in vitam aeternam. Amen.

"May the Body of our Lord Jesus Christ guide your soul into life everlasting. Amen."

It wasn't guiding *his* soul to life everlasting, Brian told himself wildly.

Corpus Domini. . . . The priest was a few steps away.

The body of Christ would only send him to hell everlasting! He'd have to get away from the altar rail! But the men behind were pressing against him. He was getting panicky. He must get away from the altar rail!

Corpus Domini. . . .

Brian saw his father on his right bow his head and mumble a few prayers before receiving. The very sight of his father's piety made Brian realize the enormity of what he was about to do. But it wasn't awful, he told himself desperately. He did not believe in God!

Corpus Domini. . . .

Michael raised his head, received, and bowed his head again. Brian was next. In his agitation, for one awful moment he imagined himself stepping up in front of a mad, yelling mob and slapping the face of the figure on the cross so hard that the blow turned the head and it hung on the other side, the way Paul's head had done on the railing.

Corpus Domini. . . .

The mob surged forward to get at the figure on the cross and knocked down Brian and trampled him underfoot. . . .

Brian saw the white circle above his head. It began to shine; it turned into a gleaming disc; it was a circle of light. It became so bright, so glaring, it blinded him. It blazed into his brain so that he could no longer think of where he was, of what he was doing. Suddenly the white disc exploded in front of him and he fell backward from the altar rail. He felt his head had been split by the explosion, the way the lightning had split the tree that day he was on the run. . . .

"Can you hear me, Brian? Feel all right?"

Brian opened his eyes and looked up and again saw a white circle, but this time it was a patch of sky circumscribed by a group of figures looking down at him. His head stopped spinning and slowly he became conscious of where he was: he was lying on the pavement outside the Monastery, and his father was kneeling beside him.

"Brian, are you all right?" asked Michael anxiously.

"I think so," said Brian dully. He sat up.

"Pure weakness," commented Michael to the spectators. "He must have gone through it on the run."

There was a sympathetic murmur from the bystanders. It was the first time, thought Brian, that he had fainted in his life, and he had fainted over something he no longer believed in.

When he felt strong enough he stood up and leaned with one hand against the church railing. A few moments later he prepared to leave and the crowd opened a path for him. When he took his hand away from the railing, he was surprised to see it was coated with soft tar. A sympathetic onlooker offered him a sheet of newspaper to wipe it off.

"That's tar," said the man unnecessarily. "Fellow was tarred and feathered here last Sunday. A rotten traitor he was. Betrayed his own brother."

Brian and his father walked home slowly together. Along the way they agreed not to mention to Mary that he had fainted in church, for it would only upset her.

After breakfast Brian decided to take a walk in the fresh air to settle his disturbed state of mind. A ten-minute walk along the Falls Road brought him to a bend that hid the rest of the road in front of him. There were not many people in sight at that hour. Suddenly from around the curve a man in a navy-blue suit and a check cap came running in his direction. The man was holding his coat pockets tightly to him as he ran and was swinging his shoulders from side to side in a way that reminded Brian of how he had often run down to the stable with his pockets full of apples for Stardust. When the man came up Brian saw that his face was deathly pale.

"What's up?" he asked.

"Four I.R.A. men escaped from Crumlin Road Jail," panted the man. "The Specials are leppin' mad and are searching high up and low down for them. They're stopping everybody on the Falls Road and I have some stuff on me. For God's sake, tell me where I can hide!"

"Go into any of these houses," said Brian quickly. "You'll be safe enough till the Specials blow off."

"Thanks, Mac!" said the man, relieved. Without knocking, he pushed open the door of a house in the middle of the row and disappeared inside.

For a moment Brian thought of following him, but before he had made up his mind it was already too late. The door of the house had no sooner closed than Brian saw, rather than heard, the familiar squat body of a whippet rip around the bend. After it lumbered two cages, with Lewis guns mounted over the drivers' cabins. About twenty yards ahead of Brian the whippet pulled up in the middle of the road and the two cages pulled up level with it. Metal doors clanged and black-clad Specials began to pour out of the cages, drawing revolvers. Three of them stopped the people in front of Brian and put them into line. A second group of Specials did the same thing on the other side of the road. An Inspector now climbed down from the nearest cage. He was a dapper man in a smart, well-fitting uniform, with polished leather leggings. Brian wondered if it was the same man who had ordered him thrown out of Albert Street Barracks. He hoped not. The Inspector kept fingering the corner of his mustache as he placed the Specials at various points. He evidently did not wish to overexpose himself, for he stayed close to the cage under the protecting shadow of the Lewis gun that glared at the line of men with its dark, threatening pupil and iris of glinting steel.

Brian glanced up at the crisp, blue sky and at the single white cloud floating across it like a boat drifting lazily down a slow stream, and all at once the meaning of freedom had never seemed so clear to him. Everything took on a new brightness, a new interest for him, a new beauty. He remembered that as a boy he had been confined to his bed for two long weeks, and on his first day outside the house the simple fact that he could walk in the open air again had foolishly exhilarated him. To enjoy his freedom to the full he had walked to nearby Dunville Park to mix with the people, mostly women and children and old men, and had watched the birds dashing in and out among the trees as free as the wind. Even the scowling, black-streaked goldfish, gliding and darting about in the rippling waters of the pond, had seemed unconfined.

Now his heart went out to the four men who had escaped from jail. He could imagine them in some secret place, glancing up at the same sky, throwing back their heads, and breathing deeply. In sympathy with them he threw back his own head and took in a deep breath. But just then a haunting fear came to him that perhaps the net was closing in about himself and that it was only a matter of time before the Specials caught up with him and took away *his* freedom.

As he joined the line of men he began to go over the objects he had in his pockets to see whether he might not have something incriminating on him. But he was sure he had nothing to fear from a search. He was thankful he had not been long from chapel and had left his revolver at home. The men were superstitious about bringing guns into chapel.

"Put 'em up!"

Brian obeyed and noted the upcountry accent the Special was trying to hide. They were always anxious to preserve their anonymity so as not to become marked men.

Just before he stepped out of the line up to the Special who was searching there came to him, like an unexpected blow, the sudden recollection of a notebook he always carried in his hip pocket. It was a cheap little notebook with names and addresses, but it still had a few pages of the notes and simple designs he had used for one or two talks he had given on what they had pompously called at the Huts "military engineering." A book like that in these days of terror, Brian knew, was enough to condemn a man and all those whose names were in it. Papers had assumed a dread significance, for they led from one suspect to another. He wondered if he was now carrying that notebook and, not daring to look, for fear of drawing attention to it, tried to recall his movements before he had left the house. One moment he was sure the notebook was still at home; the next moment he was certain it was in his hip pocket. At the thought of this he went weak and his knees almost buckled under him. With a painful effort he pulled himself together. If the worst came to the worst he could either take the Specials by surprise and run for it, risking a burst from the Lewis gun. Or else he could snatch the revolver from the Special assisting the searcher. That might be better. He could shoot it out with them and take his chance of escaping in the confusion.

As he stepped up to be searched his muscles stiffened; the skin on the top of his head tightened; his feet and the tips of his fingers tingled; he drew in a deep, deep breath.

The searcher passed his hands cursorily at first along Brian's sides, under his armpits, up and down his thighs. Brian was half afraid the searcher would sense the overpowering current of hatred that flowed through him for the man. The searcher shoved his hand into Brian's right coat pocket; nothing there; tried the left coat pocket, and began to unbutton Brian's jacket to get at the trouser pockets. This was when Brian decided to risk everything in his attempt to escape. There was no other way.

Noting well the loose hold the Special who accompanied the searcher had on his gun, Brian clenched his fist and prepared to bring it down as hard as he could on the searcher's neck and disable him with the shock of the blow. Then he would . . .

"Inspector."

Brian held himself in for the fraction of a second. . . . The searcher withdrew his hands, straightened up, and looked across to where the call came from.

"Inspector."

On the other side of the road the second searcher and his covering Special were struggling with a man in a brown suit.

The struggle was soon over, however, for several other Specials rushed up, pulled the man out of the line, and pinioned his arms behind his back.

Brian did not recognize the man the Specials had surrounded. He was rather young, had a reddish complexion and wavy, auburn hair. The cold, bright sun was shining on him at the time, and all at once Brian thought of how this sunshine would be shut out, perhaps forever, from this young man's life. He earnestly wished he could have done something to help him, but there was little anyone could do in the face of those alert, threatening guns.

The Inspector, who up to then had been observing everything rather nonchalantly, suddenly tautened and his jawbones showed in his cheeks. He had been the only one besides the searchers without a weapon in his hand. Now he drew a large Webley from its shining leather holster and held it waist-high as he crossed the road, nibbling at the corner of his mustache.

Three Specials forced the man in front of the Inspector and one of them handed some papers to him. The Inspector glanced at the papers, then looked up sharply at the man. The victim must have been someone of importance, for the Inspector nodded toward the cage and immediately afterward gave the signal for the rest of the Specials to withdraw. Brian guessed that he was afraid the men's comrades might stage a rescue. It had happened before. The man drew back instinctively and shot a mute appeal at the other men still waiting to be searched, but he was quickly hustled to the door of the cage. Uniformed arms reached down and pulled him up while the rest of the Specials leveled their weapons and began to withdraw. Brian felt the air grow so charged he had difficulty breathing. The Lewis guns traced wicked designs over the fidgeting, restless men until the last Special had been pulled on board. The steel doors clanged shut; the whippet and the cages roared into life, moved forward, and sped down the Falls Road.

It was only then that Brian remembered the notebook. His hand reached quickly to his hip pocket: the notebook was not there. Relief now flooded over him and burst out through a million pores all over his body, and he sat down on the curb until the noises that thundered in his ears had ceased. Then he rose shakily, knocked at the nearest door, and asked for a glass of water. When he had gulped down the water, he walked home, feeling like a man whose blood had been drained out of him. His luck had held again, all right, he told himself, but it was running out. Before long he would either betray himself by a slip such as the notebook, or else the Specials would eventually catch up with him as they drew the net tighter round Belfast.

At home that afternoon, reflecting that it had been anything but a pleasant day, he gave a last rub at the green tank of the motorcycle, straightened his aching back, and looked up at the dull sky. Since morning it had turned to a kind of concrete gray, as if it might rain. Even as he admired the shining tank, one or two tiny drops of rain fell on its polished surface and, unable to spread, settled there like minute emeralds. Brian picked the waterproof cover off the ground, threw it across the machine, and pulled it well down over the sides to make sure that no part of the machine was exposed. The better the motorcycle looked, the more he could ask for it, and he had spent the afternoon making it look its best. He never thought he'd see the day when he'd have to sell it except to buy a new one. But he didn't have much choice. He couldn't use it, for he had no money to buy petrol with, and he needed every penny it would bring.

God, how hopeless it was! One by one his friends were disappearing from the streets, and the Specials were discovering the ammunition dumps hidden in the city, leaving the Catholics without arms. The strain of fighting against impossible odds was beginning to tell. Last Sunday morning at the Huts Brian knew he had been no longer looking at the enthusiastic young men he had met in the days when he had first visited the place with Sandy.

Sean had gone, and so had many others gone with him. Their lives had been taken in street battles, ambushes, night raids, reprisals. . . . One by one these Gaels had flown. Were they martyrs? He wondered. He didn't think so. Not even his idealistic brother had died in all the right circumstances to be a martyr. Sean hadn't had all the right people on his side, he concluded morosely.

In an attempt to cheer himself a little he lifted a corner of the waterproof cover and gave the tank of the machine a friendly pat. The shining tank made him think of the smooth back of a pig.

"Now that I've fattened you," he said, laughing at the idea, "I hope you'll fetch a good price!"

Slowly, however, the laughter went out of him, and like water bubbling up into an empty well, the anger and frustration rose up in him, flooding his whole being until the feeling became unbearable, almost suffocating. He stooped down, seized a heavy spanner, and flung it with all his might against the yard wall. The spanner struck the wall, dislodging some of the rough gray plaster, and clanged to the ground. Then he bent over the motorcycle and stayed there until the bitter mood left him, letting the rain fall on him unheeded.

When he felt better he went inside the house, wiping his hands with a piece of sweat rag he still had left from the shipyards. As he splashed some water over his face at the sink, he stared into the mirror at the black V that dug deep into his brow and the sharp outline of his face. He *was* getting thinner. Turning away from the mirror, he threw the towel carelessly on the table and walked into the parlor, rolling down his shirt sleeves.

His father was reading the Sunday papers and his mother had already set the table and was about to bring in the tea. Sitting down, Brian stared absently at the fire, thinking that ordinarily it should have been stacked high and glowing and Mary should have been chiding Michael for "piling on the coals even when the sun was splittin' the trees!" Today, however, despite the chill, the fire was low. Michael took up the poker to rake it and at that moment Mary came in with a pot of tea.

"Would you look at him trying to choke what little fire we can spare!" she said. "How do you think we'll last out the winter if you waste the coal now when the sun's . . . when it's not that cold."

Brian watched his father. As a rule, when his father raked the fire he would rake it so vigorously he would send up tiny spirals and volcano spouts of white ash dust that settled again slowly on the polished grating. This time, however, he must have caught the new note of asperity in Mary's voice. He tapped the caked coals lightly and, when they collapsed into the grate, pursed his lips and put the poker down without a word.

Mary went out again and came back with a plateful of buttered toast, potato farls, and sausages. Brian remembered how he used to relish this high tea every Sunday. Now he eyed the food without interest. He never had much appetite these days.

"I'm afraid you'll have to get used to the taste of margarine," his mother said apologetically. "I never liked to put it on the table, but now it's the only thing we can get." She poured out the tea, adding wearily: "I wonder when it's all going to end."

There was very little said at the meal, and when it was over Brian rose, went to the dresser, and took out pen and paper.

"Who are you writing to, son?" his mother asked.

"A friend of mine who went to the States before the riots started," said Brian.

"What's he doing out there?" asked Michael.

"I heard he was trying to get on the police."

"You'd think he'd had enough of the police after living in Belfast!" said Michael acidly.

"Seems half the police in America are Irishmen," said Brian. "He says he hopes later to join the F.B.I."

"What's that?"

"Some kind of special detective," said Brian.

"A Special, and a detective!" exclaimed Mary. "Imagine a Catholic joining anything like that!"

"I'm telling him how all his friends are disappearing from the Falls Road," said Brian.

"You'll hardly get a letter like that past the post-office censors," said Michael.

"The way I'll write it," said Brian, "they won't know what it's all about or where it came from."

Brian continued writing. After a while he looked up again and tapped the end of the penholder against his teeth. "From what he says, America must be a grand country," he mused. "Imagine being treated like everybody else even though you are a Catholic! But why do I have to leave my own country to be free?" he burst out suddenly. "Why can't I be free in the land where I was born?" Neither Michael nor Mary looked up or answered him and he did not speak again until he had finished the letter. But once he glanced up suddenly and caught his father studying him.

"This morning at the sermon," said Mary after a while, "Father McGuire spoke out against the men that burnt down the Protestant school at the bottom of the Falls. He said he wasn't at liberty to say from the pulpit all he wanted to say but that it would be a lot better if the men who did it gave their time to something more important than burning down a school, whether Protestant or Catholic."

"Did it ever dawn on Father McGuire," asked Brian heavily, "that there must have been a good reason for burning it down? The Specials very likely were getting ready to turn it into another barracks. Sometimes I think that up at the Monastery they're living in another world."

"Don't say things like that about God's holy priests!" said Mary, shocked. "You can't expect them not to speak out against all this bloodshed!"

"I'm only trying to make it clear"—Brian was aware that his temper was getting the better of him, but he seemed incapable of controlling it—"that the priests had better keep out of this or they'll stop the boys from going to chapel altogether."

"Brian!" Mary was so distressed at this statement she could not say another word.

Michael stepped in to take her part. "I hope you're not including yourself in that," he said.

"It's no time," went on Brian stubbornly, "to go spouting about turning the other cheek where the Specials are concerned." He was not sure that he was stating his thought exactly. But he did not care overmuch. The discussion, any discussion nowadays, set his nerves on edge. "I told Father McGuire that to his face," he added hotly.

"What did he say?"

"He nearly jumped down my throat!" said Brian. "Told me that it was playing into the hands of the foreigners to make a religious issue out of Ulster's troubles. Asked me if I couldn't see that as long as one Irishman, whether Protestant or Catholic, was at another Irishman's throat, they'd never amount to anything. Started to wave his hands and shout about Robert Emmet, Wolfe Tone, Henry Joy McCracken, and God knows who!"

"And is he wrong?" Michael's voice rose. He took the pipe from his mouth and Brian could see that his hand was shaking. "Is he wrong?"

"I'm not saying he's right or wrong, am I? Don't I feel the very way he does?" Brian's reply was almost a shout. "But why did he pick on me? I never wanted to fight Protestants, did I? I never wanted to fight anybody. All I'm saying is that I wish to God they'd leave us alone. They're all at us and we don't know where to turn. Leave us alone, will you? Do you hear? Leave us alone. All of you!"

Angry and agitated, Brian rose and shuffled the sheets of paper together. Throwing them down noisily on top of the dresser, he snatched up his hat and went out into the hall.

He stood there debating with himself where he could go to spend the evening before he went to the Mooneys' and heard his father ask:

"Where's he off to?"

Brian sensed that his father was sorry he had let the discussion get so much out of hand. "If the Specials see him he'll be in trouble." Then: "He won't last long the way he's going now."

"He can't go anywhere," his mother answered sadly. "God help him, Michael dear. He and the rest of them are only boys and they've nothing to do and nowhere to go. They're lost and lonely in their own country, dear. In their own country."

22

The following Monday evening, nine days after his return to Belfast, Brian called in home. He had spent the morning and afternoon looking for a job but had found that there were too many Catholics available for the few jobs open to them.

His father and mother were sitting around the fire when he came in. Michael was reading and Mary was knitting. His mother looked up quickly and then glanced at her husband. Michael put down his book, took off his spectacles, reached up, and placed both on the mantelpiece above his head. He rubbed his hands together.

"Mary," he said.

Mary obediently laid her knitting aside and began to clasp and unclasp her hands before finally settling them on her lap.

By this time Brian had seated himself between them.

"Brian," began his father, "the mother and I have been waiting to talk things over with you."

Brian folded his arms tightly about him. Then, aware of the timid glance his mother darted at him, he tried to relax.

"Last night, son," went on Michael, "the Specials made a quick raid on the house in the dead o' night. When they found nobody they asked where you were. They said that they had word you were back in Belfast. They got no satisfaction from your mother or me and they left. Now, son, since this visit from the Specials, we have been thinking, your mother and me, about what's going to happen to you if you stay here any longer. Matter of fact, last week when you started writing to the States we began thinking along the lines of you having to leave the country. And now that the Specials know you're around again . . . things don't look too good, to say the least. Your mother and me think you ought to get away. If you don't, one of two things is bound to happen: the Specials will get you or else your health will give. You look mighty thin as it is. Don't you agree?"

Brian pressed his lips tightly together once or twice but he said nothing. His mother gave him another sidelong glance as she folded and unfolded her hands. Brian was moved with sympathy. Poor Mother! he thought. All three of her sons gone!

"So," went on Michael, since Brian did not answer, "we thought it'd be better if you left Belfast for a wee while, at least until things have settled down and they've forgotten about you and there's plenty of work again."

"Where can I go?" Brian asked the question mostly to relieve the tension he knew his silence had built up. "To the States?"

"No," said Michael. "I made inquiries and found out that you'd need all sort of papers and permits—things you have no hope of getting."

"Then where?" asked Brian, regretting the hardness in his voice.

"The only place you could get into now," said Michael slowly, "would be England."

Brian tried to laugh. "If I can't get to the States without papers and permits how am I supposed to get to England—of all places?" he added ironically.

"It happens, son," said Michael, "that I have a friend, Paddy Ryan, who's captain of one of Kelly's coal boats, and he told me it would be no bother at all to get you to Liverpool. I can also give you the address of another good friend of mine in Liverpool, Pat Cassidy. When I was younger I used to travel a lot more than I do now," he added by way of explanation, "and that's how you meet——" He caught Brian's eye. "Well, as I was saying, this friend o' mine will put you up for a couple of days till you get settled. Now what do you say to that?"

Brian rubbed his chin for a few moments without replying, then, embarrassed by the glances of his parents—it hurt him to see how his father was almost timidly waiting for his answer—he stood up and dug his hands deep into his trouser pockets. "I don't know yet," he said at last. "I must have time to think." He went outside to the yard and gazed up at the starless sky, trying to arrange the thoughts that were crowding into his mind. What his father had said was true. The Specials were closing in and it was only a matter of time before they lifted him. One thing stood out clearly: His father had merely put into words the thought that had been haunting Brian since he had returned to Belfast: he would have to leave the country. But why should he have to leave Ireland at all? he asked himself. They had forced him into their struggle of brother against brother; they had forced him to leave the farm, and now they were forcing him to leave the country! And where did they want him to go? To England, of all places!

"Brian." He turned and saw his mother standing by his side, holding a clothesbasket. Mary pointed to a line of ghostly shapes hanging in the shadows of the yard. "Give me a hand to take down the clothes, son. The line is too high for me."

Brian began taking down the stiff clothes and handing them to her. "Why don't you like the offer, dear?" Mary asked.

Brian crumpled the stiff, frosted clothes and stuffed them into the basket. "Why should I have to leave the country?" he objected.

"But why do you want to stay?" insisted his mother.

"I want to stay because . . ." began Brian. He hesitated. Then it rushed out of him. "I want to stay because I love my country in spite of what Belfast has done to me. I'll always love it and I'm afraid that if I ever leave it I'll never see it again! Like the others who left in bitterness and despair, and whom I used to blame for going, I'll sink my roots in some other land I'll never love! Another wild goose that never flew home again!"

He took the striped shirt he was holding, crushed it fiercely between his hands into a ball, and threw it violently into the basket. In a fit of depression he sat down on a little stool Mary used and stared moodily at the dark cracks in the old slate tiles of the yard. His mother came and stood over him. She combed his hair gently with her fingers.

"Is there any other reason, Brian?" she asked.

"What do you mean 'other reason'?" asked Brian.

"Sheila?"

"Aye," agreed Brian. "There's also Sheila."

"Whatever happens, Brian, you won't be able to do much if you stay in Belfast." She took the shirt Brian had crumpled, shook it out, rolled it up loosely again, and placed it in the basket. "Look, son," she said. "If you do go away for, say, a couple of years at the most, what difference will that make? And as for Sheila—your father went across the water for five long years and I waited all that time for him. I know it's not too safe now for you to be about, but it might be worth while to risk a run down to Drumree to see her."

"Yes." Brian stood up suddenly. "That's just what I'll do. Sheila will know how to help me."

He left for Drumree around noon next day on the motorcycle. At that time of day he would attract the least attention from the Specials. As he roared along the road he reminded himself that this was the last time he would use the motorcycle. Probably it would also be the last time he would see Sheila, the farm, and his friends at Drumree.

When he reached the house he ran the motorcycle into the tool shed to hide it from strangers and closed the door. He was about to set out across the fields when Cathey, attracted by the noise, came out and greeted him affectionately. But Brian's mind was on other things, and, telling Cathey that he had something very important to do, he turned to go.

"But why won't you drop in for a wee moment before you go?" pleaded Cathey. "Meg isn't in right now. She spends most of the afternoons down at the shop."

"Her," said Brian contemptuously. "Don't worry, Cathey, I'll be back later." He wondered if he should confide in Cathey. He might as well. She'd find out anyhow. "I'm going up to the Reillys'," he said, "to see Sheila."

"Good luck, Brian," was all Cathey said. But she watched him climb the rising land and she stood there until he had made the top of the ridge. When he turned round to wave at her she waved back at him.

Sheila was at home with her mother when Brian called and they were delighted to see him. After a cup of tea together, Brian embarrassedly asked if he could see Sheila alone, and from that moment on all three were at great pains to act casually. After an uncomfortable ten minutes of waiting Brian finally helped Sheila into her overcoat of green-and-black plaid, and they left the house.

Brian pulled his hat tightly down against the wind, took Sheila's arm with one hand, and dug the other deep into his coat pocket. By unspoken consent they walked toward Tara Hill, but when they started up the rough slope, Brian reluctantly had to release Sheila's arm. Their strong young strides soon brought them to the top of the hill and they looked westward where the land swept away beneath them and buried itself in the distant blue hills. Brian turned to Sheila. The walk had brought out her fresh complexion and the wind now caught her dark brown hair and swept it back from her pink ears, making Brian think of a face that had been sculptured; her lips were parted in a quiet, exultant smile. She was leaning against a tree at the time, pausing to catch her breath, and that was how, he knew, he would always remember her. At that moment, for the first time, she appealed to him as the most desirable thing in the world. Suddenly she noticed that he was staring at her. She blushed and self-consciously brushed back a wild strand of hair.

Brian leaned back against the tree beside her. "Sheila, darling," he began a little nervously, "I came to say good-by."

"Good-by?" Sheila was taken by surprise. She puckered her brow in concern. "Where to, dear?"

"To England," said Brian. He tried to make the idea laughable. "To England. Can you beat that?"

"But why do you have to leave at all?"

"The Specials are on my tail and they'll lift me sooner or later."

"But won't the I.R.A. protect you?"

"I don't belong to the I.R.A. I have nothing to do with them. I joined them for my own reasons, and when I got what I wanted I left." He told Sheila why he had taken part in the trouble, and because he had long waited for someone to tell everything to, he told her also of the way in which his life had gone and how he had gradually turned from the Faith. But the more he talked, the more he confessed, the stronger became his impression that Sheila was inwardly retreating from him.

When he had finished his story there was a long silence and Sheila kept her gaze fixed on the distant hills. He was glad when she turned her head again to look at him; he was glad to hear again the sound of her voice.

"But, Brian," she said, "it was wrong to come into the movement with the terrible motives that you had. We're not a gang of murderers; we're not out for revenge. We're patriots, decent people with a just cause. If we only seek revenge, God will never bless our cause. And then you say you've lost the Faith. I can't believe that. How could you, Brian? You're only too upset by everything. You can't really mean it."

"I mean every word of it," said Brian stubbornly.

"Then you're no longer the same Brian that I knew."

"I don't care a rap whether I am or not," Brian's two fists clenched tightly in his pockets.

"But don't you see, Brian?" insisted Sheila. "If you act that way you're . . . you're nothing but another Special on the wrong side of the Falls Road."

"Oh, for God's sake, Sheila," he protested. "Don't *you* start preaching! Leave that to the priests. Who cares what I am?"

Sheila spoke slowly but with all her self-possession. "I care a great deal," she said. At another time it would have thrilled him to hear her low, sweet voice say that. But now there was no affection, no warmth, in her voice, only an odd, distant quality that warned him. Instinct told him that she was leaving him again and that if he did not act at once he might never be able to call her back. He made his decision. Stepping over to her and seizing her arms, he brought her close to him, so close that he could feel her warm breath on his face. As she gazed at him the familiar softness crept into her eyes and they half closed.

"Sheila," said Brian with whispered urgency, "I know that it can't be now, but will you at least wait for me? Will you promise, just promise, to marry me some day?"

Sheila's half-closed eyes opened and cleared again, and Brian grew desperate, for he was aware that she was withdrawing from him, shutting herself off from him, leaving him alone again to face a world that held no joy for him. He made a final effort to hold her. "Sheila," he pleaded desperately, tightening his grip on her. "Promise, promise." But it was useless. They struggled and he felt her body stiffen as, despite his firm hold on her, she broke away from him.

"Brian!" she gasped, breathless from the effort. "Please don't! I'm not sure. . . . I must see where I'm going."

"What do you mean?"

"I'm confused just now, Brian darling," said Sheila. "And afraid," she added nervously.

"Afraid? Afraid of what?" asked Brian, angry at his sense of loss.

"I'm afraid of—" Sheila stopped speaking until she had completely recovered her composure. Then she went on. "I think that you have changed, Brian. I feel you're not the same Brian, the Brian that I loved. I'm too confused to make up my mind now."

So she was gone. So when he most needed her she was leaving him. So he had lost her. So he was alone. Maddened by despair at the thought of what lay ahead of him, he shouted: "Will you or will you not marry me?"

"I don't know, Brian. I need more time to think." Sheila bent her head and, taking a tiny handkerchief from her pocket, put it to her eyes.

Brian took a determined step toward her, intending to seize her again, for a strange feeling now came over him and he wanted to hurt her. But at this new move a look of something so akin to fear suddenly appeared on Sheila's face it caught him up sharply. For an eternity he stared at her, embarrassed, bewildered, shocked, and all the time wondering what was going on in her mind, wondering what was happening to her, to himself, to the world about him. Then, like the surge of the wild sea he had watched that day he had met the piper, a flood of anger rushed over him, swirled riotously within him, and filled the dark pits, the clefts and crevices of his tormented soul.

"All right," he said hoarsely, his lips working. "All right. Join the rest of them. Turn against me. That makes the picture complete. To blazes with the lot of you!" He wheeled around and, only vaguely aware in his disturbed state of mind that Sheila was calling after him entreatingly, endearingly, he half ran, half stumbled his way down the east side of Tara Hill.

In a black mood he reached the farmhouse and went directly to the tool shed to get out the motorcycle and ride off to Belfast without a word to anyone. Cathey, however, was waiting for him at the door of the house. She ran forward to meet him.

"Brian," she called out, "Jamie's inside and wants to see you. I told him you were up at the Reillys'. Won't you come and speak to him? He always talks about you. Please, Brian!"

When she said this Cathey put her head slightly to one side and scrutinized him. She probably guessed from his appearance and his behavior, thought Brian, what had been the outcome of his meeting with Sheila. Her presence and her serene air brought a measure of calm back to him. What a wonderful world it would be, he told himself, if everybody were like Cathey! He followed her inside the house.

"Well, well, well!" greeted Jamie. "And how's me bold Sir Gallyhad? How did it go?"

"How did what go?"

"Come on, man," said Jamie, hugging Brian with good-natured impatience. "Quit the coddin'! I know well enough what you went up there for. Uncle Jamie's not the fool some of them take him for. You went up there to ask Sheila Reilly if she'd marry you. Right?" He pulled back his head as if to read the signs on Brian's face. "So out with it. What happened?" He was evidently filled with happy prospects.

"We went for a stroll together on this side of Tara," said Brian reluctantly, "where we could see the grand sweep of Irish land to the west——"

"You must take that gab after your father," interrupted Jamie shortly. "You went out there to ask the girl to marry you. Did you do it?"

"I did."

"What did she say?"

"No."

"No?"

"Yes."

"Oh, *yes.*"

"*No.* I said she said no. She wouldn't marry me."

"That's damned odd! You mean to tell me that she didn't grab at the chance?"

"Of course not, Uncle! I don't think she's that kind of a girl."

"Don't you try to tell me what kind of a girl any of them is, my lad. I know what I'm talking about. But what had you to say to that?"

"I told her that if she loved me she'd marry me no matter what." Brian stopped. He did not want Jamie or anyone else in the family to know too much about himself. "She talked a lot about changes," he ended vaguely.

"Changes?" Jamie pursed his lips, waiting for the rest. Since Brian did not venture further information, Jamie encouraged him. "And then?"

"Oh, I got mad. I know I shouldn't have, but an odd feeling came over me and I wanted to hurt her."

"Don't worry about that," interrupted Jamie. "As soon as ever you can wind yourself up enough—let them have it! Later on you don't seem to have—— They get harder to handle as time goes by, I suppose," he concluded lamely.

"I don't know," mused Brian, half to himself. "I shouldn't have said all I did say. But I was upset and I took a kind of satisfaction in causing her pain."

"Pain? Them?" said Jamie, shaking his head. "Don't you believe it! Man alive! If only I'd known when I was courtin' what I know now! . . . They must think a man's head's full o' bran!"

"Oh, Jamie," protested Cathey. "Stop talking that sort of nonsense!" She turned to Brian. "But what's all the hurry, Brian? Give the girl a little time to think things over. After all, the world's a bit upside down now, and besides, I don't see how you could get married and you in trouble with the Specials. What's your hurry, so?"

"It isn't the trouble that's stopping her," said Brian. "And as for the hurry—I'm going across the water."

"Oh." Cathey said this in a small, hushed voice.

"What?" cried Jamie. "You're leaving the country, the land?"

"What else is there for me to do?"

The three of them stood for a moment with nothing to say.

"When are you leaving, then?" asked Jamie at last.

"I'm not sure yet," said Brian. "When it's settled I'll let you know." He walked toward the door. "I must be off now."

"Indeed I suppose you must," said Jamie with a trace of sadness. Brian shook Jamie's limp hand, but Cathey went out in front of him and wheeled his motorcycle out of the tool shed, facing it toward the road.

"Thanks, Cathey," said Brian.

He seated himself on the cold leather seat and Cathey came over close to him. He looked up into her soft brown eyes, full of concern for him. She put her arms around him, kissed him on the cheek, and hugged him tightly for a moment.

"Poor Brian!" she said.

"Good-by, Cathey," said Brian abruptly, for he was afraid her sympathy might affect him too much. He kicked the machine into gear and, balancing it with his feet, moved it down the lane until it picked up speed. At the end of the lane he looked back, waved to Cathey, and then roared defiantly along the road to Belfast.

23

For the next few days Brian was completely taken up with preparations for leaving. He sold his motorcycle for a few pounds, money that would come in handy when he landed in England. Michael wrote to his friend, Pat Cassidy, in Liverpool, saying that Brian was coming, but did not mention the circumstances that were forcing him to leave the country. Since Brian would have to travel without luggage, his few belongings would be sent on to this friend.

The most important item of the arrangements was meeting Captain Patrick Ryan of the coal boat, *Gaelic Prince.* Captain Ryan was a stocky man with a red, pimply face and straw-colored hair. Brian and Michael met him in the cubicle of a pub near the docks. They ordered Guinness's during this meeting, but the captain called for a "bubble." Brian wondered what a "bubble" was, until the bartender in shirt sleeves brought out a rum-and-soda and set it down in front of the captain.

The captain was a willing talker and told them he had spent most of his life at sea and that he had taken the job he had now on one of Kelly's "floatin' coffins" because the wife wanted to see more of him. He said he looked on Brian as a fleeing patriot and confided to him inconsequentially that, no matter what the drink was, he always put a shot of soda in it. "It lightens the load." He also confided to Brian that in his days he had hidden patriots fleeing from Africa, India, South America, Ireland, and God knows where. "Could make a regular business of it if I wanted, helping patriots skedaddle." The captain stopped and stared at his third nearly-finished "bubble." Brian did not know if this was a hint. But evidently the captain had merely been thinking, for he went on, "Yep," he mused, "'sa funny thing, but every cussed moment of the day somebody's being pushed around by somebody else and has to skedaddle. And there's no reason for it, either. Strikes me they could learn to live together with half the trouble."

"Captain," said Brian, suddenly self-conscious, "I was wondering what we . . . how much——"

"What you're trying to ask," interrupted the captain with an air of hauteur, "is how much I expect for taking you?" The hauteur suddenly vanished. "Don't worry on that score, son. I'll do this one for nothing. I like the looks o' you. Damned if I wouldn't mind keepin' you on the old floating coffin for good! But that's not to be your life, I suppose. So I'll have one more bubble and that'll be payment enough for Paddy Ryan." He ruffled Brian's black hair good-naturedly. In one gulp he finished the final drink and wiped his mouth with his thumb and forefinger, starting from the edges and working to the center of his lips. "We shove off day after tomorrow at two bells, about 9 P.M. I'll be watching in case anybody tries to stop you from coming aboard. Although to tell the God's honest truth, all the animals in Noah's ark could come aboard our coal boats and nobody'd be a whit the wiser. So you just come to Dock 15, walk on board the *Gaelic Prince*—and a poor, broken-down, ill-used, ready-to-flounder *Gaelic Prince* she is!—and go straight down to the boiler room. And don't poke your bloody nose on deck till we've slipped our moorings! Night and good luck t' you."

On the evening of Brian's departure the house on the Falls Road began to fill with visitors. The original intention of the Traceys had been to invite only a few close friends, for they were anxious not to attract too much attention. But one had told the other, and there must have been thirty people at the send-off. Some drinks for a farewell toast had been provided by the Traceys, but many of the guests, invited and uninvited, had brought their own.

Brian noticed that his father was paying frequent visits to the scullery where the drink was kept and was gradually becoming more moody and less coherent. He was beginning to worry about his father when he heard a fresh commotion in the hall, and moments later in strode Jamie and Dinny, both smiling in a very relaxed fashion and both effusive in their greetings. Brian wondered how many times they had stopped to ask the way to Belfast.

"He's running away from the girl," Jamie laughed thickly, after holding Brian in a silent, dramatic embrace. "Smart boy, eh, Dinny? All th' Traceys smart boys, eh, Dinny? Told you Brian was a smart boy, eh, Dinny?" At each "eh, Dinny?" Jamie playfully poked Dinny in the ribs and Dinny in reply spread out his lips in a lugubrious smile.

"I'm glad you came, Jamie, and I'm glad you came too, Dinny," said Brian. "I'll always remember this. But why don't you have something with the others?"

"Sure we'll have something with the others, eh, Dinny?" said Jamie. He moved away toward the scullery, pulling Dinny along with him.

Finally the Monastery bell boomed out eight times, and Brian heaved a heavy sigh as its notes died away. How things had changed since he had first heard that bell! And how alone he felt in that gay crowd. The only one he would have wanted near him at that moment was not there, would never be close to him again. Just then another sound broke into his sad thoughts. It was the sound of a car drawing up outside the door, and a moment later Curly Downey, who had borrowed the car for the occasion, bounced into the room. It was the signal for Brian to get ready, and he was glad that the hour had come. He went up to his mother. She embraced him, letting her hands stray about his head and shoulders the way Brian had seen the blind do. She kissed him, sat down on the nearest chair, and with eyes opened wide stared in front of her.

Brian had rehearsed in his mind these partings and had planned to lighten them with a smile or a joke. But the sight of his mother staring with unseeing eyes made him turn around quickly and handshake his way roughly through a crowd of faces to the door. Once in the car he took a cloth cap out of his pocket and put it on his head, tugged off his collar and tie and in their stead wrapped a thin muffler round his neck. The cap and muffler were the standard garb of a dock worker. After that he huddled himself up in his overcoat and waited for the car to move. Michael and Jamie came in beside him and Dinny sat in the front seat. Curly got into the driver's seat and they moved off down the Falls. The car had barely moved when Michael leaned over, put his arm round Jamie, and broke out into song.

"Adieu! The snowy sail, swells her bosom to the gale
As our barque from Innisfail bounds away!"

"Both of them footless," Brian heard Dinny remark to Curly. "As tight as two drums!" added Curly. But Brian saw no humor in the two men's absurd antics.

"So the wild geese are on the wing again!" said Jamie gaily.

"The Flight of the Earls," said Michael with drunken solemnity. "Remember the story about the earls, Brian?" He threw out his right hand and began to recite:

"A half of pathos is the past we know,
A half the future into which we go!
Or present joy broken with old regret,
Or sorrow saved from hell by one hope yet.
There once was pleasant water and fresh land
Where now the Sphinx gazes 'cross the sand;
Yet may she hope, though dynasties have died,
That Change abide while Time and she abide."

"What's the matter with the country anyway?" asked Jamie, suddenly cross again. "Why can't they stay at home once in a while? Have they a flea in their pants that makes them go gallivanting around the world and forgetting the people at home?"

"Aye," said Michael. He tried to fill his pipe with shredded tobacco, but the movement of the car and his unsteady hands caused the tobacco to fall through his fingers. And Brian remembered the day many years ago when he, his father, and Jamie had first come to Belfast in the trap with Stardust. "The wild geese have been flying away for nigh on five hundred years," said Michael. "When will they ever fly home?"

"They must have a big flea in their pants!" said Dinny.

"Go, go, go!" Michael's voice rose above the sound of the car's engine. "Let them all go! Three of mine have gone! Mother Erin is prodigal of her seed and fills the earth with greatness. But children yearn for the mother's breast again when they grow old and tired and sad. They must . . ."

"They must have a *very* big flea in the seat of their pants," said Jamie.

". . . be a great people, for the powerfullest empire the world has ever seen could not subdue them through centuries of suffering and sorrow. Oh, Mary . . ."

"They must have a . . ." began Jamie. Then he stopped and added: "I think I'll take a nap! I've had a hard day. Though why I kill myself for a woman like Meg Tracey and that mollycoddle of a son, I don't know."

". . . of the Gael, why have you made those who loved you wander the face of the earth? Wandering Jews, wandering Gaels. Both on a pilgrimage along life's way. Oh, Mary of the Gael, show us the way in the dark! Why has God . . ."

"If the boat was to take off with me and Michael, it'd be a hellava while afore Meg'd catch up with us, eh, Dinny?" Jamie reached forward in the car to poke Dinny, but Dinny's head was now slumped forward in sleep.

". . . made the Jews suffer because they rejected Christ and the Gaels suffer because they accepted Him? There's a riddle for you! I'd like to hear McGuire answer me that! I'll lay two to one he— What in the name o' God is all the blowin' about? Are we not free even to talk in our own country?"

"That's the ship's horns, Dad," said Brian. "I'll soon be leaving you."

"Well, I've news for you," cried Michael. He struggled to sit up straight. "I'm not leaving *you!* Put that in your pipe and smoke it! I'd have you know that when I was a young man I . . ."

"Are you going with him, Mike?" asked Jamie in pleased surprise. "Bully for you! When you have a drink taken you always get a flea in your pants!" He slapped his thigh and began to laugh.

". . . I covered more ground than the lot of you will ever cover, and I . . ." Michael lapsed into silence, his head dropped forward to one side, and he began to snore.

The car by now was close to the docks. It was a dark area at that time of the night, for everything was closed except the bars. Curly stopped the car a few streets away and they walked until they came up to the water front. On the side of the wide road opposite the docks there was a line of ships' chandlers and warehouses. To the left Brian saw the brightly-lit steamers that ran each night between Belfast and the cross-channel ports, their decks bustling cheerfully with passengers. Even as he watched, a horn blew one long blast and one of the steamers edged away from the pier and slid down the harbor, her lights dancing gaily on the dark waters.

The steamer glided past Dock 15 and Brian saw, across the wide road, coal wagons, railway tracks, huge mounds of machinery covered with tarpaulins, and behind these a dimly-lit area, and finally a small coal boat of around five thousand tons leaning wearily against the wharf. He supposed it was the *Gaelic Prince*.

The little party took shelter in the shadow of a doorway opposite Dock 15. There were a few moments of meaningless conversation, mostly from Michael about life on board ship, during which Brian was completely forgotten. Impatiently, almost angrily, Brian decided it was time to go.

Shaking hands with each one of them seemed to sober them. Michael could not speak as he embraced Brian and kissed him with a mouth that smelled of whisky, and the other three were sincerely moved when they said good-by. Brian was in no mood to look back and acknowledge their sentimental wavings of the hand as he slipped into the dark area separating the dock from the roadway, and threaded his way among the heavy machinery and the wagons smelling of coal dust. He was about to leave these shadowy areas and cross the open ground to the boat when he stopped. He was not sure if he had really heard something or if it was just instinct that warned him; but he did not step out from the shadows. Instead he huddled closer to a coal wagon, his ears cocked. Then he bent down and, crawling in under the wagon, stretched out his body along the cold metal axle. Although he could not see where he was lying, he thought of the dirt and oil and grime his clothes must be gathering as he lay there. He dug into his trouser pocket for his revolver. It was a small .32, not a very effective weapon, but it did give him a feeling of greater security.

He waited, listening. Then he heard a telltale sound. Not the sound of an engine, but the sound of tires rippling along the smooth set-squares of the roads. It was a whippet. He saw the two slits of headlights that from the day of the ambush in Raglan Street had made him think of the narrow, wicked eyes of a panther. Now the panther was stalking its prey to the edge of the jungle, beyond which its ferociousness could not harm. Suddenly a bar of light, intensely white in the darkness, shot from the turret. Silent and catlike, the light crawled along the ground, across openings, along the sides of the wagons, and up and down the tarpaulins, giving them eerie, ghostlike shapes. As it crept silently toward the wagon where he was, Brian felt every nerve in his body tingle painfully and every pore open and exude a chilling dampness. He felt he had no longer any control over the muscles of his body and for a moment he thought his bowels would move from fear.

The light snapped out again and he heard the ripple of the tires. The low, quiet hum of the engine continued for a while until for the second time the solid beam of white light shot from the whippet. In his taut state of mind, Brian could almost imagine it made a sound as it struck the little group he had just left, bathing them in deathly pallor. The turret of the whippet swung round until the machine gun was trained on the four men who were now crouching in the doorway as if bending their necks to the sword. For one dread-filled moment Brian waited to hear a sickening crash of gunfire smash into the hearts of the four cowering figures, spilling out their lives and hurtling them into eternity.

The thought that his father and the others were in danger quickened him. But what could he do? He had only a revolver, and what was that against the armored hide of the whippet?

Fuming at his helplessness, he decided on the instant that there was only one thing to do. He would dash out of his hiding place, rush up to the whippet, and shove the muzzle of his gun into the narrow slit the driver used and empty it blindly, leaving the rest to chance. At least one Special wouldn't drive for a long time after a blast like that! He began to wriggle his body free of the cold axle when he was brought up short by the sound of a voice muffled by the turret shouting, "Come out with your hands up and turn to the wall."

Curly, Dinny, his father, and Uncle Jamie, in that order, slowly edged out of the doorway and did as they were told. The door of the whippet clanked open; three hatless Specials stepped down on the roadway and advanced on the men. Two carried revolvers, and they covered the four men while the third Special searched. All this time the machine gun, like a viper's black, venomous tongue, glinted under the searchlight and pointed its small, obscene mouth at the men.

The search did not take long. It was cold for the Specials, too, reflected Brian, as he shifted uncomfortably under the wagon, and they wanted to get the job over with. He heard one of them order the four men to be home before curfew, or they'd be in trouble, and the four moved off stiffly, turned a corner, and disappeared. Waiting until they had turned the corner, the Specials walked back to the whippet and clambered on board, their heavy boots scraping noisily against the metal sides. The door slammed shut, the searchlight went out, and again Brian heard the ripple of tires and the quiet, almost noiseless hum of the engine. Finally that also died away and the dark form of the whippet dissolved into the shadows.

He wormed free of the undercarriage of the wagon. Then he dashed across the area lighted by yellow lamps to the *Gaelic Prince*, a small, dirty coal vessel alongside the dock. Her Plimsoll line was high above the water, and both her gangway and deck were covered with coal dust that shone like silver speckles in the murky light. He took in lungfuls of air laden with coal dust as he walked quickly down the gangplank and stepped onto the deck.

Two men were coiling ropes near the gangway but they ignored him.

"Hey, Tracey boy!"

Brian looked up. Leaning out of the window of the little bridge was a stocky figure dressed in a brown sweater and peaked cap. Captain Ryan waved to him. Brian waved back curtly and looked around for the ladder to the boiler room. Meanwhile he heard Ryan shout: "Haul in the gangway!" and the two men who had been coiling ropes prepared to obey. This was followed by two hoarse blasts on the ship's horn.

He found the companionway to the lower deck and from there the ladder to the boiler room. Everywhere he saw nothing but dirt and grease and smelled nothing but coal, heavy oil, and lavatory. Finally he reached the boiler room. Two furnaces were going, and opposite them lay a pile of glinting coal nuggets slanted against the bulkhead. Two men in trousers and shoes were shoveling coal into the open furnaces, scooping it up with clean strokes of the shovel along the floor under the coal pile and slinging it neatly into the open furnace.

The third, a lean man, was sitting on the coals smoking a cigarette. He was the one that spoke to Brian. "What have you done, my friend," he asked, "to be condemned to hell?"

Brian ignored him and hung his cap and coat on a hook near the door. Stripped down to his waist and with an unfriendly scowl on his face, he asked nobody in particular: "What do I do?"

One of the men who had been stoking handed him his shovel. Brian took the shovel, scraped it along the iron deck, clumsily scooped up a heavy shovelful, and slung it in an ungainly way among the wildly dancing, white-red flames. The man who was already stoking stared at Brian for a moment. Then he stopped, leaned on his shovel, and gave all his attention to him. Finally he turned to his companions and tapped his head with his forefinger. Brian saw the maneuver but kept on stoking the roaring fire.

At last he heard the quick, throbbing sound he had been waiting for. The ship rolled slightly under him.

"She's moving!" said one of the men. The ship rolled again.

"And that's what these floating coffins do on the river!" said the lean young man. "Just think—but, oh, just think what she'll do when she hits the Irish Sea!"

Brian imagined that they must be moving down the harbor. That meant it was safe to go on deck. With a rebellious gesture he threw down his shovel, put on his clothes, and spat out some of the choking coal dust. He completely ignored the three men who were still staring at him as he stepped into the passageway.

When he got on deck the *Gaelic Prince* was sailing down the quiet waters of the harbor. She swung around a slow bend, bringing a cluster of lights into view. Brian caught his breath. They were the lights of the shipyards. Oh, how he remembered the first day he had gone there to work and the boyish dreams he had had of heading the great shipbuilding firm! He smiled, but ceased to smile when he remembered his other dream of owning the farm and the repair shop; for that dream, too, had been shattered on the day he had had to run for his life from those very shipyards. His bitterness was now increased by the thought that, in passing by those shipyards on his way out of the country, he was acknowledging his defeat; and his bitterness was mingled with shame, for in a way he looked upon himself as a deserter.

Defeat and death, frustration and despair. It had always been that way with Ireland. As a boy he had been an avid reader of stories about Ireland but had always begun each story with a certain reluctance: he knew that the story would have a melancholy ending with the death or flight, but never the triumph, of the hero. He could not understand that. Nor could he understand now why he should have to leave his own country when all the time he wanted to stay. It was as if the city, like some great machine, had sucked him in at one end and had delivered him, a different product, a different person, at the other, like a young tree swallowed up in the huge maws of a mill and churned and tossed and finally transformed. Now he was being delivered at the other end —and for export. Like a child being denied something it sorely wanted, Brian kept repeating to himself that he wanted to stay in Ireland. Sheila was there; the farm was there; his home was there; everything he loved was there. But the throbbing deck of the *Gaelic Prince* kept bearing him relentlessly down the waters of the harbor, farther and farther away from the Irish shore, from Sheila, from the farm, from his home. What with all the powers of his soul he wished would not happen was happening in spite of him. Wasn't there anything he could do to stop it? He looked around helplessly and saw the dark mist settle over the lights of the vanishing headland. There were no longer any lights in front of him, for now the mist had settled on them, too. Wasn't there any way out of this despair? Couldn't anyone do anything to help him? Couldn't he do anything to help himself? He would have to do something, no matter how desperate, for he could not bear much longer this bitter frustration.

He dug his hands angrily into the pockets of his trousers . . . and the fingers of his right hand encountered the revolver. His palm, closing over the handle, felt every line and marking on the stock. A wave of wild thoughts rushed upon him, flooding his mind, blotting out all reason. He drew out the revolver and stared at the dark shape, fascinated by its deadliness as a man is fascinated when he looks down from an unaccustomed height. With a dread slowness, half unwilling, half protesting to himself as he did so, he raised the gun and held it so tightly to his temple that he could distinguish the cold, steel circlet of the bore. His grip tightened on the handle; his forefinger curved around the trigger and kept pressing until the slight play in it ceased and he felt the trigger stiffen against the joint of his finger bone.

How long he stood like that he did not know. He was not aware of time. Oddly enough, he was aware only of the throbbing engines under his feet and the quiet swish of waters past the stern. Dazed and motionless, he stood staring at the brown-black waters tossing and tumbling and swirling madly about the churning screws, finding a strange consolation and companionship in the tormented waters. Sweat broke out on his forehead and turned ice-cold in the chill wind.

It seemed that he was living through a dream, a horrible dream, and just as he had done in such dreams as a boy, he now sought strength from somewhere in his being to shake it off.

A suicide? he asked himself after an age. He, Brian Tracey, a suicide? Had he allowed himself to sink into such despair? Was he about to kill himself? What would Sheila think of him, and his mother and father, and Sean? And when he died he would have to meet his God . . . his God. But he did not believe in God any more! He—did—not—believe—in—God—any—more! Oh, why could he not convince himself? He—did—not—believe—in—God—any—more!

Something between a gasp and a moan escaped him. "God help me!" He did not know whether it was a cry of hopelessness or a prayer. But with a supreme effort he fought against the strange outside, evil power that held his gun to his head, tried to shake off this nightmare of horror. At last he succeeded in pulling the gun away and with a desperate gesture threw it far out into the ship's wake. He neither heard it strike the water nor saw it sink into the black sea. Covering his face with his hands, he rested them on the rail and then from sheer weakness slid to his knees. While the pounding of his temples made rhythm within the chugging of the ship's tired engines, he began to pray. And the prayer he kept repeating humbly in his dazed mind was one that had come down to him and his people through the ages with a legacy of grief. "O Mary of the Gael," he moaned, "show us the way through the dark."

After a while he raised his head wearily and the rising wind cooled his hot cheeks, the same wind that swept the mist far out to sea and let the stars shine brilliant and clear against the wintry sky. Lights were again glowing on both sides of the widening mouth of the harbor, and as the ship cleared the mainland and headed for the open sea, the chaste beam of a lighthouse swept her decks.

Slowly, painfully, Brian regained something of his calm, and, like the mist, the doubts and fears that had tormented him lifted, and he saw himself as he had not seen himself since the beginning of the dreadful nightmares that had changed his life . . . the riots at the shipyard, the shooting at the Monastery, Sean's death, the ambush. . . .

Oh, God, what a fool he had been! What a stupid, insane fool! What a fool in the first place ever to have fired that shot at the

Monastery! He had been worse than a fool, when Sean had died, to have let hate a second time gain mastery over him and force him to seek revenge in murder. By spilling blood he had put himself outside the pale of the brotherhood of man; by rejecting forgiveness he had put himself outside the friendship of God. He had not believed in God! How childish of him! He had merely tried to push God out of his life so that the thought of God would not interfere with his plans for revenge. Sheila was right when she had said that there was no place for such as he in Ireland's cause. And the old priest had been right, too, about God having His own plans for Ireland.

By this time he had left the stern of the ship with its churning, tormented waters and walked along the narrow deck, holding on now to the rail, now to the iron grips welded to the bulkhead, for the little ship had begun to roll in the rougher waters of the Irish Sea. Passing under the bridge, he made his way forward.

"Tracey boy, that you again?" The voice hailed him from the darkened bridge.

"Aye, Captain Ryan," he answered cheerfully enough.

"Come on up and have a 'bubble.'"

"Just a minute, Captain," shouted Brian back. "I want to look ahead for a while."

"Suit yourself, son."

Crossing the space between the bridge and forecastle, he climbed the ladder to the prow and soon stood erect against the wind, holding on to the forecastle head. Here he felt one with the ship in her forward and side rolls. The wind sang in his ears and tugged sportively at his clothes and he could hear its high-pitched whistle through the rigging at the masthead. He breathed in deeply of the invigorating air. He seemed to have left another self back at the stern, a sort of phantom Brian that had haunted him during the long months of the past year. He was different now; he was his real self again. He was an Irishman; he was of a race that in all its long history of suffering and sorrow had never known defeat or despair, of a race whose spirit had always conquered, no matter what the odds, no matter what the obstacle.

Like a bird released from its cage, he exulted in his new freedom, seeking the heights where he once used to dwell. "I am young!" he shouted into the winds. "I am strong! And with God's help I can still fight my way back." I can still have Sheila, he told himself, my home, my farm, and my country. The day came back to him when his father had thrashed him for running back to the farm and how even while he was being beaten he had cried out that he would go back. Now he repeated defiantly: "I *will* go back! Though misfortune is on me now, I still repeat, I *will* go back!"

The chug-chug, chug-chug of the *Gaelic Prince's* engines took up the refrain. *I will go back! I will go back! I will go back!*

I'll not be like another Sarsfield, he thought, giving my life in vain on some foreign field of battle and lamenting that it was not spent for Ireland. I'll give my life *for* Ireland but not in an attempt to shed more Irish blood. Oh no! There must be some way to stop the spilling of blood and I swear I'll find it, so help me God!

"Able-seaman Tracey! Your bubble's goin' flat! Com'on up!"

"Coming, Captain! I'm coming up!"

Yes, Captain, he was coming up, up from the lowest reaches of despair into which he had plunged himself. Perhaps, he reflected, God had wanted it that way to humble him, to purify him, to make him a more suitable instrument in His hands. If that was so then he had been humbled, he had been purified: he hoped he would now be a suitable instrument. Yes, he was coming up!

Leaving the foredeck, Brian gave a last look at the fading glimpse of the Irish shore. The roll and the dip of the *Gaelic Prince* became more pronounced, and she thumped against the sea, warning him that a rough voyage lay ahead. But as he climbed the ladder to the bridge, he told himself that the little ship had gone out often in such rough weather and just as often had returned, laden with the riches of her travels. After this voyage she would come back again to the Irish shore and so, he assured himself, in God's good time, would he.